Peccavi by E. W. Hornung

Ernest William Hornung was born in Middlesbrough, England on 7th June 1866, the third son and youngest of eight children.

Although spending most of his life in England and France he spent two years in Australia from 1884 and that experience was to colour and influence much of his written works.

His most famous character A. J. Raffles, 'the gentleman thief', was published first in Cassell's Magazine during 1898 and was to make him famous across the world as the new century dawned.

Hornung also wrote several stage plays and was a gifted poet.

Spending time with the troops in WWI he published Notes of a Camp-Follower on the Western Front during 1919, a detailed account of his time there. This was especially close to his heart as his son, and only child, was killed at the Second Battle of Ypres on 6th July 1915.

Ernest William Hornung died in Saint-Jean-de-Luz, in the south of France on 22nd March 1921.

Index of Contents

CHAPTER I

DUST TO DUST

Long Stow church lay hidden for the summer amid a million leaves. It had neither tower nor steeple to show above the trees; nor was the scaffolding between nave and chancel an earnest of one or the other to come. It was a simple little church, of no antiquity and few exterior pretensions, and the alterations it was undergoing were of a very practical character. A sandstone upstart in a countryside of flint, it stood aloof from the road, on a green knoll now yellow with buttercups, and shaded all day long by horse-chestnuts and elms. The church formed the eastern extremity of the village of Long Stow.

It was Midsummer Day, and a Saturday, and the middle of the Saturday afternoon. So all the village was there, though from the road one saw only the idle group about the gate, and on the old flint wall a row of children commanded by the schoolmaster to "keep outside." Pinafores pressed against the coping, stockinged legs dangling, fidgety hob-nails kicking stray sparks from the flint; anticipation at the gate, fascination on the wall, law and order on the path in the schoolmaster's person; and in the cool green shade hard by, a couple of planks, a crumbling hillock, an open grave.

Near his handiwork hovered the sexton, a wizened being, twisted with rheumatism, leaning on his spade, and grinning as usual over the stupendous hallucination of his latter years. He had swallowed a rudimentary frog with some impure water. This frog had reached maturity in the sexton's body. Many believed it. The man himself could hear it croaking in his breast, where it commanded the pass to his stomach, and intercepted every morsel that he swallowed. Certainly the sexton was very lean, if not starving to death quite as fast as he declared; for he had become a tiresome egotist on the point, who, even now, must hobble to the schoolmaster with the last report of his unique ailment.

"That croap wuss than ever. Would 'ee like to listen, Mr. Jones?"

And the bent man almost straightened for the nonce, protruding his chest with a toothless grin of huge enjoyment.

"Thank you," said the schoolmaster. "I've something else to do."

"Croap, croap, croap!" chuckled the sexton. "That take every mortal thing I eat. An' doctor can't do nothun for me—not he!"

"I should think he couldn't."

"Why, I do declare he be croapun now! That fare to bring me to my own grave afore long. Do you listen, Mr. Jones; that croap like billy-oh this very minute!"

It took a rough word to get rid of him.

"You be off, Busby. Can't you see I'm trying to listen to something else?"

In the church the rector was reciting the first of the appointed psalms. Every syllable could be heard upon the path. His reading was Mr. Carlton's least disputed gift, thanks to a fine voice, an unerring sense of the values of words, and a delivery without let or blemish. Yet there was no evidence that the reader felt a word of what he read, for one and all were pitched in the deliberate monotone rarely to be heard outside a church. And just where some voices would have failed, that of the Rector of Long Stow rang clearest and most precise:

"When thou with rebukes dost chasten man for sin, thou makest his beauty to consume away, like as it were a moth fretting a garment: every man therefore is but vanity.

"Hear my prayer, O Lord, and with thine ears consider my calling: hold not thy peace at my tears.

"For I am a stranger with thee: and a sojourner, as all my fathers were.

"O spare me a little, that I may recover my strength: before I go hence, and be no more seen . . ."

The sexton was regaling the children on the wall with the ever-popular details of his notorious malady. The schoolmaster still strutted on the path, now peeping in at the porch, now reporting particulars to the curious at the gate: a quaint incarnation of conscious melancholy and unconscious enjoyment.

"Hardly a dry eye in the church!" he announced after the psalm. "Mr. Carlton and Musk himself are about the only two that fare to hide what they feel."

"And what does Mr. Carlton feel?" asked a lout with a rose in his coat. "About as much as my little finger!"

"Ay," said another, "he cares for nothing but his Roman candles, and his transcripts and gargles."[1]

[Footnote 1: Transepts and gargoyles.]

"Come," said the schoolmaster, "you wouldn't have the parson break down in church, would you? I'm sorry I mentioned him. I was thinking of Jasper Musk. He just stands as though Mr. Carlton had carved him out of stone."

"The wonder is that he can stand there at all," retorted the fellow with the flower, "to hear what he don't believe read by a man he don't believe in. A funeral, is it? It's as well we know—he'd take a weddun in the same voice."

The schoolmaster turned away with an ambiguous shrug. It was not his business to defend Mr. Carlton against the disaffected and the undevout. He considered his duty done when he informed the rector who his enemies were, and (if permitted to proceed) what they were saying behind his back. The schoolmaster made a mental mark against the name of one Cubitt, ex-choirman, and, forthwith transferring his attention to the audience on the wall, put a stop to their untimely entertainment before returning softly to the porch.

In Long Stow churchyard there was shade all day, but in the church it was dusk from that moment in the forenoon when the east window lost the sun. This peculiarity was partly temporary. The church was in a transition stage; it was putting forth transepts north and south; meanwhile there was much boarding within, and a window in eclipse on either side. The surrounding foliage added its own shade; and each time the schoolmaster stole out of the sunlight into the porch, to peer up the nave, it was several moments before he could see anything at all. And then it was but a few high lights in a sea of gloom: first the east window, as yet unstained, its three quatrefoils filled with summer sky, the rest with waving branches; next, the brass lectern, the surplice behind it, the high white forehead above. Then in the chancel something gleamed: that was the coffin, resting on trestles. Then in the choir seats, otherwise deserted, a figure grew out of the shadows, a solitary and a massive figure, that stood even now when everybody else was seated, finely regardless of the fact. It was a man, elderly, but very powerfully built. The hair stood white and thick upon the large strong head, less white and shorter on the broad deep jowl. The head was carried with a certain dignity, rude, savage, indomitable. The eyes gazed fixedly at the opposite wall; not once did they condescend to the thing that gleamed upon the trestles. One great hand was knotted over the knob of a mighty stick, on which the old man leant stiffly. He was dressed in black, not quite as a gentleman, yet as befitted the most substantial man but one in the parish. And that was Jasper Musk.

The parson finished the lesson, and his white brow bent over the closed book; the face beneath was bearded and much tanned, and in it there burnt an eye that came as a surprise after that formal voice; and the hand that closed the book was sensitive but strong. Stepping from the lectern, the clergyman declared his calibre in an obeisance towards the altar, then led the way slowly down the aisle. Bearers rose from the shades and followed with the coffin; they were almost at the porch before Jasper Musk took notice enough to limp after them with much noise from his stick. The congregation waited for him, swarming into the aisle in the big man's wake. So they came to the grave.

And there broad daylight revealed a circumstance that came as a shock to most of those who had followed the body from the church, but as an outrage to the officiating clergyman: the coffin bore no plate. Mr. Carlton coloured to the hair, and his deep eye flashed upon the chief mourner; the latter leant upon his stick and replied with a grim glare across the open grave. For a moment the wind washed through the trees, and every sparrow made itself heard; then the rector's eyes dropped to his book, but his voice rang colder than before. And presently the earth received its own.

Mr. Carlton had pronounced the benediction, and a solemn hush still held all assembled, when a bicycle bell jarred staccato in the road; a moment later, with a sharp word for some children who had tired of the funeral and strayed across his path, the rider dismounted outside the saddler's workshop, a tiny cabin next his house and opposite the church. The cyclist was a lad in his teens, dark, handsome, dapper, but small for his age, which was that of high collars and fancy ties; and he rode a fancy bicycle, the high machine of the day, but extravagantly nickelled in all its parts.

"Well, Fuller," said he, "who are they burying?"

Fuller, the saddler, who enjoyed a local monopoly in the exercise of his craft, but whose trade was the mere relaxation of a life spent in reading and disseminating the news of the day, was spelling through the Standard at his bench behind the open window. He dropped his paper and whipped the spectacles from a big dogmatic nose.

"Gord love yer, Mr. Sidney, do you stand there and tell me you haven't heard?"

"How could I hear when I'm only home from Saturdays to Mondays? I'm on my way home now. Old Sally Webb—is it—or one of the old Wilsons?"

"No, sir," said the saddler; "that's no old person. Gord love yer," he cried again, "I wish that was!"

"Who is it, Mr. Fuller?"

"That's Molly Musk," said Fuller, slowly; "that's who that is, Mr. Sidney."

The boy had not the average capacity for astonishment; he was not, in fact, the average boy; but at the name his eyebrows shot up and his mouth grew round.

"Molly Musk! I thought nobody knew where she was? When did she turn up?"

"Tuesday night, and died the next."

"But I say, Fuller, this is interesting!" Perhaps the average boy would have been no more shocked; he might not even have found it interesting. This one leant his bicycle against the wall, and his elbows on the bench within the open window. "Where's she been all this time?" he queried, confidentially. "What did she die of? What's it all mean?" And there was a knowing curl about the corners of his mouth.

"Mean?" said the saddler; "there's more than you want to know that, Mr. Sidney, but want must be their master. That old Jasper, he know, so they say; but I'm not so sure. It was he fetched her home, poor old feller; got the letter Monday morning, had her home by Tuesday night. That's a man I never liked, Mr. Sidney. I've said it to his face, and I'll say it as long as I live; but, Gord love yer, I'm sorry for him now! That's given him a rare doing and no mistake, and less wonder. A trim little thing like poor Molly Musk! Not that I'm so surprised as some; a man of my experience don't make no mistake, and I never did care for the breed. But there, even my heart bleed when that don't boil; as for the reverend here, he feel it as much as anybody else, and that I know. That young Jim Cubitt, he come by just now, and says he, 'He's taking the service as if it was a wedding.' 'You've been kicked out of the choir,' I says; 'that's what's the matter with you still, or you wouldn't want a man to be a woman. Thank goodness there's one live man in the parish,' I says, 'though I don't fare to hold with him.' And no more I do, Mr. Sidney; but, Gord love yer, that make no difference to men of our experience. I like the reverend's Popery as little as the squire like it, and I tell him so, yet he go on bringing me the Standard every day when he've done with it. Is there another clergyman that'd do the like to a man that went against him in the parish? Would the Reverend Preston at Linkworth? Would the Reverend Scrope at Burton Mills? Or Canon Wilders, or any other man Jack of 'em? No, sir, not one!"

"But if he doesn't read them himself," said the boy, "it doesn't amount to so very much." And he laid his hand on three more Standards, unopened, with the parson's name in print upon the wrapper.

"What I was coming to," cried the saddler; "only when I get on the reverend my tongue will wag. They say he don't feel. I say he do, and I know: all this week I've had no Standard, so this morning I was so bold as to up and mention it, and there was all six unopened. 'Reverend,' I says, 'you must be ill—with that there Egyptian Question to argue about'—for we're rare 'uns to argue, the reverend and me—'and no trace yet o' them Phœnix Park varmin!' But he shake his head. 'Not ill, Fuller,' he says; 'but there's tragedy enough in this parish without going to the papers for more. And I haven't the heart to argue even with you,' he says. So that's my answer to them as says our reverend don't feel."

The boy had been patiently pricking the bench with a saddler's punch; now he raised his deliberate dark eyes and looked at the other point-blank.

"You talk about a tragedy," he said, "but you won't say where the tragedy comes in. What has killed the girl?"

"I hardly like to tell a young gentleman like you," said the saddler; "though, to be sure, you'll hear of nothing else in the village."

"Perhaps," said the boy, with a rather sinister smile, "I'm not quite so innocent as I ought to be. Come on, out with it!"

"Well, then, the poor young thing was brought home in trouble," sighed the saddler. "And in her trouble she died next night."

The boy looked at the man through narrow eyes with a knowing light in them, and the curves cut deep at the corners of his mouth.

"In trouble, eh? So that's why she disappeared?" he said at length. "Molly—Musk!"

CHAPTER II

THE CHIEF MOURNER

Jasper Musk remained some minutes at the grave, alone, and more than ever a mark for curious eyes; his own were raised, and his lips moved with a significance difficult to mistake, but in him yet more difficult to accept. The infidelity of the man was notorious, and, indeed, the raised face was not the face of prayer. It was flint bathed in gall, too bitter for faith, too savage for sorrow; it was a frozen sea of wrinkles without a single ripple of agitation. Yet the lips moved, and were still moving when Jasper Musk passed through the crowd now assembled about the gate, erect though halt, a glitter in his eyes, but that was all.

As the folk had waited and made way for him in the church, so they waited and made way outside. Thus, as he limped down into the road, Musk had the village almost to himself. He turned to the right, and the west wind blew in his face, strong and warm, with cloud upon cloud of yellow dust; overhead the other clouds flew high and white and broken, a flotilla of small sail upon the blue. But Musk was done gazing at the sky, neither did he look right or left as he trudged in the middle of the road. So the saddler's place, and then the woody opening of the road to Linkworth, with the white bridge gleaming through the trees, and the ripe leaves purling in the wind like summer surf, all fell behind on the left; as, on the right, did the rectory gate, terminating that same flint wall which had been the children's grand stand. Rectory, church, and glebe stood all together, an indivisible trinity, with open uplands east and north. Westward began the cottages, buff-coloured, thatched; and it was cottages for half a mile, but healthy cottages, with plenty of space between, here a wheatfield, there a meadow; for every householder of Long Stow has also his holding of land, and there is no more independent parish in East Anglia. Of private houses that are not cottages, however, the village has only three: the rectory at one end, the hall near the other, and the Flint House between the two.

The Flint House now belonged to Jasper Musk. Report said that he had bought it outright for nine hundred pounds, with the meadow he was now passing on his left, and the wild garden reaching to the river. Originally part and parcel of the Long Stow estate, the place had been let for years, with a good slice of land, to London sportsmen who spent just two months of the twelve there. Musk had been the lessee's bailiff, and had feathered his nest so well that when the whole estate changed hands, and the part went with the whole, the ex-bailiff was in a position to buy a house and grounds for which the new squire had no use. None knew how he could have come honestly by so much profit; yet he was a man of tried integrity, but a hard man, and the last to get fair treatment behind his back. A more genuine marvel was the way in which he had spent his money, on a house that could scarcely fail to be a white elephant to such a man, and a hideous house into the bargain. It abutted directly on the road, grim and rambling, with false windows like wall-eyes, and facets of flint so sharp that to brush against the wall was to rip a sleeve to ribbons. There were many rooms, musty and mice-ridden, and now only two old people to inhabit them. Musk had driven all his sons from home, thus doing his country an unwitting service, for there was the stuff that knits an empire in the blood. But only one daughter had been born to him, and now he had left her in the ground, and would wash his mind of her for ever.

The resolution was easier than its accomplishment: on his very threshold a shrill small cry assailed and insulted Jasper Musk. And in the parlour walked his wife, meek-spirited, flat-chested, leaden-eyed; too weary for much grief, as he was too bitter; in her thin arms an infant not four days old.

Musk put himself in her path.

"Stop walking!"

"That'll set him off again," sighed Mrs. Musk, though not before she had obeyed.

"I don't care," said Jasper. "That can cry till that die," he added brutally, as the fit returned; "and the sooner the better. Hold it up a bit. There, now! I want to have a look at the brat. I want to see who that's like!"

"It's like poor Molly," whimpered the grandmother, shedding tears that she could neither check nor hide.

Musk thumped his stick on the floor.

"Molly? Molly? You let me hear that name again! Haven't I told you once and for all never to lay your tongue to that name, in my hearing or behind my back, as long as you live? Then don't you forget it; and none o' your lies. That's no more like her than that's like you. But a look of somebody it have, though I can't for the life of me think who. Wait a bit. Give me time. That'll come—that'll come!"

But the thin shrill screaming continued till the little red face grew livid and wrinkled almost beyond resemblance to its kind; then Musk relinquished his futile scrutiny, and signed to his wife to resume the walking, but himself remained in the room. And he leant on his stick as he had leant on it at the funeral; but here in his house he wore his hat; and from under its broad brim he followed them, backward and forward, to and fro, with smouldering eyes.

"Do you know what I've vowed?" he presently went on. "Do you know the oath I took, there at that open grave, when all the tomfoolery was over, and that Jesuit jerry-builder had taken his hook?"

"I'm sure I don't," sighed Mrs. Musk, as the child lay once more still against her withered bosom.

"I stood there," said Jasper, "and I swore I'd find the man. And I swore I'd tear his heart out when I've found him. And I'll do both!"

His voice rose so swiftly to so fierce a pitch that the woman started violently, and the infant wailed again. Instantly the room shook, and with one stride, paid for by a spasm of pain, the husband towered above the wife; and this time it was a heavy hand upon her shrunk and shrinking shoulder that put a stop to the walk.

"Do you know who it is?" he cried. "My God, I believe you do!"

"I don't, indeed!"

"She never told you?"

"God knows she did not."

"Or anybody else?"

"I don't know."

"But you think—you think! I see it in your face. Who is it you think she may have told? I'll soon find out from him or her; trust me to wring that out!"

For answer, the woman subsided in sobs upon the horsehair sofa, rocking herself and the baby in her grief and terror. "You'll be that angry with me," she moaned; "you'll be right mad!"

"Oh, no, I sha'n't," said Musk, in a kindlier voice. "I'm not so bad as all that, though this do fare to make a man crazy. Tell away, old woman, and don't you be afraid."

"Oh, Jasper, it was when you were gone to Lakenhall for the doctor—that last time!"

"Well?"

"She knew the end was near. Poor thing! Poor thing!"

"What did she say?"

"That she'd die more happier if only she could speak—if only I would send—"

"Not for Carlton?"

The wife could only nod in her fear and desperation.

"You sent for that man the moment my back was turned?"

"Oh, I knew that'd make you right wild—I knew—I knew!"

Musk controlled himself by an effort.

"That don't. That sha'n't. I'll have it out of him, that's all; he's not the Church o' Rome yet! Go on. Go on."

"I went myself. No one knew. I left her alone time I was gone."

"And you brought him back with you?"

"Well, he got here first. He ran all the way."

"He knew better than to let me catch him. Jesuit! How long was he with her?"

"Not long, Jasper, not long indeed!"

"And you heard nothing?"

"Not a word. I stayed downstairs. I had to promise her that before I went. She had something to say to Mr. Carlton that nobody else must know."

"But somebody else shall!" said Jasper grimly. "That was it, you may depend; you should have listened at the door. But that make no matter. Somebody else is going to know before he's many minutes older!"

And an ugly smile broadened on the thick-set face; but the woman gasped. Quick as thought the child was on the sofa, the grandmother on her feet. Trembling and terrified, she stood in her husband's path.

"Jasper! You're never going up to the rectory?"

"I am, though—this minute!"

"Oh, Jasper!"

"Do you let me by."

"But I promised you should never know! You've made me break my solemn word! He'll know I've broken it!"

"Yes, I'm going to learn him a thing or two. Will you let me by?"

"She'll know—too—wherever she has gone to!"

"You'd better not keep me no more."

"Jasper! Jasper! On her death-bed I promised her—"

"Out of my light!"

CHAPTER III

A CONFESSION

The rector's study was on the ground floor, facing south. It was a long room, but narrow, and so low that the present incumbent, who stood six-feet-two, had contracted a stoop out of continual and instinctive dread of the ancient beams that scored his study ceiling, combined with a besetting habit of pacing the floor. There were two doors; one led into the garden, providing parishioners with immediate access to the rector when he was not to be found at the church; the other terminated an inner passage. Both were of immemorial oak, and, like the lattice casement over the writing table, both rattled in the least wind. Such was the room which the Reverend Robert Carlton haunted when driven or detained indoors: rickety, ill-lighted, and draughty when it was not close, it was still a habitable hole enough, and picturesque in spite of its occupant.

Optional surroundings afford a fair clue to the superficial man, but no real key to character; thus Mr. Carlton's furniture suggested a soul devoid of the æsthetic sense. He had the sense in all its fineness, but it found expression in another place. Like many ritualists, Carlton was a religious æsthete; none more fastidious in the service of the sanctuary; on the other hand, after the fashion of his peers in two Churches, the trappings of his own life were severely simple. They had nearly all been purchased second-hand, those wire-covered shelves and the books they bore, that oak settle, and the huge arm-chair filled with miscellaneous lumber. Two baize-covered forms were there for the accommodation of various classes which the rector held; a prayer desk faced east in the one orderly corner of the room. Only three pictures hung on the walls; a Holy Family and Guido Reni's St. Sebastian, ordinary silver prints in Oxford frames, mementoes of a pilgrimage to Rome; and an ancient cricket eleven, faded from age, and fly-blown for long want of a glass. There were also a couple of tin shields, bearing the heraldic devices of Robert Carlton's public school and of his Oxford college, while a crucifix hung over the prayer desk. Among the books two volumes on Building Construction might have been remarked upon the settle, together with a tattered copy of Parker's Introduction to Gothic Architecture; among the lumber, a mason's trowel and a cold-chisel. Lastly, the study smelt, but did not reek, of common birdseye.

Jasper Musk, passing the open lattice, caught the parson hastily rising from his knees, not at the prayer desk, but beside his writing table, upon which a large book lay open. A newspaper lay on top of the book when Musk was admitted some moments after he had knocked.

He entered with his heavy, uneven steps, but took up a position barely within the threshold, and began by declining a seat with equal emphasis and stiffness.

"No, I thank you, Mr. Carlton. I've never been here before in your time, and I'm never likely to come again. I'm only here now to ask a question—and return a compliment!"

And the visitor's eye gleamed as Mr. Carlton creased the forehead that was so white in comparison with his face: at the moment this contrast was not conspicuous.

"From what I hear," explained Musk, "you've done me the kindness of coming to my house when my back was turned."

"And you have only heard of it now?"

"Within the last ten minutes; and I come here right straight. You may think I wouldn't come for nothing, me that's never darkened your door before to-day. I don't hold with you, Mr. Carlton, and I'm not the only one. That's true—I'm not a religious man, and never was; but, if I ever was to be, it wouldn't be your religion. No, sir, when I fare to want Christmas-trees in church I'll go to Rome and be done with it; and that's where you ought to be, Mr. Carlton, before you get a parcel of women to confess their sins to you as though you was God Almighty!"

Mr. Carlton sat quite still under this uncalled-for criticism; he even looked relieved, and one sensitive finger brushed the brown moustache to either side of his mouth.

"I have never advocated auricular confession," said he, "whatever I may think. I have merely said, to those in doubt, in difficulty, or in trouble, I will help them with God's help if I can."

"In trouble!" cried Musk scornfully. "I know one that never might have got herself into trouble if she'd never listened to you! And that's what brings me here; I'll beat about the bush no more. My wife said she fetched you the other night. I don't blame you for going, I won't go so far as that. What I want to know, and what I mean to know, is this: did my—that young woman lying there—confess to you or did she not?" It was a fist that he had flung in the direction of the churchyard.

"Confess what?"

And the parson's voice was cold and constrained, as it had been beside the grave; but that white forehead glistened like a dead man's.

"The name of the father of her child!"

Carlton took an ivory paper-knife from his desk, and the thin blade snapped in two between his fingers. A pause followed. Musk stood like granite, stick and hat in hand, frowning down on the clergyman seated at his writing table. At length the latter looked up.

"I might say that is a question you have no right to ask, Mr. Musk; what is certain, had there been any question of confession, I should have no right to answer you. There was none. Your daughter sent for me, to speak to me; and speak we did; but she did not tell me that—scoundrel's—name."

"But you know!"

"How dare you say that?" cried Carlton; and a flash of anger played for an instant on his pallor.

"I see it in your face; but I'll have it out of you! I'll have it out of you," roared Musk, in a sudden frenzy, striking his stick to the floor, "if I have to tear your smooth tongue out along with it! So smooth you could read over that murdered girl, and know all the time who'd murdered her, and think to keep that to yourself! But you sha'n't; no, that you sha'n't; not if I have to stand here till midnight. You know! You know! Deny it if you can!"

"I shall deny nothing," retorted the other. "No, I shall deny nothing!" he reiterated as if to himself. "But think for a minute, Mr. Musk—I entreat you to think calmly for one minute! Suppose I could tell you what you ask, could it serve any good end for you to know?"

"Good end!" cried Musk. "Why, you know it could. I could kill the man who's killed my daughter—and kill him I will—and swing for him if they like. That'll be a wonderful good end all round!"

"Then is it for me to throw temptation in your way? Is it for me to spoil a life, if not to end it? For all you know, Mr. Musk, it may be a life otherwise honest, useful, and of good report. Nay!" exclaimed Mr. Carlton, as if suddenly impatient of his own reticence, "I'll go so far as to say that it once was all three. And the man would do such duty—make such amends—"

A groan admitted that there were none to make, and finished a sentence to which Musk had not listened; the one before was sufficient for him; and his broad face shone with the satisfaction of a point gained.

"Come," said he, "that's fairer! So you do know him, and you say so like a man. I always took you for a man, sir, though there's been no love lost between us; and I'll say I'm sorry I spoke so harsh just now, Mr. Carlton; for I had a hold of the wrong end o' the stick—I see that now. It was the man that confessed—it was the man. Sir, if you're the Christian gentleman that I take you for, and this here Christianity o' yours ain't all cant an' humbug, you'll tell me that man's name; for I can't call to mind a single one she so much as looked at—unless it was that young Mellis."

"No, no; poor George is innocent enough, God knows!"

"He's like to be, for all I hear. They say he carries a cross for you o' Sundays—but I won't say no more about that. If he's your right hand in the parish, as they tell me he is, at least I should hope he'd be straight."

A puff of wind came through the open window. It lifted the newspaper from the open book, but the rector's hand fell quickly upon both. And there it rested. And his wretched eyes rested upon his hand.

"So I've never thought twice about George Mellis. I'd as soon think o' you, sir. Then who can it be?"

Mr. Carlton bounded to his feet, white as his collar, and quivering to his nostrils.

"You want to know?"

"I mean to know, sir."

"And to kill him—eh?"

"I reckon I'll go pretty near it."

"Ah, don't do it by halves!" cried Carlton in a strange high voice. "Kill him now!" His hands fell open at his side; his head fell forward on his breast; and he who had sinned grossly against God and man, yet was not born to be a hypocrite, stood defenceless, abject, self-destroyed.

Moments passed; became minutes; and all the sound in the rectory study came from the rattling of its inner door, or through the outer one from the garden. Then by degrees a hard breathing broke on Robert Carlton's ears; but he himself was the next to speak, flinging back his head in sudden misery.

"Why don't you strike?" he cried out. "You've got your stick; strike, man, strike!"

It seemed an hour before the answer came, in a voice scarcely recognizable as that of Jasper Musk, it was so low and calm; yet there was an intensity in the deep, slow tones that matched the fearful intensity of the fixed light eyes; and the massive face was still and livid from the short steel beard to the virile silver hair.

"Oh, yes, I'll strike!" hissed Musk. "I'll strike! I'll strike!" And he struck with his eyes until the other's fell once more; until the guilty man collapsed headlong in his chair, his arms upon the table, and his face upon his arms. "But I'll strike in my own way, thank you," Musk went on, "and in my own good time. You shall smart a bit first—learn what it's like to suffer—taste hell upon earth in case there's no hell for bloody murderers beyond! How I wish you could see yourself! How I wish your precious flock could see you—and they shall. Whited sepulchre . . . filthy hypocrite . . . living lie!"

Deliberately chosen, with long pauses between, with many a rejection of the word that came uppermost—the worse word that was too strong to sting—these measured epithets carved round the heart that unbridled abuse would have stabbed and stunned. Carlton could hide his face, but he quivered where he sprawled, and the other nodded in savage self-esteem.

"Not that I had ought to be surprised," continued Musk; "it's what might have been expected of a Jesuit in disguise; the only wonder is I didn't suspect you from the first. I never set up for being a charitable man; but that seems I was a damned sight too charitable towards you. I thought no wrong, whatever else I may have thought of you and your ways. No; I may have jeered, I may have been vexed, but my mind wasn't nasty enough for that. God! that I can keep my stick off you, when I remember the choir practices, and the organ practices, and the Bible classes, and the Young Women's Christian Association. Sounds well, don't it? Young Women's Christian Association! Now we know what it meant; now we know what it all means, church and parsons, religion and all; a sink of iniquity and a set of snivelling, whining, licentious—"

"Stop!" cried Carlton, manned at last, and on his feet to enforce the word. "Say what you please of me, do what you will to me. Nothing is too bad for me—I deserve the very worst. But abuse my Church you shall not, in my hearing."

"His Church!" sneered Musk. "A lot you've done to make me respect it, haven't you? My God, can you stand there looking at me as if I were in the wrong instead o' you? Do you know what you've done, and confessed to doing? You've murdered my girl, just as much as though you'd taken and cut her throat, you have: more, you've murdered her body and soul, you that snivel about the soul! And you can stand there and whine about your Church! Is that all you've got to say for yourself—to the father of the woman you've ruined to her grave?"

"That is all I have to say to you, Mr. Musk. I will not insult you by asking your forgiveness, much less by attempting to make the shadow of an excuse; there could be none; nor can there be any forgiveness for me from you or your wife; nor do I look for any mercy in this parish, or this world. Go, spread the news, and ruin me in my turn; it's what I deserve, and mean to bear.."

"Not so fast," said Musk—"not so fast, if you please. So I'm to spread the news, am I? And do you think I'm so proud that's the reverend? By your leave, Mr. Carlton, I'll keep that same news to myself till I've had all I want from it."

"Any refinement you like," said Carlton. "It will not be too bad for me—or too much—please God!"

Jasper Musk put on his hat, but came close up to the clergyman before taking his leave.

"I wish I knew you better!" he ground out through his teeth. "I wish I'd made up to you like the women, instead of giving you the wide berth I have. Do you know why? Because I'd have known how to hit you hardest," said Musk, hissing like a snake; "because I'd have known where to hurt you most!"

Carlton stood a trifle more upright: his enemy's malice ministered subtly to his remnant of self-respect.

"I wish I'd been a church-goer," continued Musk; "but it's never too late to mend! I may be there to-morrow to hear you preach; maybe I'll have a word to say myself; maybe I shall not. You'll know when the time comes, and not before."

Carlton quailed, for the first time at a threat, and his visible terror seemed to intoxicate the other. Seizing him by the shoulder as he had seized his wife, clutching him like a wild beast, and thrusting his great face to within an inch of that of the unhappy clergyman, Jasper Musk spat lewd names, and foul insult, and wanton blasphemy, until breath failed him. All the vileness he had heard in sixty years, and could recall in half as many seconds, poured from him in a very transport of insensate ribaldry; words that had never left his lips before, crowded to them now; and were still ringing in a swimming head when Robert Carlton woke to the fact that he was once more alone.

His first sensation was one of overwhelming nausea. His very vitals writhed; and he reeled heavily against an open bookcase, casting an arm along one of the upper shelves, and resting his face upon the sleeve. For a few moments all his weight was upon that arm; then he opened his eyes, and the titles of the books engaged his dazed attention. None was apt, but all were familiar, and the familiarity maddened the stricken man. He stood glaring from one low wall to another, filled with those doubts which are the cruel satellites of transcendent anguish. Had it really happened after all? The room was so unchanged, from the few things on the walls to the many in the chair! All was so homely, so intimate, so reassuring; and no visible trace of Musk! Had he ever been there at all?

Ah, yes, for he had gone! In the distance a gate had squealed, and shut with a rattle; the sound had lain in his ear; now it sank to the brain. Now, too, another sound, intermittent all this time, but meaningless hitherto, assumed a like significance. This was the continued rustling of a newspaper, as the wind whisked in at the open door and out by the open window in invisible harlequinade. The man's mind fled back a little lifetime of minutes. And he recalled the last puff and rustle, and the quick falling of his own hand upon the paper, which lay on his desk, as the last event of a past era of his existence—the last act of Robert Carlton, hypocrite!

And what was the peril that had made the final demand upon his caution and his cunning? It was a new irony to perceive at once that it had existed chiefly in guilty imagination; to remove the paper, and to reveal nothing more incriminating than the parish register of deaths, with an unfinished entry in his own hand, a spatter of ink in place of a name, and some round white blisters lower down the leaf. Yet this it was that had brought Carlton to his knees an hour ago; and it brought him to his knees again, not at the desk of formal prayer, but here at his table as before.

"Father have mercy on me," he prayed, "for I neither deserve nor desire any mercy from man!"

CHAPTER IV

MIDSUMMER NIGHT

And while he knelt the situation was developing, with unforeseen and truly merciful rapidity, in an utterly unsuspected quarter; thus an aggressive knock at the inner door came in a sense as an answer to the prayer it interrupted.

The rectory servants consisted at this time of a small but entire family employed wholesale out of pure philanthropy. And this was the mother, red-hot in her cheap crape, to say that she had heard everything—could not help hearing—and that house was no longer any place for respectable women and an honest lad—no, not if they had to sleep in the fields. So the lad had got their boxes on a barrow, but he would bring it back. And they would go, all of them, to Lakenhall Union, sooner than stay another hour in that house of shame.

Mr. Carlton produced his cash-box without a word, and counted out a month's wages for each in addition to arrears. The poor woman made a gallant stand against the favour, but, submitting, returned to her kitchen of her own accord, and to her master's study in a quarter of an hour, to tell him she had laid the table, and there was a wire cover over the meat.

"And may God forgive you, sir!" cried she at parting. "I couldn't have believed it if I hadn't heard it from your own lips with my own ears!"

There was much that Carlton himself could not believe. He sat half stupefied in his deserted rectory, like a man marooned, his one acute sensation that of his sudden solitude. What was so hard to realize was that the people knew! that the whole parish would know that night, and his own family next week, and the whole world before many days. He was well aware of the certain consequences of this scandal and its disclosure; he had faced them only too often during the nightmare of the past week, imagining some, ascertaining others. What seemed so incredible was that he had made the disclosure himself, that the very father had not suspected him to the end!

The last reflection convulsed him with self-contempt. What a hypocrite he must be! What an unconscious hypocrite, the worst kind of all!

Here he was eating his supper; he had no recollection of coming to the table; yet, now that he had caught himself, the food did not choke him, he was not sick with shame; he only despised himself—and went on.

It was dusk. He must have lit the lamp himself; as he lifted it from the table, having risen, he caught sight of its reflection and his own in the overmantel, and set the lamp upon the chimneypiece, and by its light had a better look at himself than he could remember having taken in his life before. There was no vanity in the man; he was studying his face out of sheer curiosity, from a new and quite impersonal point of view, as that of an enormous hypocrite and voluptuary.

Human nature was very strange: he himself would never have suspected such a face. The forehead was so broad and high, the deep-set eyes so steadfast, and yet so fervid! They were the eyes of a zealot, but no visionary: wisdom and understanding were in that bulge of the brow over each. But the evil writing is lower down, unless you look for positive crime or madness; yet these nostrils were sensitive, not sensual; and the mouth, yes, the mouth showed between the short brown beard and the heavy brown moustache; but what it showed was its strength. No; neither weakness nor wickedness were there; even Robert Carlton admitted that. But to be strong, and yet to fall; to mean well, and do evil; to look one thing, and to be another: all that was to embody a type for which he himself had ever entertained an unbridled loathing and contempt.

He carried the lamp to his study, and as he entered from within there was a knock at the outer door. One was waiting to see the rector, one who had waited and knocked there oftener than any other in the parish.

Carlton drew back, and the impulse of flight was strong upon him for the first time. It needed all his will to shut the inner door behind him, and to cry with any firmness, "Is that George Mellis?"

In response there burst into the room a lad in knickerbockers, broad-shouldered, muscular, yet smooth-faced, and mild-eyed all his nineteen years; but this was the supreme moment of them all; and his woman's eyes were on fire as he planted himself before the rector and his lamp, pale as ashes in its rays.

"Is it true?" he gasped. "Is it true?"

This lad was Carlton's chief disciple, his admirer, his imitator, his enthusiastic champion and defender; his right hand in all good works; nay more, his acolyte, his lieutenant of the sanctuary; and, before a broad chest so agitated, and innocent eyes so wild, the culprit's courage failed him at last, so that the truth clove to his tongue.

"It's all over the village," the lad continued in gasps. "You know what I mean. They're all saying it. They say you've admitted it; for God's sake say you haven't! Only deny it, and I'll go back and cram their lies down their throats!"

But by this Mr. Carlton had recovered himself, and was looking his last upon the anxious eager face of the lad who had loved and honoured him: his final pang was to see the eagerness growing, the anxiety lessening, his look misunderstood. And this time the admission was halt and hoarse.

What followed was also different; for, with scarcely a moment's interval, young Mellis burst into tears like the overgrown child that he was, and, flinging himself into the rector's chair, sobbed there unrestrainedly with his smooth face in his strong red hands. Carlton watched him by a prolonged effort of the will; he would shirk no part of his punishment; and no part to come could hurt much more than this. His fixed eyes were waiting for the boy's swimming ones when at length the latter could look up.

"You, of all men!" whispered Mellis. "You who have kept us all straight—me for one. Why, the very thought of you has helped me to resist things! You, with your religion: no more religion for me!"

At that the other broke out; his religion he could still defend; or thought he could, until he came to try, and his own unworthiness slowly strangled the words in his throat.

"Say what you like," said Mellis; "it was you brought me to church; it's you who turn me away; and I'll go to no other after yours. Only to think—"

And he plunged into puerile reminiscences of their religious life in common, quoting extreme points in the rich ritual in which he had been privileged to assist, as though they aggravated the case, and made it more incredible than it was already.

"If our Lord Himself—"

It did not need the rector's finger to check that blasphemy; but the thing was said; the thought was there.

"Yes; better go," said Carlton, as the lad leapt up. "Go; and let no one else come near me who ever believed in me; for I can better face my bitterest enemies. Yet you—you must be one of them! After her own father, no man should hate me more!"

And there was a new pain in his voice, a new agony of remorse, as memory stabbed him in a fresh place. But the boy shook his head, and hung it with a blush.

"You think I cared for her," he said. "I thought so, too, until she went away. I should have cared more then! It troubled me for a time; but I got over it; and then I knew I was too young for all that. Besides, she never looked at me after you came; that's another thing I see now; and I know I ran less after her. Yes, I was too young to love a woman," cried this village lad, "but I wasn't too old to love you, and look up to you, and follow you in all you did. I tell you the honest truth, Mr. Carlton," and his great eyes flashed their last reproach: "I'd have died for you, sir, I would! And I'd die now—thankfully—if it could make you the man I thought you were!"

This interview left Carlton's mind more a blank than ever. It might have been an hour later, or it might have been in ten minutes, that the thought occurred to him—if his dearest disciple felt thus, what must the enemy feel? And he was a man with enemies enough in the parish, having followed the old order of country parson, and that with more vigour than diplomacy. In eighteen months his reforms had been manifold and drastic beyond discretion. It is true that his preaching had won him more followers than his priestcraft had turned away. Yet a more acute ecclesiastic would have tapped the wedge instead of hammering it; the consummate priest would have condescended further in the direction of a more immediate and a wider popularity. Carlton had gone his own way, consulting none, attracting many, offending not a few. And he expected the speedy settlement of many a score.

Nor had he long to wait. Lamp in hand, he was locking up the house as mechanically as he had fed his body; but one thing had pricked him in the performance, and he tingled still between gratitude and fresh grief. He had a Scotch collie, Glen by name, a noble dog, that was for ever at its master's heels. So, during any service, the chain was a necessary evil; but straight from his vestry, in cassock and biretta, the rector would march to his backyard to release the dog. To-day he had forgotten; nor was it till the master's round brought him to the back premises that the poor beast barked itself into notice. Then, indeed, the dazed man realized that his outer ear had been calmly listening to the barking for some time; and, with a small thing to be sorry for again, and one friend behind him, he continued his round, a sentient being once more.

It was upstairs that the dog barked afresh, causing Carlton to snatch his head from the basin of cold water in which he had sought to assuage its fever, and to go over to his open window, towel in hand. No sooner had he reached it than he started back, and stood very still with the water dripping from his beard. When he did dry his face it was as though he wiped all colour from it too. And it was six feet of quivering clay that returned on tip-toe to that open window.

The new moon was setting behind the trees towards Linkworth; there was no need of its meagre light. Lanterns, bright lanterns, were closing in upon the rectory: at first the unhappy man had seen lanterns only, swinging close to the ground, swilling the lawn with light. Stealthy legs, knee-deep in this light, he remembered after his recoil. But not till he had driven himself back to the window did he see the set faces, or realize the fury of his people, kindled against him by his own confession of his own guilt.

When he saw this his nerve went, and he stood with clasped hands, the perspiration bursting from his skin. And the lanterns shook out into a chain along the edge of the lawn, and were held up to search the face of the house, all as yet without a word.

"That's his room," whispered one at last; "that—where the light is!"

It was the voice of the schoolmaster, himself a churchwarden, and withal an honest creature who was merely as many things as possible to as many men. His part had been a little difficult lately. "This has simplified it," thought the rector; and the twinge of bitterness did him good.

He was a man again for one moment; the next, "He's in his room," cried another, aloud; "that's him standing at the window!"

And there burst forth a howl of execration, that rose to a yell as the delinquent disappeared and in his panic put out the light.

"You coward!"

"Ah, you skunk!"

"Bloody Papist!"

"Hypocrite!"

They were the better names; each shot his own, and capped the last; the schoolmaster, mad with excitement, blaspheming with the best.

"Come down out of that, ye devil!"

"Do you show yourself, you cur!"

And this command Robert Carlton obeyed, his manhood rising yet again. But no sooner was he at the window than both panes crashed to powder over his head, and the surrounding bricks rang with the volley. The clergyman had a scratch from the falling glass, and a stone stung him on the hand. The blood bubbled in his veins.

"Cowards and curs yourselves!" he shouted down, shaking his fists at the crowd; and in ten seconds he was at the front door, with a couple of walking-sticks snatched from the stand. But he himself had turned the key and shot the bolt within the last few minutes, and this gave him time to think.

"Quiet, sir—quiet!" he cried to the dog at his heels. "They've right on their side," he groaned, "after all! Quiet, old doggie; come back; it's all deserved. And it's only the beginning of what we've got to bear!"

So he bore it, sitting on the stairs, where no window overlooked him, and soothing Glen with one hand, restraining him with the other; and yet, for his sin, despising his forbearance, even while he continued telling himself it was his duty to forbear.

And now breaking glass and barking dog made night a nightmare in the dark and empty house: the infuriated villagers were smashing the rectory windows one by one. Where the blind was up, the glass spread, and the stone flew far into the room; where the blind was down, stone and glass rattled against it, and fell in one heap with one clatter. So dining-room and drawing-room were wrecked in turn, at short range, with the heaviest available metal, and much interior damage. And still the master of the house sat immovable within, nodding grimly at each crash; wincing more at the curses; and once releasing the dog to stop his ears altogether.

It was no use; curiosity compelled him to listen; he was forbidden to shirk one stripe. And that was a communicant, that cursing demon; this was the schoolmaster, yelling like one of his own boys; the other Palmer, of the Plough and Harrow, a very old enemy, hoarse as a crow with drink and triumph. Young Cubitt, again, who cheered each crash, was one of the disaffected; but till to-night most of this howling mob had been his flock. Now all the good work was undone, was stultified, the good seed poisoned in the ground; and not for the first, and not for the fiftieth time that week, the confessed rake asked himself whether more harm than good would not come of his confession.

Meanwhile, of all the voices that he heard and could distinguish, only one diverted his self-contempt for an instant. This was the soft, passionless voice of a young gentleman, evidently not himself engaged in the stone-throwing, pointing out panes still to break to those who were. This was the voice of Sidney Gleed.

The thing had gone on for ten minutes or more when the outcry altered in character: an interruption had occurred: was it the police? No, the rector of the parish was too well acquainted with the character of its solitary constable. He would come up when all was over. Then who could this be?

The shower of stones had ceased as suddenly as it had begun. New oaths were flying in a new direction, and a voice hitherto unheard was heaping abuse on the abusers; with a strange thrill, the clergyman recognised it as the voice of Tom Ivey, the young contractor who was building the transepts; and he could remain no longer on the stairs. Stealing into the drawing-room, he stumbled across a crackling drift of glass, and, unnoticed now, stood in the wrecked bow-window, with the fresh air upon his face once more.

Lanterns were skipping right and left, their erratic rays giving momentary glimpses of a stalwart figure in pursuit, a stick whirling about his ears, and resounding on the backs and shoulders of the retreating rabble. Some stayed to stone the new foe before they ran; and one, Palmer the publican, set his lantern on the gravel and squared up in style. Robert Carlton never saw what followed; for at this moment his maddened dog, which had been tearing about the house in search of an outlet, bounded past him through the shattered window; and, when the rout was complete, the inn-keeper's lantern was a solitary star in the nether darkness. Then the gate clattered, a swinging step approached, and Tom Ivey caught up the lantern in his stride.

Carlton sprang through the window to meet him, every other emotion sunk for the moment in one of overflowing gratitude.

"Tom," he cried, "how can I thank you—"

"Keep your thanks to yourself."

"But—Tom—"

"Don't 'Tom' me! Keep your distance too. Do you think I haven't heard about it? Do you think I'd lift a finger for you—let alone a stick? No, sir, I'd liefer take that to your own back; but I fare to mind when the Rector of Long Stow was a good man, who didn't preach too tall, but acted up to what he did preach; and I won't see the house he lived in wrecked and ruined because a blackguard's followed him."

"I am all that," said Mr. Carlton. "Go on!"

The other stared, not so much disarmed as confounded.

"I'm sorry to open so wide, and you know I'm sorry," he at length burst out. "'Tain't for me to call you over, sir, and I won't tell you no more lies. I couldn't bear to see them snarling curs setting on you the moment you was down, and that's the truth! But it wasn't what I come back to say," continued Ivey doggedly. "I come back to say you can get another party to go on with that there building, for I won't work no more for you. The plant's yours; you found that for the job; you can find more men. I throw up the contract: take the law of me if you like."

Robert Carlton was back in his study. It was the one front room which had escaped inviolate; the open lattice had saved it; not a pebble added to the old disorder. The rector sighed relief as he held up the lamp on entering; then he shot the rubbish out of the big arm-chair, and himself lay back in it like the dead. A bloody smear, where the glass had grazed his cheek, enhanced his pallor; his eyes were closed; no muscle moved. And yet his wits clung to him like wolves, till presently the white brow wrinkled, the heavy eyelids twitched.

"May I come in, reverend?" said the saddler's voice.

Carlton assented with a sigh, but did not raise himself to greet the visitor, who came in mopping his forehead, reversed the chair at the writing table, and seated himself with ominous deliberation. Then he mopped again, and was slow to speak; but his scornful expression prepared the clergyman for more of that which he was resolved to bear.

"Pharisees!" cried Fuller at last. "Humbugs and hypocrites!"

The words were precisely those which Robert Carlton expected and must endure, but against the plural number he felt bound to protest. "We are not all alike, Mr. Fuller," he said; "thank God, I am but one out of many thousands."

"You?" cried the saddler. "Gord love yer, reverend, did you think I meant you? No, sir, it's the stupid fools and canting cowards I mean, that take and hit a man as soon as ever he's down; not the man they hit."

Mr. Carlton sat silent, astounded, and tingling between pain and pleasure. He fancied he had run through the gamut of the emotions, but here was a new one that he feared to dissect.

"Not the man," proceeded the saddler in raised tones—"not the man who is worth the rest of the parish put together—saint or sinner—guilty or innocent!"

Yes, it was pleasure! It was pleasure, acute and lawless, wicked, ungovernable, and yet to be governed. To have one man's sympathy, how sweet it was, but how shameful in a guilty heart that would be contrite too! It had brought a colour to his face, a light to his eyes; ere the one had faded, and the other failed, Robert Carlton's will had frozen that tiny rill of comfort at its fount.

"You mustn't say that," was his belated reply; but it came curt and cold enough to please himself.

"But I do say it," cried old Fuller, "and I will say it, and I won't say a word more than I mean. Let there be no mistake between us, reverend: I don't deny I felt what is felt when first I heard; but when I come to think of it, that fared to break my heart more'n to make that boil; and when I thought a bit deeper, I see how easy that is to make bad worse. Not as it ain't right bad; but that wasn't for us to make it worse. So it was me fetched Tom Ivey. And now he tells me what he ups and says himself when all was over. 'Gord love yer, Tom,' says I, 'you'll be ashamed of that when you're a man of my experience! You forget the good our reverend's been doing amongst us all this time, and you think only o' this here evil. I'll go up,' says I, 'and I'll show him there's one fair-minded, level-headed man o' the world in this here hotbed o' fools and Pharisees.'"

"But Tom was right, and you were wrong."

"Don't tell me, reverend," said the saddler, edging his chair nearer to the long limp figure under the lamp. "You can't undo the good you've once done, not if you try. Leave religion out of it, and look at all you've done for the poor: look at the coal club, and the book club, and the dispensary, and the Young Man's—"

"Unhappily, Fuller, all this is beside the question."

And the cold tone was no longer put on; neither did it cover an emotion which called for conscientious suppression; for these officious sallies only fretted the spirit they were intended to soothe.

"Well, then," rejoined Fuller, "if you prefer it, and for the sake of argument, look at a poor old feller like me. What should I ha' done without you, reverend? I don't come to church, yet you take no offence when I tell you why, but you argue the point like a rare 'un, and you lend me the paper just the same. The Reverend Jackson wouldn't ha' done it, though I durs'n't stay away in his day; he'd have stopped my livelihood in a week. So don't you fare to make yourself out worse than you are, reverend; you've done wrong, I allow, but so did Solomon, and so did David; and weren't so quick to own up to it, either! Like them, you've done good, too, and plenty of it, and that sha'n't be forgotten if I can help it. As for the poor young thing that's gone—"

"Don't name her, I beg!"

"Very well, sir, I won't. I'm as sorry as the rest o' the parish; but we shouldn't be unfair because we're sorry. They may say what they like, but a man of my experience knows that nine times out of ten the woman's more to blame—"

"Out of my house!"

Carlton had leapt to his feet, was standing at his full height for the first time that night, and pointing sternly to the door. His face was white with passion. The saddler's jaw dropped.

"What, sir?" he gasped.

"Out of my sight—this instant!"

"For sayun—"

"For daring to say one half of what you have said! It's my own fault. I've spoilt you; but out you go."

Fuller rose slowly, amazed, bewildered, and mortified to the quick. He was a kind-hearted man, but he had all the superior peasant's obstinacy and self-conceit: the one had helped to bring him to the clergyman's side, the other to wag his tongue. Yet his sympathy was genuine enough; and the theory, of which the bare hint had spilled vials of wrath upon his head, was in fact his profound conviction. Smarting vanity, however, was the absorbing sensation of the moment. And for the next hour the saddler could have returned every few minutes with some fresh retort; but in the moment of humiliation he could not rise above a grumble:

"I might as well have thrown stones with the rest!"

"Better," the clergyman cried after him. "You had a right to punish me; to pity and excuse me you had none. Least of all—"

He broke off, and stood at his door till the quick steps stopped, and the gate clattered, and the steps died away. The night was dark, and this end of the village already very still: the Plough and Harrow was nearer the other. The wind had not fallen; a murmur of very distant thunder came with it from the west. Nearer home a peewit called, and Robert Carlton caught himself wondering whether there would be rain before morning.

CHAPTER V

THE MAN ALONE

At midnight he was still alone, and the slow torture of his own thoughts was still a relief. As the dining-room clock struck—he noted its preservation—and the thin strokes floated through those broken windows and in at that of the study, he gave up listening for the next step. His privacy seemed secure at last. He could abandon his spirit to its proper torments; he could enter upon another night in hell. Yet, even now, the worst was over, and there would be no more nights of secret grief, secret remorse, secret shame. He had confessed his sin, and thereby earned his right to suffer. No more to hide! No more deceit! He could not realize it yet; he only knew that his heart was lighter already. He felt ashamed of the relief.

Yet another night came back to him as he paced his floor: a last year's night when the full moon shone through ragged trees. It also had been worse than this: it was the inner life that lay in ruins then. He remembered pacing till sunrise as he was pacing now: such a still night but for that; one had but to stand and listen to hear the very fall of the leaf. He remembered thus standing, there at the door, in the moonlight, and a line that had buzzed in his head as he listened.

"And yet God has not said a word!"

God had spoken now!

And the man was glad.

Glad! He almost revelled in his disgrace; it produced in him unexpected sensations—the sensations of the debtor who begins to pay. Here was an extreme instance of the things that are worse to dream of than to endure. He felt less ignominious in the hour of his public ignominy than in all these months of secret shame. He was living a single life once more. The wind roamed at will through the damaged house as through the ribs of a wreck; and its ruined master drew himself up, and his stride quickened with his blood. He was no longer lording it in his pulpit, the popular preacher of the countryside, drawing the devout from half a dozen parishes, a revelation to the rustic mind, a conscious libertine all the while, with a tongue of gold and a heart of lead. More than all, he was no longer the one to sit secure, in loathsome immunity, in sickening esteem: he, the man! The woman had suffered; it was his turn now. Woman? The poor child . . . the poor, dead, murdered child . . . Well! the wages of his sin would be worse than death; they were worse already. And again the man was glad; but his momentary and strange exultation had ended in an agony.

The poor, poor girl . . .

No; nothing was too bad for him—not even the one thing that he would feel more than all the rest in bulk. He put his mind on that one thing. He dwelt upon it, wilfully, not in conscious self-pity, but as one eager to meet his punishment half-way, to shirk none of it. The attitude was characteristic. The sacrificial spirit informed the man. In another age and another Church he had done barbaric violence to his own flesh in the name of mortification. Living in the latter half of the nineteenth century, a mere Anglican, he was content to play tricks with a fine constitution in Lent.

"I will look my last upon it," he said aloud: "it would be insulting God and man to attempt to take another service after this; I have held my last, and laid my last stone. Let me see what I have sown for others to reap."

And he picked his way through the darkness to the church.

The path intersected a narrow meadow with the hay newly cut, and lying in tussocks under the stars; a light fence divided this reef of glebe from the churchyard; and, just within the latter, a lean-to shed faced the scaffolding of the north transept, its back against the fence. The shed was flimsy and small, but it had come out of the rector's pocket; the transepts themselves were to be his gift, because the living was too good for a celibate priest, and it was his sermons that had made the church too small. So he had paid for everything, even to the mason's tools inside the shed, because Tom Ivey had never had a contract before and lacked capital. And the out-door interest of the building had formed a healthy complement to the engrossing affairs of the sanctuary; and, indeed, they had developed side by side. Perhaps the material changes had proved the more absorbing to one who threw himself headlong into whatsoever he undertook. Of late, especially, it had been remarked that the reverend was taking quite an extraordinary part in these proceedings: cultivating a knack he had of carving in stone; neglecting cottages for his mason's shed; and tiring himself out by day like a man who dreads the night. How he had dreaded it none had known, but now all might guess.

Yet he had loved his work for its own sake, not merely as a distraction from gnawing thoughts; there was in him something of the elemental artist: the making of anything was his passionate delight. And now the scene of his industry inflicted a pang so keen that he forgot to appreciate it as part of his deserts; and, for the moment, priest and sinner disappeared in the grieving artist, bidding good-bye not only to his studio, but to art itself. It was very dark; the place was strewn with uncut boulders, poles, barrows, heaps of rubble; but he knew his way through the litter, and, in the double darkness of the shed, could lay his hand on anything he chose. He took something down from a shelf. It was a gargoyle of his own making, meant for the vestry door in the south transept. He stood with it in both hands, and his thumbs felt the eyes and his palms the cheeks, at first as gently as though the stone were flesh, then suddenly with all his strength, as if to crush the grotesque head to powder. It was not a useful thing: no water could spout from the sham mouth which he had wrought with loving pains. It was only his idea for finishing off the label moulding of the vestry door; it was only something he had made himself—for others to throw away, or to keep and show as the handiwork of the immoral rector of Long Stow. He restored it to its place; and retraced his sure steps through the rubbish, artist no more. Good-bye to that!

He crossed over to the church, went round to the porch, and entered by the only door in use during the alterations. Eighteen months ago he would have found it locked. It was he who had opened the House of God to all comers at all hours, and made every sitting free. He stole up the aisle as one seeing in the dark. His feet fell softly on the matting, where in early days they had clattered on bare flags, and yet more softly when they had mounted a step without stumbling. The matting in the aisle was his addition, the rich carpet in the chancel was his gift. All his innovations had not provoked dissension. Presently he lit a lamp, a Syrian treasure, highly wrought, that hung over the lectern: he had bought it at Damascus, years before, for his church when he should have one. Yes; he had given freely to God's House, to make it also the House Beautiful, though he took no trouble to adorn his own.

And this was to be the end! For events could take but one course now: a complaint to the bishop (all the parish would sign it), a summons to the palace, a trial at the consistory court; suspension certainly; deprivation, perhaps; he had been at some pains to inform himself on the subject. The bishop would be sore. He had taken such an interest in everything at the confirmation, his sympathy had been so full and unexpected, his approval so stimulating, so hearty and frank! Carlton was ashamed of thinking of his bishop instead of praying to God upon his knees. He longed to kneel and pray, for the last time, there at the table which he chose to call the altar, but which he had found ugly and bare, and was leaving richly laden and richly hung. In the small and distant light of the lectern lamp he stood gazing at the damask hangings, the green frontal, the silver candlesticks, the flowers from his own garden—the flowers he grew for this. He longed to kneel, but could not. He could not pray. He could not weep. His heart was a grave, and the grave filled in and the weight of the earth upon his spirit. He had been quite wrong an hour ago. This was the blackest hour of all. To have done and given so much, and to lose it all! To have set his whole soul for years towards the light, to have striven so to turn the souls of others; and to be thrust into outer darkness for one sin!

This wave of bitterness, of blind rebellion and human egotism, bore him out of his church, for the last time, in a passion of defiance and self-defence: a sudden and deplorable change in such a man at such an hour. Happily, it was short-lived. His angry stride brought him tripping into fresh earth, and he started back, aghast at his egotism, stunned afresh by his sin, and overwhelmed by such a flood of penitence and remorse as even he had not endured before. Under his eyes the new grave was growing clearer in the starlight, and not less cruel, and not less cold. An hour later he was still kneeling over it, and his tears had not ceased to flow.

CHAPTER VI

FIRE

Witnesses have differed as to the exact hour at which the inhabitants of Long Stow, sound asleep after excitement enough for one night, were frightened from their beds by a sudden and violent ringing of the church bells. The midsummer night was as dark as ever, and so it remained or seemed to remain for a considerable time. It cannot have been more than two o'clock.

A few minutes before the alarm, Robert Carlton had forced himself to his feet, to be struck with fresh shame at two apparent evidences of the mood in which he had quitted the church. He had left the door wide open and the church lit up. Every stone showed on the path, in the stream of light poured upon it from the porch, into which, however, it was impossible to see from where the rector stood. The porch projected from the south side, while the new grave was directly opposite the west window, every square of which stood out against the glare within. An instant's reflection showed Carlton that this could not be the light which he had left; he went to see what it was. A sudden heat upon his face broke the truth to him in the porch, and in a stride he knew the worst. A little fire was raging in the church: two or three pews were in flames.

Robert Carlton stood inactive for a score of seconds. It looked the kind of fire that a vigorous man might have beaten out with his coat. Yet one in the full vigour of his manhood stood thinking a score of thoughts while the flames bit through the varnish into the wood. Nor was this the fascination of horror: the fire looked such a little fire at the first glance. It was rather the obsession of an astounding puzzle: what in the world could have caused a fire at all?

A guilty feeling came in answer: he must have dropped the match with which he lit that lamp. The feeling escaped in the simultaneous discovery that the lamp in question had been extinguished, but that it and others were slightly awry, and one or two still swaying on their chains, as though all the lamps had been rudely meddled with. And now horror came. The flames were spreading with curious facility, shooting their blue tongues over the woodwork before the yellow fangs took hold, but all so quickly that the burning area seemed to have doubled itself in these few seconds, while from the heart of it there came the crisp crackle of quicker fuel, culminating in a blaze as though a rick had caught; and, sure enough, as these flames leapt high, their source was revealed in a pile of the rector's new straw hassocks.

The puzzle was one no more: plainer work of incendiary was never seen. Through the smoke now swinging in black coils to the roof, the east window showed in holes made within the last hour, obviously to promote the draught that blew in Carlton's face as he rushed back to the open door and laid hold of all the bell-ropes at once.

The bells were small and jangling; a new peal, and a tower to hang them in, were among the things which the rector had said that he would have some day. But as the old bells clanged for the last time, in the dead of that summer night, they were heard at Linkworth, a mile and a half across the wind, but down the wind they rang up half Bedingfield, which is three good miles from Long Stow.

The first inhabitant to reach the scene was the fleet and sturdy Tom Ivey, whose mother kept the post-office in the middle of the village; as he ran the ringing stopped, and the first glass smashed with the heat, flame and smoke making a mouthpiece of the mullioned window in the north wall as Tom dashed up by the short cut through the rectory garden. He was greatly alarmed at finding no one in the churchyard, and rushed into the church with the full expectation of discovering the ringer senseless at his post. What he did find was the rector, standing within the church, to windward of the conflagration, his back to the door, absorbed, as it seemed, in a perfectly passive contemplation of the fire.

"Mr. Carlton!" shouted Tom.

Before replying, the clergyman spun something into the heart of the flames; in the thickening smoke it was impossible to see what; but the same second he was round upon his heel, coughing and choking, his face black, his eyes fires themselves, purpose and determination in every limb.

"Tom? Thank God it's you! We must get this under. Out of it before we suffocate!" And with his own rush he carried the builder into the open air.

"What's done it, sir?"

"Done it? Wait till we've undone it! We can if we work together. Ah! here are more of you. Buckets, men—buckets!" cried Carlton, rushing to meet a half-dressed medley at the gate, and commanding them as though there had been no other meeting earlier in the night. "You who live near, run for your own; the rest into my kitchen and find what you can; buckets are the thing! One of you pump; the rest form line from my well to the church, and keep passing along. You see to it, Mr. Jones!"

And for a while the schoolmaster and churchwarden, carried away as usual by his feelings and self-importance, was as busy enforcing the rector's orders as he had made himself in breaking his windows an hour or two before.

"Let one man ride or run for the Lakenhall engine; not you, Tom!" exclaimed the clergyman, seizing Ivey by the arm. "They'll be all night coming, and I can't spare you."

"I'll stay, sir."

"Water's no use to windward of a fire; it's spreading straight up the church. We want to be on the other side to stop it."

"The aisle's not afire!"

"But they couldn't get the water to us, even if we got through alive. No; where the walls are down for the transepts—that's the place. Which side's boarded strongest?"

"Both the same, sir."

"Then we'll hack through the nearest! A saw and an axe, and we'll be through by the time the first bucketful's ready for us."

And, friends again, but both unconscious of the change, they rushed together to the shed of which Robert Carlton had so lately taken leave: in the fever of the moment even that leave-taking was forgotten.

It was the north transept which faced the shed. Already the walls were a dozen feet high, but a doorway had been left. The greater gap between transept and nave was vertically boarded over within the church, and on these boards fell the rector with his axe, to make an opening for Tom's saw. They had light enough for their work. The interstices between the boards were as the red-hot strings of a colossal harp; quickly a couple were cut, and the boards beaten in; and it was as though the wind had come down a smoking chimney. The pair fell back on either side of the black stream that gushed out like water. Then cried Carlton in his voice of command:

"Look here! you stay where you are, Tom."

"With you, sir?"

"No, I must have a look; but one's enough."

"Not for me, Mr. Carlton. I follow you."

"Then you keep me where I am," said Carlton, sternly.

"All right, sir! You follow me!"

Next instant they were both through the breach, the builder first by the depth of his chest. And they stood up within, but were glad to crouch again out of the smoke. Already a dense reek hid the roof, and every moment added to the depth of that inverted sea. It was a sea of ineffectual currents, setting towards the smashed windows, the new breach, the open door, but caught and diverted and sucked into the inky whirlpool that the wind made under the roof, and escaping only by chance fits and sudden starts. On the other hand, there was still air enough to breathe within a few feet of the ground, and with water it seemed as if something might yet be done. But it was no longer a very little fire: at best the nave must be gutted now; to save roof and chancel was the utmost hope. Yet here and there the worst seemed over. The blazing hassocks were now only a glowing heap, and still the roof had not caught. As the two men crouched and watched, the flames felt the front pews with their splay blue tentacles, and the woodwork which was still untouched glistened like a human body in pain.

"You see that?" said Mr. Carlton, pointing to this moisture.

"What is it?"

"Paraffin! Look at the lamps; he's simply emptied them—"

"Who, sir—who?"

"God knows, and may God forgive him! I have enemies enough this morning, though not more than I deserve. If only they will be my friends for one hour, for the sake of the church! Are they never coming with that water? Run and tell them a bucketful would make a difference now, but cartloads will make none in ten more minutes! And tell them what I said just now: bid them for God's sake think of nothing but the fire till we get it under."

He was thinking of nothing else himself, confident still of some measure of success, only fretting for his water. In Ivey's absence he stripped to the waist, and with his long coat essayed to beat the little flames out as they spread and leapt, the blue and yellow surf of the encroaching tide; but for one he extinguished he fanned a hundred, so he retreated before he was flayed alive. And they found him stooping near the opening, half-naked, scorched, begrimed, but not disheartened; a strange figure in the place that knew him best in vestments, if any of them thought of that.

The first man had a bucket in each hand, but had spilt freely from both in his haste. Carlton would not let him in, but received the buckets through the hole, dashed their contents over the burning pews, and returned them empty without waiting to see results. When he had time to look, a little steam was rising, but the fire raged with undiminished fury. The next comer was a boy with a brimming watering-can; but it is difficult to fling water with effect from such a vessel, and pouring was impossible in the increasing heat. Then came Tom Ivey with two more buckets.

"Keep outside," cried Carlton, taking them. "There's only work for one in here. Can't they form line as I said, and pass along instead of carrying?"

"No, sir—not enough of us for the distance."

"Not enough of you who'll put the church before the parson! That's what you mean. The parson may deserve burning alive, but the poor church has done no wrong!"

And he continued his exertions in a bitter spirit not warranted by the real circumstances, for his masterful monopoly of all danger had won some sympathy outside, and many a one who had flung a stone was running with a bucket now. More, however, stood with their hands in their pockets; for East Anglia is constitutionally phlegmatic, and not all the village had joined in the indignant excesses of the evening.

The saddler came no farther than the fence in front of his house and workshop. He was that implacable creature, the offended countryman.

George Mellis did not even see the fire; already he had shaken the dust of Long Stow from his feet for good.

Thus, of the three types, as far removed from one another as the points of an equilateral triangle, who had put in their individual word of reproach, of denunciation, and of sympathy more insufferable than either, only one was present on this lurid scene; but that one was doing the work of ten.

"That there Tom Ivey," said one of a group on the safe side of the rectory fence, "he fares all of a wash. Yet I do hear as how he come up to the rectory when he'd cleared the garden and called Carlton over somethun wonderful."

"I lay it was nothun to the calling over he had from Jasper."

"Where is Jasper?"

"Been indoors ever since: a touch of the old trouble, the missus told Jones when he called."

"That's a pity. This would've soothed his sore."

One or two observed that that fared to soothe theirs; for there was no reaction on the safe side of the fence. But the worst said in the Suffolk tongue was invariably capped by a different order of voice, which chimed in now.

"The best thing Carlton can do is to cockle up with his church. The governor'll build you a new church and find a new man to fill it. There's nobody keener on a change as it is. I should like to be there when he hears . . ."

The speaker was smoking a cigarette on a barrow wheeled from the shed. He might have been watching a display of fireworks, and one which was beginning to bore him. His unmoved eye sought change. It found the sexton hobbling in the glare.

"Hi, Busby! Come here, I want you. What the dickens do you mean by setting fire to the church?"

"Me set fire to it, Master Sidney? Me set a church afire? He! he! you allus fare to have yer laugh."

"It will be no laughing matter for you when you're run in for it, Busby."

"Go on, Master Sidney; you know better than that."

"I wish I did. They hang for arson, you know! But I say, Busby, how's the frog?"

The wizened face grew grave, but only as the screen darkens between the pictures; next instant it was alight with the ineffable joy of gratified monomania. The sexton hobbled nearer, clawing his vest.

"Oh, that croap away; that's at that now! Would 'ee like to listen, Master Sidney?"

"No, thanks, Busby; don't you undo a button," said the young gentleman, hastily. "I can hear it from where I am."

The sexton went into senile raptures.

"You can hear it? You can hear it? Do you all listen to that: he can hear it, he can hear it from where he sit. The little varmin, to croap so loud! That must be the fire. That fare to make him blink! An' Master Sidney, he can hear him from where he sit!"

The sexton hurried off to spread his triumph; but he boasted to deaf ears. There was a sudden light below the sharp horizon between black roof and slaty sky, yet no flame rose above the roof. It was as though the southern eaves had caught. Ivey rushed out of the north transept. Mr. Carlton followed, axe in hand. His chest and arms were smudged and inflamed, his blinking eyelids were burnt bare, and the sweat stood all over him in the red light leaping from the shivered windows.

"It's no use, lads!" he called to those still running with the buckets; "the boards have caught on the other side. Come and help me smash them in, and we may save the chancel yet! Every man who is a man," he shouted to the group across the fence, "come—lend a hand to save God's sanctuary!"

And he led the way with his axe, stinging to the waist in the open air, but drunk with battle and the battle's joy. And there was no more talking behind the rectory fence; not a man was left there to talk; even Sidney Gleed had dropped his cigarette to follow the inspired madman with the axe.

The south transept was a stage less advanced than the north. Carlton got upon one low wall, ran along it to that of the nave, and swung his axe into the burning wood to his right. A rent was quickly made; he leapt into the transept and improved it, his axe ringing the seconds, the muscles of his back bulging and bubbling beneath the scorched skin. Men watched him open-mouthed. It seemed incredible that such nerve, such sinew, such indomitable virility, should have hidden from their vengeance that very night.

"A ladder!" he cried. "There's one behind the shed."

The wood screen was rent, but not to the top. Below, the fire was checked, but above it still crawled east. Waiting for the ladder, Carlton employed himself in widening the gap that he had made; when it came, he had it held vertically against the eaves, left intact above the boarding, and ran up to finish his own work with the axe held short in his left hand. A couple of planks were smashed in unburnt. He stayed on the ladder to see whether the flames would leap the completed chasm, stayed until the rungs smoked under his nose. When the burning boards fell in on his left, and those on his right did not even smoulder, he returned quickly to the ground.

Throats which had groaned that night were parching for a cheer. The time was not ripe. A shrill cry came instead: the boarding upon the other side had ignited in its turn.

"Round with the ladder," cried the rector; "we'll soon have it out. We know more about it now. We'll save the chancel yet! Find another axe; we'll begin top and bottom at once."

And now the scene was changing every minute. A sky of slate had become a sky of lead. The tens who had witnessed the first stages of the fire had multiplied into hundreds. Frightened birds were twittering in the trees; frightened horses neighed in the road; every kind of vehicle but a fire-engine had been driven to the scene. Among the graves stood a tall and aged gentleman, with the top-hat of his youth crammed down to his snowy eyebrows, and an equally obsolete top-coat buttoned up to his silver whiskers, in conversation with Sidney Gleed.

"The damned rascal!" said the old gentleman. "But how the devil did it come out?"

"Musk seems to have smelt a rat, and went to him after the funeral. And he owned up as bold as brass; the servants heard him. There he goes, up the ladder again on this side. Keeps the fun to himself, don't he? Who's going to win the Leger, doctor? Shotover again?"

"Damn the Leger," said Dr. Marigold, whose sporting propensities, bad language, and good heart were further constituents in the most picturesque personality within a day's ride. "To think I should have stood at her death-bed," he said, "and would have given ten pounds to know who it was; and it's your High Church parson of all men on God's earth! The infernal blackguard deserves to have his church burnt down; but he's got some pluck, confound him."

"Sucking up," said Master Sidney: "playing to the gallery while he's got the chance."

"H'm," said the doctor; "looks to me pretty badly burnt about the back and arms. If he wasn't such a damned rascal I'd order him down."

"He's doing no good," rejoined the young cynic, "and he knows it. He's only there for effect. Look! There's the roof catching, as any fool knew it must; and here's the Lakenhall engine, in time for 'God save the Queen.'"

Dr. Marigold swore again: his good heart contained no niche for the heir to the Long Stow property. He turned his back on Sidney, his face to the sexton, who had been at his elbow for some time.

"Well, Busby, what are you bothering about?"

"The frog, doctor. That croap louder than ever."

"You infernal old humbug! Get out!"

"But that's true, doctor—that's Gospel truth. Do you stoop down and you'll hear it for yourself. Master Sidney, he heard it where he sit."

"Did he, indeed! Then he's worse than you."

"But that steal every bit I eat; that do, that do," whined the sexton. "I've tried salts, I've tried a 'metic, an' what else can I try? That fare to know such a wunnerful lot. Salts an' 'metics, not him! He look t'other way, an' hang on like grim death for the next bit o' meat. That's killin' me, doctor. That's worse nor slow poison. That steal every bite I eat."

"Well, it won't steal this," said the doctor, dispensing half-a-crown. "Now get away to bed, you old fool, and don't bother me."

And neither thanks nor entreaties would divert his eyes from the burning church again.

The antiquated doctor was one of Nature's sportsmen: his inveterate sympathies were with the losers of up-hill games and games against time; and this blackguard parson had played his like a man, only to lose it with the thunder of the fire-engine in his ears. The roof had caught at last; in a little it would be blazing from end to end; and half-a-dozen country fire-engines, and half a hundred Robert Carltons, could do no good now. Carlton came slowly enough down his ladder this time, and stood apart with his beard on his chest.

"Hard lines, hard lines!" muttered Dr. Marigold in his top-coat collar; and "Those slow fools! Those sleepy old women!" with his favourite participle in each ejaculation.

A sky of lead had turned to one of silver. Across the open uplands, beyond the conflagration, a kindlier glow was in the east. And in the broad daylight the fire reached its height with as small effect as the firemen plied their water. Nothing could check the roof. Ceiling, joists, and slates burnt up like good fuel in a good grate. Now it was a watershed of living fire; now an avalanche of red-hot ruin; now a column of smoke and sparks, rising out of blackened walls; a column unbroken by the wind, which had fallen at dawn with a little rain, the edge of a shower that had shunned Long Stow.

When the roof fell in there were few of the hundreds present who had not retreated out of harm's way. Only the helmed firemen held their ground, and two others with bare heads. Of the pair, one was standing dazed, with his beard on the rough coat thrown about him, and an ear deaf to his companion's entreaties, when the crash came and the sparks flew high and wide through rent walls and gaping windows. The sparks blackened as they fell. The first smoke lifted. And the dazed man lay upon his face, the other kneeling over him.

Dr. Marigold came running, for all his years and his long top-coat.

"Did anything hit him, Ivey?"

"Not that I saw, sir; but he fared as if he'd fainted on his feet, and when the roof went, why, so did he."

Marigold knelt also, and a thickening ring enclosed the three.

"He's rather nastily burnt, poor devil."

And the old doctor lifted a leaden wrist, felt it in a sudden hush, examined a burn upon the same arm, and looked up through eyebrows like white moustaches.

"But not dangerously, damn him!"

CHAPTER VII

THE SINNER'S PRAYER

The bishop of the diocese sat at the larger of the two desks in the palace library. It was the thirteenth of the following month, and a wet forenoon. At eleven o'clock his lordship was intent upon a sheet of unlined foolscap, with sundry notes dotted down the edge, and the rest of the leaf left blank. The bishop's sight was failing, but against glasses he had set his face. So his whiskers curled upon the paper; and the wide mouth between the whiskers was firmly compressed; and this compression lengthened a clean-shaven upper lip already unduly long. But the pose displayed a noble head covered with thin white hair, and the broad brow that was the casket of a broad mind. Seen at his desk, the massive head and shoulders suggested both strength and stature above the normal. Yet the bishop on his legs was a little man who limped. And the surprise of this discovery was not the last for an observer: for the little lame man had a dignity independent of his inches, and a majesty of mind which lost nothing, but gained in prominence, by the constant contrast of a bodily imperfection.

The bishop stood up when his visitor was announced, a minute after eleven, and supported himself with one hand while he stretched the other across his desk. Carlton took it in confusion. He had expected that shut mouth and piercing glance, but not this kindly grasp. He was invited to sit down. The man who complied was the ghost of the Rector of Long Stow, as his spiritual overseer remembered him. His whole face was as white as his forehead had been on the day of the fire. It carried more than one still whiter scar. Yet in the eyes there burnt, brighter than ever, those fires of zeal and of enthusiasm which had warmed the bishop's heart in the past, but which somewhat puzzled him now.

"I am sorry," said his lordship, "that you should have such weather for what, I am sure, must have been an undertaking for you, Mr. Carlton. You still look far from strong. Before we begin, is there nothing—"

Carlton could hear no more. There was nothing at all. He was quite himself again. And he spoke with some coolness; for the other's manner, despite his mouth and his eyes, was almost cruel in its unexpected and undue consideration. It was less than ever this man's intention to play upon the pity of high or low. He had an appeal to make before he went, but it was not an appeal for pity. Meanwhile his back stiffened and his chest filled in the intensity of his desire not to look the invalid.

"In that case," resumed the bishop, "I am glad that you have seen your way to keeping the appointment I suggested. In cases of complaint—more especially a complaint of the grave character indicated in my letter—I make it a rule to see the person complained of before taking further steps. That is to say, if he will see me; and I don't think you will regret having done so, Mr. Carlton. It may give you pain—"

Carlton jerked his hands.

"But you shall have fair play!"

And his lordship looked point-blank at the bearded man, as he had looked in his day on many a younger culprit; and his voice was the peculiar voice that generations of schoolboys had set themselves to imitate, with less success than they supposed.

Carlton bowed acknowledgment of this promise.

"In the questions which I feel compelled to put"—and the bishop glanced at his sheet of foolscap—"you will perhaps give me credit for studying your feelings as far as is possible in the painful circumstances. I shall try not to leave them more painful than I find them, Mr. Carlton. But the complaint received is a very serious one, and it is not made by one person; it has very many signatures; and it necessitates plain speaking. It is a fact, then, that you are the father of an illegitimate child born on the twentieth of last month in your own parish?"

"It is a fact, my lord."

"And the woman is dead?"

"The young girl—is dead."

The bishop's pen had begun the descent of the clean part of his page of foolscap; when the last answer was inscribed, the writer looked up, neither in astonishment nor in horror, but with the clear eye and the serene brow of the ideal judge.

"Of course," said he, "I am informed that you have already made the admission. Let there be no affectation or misunderstanding between us, on that or any other point. But as your bishop, and at least hitherto your friend, I desire to have refutation or confirmation from your own lips. You are at perfect liberty to deny me either. It will make no difference to the ultimate result. That, as you know, will be out of my hands."

"I desire to withhold nothing, my lord," said Robert Carlton in a firm voice.

"Very well. I think we understand each other. This poor young woman, I gather, was the daughter of a prominent parishioner?"

"Of a prominent resident in my parish—yes."

"But she herself was conspicuous in parochial work? Is it a fact that she played the organ in church?"

"It is."

The fact was noted, the pen laid down; and the little old man, who looked only great across his desk, leant back in his chair.

"I am exceedingly anxious that you should have fair play. Let me say plainly that these are not my first inquiries into the matter. I am informed—I wish to know with what truth—that the young woman disappeared for several months before her death?"

"It is quite true."

"And returned to give birth to her child?"

"And to die!" said Carlton, in his grim determination neither to shield nor to spare himself in any of his answers. But his hands were clenched, and his white face glistened with his pain.

The bishop watched him with an eye grown mild with understanding, and a heart hot with mercy for the man who had no mercy on himself. But the tight mouth never relaxed, and the peculiar voice was unaltered when it broke the silence. It was the voice of justice, neither kind nor unkind, severe nor lenient, only grave, deliberate, matter-of-fact.

"My next question is dictated by information received, or let me say by suspicions communicated. It is a vital question; do not answer unless you like. It is, however, a question that will infallibly arise elsewhere. Were you, or were you not, privy to this poor young woman's disappearance?"

"Before God, my lord, I was not!"

"I understand that her parents had no idea where she was until the very end. Had you none either?"

"No more than they had. We were equally in the dark. We believed that she had gone to stay with a friend from the village—a young woman who had married from service, and was settled near London. It was several weeks before we discovered that her friend had never seen her."

"And all this time you did not suspect her condition?"

"Yes; then I did; but not before."

"She made no communication before she went away?"

"None whatever to me—none whatever, to my knowledge."

"And this was early in the year?"

"She left Long Stow in January, and we had no news of her till the middle of June, when strangers communicated with her father."

Again the bishop leant over his foolscap.

"Did you ever offer her marriage?" he asked abruptly.

"Repeatedly!"

The clear eyes looked up.

"Did you not tell her father this?"

"No; I couldn't condescend to tell him," said Carlton, flushing for the first time. "My lord, I have made no excuses. There are none to make. That was none at all."

His lordship regarded the changed face with no further change in his own.

"So you loved her," he said softly, after a pause.

"Ah! if only I had loved her more!"

"If excuse there could be . . . love . . . is some."

It was the old man murmuring, as old men will, all unknown to the bishop and the judge.

"But I want no excuses!" cried Carlton, wildly. "And let me be honest now, whatever I have been in the past; if I deceived myself and others, let me undeceive myself and you! Oh, my lord, that wasn't love! It's the bitterest thought of all, the most shameful confession of all. But love must be something better; that can't be love! It was passion, if you like; it was a passion that swept me away in the pride of my strength; but, God forgive me, it was not love!"

He hid his face in his writhing hands; and, with those wild eyes off him, the bishop could no longer swallow his compassion. The lines of his mouth relaxed, and lo, the mouth was beautiful. A tender light suffused the aged face, and behold, the face was gentle beyond belief.

"Love is everything," the old man said; "but even passion is something, in these cold days of little lives and little sins. And honesty like yours is a great deal, Robert Carlton, though your sin be as scarlet, and the Blood of our Blessed Lord alone can make you clean."

Carlton looked up swiftly, a new solicitude in his eyes.

"In me it was scarlet: not in her. She loved . . . she loved. Oh, to have loved as well—to have that to remember! . . . She thought it would spoil my life; and I never guessed it was that! But now I know, I know! It was for my sake she went away . . . poor child . . . poor mistaken heroine! She died for me, and I cannot die for her. Isn't that hard? I can't even die for her!"

His bodily weakness betrayed itself in his swimming eyes; in the night of his agony no tear had dimmed them before men. But his will was not all gone. With clenched fists, and locked jaw, and beaded brow, he fought his weakness, while the good bishop sat with his head on his hand, and closed eyes, praying for a brother in the valley of despair. When he opened his eyes, it was as though his prayer was heard; for Robert Carlton was bearing himself with a new bravery; and the incongruous unquenched fires, which had caused surprise at the outset of the interview, burnt brightly as before in the younger eyes. The old man met them with a sad, grave scrutiny. But the lines of his mouth remained relaxed. And, when he spoke again, his voice was very gentle.

"You may think that I have put you to unnecessary pain," he said, "when I give you fair warning that your case must form the subject of further proceedings in another place. But I had heard that your conduct was indefensible, root and branch, from beginning to end. Of that I am now able to form my own opinion. Yet my individual opinion can make no difference in the result, since absolute deprivation I had never contemplated in your case, and it is only the extreme penalty which rests with me. On the other hand, it will be my duty to set the ecclesiastical law in motion; and the ecclesiastical law must take its course. I take it that you do not propose to defend your case?"

A grim light flickered for an instant in Robert Carlton's eyes. "Have I defended it hitherto, my lord?"

"Then there can only be one result; and you must make up your mind, as you have doubtless already done, to suspension for a term of years. If word of mine can lessen that term, it shall be spoken in your favour, both out of consideration of the great work that you were doing, and have done, and in view of certain circumstances which our conversation has brought to light."

"But can you want me back in the Church?" cried Carlton; and his heart beat high with the question; but turned heavier than before in the interval of prudent deliberation which preceded any answer.

"I would punish no man beyond the letter of the law," declared the bishop at length, "even if it were in my power to do so. The Act debars suspended clergymen from all exercise of their divine calling and from all pecuniary enjoyment of their benefice until the term of such suspension is up. I would not, if I could, prolong the period of disability by throwing further let or hindrance in the way of an erring brother who repents him truly of his sin. I would rather say, 'Come back to your work, live down the past, and, by your example in the years that may be left you, pluck up the tares that your bad example has surely sown. Retrieve all but the irretrievable. Undo what you can.'"

Carlton's eyes melted in gratitude too great for speech, but plain as the benediction which his trembling lips left eloquently unsaid.

"That," continued the bishop, "is what I should say to you—because I think we understood each other. You have not sought to palliate your offence; nor are you the man to misconstrue the little I may have said concerning the offence itself. What is there to be said? You know well enough that I lament it as I lament its mournful result, and deplore it as I deplore the blot on the whole body of Christ's Church militant here on earth. You have committed a great sin, against humanity, against God, and against your Church; yet he would commit a greater who sought on that account to hound you from that Church for ever. Courage, brother! Pray without ceasing. Look forward, not back; and do not despair. Despair is the devil's best friend; better give way to deadly sin than to deadlier despair! Remember that you have done good work for God in days gone by; and live for that brighter day when you have purged your sin, and may be worthy to work for Him again."

"And meanwhile?" whispered Carlton, for fear of shouting it in his passionate anxiety. "Is there nothing I may do meanwhile—among my own poor people—before the tares come up?"

"If you are suspended you will be unable to hold any service; and I hardly think you will care to go among your parishioners while that is so."

"But I shall not be forbidden my own parish?"

"Not forbidden."

"Nor my rectory?"

"No; so far as I am aware, at least, you retain your right to reside there; but I can hardly think that it would be expedient."

"And the church! They must have their church back again. Who is going to rebuild it for them?"

Carlton was on his feet in the last excitement. The bishop regarded him with puzzled eyebrows.

"I have heard nothing on that subject as yet; it is a little early, is it not? But I have no doubt that it will be a matter for subscription among themselves."

"Among my poor people?"

"With substantial aid, I should hope, from men of substance in the neighbourhood."

"But why should they pay?" cried Carlton, impetuously. "The church was not burnt down for my neighbours' sins, nor for the sins of the parish, but for mine alone . . . Oh, my lord, if I could but go back among my people, and be their servant, I who was too much their master before! I was not quite dependent—thank God, I had a little of my own—but every penny should be theirs!"

And the profligate priest stood upright before his bishop—his white hands clasped, his white face shining, his burning eyes moist—zealot and suppliant in one.

"You desire to spend your income—"

"No, no, my capital!"

"On the poor of your parish? I—I fail to understand."

"And I scarcely dare make you!" confessed Carlton, his full voice failing him. "I so fear your disapproval; and I could set my face against all the world, but against you never, much less after this morning . . . Oh, my lord, I have set my poor people a dastardly example, and brought cruel shame upon my cloth; for its sake and for theirs, if not for my own, let me at least leave among them a tangible sign and symbol of my true repentance. I have the chance! I have such a chance as God alone in His infinite mercy could vouchsafe to a miserable sinner. My church at Long Stow has been burnt down through me—through my sin—to punish me—"

"Are you sure of that, Mr. Carlton?"

"I know it, my lord. And I want to do what only seems to me my bounden and my obvious duty, and to do it soon."

The bishop looked enlightened but amazed.

"You would rebuild the church out of your own pocket? Is that really your wish?"

"It is my prayer!"

CHAPTER VIII

THE LORD OF THE MANOR.

Wilton Gleed owed his success in life to a natural bent for the politic virtues, and to the quality of energy unalloyed by enterprise. He was a man of much shrewdness and extraordinary tenacity, but absolutely no initiative; so he had taken his opportunities and held his ground without running a risk that he could remember. Not a self-made man, he was, however, the son of one who had made himself by dint of that very enterprise which was lacking in Wilton Gleed. The father had seen a certain want and filled it to the satisfaction of the wide world; the son had extended the business without meddling with the product of the firm. Monopolies die hard. Gleed & Son did nothing to deserve a swift demise. They just stalked behind the times, and appeared to thrive on a sublime contempt of competition. And those who knew him best were the most surprised when Wilton Gleed turned the great concern into a limited liability company, and made a fortune out of the transaction alone; it was the most daring thing that he had ever done.

The reason for the step may be related as characteristic of the man. Age had given the firm a certain aristocracy of degree—not of kind—even age could not soften the fact that Gleed & Son sold things in tins. And the tins it was that turned plain Gleed & Son into Gleed & Son, Limited. Some innovator was making tins with cunning openers attached; the lesser firms jumped at the improvement. The lesser firms were already doing Gleeds' some slight damage in their go-ahead little way; but the worst they could all do together was as nothing compared with the extra expenditure of an appreciable fraction of a farthing per tin on an output of millions in the year. Wilton Gleed could not face the immediate hole in his profits. He had never taken a risk in his life, and was not going to begin. He had increased his expenses by going into Parliament, and he was not such a fool as to play tricks with his income. He faced the situation as though it were ruin staring him in the face, and lost a discernible measure of flesh before his big resolve. It was all he did lose over the ultimate operation. He retired into private and public life with more money than he knew how to spend.

The average man is at his best as host, and in that capacity Wilton Gleed was popular among his friends. He was an excellent sportsman of the selfish sort; cherished a contempt for the various games which involve playing for one's side; but was a first-rate shot, a fine fisherman, and a good rider spoilt by his great principle of refusing the risks. To shoot and dine with him was to see Gleed at his very best. He was a bald little man, with silver-sandy moustache and close-cropped whiskers; but his full-blooded face was still pink with health, his fixed eye unerring as ever, his step elastic as the heather he loved to tread. Gun in hand, in his tweeds and gaiters, and with his cap pulled well over his head, Wilton Gleed never passed the prime of life; it was late in the evening before he collected the years blown away on the moor; and in its way the evening was as delectable as the day. The dinner was a good one, and the host abandoned himself to its joys with a schoolboy's ardour. Irreproachable champagne flowed like water, more especially at the head of the table. Gleed carried it like a gentleman, also the port that followed, though a little inclined to be garrulous about the latter. As he sipped and gossiped, and settled the Eastern Question in two words, and Mr. Gladstone's hash in one, the skin would shine as it tightened on the bald head, and the always intent eye would fix the listener beyond the needs of the conversation. It was very seldom, however, that a syllable slid out of place, or that Wilton Gleed went to bed looking quite his age.

For some years he had leased various shootings in the autumn, spending the other seasons at a lordly but suburban retreat inherited from his father, with an occasional swoop abroad—the correct place at the correct time—less for enjoyment than for other reasons. Gun, rod, and cellar were what he did enjoy, and of these delights he vowed to have his fill after getting out of Gleeds with unexpected spoils. A sporting estate was in the market within two hours and a half of town; and for forty thousand pounds Wilton Gleed became squire of Long Stow, patron of an excellent living, and a large landowner in a country where he had a nucleus of friends and soon made more. As Member of Parliament for that division of London in which Gleeds had employed hundreds of hands for half a hundred years, he at the same time bought a house in town, and let the place outside. Subtler investments followed. The man was becoming a gambler in his old age; but he played his own game with ineradicable care and foresight, and rose Sir Wilton Gleed when his side lost in the General Election of 1880. It was only a knighthood, and Sir Wilton might have entertained justifiable hopes of his baronetcy; but one or the other had been a moral certainty for some time.

It was in Hyde Park Place that Sir Wilton first heard of the Long Stow scandal and its immediate sequel. The news came in a few dry lines from Sidney, by the first post on the Monday morning, June 26, 1882. It fell like a firebrand in a keg of gunpowder. Sir Wilton, however, had even better reasons than were obvious for his paroxysm of rage and indignation; personal mortification was not the least of his emotions. He would have gone down by the next train to "horsewhip the hound within an inch of his life," but the cur had taken refuge in Lakenhall Infirmary, "with very little the matter with him," in Sidney's words. And just then the House was an Aceldama which no good soldier could desert for a night, with the Government satisfactorily on the spit between Phœnix Park and Alexandria, and the Opposition creeping up vote by vote. Sir Wilton decided to run down on the Wednesday for twenty-four hours, and talked of having the rectory furniture thrown into the street if the rector was not there to take it and himself away for good. Sir Wilton had his own impression as to his powers as patron of the living, and he very naturally swore that he would "have that blackguard out of it" within the week. A friend at the Carlton put him right on the point.

"You can't do that, Gleed. A living's like nothing else. My lord gives, but my lord can't take away."

"Then what on earth am I to do?"

"Get him inhibited and make him resign. It will come to the same thing."

The fire was in all the newspapers, with the hint of a scandal at the end of the paragraph. Among those who spoke to Sir Wilton on the subject was a jaunty politician who had never yet recognised him at the club.

"Sir Wilton Gleed, I think? I fancy we have met before?"

"Indeed, my lord?"

It was the noble who had chosen to forget the circumstance hitherto; to-day he was all courtesy and confidential concern. What was this about the church that had been burnt down? He had heard it was on the other's estate. Sir Wilton professed to know no more as yet than the papers told him.

"I ask because it reads to me—don't you know? Some scandal—what? And I'm sorry to say—fellow Carlton—sort of connection of mine."

"To be sure," said Sir Wilton. "I remember hearing it."

"Odd fish, I'm afraid. Here in town for years, at that ritualistic shop across the park—forget my own name next. Might have had a good time if he'd liked. Never went out. Preferred the mews. Made a specialty of footmen and fellows. Had a night club somewhere, where he taught 'em to box, and brought my own man home himself one night with an eye like your boot. It was about the only time we met. Remember hearing he could preach, though; only hope he hasn't been making a fool of himself down there!"

"I hope not also," said the discreet knight; "but I am going down to-morrow, so I shall hear."

He went down very grim: for Robert Carlton had not only been a thorn in his side that twelve-month past; he actually stood for the one false move, of importance, which Sir Wilton Gleed was conscious of having made in all his life. Yet he had taken no step with more complete confidence and self-approval. A gentleman and man of brain, reported by Lady Gleed and their daughter, and duly admitted by himself, to be the best preacher they had ever heard; a man of family into the bargain, and not such a distant cadet as the head of that family implied; could any combination have promised a more suitable successor to the venerable sportsman who had scorned white ties and caught his death coursing in mid-winter with Dr. Marigold? And yet the fellow had proved a perfect pest from the beginning. He had gone his own gait with a quiet independence only less exasperating than his personal courtesy and deference in every quarrel. In fact there had been no regular quarrel: the squire had only been rather rude to the rector's face, and very abusive behind his back. Nor was Sir Wilton's annoyance in the least surprising. Devoid himself of a single religious conviction, but the natural enemy of change, he viewed the inevitable, but too immediate, innovations in the light of a personal affront; but when his own expostulations were met with polite argument on a subject which he had never studied, and he found himself at issue with a cleverer and a stronger man, who put him in the illogical position of objecting in the country to what his family approved in town, then there was no alternative for the squire but to withdraw from the unequal field and wait upon revenge. Too politic to break with one who after all had more followers than foes, and who speedily made himself the first person in the parish, Sir Wilton very naturally hated his man the more for those very considerations which induced him to curb his tongue. But his disappointment was manifold. It was not as if the fellow had proved personally congenial to himself. He preferred teaching the lads cricket to shooting with the squire, and he was a poor diner-out. His predecessor had shot almost (but not quite) as well as Sir Wilton himself, and had the harder head of the two for port. Carlton was not even in touch with his own people. There was no advantage in the man at all.

But now the end was in sight—the incredibly premature and disgraceful end. Sir Wilton went down grim enough, but much less angry and indignant than he supposed. Most of his wrath was the accumulation of months, free for expression at last. He was, however, a good and clean citizen according to his lights, and he did undoubtedly feel the rightful indignation with which the story from Long Stow was calculated to inspire many a worse man. Arrived at Lakenhall, where the stanhope was waiting for him, he asked but one question on the way to Long Stow, and then drove straight past the hall to the church. Here he got down, and examined the black ruins with his hands in his pockets and his shoulders very square and a fixed glare of mingled rage and exultation. Then he walked past the broken windows, and the stanhope met him at the rectory gate. He drove home without a word. His one question had elicited the fact that the rector was still in the infirmary.

The village street cut clean through the high-walled hall garden, and the brown-brick hall itself stood as near the road as the mansion in Hyde Park Place, and was the uglier building of the two, from the dormer windows in the steep slates to the portico with the painted pillars. Within was the depressing atmosphere of a great house all but empty. Sir Wilton hurried through a twilit drawing-room in deadly order, and forth by a French window into a pleasaunce of elms and plane-trees whose shadows lay sharp as themselves upon the shaven sward. A girl was coming across the grass to meet him, a girl at the awkward age, with her dark hair in a plait and her black dress neither long nor short. Sir Wilton brushed her cheek with his bleached moustache.

"Where's Fraulein?" he said.

"In the schoolroom, I think, uncle."

"I want to speak to her. I'm only down for the night and shall be busy. I'll be looking round the garden, tell her."

And he walked away from the house, treading vigorously on the cropped grass; and presently a little middle-aged lady, with a plain, shrewd face, flitted over it in her turn. She found Sir Wilton between the four yew hedges and the mathematical parterres of the Italian garden at the further end of the lawn. He shook hands with her, but gave free rein, for the second time in five minutes, to his idiosyncrasy of hard staring.

Fraulein Hentig had been many years in the family, and had taken many parts; at present she was permanent housekeeper in the country, but had lately also recommenced old schoolroom duties on the adoption by Sir Wilton of his only brother's only child. There was no nonsense about Fraulein Hentig. She told Sir William all that she had heard and all that she believed was true, without mincing facts or wincing at the expletives which more than once interrupted her tale. As it proceeded the fixed eyes lightened with a vindictive glitter; but the end found Sir Wilton scowling.

"I wish I'd been here! I wouldn't have let them break his windows; no, I should have claimed the privilege of horsewhipping him with my own hands. I'd do it still if he were here; but he'll never show his nose in Long Stow again. I suppose there's no doubt the church was wilfully set fire to?"

"None at all from what I hear, Sir Wilton."

"Is nobody suspected?"

"George Mellis was. They say he was in love with the girl, and he disappeared on Saturday night. However, it turns out that he was already in Lakenhall hours before the fire, and he never came back. It appears he went straight to the rectory when he heard the scandal, and almost as straight out of Long Stow when Mr. Carlton admitted everything. Already I hear that he has enlisted in London."

"You don't mean it! That's another thing at that blackguard's door; it's a nice list! But it's enough to send the whole parish to the dogs. By the way, you would get Lady Gleed's letter?"

"Yes, Sir Wilton. I wrote last night to tell her ladyship that she might make her mind easy about her niece. She is very innocent, and when I told her the windows had been broken because Mr. Carlton had done something dishonourable, she was amazed of course, but she asked no more questions. I spoke at once to the servants, and I made Gwynneth promise not to go among the people at present; they have already typhoid fever in one of the cottages, and that was my excuse."

"Excellent!" said Sir Wilton. "I won't have her in and out of the cottages in any case, and I shall tell her so before I go. She's much too young for that kind of nonsense. And she mustn't read just exactly what she likes. She had a book in her hand just now—I couldn't see what—but she seems inclined to fill her head with any folly. We must find a school for her, and meanwhile bring her up as we've brought up our own child."

Fraulein Hentig smiled judiciously.

"They are already rather different characters," she said. "But I will do my best, Sir Wilton."

When the pair quitted the Italian garden, the gentleman hurrying to make other inquiries before dinner, while the German gentlewoman dropped behind, two brown eyes saw them from an upper window, whither the girl had carried her book in vain. Her attention had been intermittent before, but now she could not even try to read. The air was full of mystery, and the mystery was more absorbing than that in any book. It was also absolute and unfathomable in the girl's mind. Yet her brain teemed with questions and surmises. She had come upstairs because she felt that they wanted her out of the way, her uncle and the good, slow, serious Fraulein. Yet that was not enough for them: they also must retire as far as possible for their talk. Of course Gwynneth knew what they had to talk about; but what was the dishonourable action that a clergyman could commit and that could not be so much as mentioned in her hearing? She was not thinking of "a clergyman" in the abstract. She was thinking of the man with the beautiful, sad face; of the passionate preacher with the voice that thrilled the senses and the words that filled the mind. She had heard him preach of sin and suffering with equal sympathy. Phrases came back to her. Now she understood. But what could he have done, that he should suffer so, and that a perfectly kind person like Fraulein Hentig should exult in his suffering?

Gwynneth was splendidly and terribly innocent, but all the more inquisitive on that account. She was unacquainted with the facts, yet not with the tragedy of life. In a tragic atmosphere she had been born and bred. Quentin Gleed had been fatally lacking in the politic virtues cultivated by his brother. He had deserted his wife and drunk himself to death within the memory of Gwynneth. The young girl recalled dim years of bitter scenes in a luxurious home, and vivid years of peace and poverty in a tiny cottage. And now her mother was gone also; the dear, independent, wilful little mother, who had taught her child all but the wickedness that was in the world! And that child sat at her bedroom window in the new home that never could be home to her; and the drooping sun could find no bottom to her dark and limpid eyes, no flaw upon her pure warm skin; and neither the cuckoo in the poplar, nor the thrush in the elm, nor the sparrows in the eaves just overhead, could tell her anything of the wickedness that was in even her small world.

CHAPTER IX

A DUEL BEGINS

Late in the afternoon of July 13, a Lakenhall fly rattled through Long Stow, and waited in the rain outside the rectory gate while one of the occupants ran up to the house. He was such a short time gone, and so few people were about in the wet, that the fly was on its way back to Lakenhall before the Long Stow folk realised that it was the rector who had upset prophecy by showing his nose among them in broad daylight. He had done no more, however, nor was anything further seen or heard of him during the month of July. It appeared that he had returned for some private papers only. The rectory was locked up by the squire's orders, but the rector had forced his own study door, and his muddy footmarks were confined to that room. The same evening he went up to town—and disappeared. But his address was known in an official quarter. And all day and every day he might have been discovered in the reading room of the British Museum: a memorable figure, stooping amid mountains of architectural tomes, and drawing or copying plans in the few inches of table-land they left him, all with a nervous eagerness of face and hand not daily to be seen beneath that dispiriting dome.

Then the call came, and he was tried in the consistorial court of his own diocese, before the chancellor thereof, at the beginning of August. No need to record more than the fact. The proceedings were brief because the accused pleaded guilty and his own word was the only evidence against him. The sentence was that of suspension foreshadowed by the bishop. The Reverend Robert Carlton was formally suspended ab officio et beneficio for the period of five years.

The result was reported in the London papers; there was only matter for a few lines. "Mr. Carlton was suspended for five years" was the concluding sentence in The Times report; and that was good enough for Sir Wilton Gleed. It was a happy omen for the holidays, which began for him that very day. The family were already in the country. Sir Wilton took the last train to Lakenhall and drove himself home for good in the highest spirits. Four miles of the five were over his own acres, and every one of them was crumbling with rabbits in the rosy dusk. Later, the larkspur and peonies on the dinner-table were as the very breath and blush of the gorgeous English country; and a thrush sang its welcome through the open window, and a nightingale trilled the tired Londoner to sleep; but he dreamt of a pheasant that he had heard calling between Lakenhall and Long Stow.

In the country Sir Wilton was an early riser, and he was abroad next morning while the shadows of the elms still stretched to the house and quivered up its bare brick walls. The great lawn was dusted with a milky dew in which Sir Wilton positively wallowed in his water-tight boots; it was not his least delight to be in shooting-boots and knickerbockers and soft raiment once more. The first few minutes of the more excellent life produced an unseasonable geniality in the breast of Wilton Gleed. The man was a human being, and he longed for companionship in his joy. But Sidney never rose before he must, nor the gardeners either, it appeared. In the stable-yard a groom was encountered, but Sir Wilton had seen his face every day in town. He went out into the village, and naturally turned to the left. The cottage doors were open, and they were filled with homely figures that touched a cap or courtesied as he passed with a pleasant word for all. It was good to be back, to be a little king again. Sir Wilton pulled the cap over his eyes because the sun was in them, and admired the ripe wheat in the field beyond the post-office, the barley in the field beyond that. So he passed the Flint House on the other side with unruffled mind, and was passing the Flint House meadow before his thoughts took the inevitable turn which led to profane mutterings through shut teeth. But this morning it did not lead quite so far; this morning, with the scented air of England in his nostrils, and a twitter in the ears from every thatch, even Sir Wilton Gleed could find it in his heart to pity the sinner fallen from his high estate in what was paradise enough for the squire.

"Poor devil!" he said as he came to the rectory gate and saw the long grass within. It was sufficiently in key with the old quaint rectory, in its rags of ivy and its shawl of disreputable tiles. The windows were still broken and the shutters shut. Otherwise the picture was as alluring as its fellows to the lord of the manor. The trees that hid the church at midsummer would screen its ruins for many a day.

Sir Wilton entered to refresh his memory as to the minor damages, and they changed his mood. Who was to pay for twenty-nine panes of glass—no, he had missed a window—for thirty-three? He was a man who did not care to spend a penny without obtaining his pennyworth; but he was not clear as to his legal obligations; and he bristled at the idea of paying for the immorality of the parson and the excesses of his flock. He had paid enough in other ways. And there was the church. Who was to rebuild the church? They might expect him to do that once he began doing things; and the man fell into premature fuming between his love of the lavish and his detestation of expense. Meanwhile he had found a whole window, that of the study, and the door beside it stood ajar. This he pushed open as though the place belonged to him (his view in so many words), and stood still upon the threshold.

"Well, I'm damned!" he cried at last.

Robert Carlton sat asleep in his chair, his hands in his overcoat pockets, the collar turned up about his ears. His boots and trousers were brown and yellow with the dust of the district. In an instant he was on his feet, scared, startled, and abashed.

"So you've come back, have you?"

"An hour or two ago. I walked from Cambridge. I don't know how you heard!"

"Heard? You must think me in a hurry for your society! No, this is an unexpected pleasure, and I use the words advisedly. It's something to find you don't come twice in broad daylight."

"I have come on business, as before, but this time the business will occupy more than a few minutes. I wished to get it in train with as little fuss as possible. Then I was coming to see you, Sir Wilton."

It was quietly spoken, without bitterness or defiance, but also without the abject humility which had trembled in the clergyman's first words. The other made some attempt to modify his manner: nothing could put him in the wrong, but he realised that it might be as well to abstain from mere brutality. And what he had just heard implied a certain reassurance.

"I see," said Gleed. "You have come to make arrangements about your furniture and effects. I am glad to hear it."

"My furniture and effects?" queried Carlton. "What arrangements do you mean?"

"Well, you can't leave them here, can you?"

"Why not, Sir Wilton?"

"Why not!" echoed the squire, turning from pink to purple with the two words. "Because you've been disgraced and degraded as you deserve; because you're the hound you are; because you've been suspended for five years, and I won't have you or your belongings cumber my ground for a single day of them! So now you know," continued Gleed in lower tones, his venom spent. "I didn't think it would be necessary to tell you my opinion of you; but you've brought it on yourself."

Carlton bowed to that, but respectfully pointed out the difference between suspension and deprivation, his tone one of apology rather than of triumph.

"I don't say which I deserved," he added, "but I do thank God for the mercy He has shown me. This gives me another chance—in five years' time. Meanwhile I am not only entitled to keep my furniture in the rectory. I believe I may live in it if I like."

Gleed stood convulsed with wrath redoubled. He had been too busy in town to prime himself upon a point which could not arise before he went down to the country; and here it was, awaiting him. His disadvantage alone was enough to put him in a passion; but the last statement was monstrous in itself.

"I don't believe it! I don't believe a word you say! A man who can live a lie will tell nothing else!"

Carlton drew himself up, his nostrils curling.

"Better go and ask your solicitor," he said. "I have forfeited the right—as you so well know—to the only possible reply."

"Rights apart," rejoined Gleed, his colour heightening by a shade, "do you mean to tell me you would seriously think of remaining on the very scene of your shame?"

"I didn't say I would do anything. I said I believed I could."

"You have done enough harm in the place; surely you wouldn't come back to do more?"

"No; if I came at all, it would be to undo a little of the harm—to live it down, Sir Wilton, by God's help!" said Carlton, and his voice shook. "But I do not mean to live here. I have spoken to the bishop, and his advice is against it, though he leaves me free to follow my own judgment. This afternoon I hoped to speak to you. There is another matter which is really a duty, so that I can be in no doubt as to what to do there. It will not involve my remaining on the spot, or obtruding myself in any way. But the church has been burnt down on my account, and I intend to rebuild it before the winter."

"The church is mine!" said Gleed, savagely.

"I don't want to contradict you, Sir Wilton; but you should really see your lawyer on all these points."

"The land is mine!"

"Not the church land, Sir Wilton; and the rector is not only entitled, but he may be compelled, to restore and rebuild within certain limits. Your solicitor will turn up the Act and show it you in black and white. And after that I think you will hardly stand between me and my bounden duty."

"I don't recognise it as your duty. Your first duty is to resign the living lock-stock-and-barrel—if you've any sense of decency left; but you haven't—not you, you infernal blackguard, you!"

Gleed was standing on the drive, his arms akimbo and his fists clenched, his flushed face thrust forward and his stockinged legs planted firmly apart. It was Carlton's lithe figure which had been filling the doorway for some minutes; but at this he strode upon his adversary, and towered over him with a hand that itched.

"Why must you insult me?" he cried. "Do you think that's the way to get me to do anything? Or are you bent upon having me up for assault? For heaven's sake remember your own manhood, Sir Wilton, and respect mine; don't trade too far upon my readiness to admit that I am all men choose to call me. Have a little pride! I am ready to take my punishment, and more. I will keep away from the place as much as possible. If I can let the rectory, that will be so much more money for the church. Don't oppose me; if you can't help me by your countenance (and I grant you it's more than I have a right to expect), at least be neutral, and let me work out my own salvation in my own way. It will make no difference to the past. It may make all the difference in the future. God knows I can't reinstate myself in His sight and in the hearts of men by building a church! But I can leave behind me a sign of my sorrow and my true penitence. I can leave behind me a name and an example, bad enough in all conscience, but yet not wholly vile to the very last. And think what even that would be to me! And think what it would be if I could but pave the way, not to forgiveness, but to some reconciliation with those whom I have loved but led amiss . . . Well, that may be too much to hope . . . no, I have no right to dream of that . . . but at least let me make the one material reparation in my power; let me do my duty! When it is done, if you and they will have no more of me, then you shall all be rid of me for good."

Gleed wavered, partly because in mere personality he was no match for the other, partly because the prospect of a new church for nothing made its own appeal to the man who had counted the cost of the broken windows. His mind ran over the pecuniary scheme and detected a flaw.

"And what's to become of the parish for the next five years?" he asked. "Who's to pay a man to do your work?"

"There's the stipend I cannot touch and would not if I could; a part of that will doubtless be set aside. Until the church is habitable, however, the case will probably be met by one of the curates coming over from Lakenhall and taking a service in the schoolroom."

"And how do you know?" cried Sir Wilton, not unjustifiably.

"The bishop sent for me," said Carlton—and his eyes fell. "I ventured to speak to him on the subject before I left. Do you think I don't care what happens here in my absence? I hope the services will begin next Sunday—the building next week. I have worked the whole thing out. I could show you the figures and the plans. The new ones are ready, if you can call them new. I shall be my own architect as before for the transepts, but the rest shall be exactly as it was."

"We'll see about that," said Sir Wilton grimly. He knew those melting eyes, that enthusiastic voice. They had brought their hundreds to this man's feet before. They might do so again. Even the squire felt their power in his own despite.

"It is my one chance!" the voice went on in softer accents. "Do not ask me to forego it altogether; but I will keep in the background as much as you like; all I want to know is that the work is going on. Suppose I did resign, and you appointed another man. Why should he give towards the church? Why should he come where there is none? Let me build the new one first!"

"Has it come to letting? I understood I couldn't prevent you?"

"No more you can; although—"

"We'll see!" cried Gleed. "That's quite enough for me. We'll see!"

"But, Sir Wilton—"

"Damn your 'buts,' sir!" shouted the other, shaking with rage. "You disgrace the parish, and you won't leave it. You come back, and set yourself against me, and think you can do what you like after doing what you've done. By God, it's monstrous! There's not a man in the country who won't agree with me; you'll find that out to your cost. Build the church, would you? I'll see you further! Law or no law, I'll have you out of this! I'll hound you out of it! I'll have you torn in pieces if you stay!"

"I have already told you I don't intend to stay," said Carlton quietly. "I only intend to rebuild the church."

"All right! You try! You try!"

And with his fixed eyes flashing, and his fresh face aged with anger, but scored with implacable resolve, Sir Wilton Gleed swung on his heel, and so down the drive with every step a stamp.

CHAPTER X

THE LETTER OF THE LAW

In the village he met Tom Ivey, but passed him with a savage nod, and was some yards further on when a thought smote him so that he spun round in his stride.

"That you, Ivey?" he called. "I wasn't thinking; you're the very man I wanted to see. How are you, eh?"

"Nicely, thank you, Sir Wilton," said Tom, coming up.

"Plenty of work, I hope?"

"Well, not just lately, Sir Wilton."

"Good! I may have some for you. I'll see you about it this evening or to-morrow; meanwhile keep yourself free. By the way, how's your mother?"

"Very sadly, Sir Wilton. I sometimes fare to think she's not long for this world."

"Nonsense, man! What's the matter with her?"

Tom hardly knew. That was old age, he thought. Then the house was that old and small; sometimes she fared to stifle for want of air. And this Tom said doggedly, for a reason.

"Ah!" cried Sir Wilton, his fixed eye brightening. "Wasn't there a question of repairs some time since?"

"There was, Sir Wilton."

"Well, I'll reconsider it. We must do what we can to make the old lady comfortable for the winter. I'll come and see her, and I'll see you again about the other matter. Keep yourself free meanwhile. Don't you let any of those Lakenhall fellows snap you up!"

And Sir Wilton went on chuckling, but again turned quickly and called the other back.

"By the way, Tom, who were those fellows you used to work for in Lakenhall?"

"Tait & Taplin, Sir Wilton."

A note was taken of the names.

"The only builders in the town, eh?"

"Well, Sir Wilton, there's old Isaac Hoole, the stonemason."

"A stonemason, by Jove!" and down went his name. "What other builders and stonemasons have we in the district—near enough to undertake some work here? I'm not thinking of the job I've got for you, Tom."

Ivey thought of three within fifteen miles, and several at greater distances, but doubted whether any of the latter would accept a contract so far afield. Their names were taken, nevertheless, and Sir Wilton stared his hardest as he put his pocket-book away.

"I shall want you all the same," he said, "and I shall expect to get you when I want you. Understand? If anybody else offers you a job, remember you've got one. And I'll see your mother this morning."

Tom went his way with his honest wits in a knot. He could not conceive what was coming. Ten minutes ago he had found a note slipped under the door in the night, and he was going straight to the rectory without his breakfast. Had Sir Wilton been there before him, and was he going to rebuild the church? Then what had the reverend to say to it, now that he was suspended for five years? And what in the world could he have to say to Tom Ivey?

He said nothing at all until they had shaken hands, and nothing then about the fire; it is with the hand alone that men pay their big debts to men, and Robert Carlton did not weaken his thanks with words.

"Have you got a job, Tom?" were his first.

"I have and I haven't, sir," said Ivey.

"You're not free to take one from me?"

"I wish I was, sir!" cried Tom, impulsively (he was not so sure about it on reflection); and in his simplicity he explained why he was not free. "But perhaps that's the same job, sir?" he added, hopefully.

Carlton shook his head, and looked wistfully on the friendly face; a few words (he knew his power) and the very man he wanted would be on his side against all odds. But he must not begin by dividing the village into factions; he must fight his own battle, with mercenaries from neutral ground, or none at all.

"Where was it you served your time, Tom?" he asked at length.

"Tait & Taplin's, sir, in Lakenhall."

"Thanks. I won't keep you, Tom. It will do you no good to be seen up here."

He held out his hand with a dismal smile. It was the other's turn to wring hard. "I care nothing about that, sir! We've been shoulder to shoulder once already; my mind don't go no further back than that; and we'll be shoulder to shoulder again!"

Carlton found flour and tea in the store-room, and in the fowl-house two new-laid eggs. He cooked his first breakfast with the sun pouring through the open kitchen window upon six weeks' dirt and dust. He was not a man of very hearty habit, but he had learnt of old the evil of exercise upon too light a diet. His pony was fattening in the glebe; but a fastidious sense of fitness forbade him to drive, and between nine and ten he set out for Lakenhall on foot.

It was an ordeal for the first half-mile: the sunlight flooding the village felt like limelight turned on him alone. Some children courtesied as though nothing was changed; their elders stared at him without further sign; only one shouted after him, he knew not who or what. He reached the open country with a raging pulse, thinking only upon circuitous ways back; but three solitary miles restored his nerve. And in Lakenhall it was only every other passer who stopped and turned and stared. Entering the town he was nearly run over by a dogcart. It was Sir Wilton driving, and Carlton caught the gleam of his eye even as he leapt to one side for his life, but mistook its significance until he was within sight of Tait & Taplin's. Then it occurred to him, and he entered fully prepared.

"No, thank you, sir—not for us! We've heard of you, and we don't deal with your sort. Do you hear, or do you want to hear more?"

Carlton searched in vain for another builder, and only got the name of a stonemason by going into the cemetery and looking at the newer gravestones. He had then to discover where the man lived, and he was ashamed to ask questions in shops. He was still scouring the town, and it was afternoon, when a gig was pulled up in the middle of the road.

"So you're back? Well, you look better than you did."

"I am," said Carlton, "thanks to you."

"Who are you looking for?"

"Hoole, the stonemason."

"Jump up and I'll drive you there."

The tone was too humane for Carlton.

"Thank you, doctor, but I like walking."

"Then find him for yourself, and be damned to you!"

And Marigold drove on, red to the hoar of his eighty years; but, as Carlton stood watching him out of sight with vain compunction, the old doctor turned in his seat and pointed up an alley with his whip in passing.

Hoole, the stonemason, was not rude, but he was as firm as Tait & Taplin in his refusal. He was an elderly man, of few words, but he admitted that Sir Wilton Gleed had been there that morning. That was enough for Carlton, who was turning away when something in his visible fatigue and dejection moved the mason to give him a hint.

"You won't get anybody in the district to work for you against Sir Wilton," he said. "That stands to reason."

"Then I must go out of the district," said Carlton. And he bought a county directory at a shop where he had been a regular customer; but they insisted on the settlement of his current bill first; and even then he had to help himself to the new book, and leave the money on the counter, because they scorned to serve him. The directory contained the names and addresses of the very few builders and master-masons within a day's journey of Long Stow. And it was all there was to show for the long day's round of retribution and rebuff when, late in the afternoon, Carlton returned as he had come, too tired and too dispirited to walk an inch out of his way; and the school-children who had courtesied in the morning knew better now, and cried after the bent figure slinking home at dusk.

The next day was Sunday, and the school-bell tinkled towards eleven o'clock, and stopped precisely at the hour. Then Carlton knew that his own idea had been adopted, and that somebody was saying matins in the parish school-room: he read the service to himself in his study, and evensong when evening came, with a sermon of Charles Kingsley's after each: for doctrine could not help him now, but brave humanity could and did.

The Monday was Bank Holiday; but Carlton only knew it when he had trudged ten miles to have speech with a builder whose premises were closed; and so another day was lost. On the Tuesday he tried again, but with as little avail. Sir Wilton Gleed had been there before him (as long ago as the Saturday afternoon), and it was the same elsewhere. The week went in fruitless visits to small contractors and working masons in this large village or in that little town; the enemy had been first in every field, with a cunning formula which Carlton reconstructed from the various answers he received.

"Of course, the church will have to be rebuilt," Sir Wilton had been saying; "but not by him. He hasn't the money, for one thing; it had better be an iron church, if he is to pay you for it. Help me to get rid of him, and you shall hear from me again. We will have a decent church when we are about it, and a local man shall get the job."

Meanwhile the boycott was nowhere more operative than in Long Stow itself, and no human being came near the rectory, where the rector subsisted on a providential store of bacon and the daily deposit of eggs, and on strange bread of his own baking, for he would risk no more insults in the shops. But one night a forgotten friend came back into his life: his collie, Glen, came bounding down the drive to meet him, and the mad uproar of that welcome was heard through half the village, and duly became the talk. The dog had been a vagabond and a rogue for six wild weeks, and it came back gaunt and hard, its brush clotted and raw underneath with the spray from a farmer's gun. Carlton washed the wound with warm water, and the two pariahs supped together, and lay that night upon the same bed, and went abroad together next morning, to try the last man left.

The day after that they stayed at home, and word reached the hall that the rector had been seen among the ruins of his church; he was, indeed, exploring them for the first time, and that both with method and deliberation. When seen, however (from the lane that runs under the fine east window of to-day, past the lawn-tennis court which was then a fowl run, and the glebe that is still the glebe), he was seated on a sandstone block in front of the little lean-to shed; and, as a matter of fact, his back was to the ruins. He was contemplating similar blocks and slabs of the undressed stone that lay where they had been lying on Midsummer Day: some were still smutty from the fire, all were slightly stained by the weather, otherwise there was no change that Carlton could see as he sat thus. At one end of the shed rose a great yellow cairn of material raw from the quarry—a stack of stones about as much of one size and shape as so many lumps of sugar; enough to finish the transepts, as matters had stood; a mere fraction of the amount required now. Carlton looked on what he had got, and his eyes closed in a calculation beyond his powers in mental arithmetic; he had to take a pencil to it, and then a foot-rule to the blackened courses, and presently a pair of compasses to the plans in the study.

In the afternoon he tidied the shed. Every tool was intact; a little rust had been the worst intruder; and the feel of the cool sleek handles quickened Carlton's pulse. Nay, the hammer rang a few strokes on the cold-chisel, for he could not help it, and the music reminded him of his poor bells, now cumbering the porch; it was almost as good to hear; and the way the soft stone peeled, in creamy flakes, thrilled the hand as it charmed the eye. But a very few minutes served to make the enthusiast ashamed of his enthusiasm; and though he spent more time in the ruins, now testing a standing wall, now scraping a charred stone, ardour and determination had died down in an eye that was looking within; a wistful irresolution flickered in their place. And that night the lonely man walked his room once more, from twilight to twilight, with long intervals spent upon his knees, in agonies of doubt and self-distrust, in passionate entreaty for a right judgment, and for the strength to abide by it. Yet his duty had not dawned upon him with the day.

Towards eleven the school-bell tinkled. It was Sunday once more; and once more he read the prayers upon his knees and the psalms and lessons standing; but no sermon to-day. No man could help him in his struggle with himself; he must trust to the strength of his own soul, to the singleness of his own heart, and to the guidance of the God who was drawing nearer and nearer to him in these days—with each prayer that rose from his heart—with each bead that stood upon his brow. And so at last, when the burden of doubt and darkness became more than the man could bear, it was as though the heavens had opened, and a beam of celestial light flooded the narrow room with the low ceiling and the cross-beams; for the peace of a mind made up had descended upon the solitary therein. And that night his sleep was sound, so that in the morning he had to ask himself why; the answer made him catch his breath; it did not shake his resolve.

"He shall have his chance," said Carlton; "he shall have it fairly to his face. And he will take it—and that will be the end!"

He hung about the ruins till it was ten o'clock by his watch, and then went straight to the hall. Sir Wilton was at home; but the footman hesitated to admit this visitor. Carlton's own hesitation was, however, at an end, and his eye forbade rebuff. He was shown into the drawing-room, where a very young girl was at the piano, evidently practising, and yet playing in a way that made Carlton sorry when she stopped. The cool room smelling of flowers; the glimpse of garden through an open window, with the court marked out and chairs under the trees; the momentary sound of a fine instrument finely touched: it was all the very breath and essence of the pleasant every-day world from which he had rightly and richly earned dismissal, and it all was branded in his brain. Then the young girl rose, and stood in doubt with the sun upon her plaited hair, and eyes great with innocent distress; but Carlton barely bowed, and the child hardly knew how she got across the room.

Sir Wilton entered with jaunty step. His whiskered jaw was set like a vice, but the light of conscious triumph danced in his fixed eyeballs. Carlton had come prepared to have his intrusion treated as his latest crime; a glance convinced him that the other was too sure of victory to object to an interview with the virtually vanquished.

"So you are quite determined that I shall not rebuild the church?"

It was a point-blank beginning. Sir Wilton shrugged and smiled. "I have told you to build it if you can," said he.

"But you mean to make that an impossibility?"

"Naturally I don't intend to make it easy."

"Admit that by foul means, since none are fair, you are deliberately preventing me from doing my duty!" Carlton pressed his point with a heat he regretted, but could not help.

"I admit nothing," said the other, doggedly—"least of all what you are pleased to consider your 'duty.' Your real duty I've already told you. Resign the living. Let us see the last of you."

Carlton met the rigid stare with one as unwavering and more acute. It was as though he would have seen to the back of the other's brain.

"Very well," he said at length. "You shall!"

"Ah!" cried Sir Wilton, when he had recovered from his surprise. But it was not the cry of victory; there was an uncharacteristic lack of finality in the clergyman's tone.

"You shall see the last of me this very morning," he continued swiftly, nervously, "if you like! But it will rest with you. I am not going unconditionally. Will you listen to what I have to say?"

Gleed shrugged again, but this time there was no accompanying smile. The other threw up his head with a sudden decisiveness—a pulpit trick of his when about to make a primary point—and his right fist fell into his left palm without his knowing it.

"Very well," said Carlton; "now I'll tell you exactly on what conditions you shall have your heart's desire, and I will renounce mine. In spite of what I hear you've been saying, I have a little money of my own—not much, indeed—but enough for me to have subsisted upon for these next years. I am not going to touch a penny of it—I shall pick up a living for myself elsewhere. Meanwhile I have turned my income into capital which is now lying in the bank at Lakenhall. It is a trifle under two thousand pounds, and I want the whole of it to go into the new church. Wherever I am I ought to be able to earn a little more, either as a coach or with my pen; so let the offer stand at a church to cost two thousand pounds. I long to have the building of it. I make no secret of that. But I have been trying to read my own heart, and I see the selfishness of such longings; and I have been trying to read your heart, Sir Wilton, and I see the naturalness of your opposition. So I come to you and I say, build the church yourself, and I withdraw. Build a better church out of your abundance, and I will resign as you wish. Give me your written undertaking, here and now, and you shall have my written resignation in exchange."

The words clung to his lips; he alone knew what it cost him to utter them; he alone, in his absolute freedom from the mercenary instinct, would have felt certain of the result. But the rich man was touched upon his tender spot. What return was he offered for his money? Who would thank him for building a church in the heart of the country? The church could be built by subscription; bad enough to have to head the list. Besides, he was flushed with triumph; he saw but a beaten man in the nervous wretch before him. Fancy bribing a beaten man to fly!

"I like your impudence," said Wilton Gleed. "Upon my word! My written undertaking—to you!"

"Do you refuse to give it?" asked Carlton quickly.

"Certainly—to you."

"Undertakings apart, do you entertain my suggestion, or do you not?"

"That's my business."

Carlton felt his patience slipping.

"Do you mean to say that you don't even yet recognise that it's mine too, as rector of the parish? Are you still so ignorant of the legal bearings of the situation? God knows, Sir Wilton, it is not for me to speak of right and wrong; but I do assure you that you're putting yourself wilfully in the wrong in this matter. You hinder me from doing my legal duty, and you refuse to assume any responsibility! Suspended or not, I am bound to keep my chancel, at all events, 'in good and substantial repair, restoring and rebuilding when necessary.'"

Sir Wilton's eyes, fixed as usual, caught fire suddenly.

"Oh, you're bound, are you?"

"Legally bound."

"You're sure that's the law?"

"The very letter of the law, Sir Wilton."

"Then see that you keep it! You come here blustering about your legal rights; but you forget that I've got mine. Where there's a law there's a penalty, and by God I'll enforce it! 'The very letter of the law,' eh? I'll take you at your word; you shall keep it to the letter. Build away! Build away! The sooner you begin the better—for you!"

This was probably the boldest move that Sir Wilton Gleed ever made in his life; it was certainly the least considered. But what satisfaction sweeter than hoisting the enemy with his own petard? It is the quintessence of poetic justice, the acme of personal triumph; and the sudden opportunity of achieving his end by means so neat was more than even Wilton Gleed could resist. Every builder and mason within reach was already on his side; not a man of them who would work for dissolute hypocrisy in defiance of might and right. No need to say another word to the masons and the builders. They could be trusted on the whole, and the untrustworthy could be bribed. Gleed had not the smallest scruple in the matter, and he was characteristically forearmed with a public defence of his private conduct. He believed that every right-thinking man would applaud his sharp practice in the cause of religion and of morality; and his confidence was not to be shaken by the way in which his challenge was received.

"Are you in earnest?" asked Carlton. "Do you seriously propose to hinder me with one hand and to compel me with the other?"

"I mean to take you at your word," Gleed repeated. "You are fond of talking about your duty. Let's see you do it."

"You set the builders against me, and then you tell me to build. May I ask if you are prepared to defend such clumsy trickery?"

"Any day you like, and glad of the opportunity!" cried Sir Wilton, cheerfully. "All I have done is to give you your proper character where it deserves to be known; you have it to thank if you can't get men to work for you; and it's your look-out. I've heard about enough of you and your church. Go and build it. Go and build it."

"I will," said Carlton. "You have had your chance." And he bowed and withdrew with strange serenity.

A parting shot followed him through the hall.

"You will have to do it with your own two hands!"

Carlton made no reply. But in the village he committed a fresh enormity.

He was seen to smile.

CHAPTER XI

LABOUR OF HERCULES

All the church had not been burnt to the ground. West of the porch (itself not hopelessly destroyed) stood thirteen feet of sound south wall, blackened on the inside, calcined in the upper courses, but plumb and firm as far as it went. A corresponding portion of the north wall, the sixteen-foot strip west of the window almost opposite the porch, stood equally rigid and erect. And, thus supported on either hand, the entire west end rose practically intact, without a missing or a ruined stone; the window was still truly bisected by its single mullion; neither head nor tracery had given the fraction of an inch; only the mangled leads, with here and there a fragment of smoked glass adhering, would have told of a fire to one led blindfold under the west window, and there given his first view of the church.

But that was the one good wall and real exception to a rule of utter ruin. The rest of the original building was either razed already or else unfit to stand. The embryonic transepts were not quite demolished, but they had never been many feet above ground. Sections of wall still stood where there were no windows to weaken them, but east of the porch nothing stood firm. Worst of all was the east end, from which the chancel walls had been burnt away on either side. It stood as though balanced, with an alarming outward list. One mullion of the great window had gone by the sill; the other was cracked and crooked, as if supporting the entire weight of the gable overhead; and it looked as though a push would send the tottering fabric flat.

Black ruin lay thick and deep within. To peep in was to see an ashpit through a microscope. The remnants of the slate and timber roof lay uppermost. Tie-beams, corbels, king-posts, ridge, struts, wall-plates, pole-plates, rafters principal and common, joists, battens, laths and fillets, half-burnt and black as the pit, save where some spilled sheet-lead shone in the sun, spread a common pall over nave and chancel, aisle and pews. It was as a midnight sea frozen in mid-storm, the twisted lectern alone rising salient like a mast. Slates lay in shallow heaps as though dealt from a pack; and certain pages, brown and brittle at the edges, which the wind had torn from the burnt Bible before Carlton rescued the remains, still fluttered in the crannies when the wind went its rounds. And the hum of bees was in the air; but there had been great distress among the sparrows, and one heard more of the rectory cocks and hens.

Upon this desolate and dead spot, in the heart of the warm, live country, Robert Carlton stood looking within a few minutes of his exit from the hall. But he did not stand looking long. He had changed into flannels at top speed, and there was still more change in the man. His eye glowed with a grim decision which lightened without dispelling the settled sadness of the face. Passionate aspiration had cooled and hardened into dogged and defiant resolve; and there was an end to all compunction and self-questioning suspense. Carlton knew exactly what he was going to do; he had known where to begin since the day before yesterday. He wore neither coat nor waistcoat, his sleeves were rolled up, he had a crowbar in one hand, and a heavy hammer in the other. He began immediately on the thirteen feet of good wall to the left of the porch.

He had tested this wall on Saturday. The upper courses were loose and crumbling; the sooner they went the better. Carlton climbed upon the wall, and, sitting astride where it was firmest, began working off the loose stones one by one with the crowbar. Iron would ring on iron twice or thrice, and then a twist of the bar send the charred stone tumbling. It was easy work, but the position was awkward, and Carlton soon went for a ladder; on the way he was surprised to find that he was already drenched with perspiration, and rather hungry.

But the next hour tired him more, or rather the time that seemed an hour to him, for it afterwards turned out to be three hours by the watch that he had left indoors. Only the topmost course, or the stones on which the red-hot eaves had rested, lent themselves to off-hand treatment; they had been burnt to cinders—the mortar binding them, to powder; it needed but a wrench to dislodge each one. But the next few courses were a different matter. Half the stones were too loose to leave, too good to chip in the removal. Carlton worked upon them with the cold-chisel first, the crowbar next, and finally with his naked fingers, removing the stones with immense care, and very deliberately dropping each into its own bed in the long grass outside. At last the little strip of wall was left without an unsound member from serrated crest to plinth: not a stone that shook or shifted at a conscientious push; and the workman took his eyes from his work. But he did not peer through the trees in search of other eyes, for he was not thinking of himself or of his work from a spectacular point of view. He merely saw that the sun had travelled the church from end to end while he had been busy. And suddenly he found himself sinking for want of food, and unable to stand upright without intolerable pain. But he was back within half-an-hour, and remained at work upon the sixteen-foot strip opposite till after sunset.

"But it hasn't been anything like a full day, old dog," said Carlton, as they crept up to bed between eight and nine. And he set his seven-and-six-penny alarum at four o'clock.

Next forenoon the sixteen-foot strip was done with in its turn; no infirm stone left standing upon another. Scraped and repointed, with the uninjured pieces replaced in fresh mortar, and an entirely new top course, these two short walls would be worthy of the gallant west end to which they acted as buttresses. Its wounds were not skin-deep, thanks to the west wind which had driven the flames the other way. It looked as though a sponge would cleanse it, and Carlton sighed as he turned his back upon the one good wall.

Elsewhere, as has been said, there were fragments fit to use again, but not to remain as they were. It cost Carlton a couple of days to take these to pieces, laying the good stones carefully in the grass, as his practice had been hitherto. The fourth day, however, he tried a change of labour to ease his aching limbs, and went round and round with a barrow, picking the sound stones from the grass, and stacking them near the shed. Next morning he fought his way into the chancel, and stood chin-deep in the wreckage, contemplating the leaning east end. And all this time no soul had come near him; through the trees he had indeed heard whispers that were not of the trees, but he had never thrown more than a glance in their direction, and the green screen was still charitably thick.

The east end must come down sooner or later—therefore sooner. Carlton was no engineer, but he was a man with a distinct turn for mechanics; had used a lathe as a lad, and taught his Boys' Friendly how to use it in their turn; had picked up much from Tom Ivey, and was himself blessed with sound instincts concerning application and control of power. Here was a tottering wall to come down altogether. It was too insecure to pull to pieces. The problem was to get it down with as little damage and as little danger as possible. One man could do it, Carlton thought, but not without considerable risk of a broken head at least. If he could but make sure of the whole wall falling in the one outward direction! He revolved about it, mentally and on his feet, till he became angry with himself for the loss of time, ceased to speculate, and went to work in desperation. He would trust to luck; he despised himself for having studied a risk so small. He had done so out of no absurd consideration for his own skin, but entirely from the depth and strength of his artistic impulse to do a thing properly or not at all. Even now he had to prepare the ground: he had to clear the chancel enough to give himself free play.

Then he found a scaffolding-pole which had not been used, and tilted at a tree for practice. The pole was unmanageable from its length. He sawed it shorter. It was still too unwieldy to use amid the débris. He shortened it until he had a battering-ram some eighteen feet long. But all these preliminaries had taken unimagined hours, and again Carlton felt sick with hunger before he thought of food, and unequal to further effort until he had some. So he turned a breaking but reluctant back upon the church, and went indoors; remembering everything on the way, and loathing himself afresh: at his work he was beginning to forget!

Thus far this outcast had subsisted chiefly on eggs; he beat up a couple now, and tossed the stuff off with a little wine and water. Then he fell upon a box of biscuits, but threw the dog as many as he munched himself, striding up and down the while, and for all his fatigue. The room was the one in which he had studied his own physiognomy. It might have been any other. He had no eyes for himself to-day, and not many thoughts, for, in the midst of his contrition for forgetting, he had forgotten again. His mind had escaped to the chancel; the flesh followed in a few minutes, having eaten and rested on its legs.

The dog bounded ahead, and presently announced an intruder at the top of its voice. Carlton quickened his pace, frowning at the thought of interruption; he was on the spot before curiosity had tempered his annoyance; and there among the ruins stood Sir Wilton Gleed, not frowning at all, but forcing a smile behind his cigar.

"How long is this tomfoolery to go on?" said he.

Carlton stood looking at him for some seconds; then he picked up his pole without replying. "You'd better stand to one side," was all he said. "Kennel up, Glen!"

"Going to do something desperate?"

"The further you get away from me the safer you'll be."

But he did not look round as he spoke, and Sir Wilton gripped his stick without occasion. Carlton's blood was boiling none the less. The enemy had surprised him at his worst. He was, for the first time, attempting single-handed the work of several men; and he might be going about it in a very ridiculous way. He could not tell till he tried; and it was one thing to experiment in private, but quite another thing to court open discomfiture of the very nature which would most delight the looker-on. And the man was worn out with hard and unaccustomed labour, dyspeptic from evil feeding, nervous and irritable from both causes combined. Sir Wilton Gleed could hardly have chosen a worse moment for renewing the duel.

In Carlton the longing to do something violent suddenly outweighed his desire to raze the east end of the church. He poised his pole and fixed both eyes on the one remaining mullion of the east window. If the mullion went, he still thought that the whole fabric should collapse, forgetting the inherent independence of arches; and his mind dwelt wistfully on the effect of the crash upon Sir Wilton Gleed. But his aim was not the less accurate, nor did his anxiety hinder him from utilising every muscle in his body at the ideal moment. The end of the ram smote the mullion fairly and powerfully, where it was already cracked. The mullion flew asunder; a quatrefoil shifted a little, robbed of its support. The whole wall seemed to shudder; but that was all.

"You remind me of Don Quixote," said Sir Wilton's voice.

Carlton spun round. The pole trailed behind him from his right hand. He took fresh hold of it, lower down, and there was no mistaking his look.

"You go about your business," said he, fiercely.

"I've come about it," was the bland reply. "I'm not trespassing either; don't put yourself in the wrong. Remember your own advice; and let's have a civil answer to a civil question. My good friend, what do you think you're trying to do?"

The artificial geniality of address, the settled malice underneath, the tone that people take with a wilful child, all galled and goaded the tired man beyond endurance.

"You had better go," he said.

"Do you really propose to rebuild the church with your own ten fingers?" inquired Sir Wilton, not to be daunted by a threat.

"You proposed it. I mean to do it."

Sir Wilton shook his head with a venomous smile. "Oh, no, you don't! You mean to pretend to try. You mean to pose."

Carlton flung the pole from him, and strode forward, swinging open hands.

"I'm not going to talk to you," he said, "and you sha'n't make me strike you; but if you don't go out you'll be put out, Sir Wilton."

Gleed smiled again. His collar was seized. He smiled no more, but lashed out with his stick. The stick was wrenched away from him. It whistled in the air. And Robert Carlton had his enemy at his mercy, still held by the collar, in the place where he had preached goodwill to men. For he was much the taller of the two and an old athlete, whereas the other was only an elderly sportsman. Carlton could have whipped him like a little dog. He did almost worse: released him without a cut, and handed him his stick without a word.

And at that moment there came the crash that would have saved this collision a few seconds before. Both men turned, rubbing their eyes; a cloud of yellow dust had filled them as it filled the chancel. The cloud dispersed, and wall and window were gone from sill to gable; what remained was nowhere higher than a man could reach.

"Now leave me in peace," said Carlton, "for I shall have my hands full; and don't trouble to come again, because I sha'n't listen to you. You've had two chances. I promised to live away and only find the money and the men; you wouldn't have it. I invited you to build the church yourself; you wouldn't hear of that. No; you would force me to do my duty, having tied my hands! You would take me at my word. I am taking you at yours. I should try fresh ground, if I were you; meanwhile you could sue me for assault."

Gleed had fully intended doing so, but the scornful suggestion killed the thought, and for once he had no last word. But his last look made amends.

CHAPTER XII

A FRESH DISCOVERY

His son was waiting for him at the gate.

"The man's mad!" cried Sir Wilton with a harsh laugh.

"What's he been doing? What was that row?"

Sidney's manner with his father was subtly disrespectful; he seldom addressed him by that name, enjoyed arguing with him (having the clearer head), and argued in slang. Yet his tongue was as dexterous and plausible as it was always smooth, and he was a difficult boy to convict of a specific rudeness.

"There's some method in his madness," was his comment on the father's account of the work accomplished under his eyes.

"But he says he's going to build it up again!"

"I wonder if he will," speculated Sidney.

"What—by himself?"

"Yes."

"Of course he won't. No man could. He's a lunatic."

They were walking home. Sidney said nothing for some paces. Then he asked an innocent question. It was a little way of his.

"I suppose one man could finish one stone, though, father?"

Sir Wilton conceded this.

"And fix it in its place, shouldn't you say?"

A gruffer concession.

"Then I'm not sure that he couldn't do more than you think," said Sidney. "The windows might stump him, and the roof would; but he could do the rest."

"Nonsense!" cried Sir Wilton. "You don't know what you're talking about."

"Of course I don't," admitted Sidney readily. "That was why I asked about the one man and the one stone."

Sir Wilton had not half his boy's brain. The cold-blooded little wretch would boast that he could "score off the governor without his knowing it." Sir Wilton's merit was his tenacity of purpose.

"I tell you the man's mad," he reiterated; "and if he doesn't take care I'll have him shut up."

"A great idea!" cried Sidney. "But, I say, if that's so we oughtn't to be too rough on him!"

"In any case I'll have him out of this," quoth Sir Wilton through his teeth; but his mind dwelt on the shutting-up notion: it really was "a great idea." And Carlton himself had given him another: he just would "take fresh ground."

He sought it that evening by a painful path. Jasper Musk and Sir Wilton Gleed were not friends; they had not spoken for years. Sir Wilton had not been long in the parish before he discovered that Musk had "cheated" him over the Flint House. The word was much too strong; but some little advantage had no doubt been taken. The quarrel had lasted to the present time; but Sir Wilton had often felt that Musk must hate the common scourge even more bitterly than he did himself, and that he would be a very valuable ally. He was a strong man and solid, the one powerful peasant in the neighbourhood. Unfortunately, sciatica had bound him to his chair from the very day of his daughter's funeral. It would have been comparatively easy to accost the old fellow in the open, and to disarm him with instantaneous expressions of sympathy and of indignation. It was more difficult for the lord of the manor to knock at the door of an enemy who was not a tenant—a door opening on the very street, and a door that might be slammed in his face for all Long Stow to see or hear. So Sir Wilton went after dinner, on a dark night; was admitted without demur; and stayed till after eleven.

Next day he went again; he was also seen at the village constable's; and the village constable was seen at the Flint House; and Sir Wilton happened to call once more while he was there. The afternoon was rich in developments, and duly murmurous with theory, prophecy, speculation. The schoolmaster was summoned from the school, the saddler from his bench: it was the latter who fetched Tom Ivey from the room that he was adding to his mother's cottage at Sir Wilton's expense. Meanwhile the village whisper became loud talk; but its arrows, shot at a venture, flew wide of any mark. For through all his dark disgrace, as now when the odium attaching to him was gathering like snow on a rolling snowball; from the night of the fire to this eighteenth day of August; there was one thing of which Robert Carlton had never been suspected by those who had loved or feared him for a year and a half.

Naturally the excitement penetrated to the hall, where Sir Wilton kept dinner waiting, but, very properly, did not refer to the unsavoury subject at that meal. He was, however, in singularly high spirits, and drank a vast amount of excellent champagne; yet his own wife left the table in ignorance of what had happened. Now Lady Gleed was a very particular person, a great stickler for restraint, her own being something strenuous and exotic. She seldom spoke of ordinary things above a whisper, and would have dealt with the village scandal in dumb show if she could. To her daughter she had genuinely preferred never to mention it at all.

But Lydia Gleed—it should have been Languish—was a more modern type. She was frankly interested in the affair. It had given quite a zest to what would otherwise have been an insufferably dull month for Lydia. The girl had the makings of a perfect woman of society, and yet the end of her second season found her still an unknown distance from the first step to the realisation of that ideal. Proposals she had received, but none such as an heiress of her calibre was entitled to expect. She had actually been engaged to an adventurer; but that had only retarded matters.

There may have been purer causes. Feeble and inanimate in her every-day life, and constitutionally bored by the familiar, Miss Gleed kept her best side for those whom she knew least; could chatter to acquaintances, the newer the better; was in her element at parties, and out of it at home. Even in her element, however, Lydia never forgot to conceal as much of her appreciation as possible, and would dance angelically with the corners of her mouth turned down, and take like medicine the wine which really did make glad her heart. This August she was feeling particularly blasée and dissatisfied; and the romantic downfall of the rector—whose sermons had kept her awake—was a French novel without the trouble of reading it or the risk of confiscation. To-night, therefore, it was Lydia who invited Gwynneth to play, and pressed the invitation with a compliment; it was her commoner practice to snub the much younger girl. And it was Lydia who drew her chair close to that of Lady Gleed, and began the whispering, to which Gwynneth was made to shut her ears with all ten fingers. Yet for once Lady Gleed was frankly interested herself.

"But what has he done?"

The music had stopped. They had not noticed it. The ungrown girl was standing in the middle of the room. She was dressed in white, and her face looked as white in the candle-light, but her eyes and hair the darker and more brilliant by contrast. And the eyes were great with a pity and a pain which were at least not less than the natural curiosity of a healthy child.

"Mind your own business," said Lydia, bluntly.

But even as she spoke the door opened.

"What's this? What's this?" cried Sir Wilton, who was beaming, and good-naturedly concerned to see the tears starting to his brother's child's eyes. "Whose business have you been minding, little woman?"

"It was about Mr. Carlton," the child said with a sob. "I hear everybody saying nothing's bad enough for him—nothing—and I thought he was so good! I only asked what he had done. I won't again. Please—please let me go!"

"In an instant," said Sir Wilton, detaining her with familiarity. "You mustn't be a little goose."

"Let her go, Wilton," whispered his wife.

"Not till I've told her what Mr. Carlton has done!"

And Sir Wilton Gleed beamed more than ever upon the consternation of his ladies.

"But, Wilton—"

Lady Gleed had risen, and was even forgetting to whisper. Lydia merely looked unusually wide-awake, and prettier for once than the child under the chandelier, who was terribly disfigured by her embarrassment and distress.

"If you want to know what Mr. Carlton has done," said Sir Wilton to his niece, "it was he who set fire to the church!"

CHAPTER XIII

Left in peace, Carlton threw himself into his task with redoubled spirit, and presently forgot the existence of Sir Wilton Gleed. He had just three hours before dark. In this time he succeeded in pulling the rest of the east wall to pieces, even to the loosened plinth, and was adding the good stones to his stack when night fell. It was a night not to be forgotten in the history of Robert Carlton's case. Nothing happened. But he had no proper food in the house, and he began to feel really ill for the want of it. Eggs and bacon he had, but the lighting of the fire fatigued him more than anything he had done all day, and he fell asleep in the kitchen, and the bacon went brittle, and his attempt at bread was become an unmasticable fossil. A very little whisky, from a bottle that had been open for months, did him more good, and enabled him to face the food problem in earnest before he went to bed. It was a very serious problem indeed. Health and strength, success or failure, continued vigour or a swift collapse, all hinged upon the inglorious question, which engrossed till near midnight one of the plainest livers on earth, as his labours had absorbed him since dawn. He had to reckon with his enemies in the matter. He had not the slightest hope of obtaining supplies in the village. But at daylight he walked some miles to see a farmer who had sometimes trudged as many to hear him preach; and the farmer gave him breakfast with a surly pity, which Carlton suffered, as he accepted the meal, for his hard work's sake.

He had explained that he came on business, and after breakfast the farmer asked him, not without suspicion, what his business was.

"Do you kill your own sheep?" inquired Mr. Carlton.

"Only for ourselves."

"When do you kill?"

"Let's see. Friday, is it? Then we kill this mornin'."

"May I wait and watch?"

The other stared.

"I want some mutton," Carlton explained.

"But I don't keep a butcher's shop," growled the farmer. "Well, we'll see what we can do; we may be able to let you have a bit of the neck-end."

"I should be very grateful for it. But I'm afraid I want more."

"What more?"

"A flock of sheep."

He was willing to pay outside prices. So a bargain was struck; and the sheep were in the glebe that night. Meanwhile he had seen one killed and dressed, and was not the less thankful that he had neck-end chops enough to last him that week.

The stacking of the stones was finished early on the Friday afternoon, and Carlton determined to take the rest of that day easily. So he set himself to retrieve the lectern from the ruins, and did finally wheel it to the rectory, on two barrows; the first broke under its weight. Moreover, this had consumed the entire afternoon, as another would have foreseen at a glance, and Carlton emerged as from a pool of ink. Since he had made himself rather hot and black, however, he thought it a pity not to clear a little more of the interior while the light lasted. It must be done some day; but again the task was more formidable than it appeared to dauntless eyes still aflame with vast endeavour. The firemen had not spared the water when all was over, so the big bones of the roof were not burnt through. Tie-beams and principal rafters, in particular, lay whole and heavy, and immovable less from their weight than from the inextricable tangle in which they had fallen. There was nothing but the saw for these, and Carlton had already sawn the lectern from its grave. He learnt to saw with his left hand that evening; and after all had very little but his own personal condition to show for his labour: only the nucleus of a wood-heap near the stack of stones, and a crooked, blackened, brass thing in the dining-room. But then he had not intended to do much that afternoon; he went indoors, and drew the water for his bath with that consolation.

Meat for the second time that day! Carlton began to feel a man. He paced his study with the old rapid step; and he determined to order and arrange his day's work so that the muscles should relieve each other in gangs: varied exertions; that was the principle of all continuous labour. You cannot sit down to rest when you are working hard; but you can do something else. Carlton never rested till he went to bed. But this evening he sat down at his desk.

A sheet of sermon paper was ruled in six columns and a margin; the columns were headed by the days of the week; down the margin the days were divided into three periods, a short and two long; it was the class-room chart of his school-days over again. In future he would rise at five; four was too early. The short period before breakfast should be daily devoted to work in the house. The place must be made and kept habitably clean; that could be left partly to the wet days. Then there was the kitchen work, the preparation of food for the day, baking two days a week, the occasional slaughter of a sheep; and here Carlton paused to grapple with the appalling problem presented by the hungriest of living men and the smallest of slain sheep . . . Salt seemed the solution . . . Salt mutton? . . . At any rate all carnal cares and menial duties should be disposed of for the day as early as possible in the early morning; not till then would he break his fast; and the real day's work should begin as near eight o'clock as might be, but as often as possible on the right side of the hour. Moreover, it should begin with the lighter labour: scraping and repointing the uncondemned walls, for example; that would take one man weeks or months; but it would not tire him out at the beginning of the day. Then there was the preparation of the stones; the careful scraping of those preserved; classification as to size for the various courses; cutting and fitting of fresh stones; the actual building with trowel and plummet. All this went under one head, and was for the body of the day; a long spell broken by a good meal and a determined rest. The day should finish, for many a day to come, with a savage attack upon the chaos within the walls. A hand too tired for skilled labour would still be fit for that.

And as Robert Carlton reached this stage in the laying of his ingenious plans, he leaned back in his chair, and stared at his dull reflection in the diamond panes above his writing table, in a sudden horror of himself and all his ways and works. He was actually happy—he! The reaction was the same in kind as that which had come to him at the shed, in the joy of touching hammer and chisel again, and which had driven him to the hall next morning. But it was greater in degree: for then he had seen how happy he might be; to-night he knew how happy he was.

"But only in my work! Only in my work!" he cried, and fell upon his knees to crave forgiveness from the Almighty for daring to enjoy the consolation which He had ordained for him.

The artist was dead in Carlton for that night. He rose a very miserable sinner, every thought a whip for his poor spirit that had dared to come to life without leave. He had committed deadly sin with deadliest result; let him never forget it! He, God's servant—the morbid rehearsal may be spared. But he did not spare himself. All the aggravating circumstances were recalled, none that extenuated; all that he had suffered he must needs suffer anew, slowly, deliberately, and in due order; that he might not forget, that he might never forget again! Now he was confessing to Musk, now to George Mellis; poor George, where was he? Now they were breaking his windows, and now Tom Ivey was refusing his hand. But at last he was before the bishop; that strong, queer voice was croaking across the desk; and all at once the croak ended, and the voice rang like a sovereign with words of refined gold.

"Courage, brother! Pray without ceasing. Look forward, not back; do not despair. Despair is the devil's best friend; better give way to deadly sin than to deadlier despair!"

And he prayed again; but not in the house.

"For I will look forward," he said as he went. "But let me never again forget!"

There was neither wind nor moon. The sparrows were still, but not the shrill little swifts. And somewhere a thrush was singing, clear and mellow and certain as a bell; and once a bat's wing brushed the bowed bare head of him who prayed not for forgiveness but for the peace of a soul; for neither was it in the ruins that Robert Carlton knelt once more.

CHAPTER XIV

THE LAST RESORT

Carlton chose a fresh stone from the heap; he was going to begin all over again. He got it in his arms, and he managed to stagger with it to the front of the shed. The stone was at least two feet long, and its other dimensions were about half that of the length; as Carlton set it down, himself all but on the top of it, he trusted it was the largest size in the heap. It was of a rich reddish yellow, roughly rectangular, but lumpy as ill-made porridge, exactly as it had come from the quarry. Carlton tilted it up against a smaller stone, smooth enough in parts, but palpably untrue in its planes and angles. This was the stone that he had been all day spoiling; it had been as big as the new one that morning, when he had begun upon it with a view to the lower eleven-inch courses; and now he had failed to make even a six-inch job of it. The stone was so soft. It cut like cheese. But he was not going to spoil another.

So he rested a minute before beginning again, and he marshalled his tools upon a barrow within reach of his hand. It was rather late on the Saturday afternoon. In the morning he had felt disinclined for violent exertion, but just equal to trying his hand at that stone-dressing which would presently become his chief labour; and his hand had disappointed him. It had the wrong kind of cunning: as amateurs will, Carlton had picked up his fancy craft at the fancy end: gargoyles were his specialty, and an even surface beyond him.

"But I can learn," he had been saying all day; and most times the dog had wagged his tail.

Ten minutes ago his tone had changed.

"I'll start afresh! I'll do one to-night! I won't be beaten!"

And that time Glen had leapt up with his master, and lashed his shins with his tail, as much as to say, "Beaten? Not you!" and had accompanied him to the heap, and was pretending to rest with him now. But Carlton was constitutionally impatient of conscious rest; and this afternoon certain sounds, louder though less incessant than those of his constant comrades, the bees and birds, informed him that the Boys' Friendly were not too proud to use the far strip of glebe land which the rector had levelled for them last year. The discovery made him glad. But it also brought him to his feet within the minute that he had promised himself; and the hammer rang swift blows on the cold-chisel as much to drown the music of bat and ball as to clear the grosser irregularities from one surface of the stone.

This done (and this much he had done successfully enough before), hammer and cold-chisel were thrown aside, and the marbling-hammer taken up, because Tom Ivey had always used it to make the rough sufficiently smooth. But it is a mongrel implement at best, being hammer and chisel in one, with changeable bits like a brace, and yet with less of these than of the pickaxe in its cross-bred composition. Like a pick you wield it, yet lightly and with the one and only curve, or at a stroke you go too deep.

Chip, chip, chip went the sharp seven-eighths-of-an-inch bit; and off curved the soft yellow flakes, to turn to powder as they fell.

Chip, chip, chip along the top; and the keen bit left its mark each time; and the finished row of these was like the key-board of a toy piano.

Chip, chip, chip, always from left to right, a tier below, and then the tier below that. The toy piano is becoming a toy organ of many manuals; and the hue of the keys is not that of the rough outer surface: as they first see the light they are nearer the colour of cigar-ash.

Chip, chip, chip—chip, chip, chip; but swish, swish, swish is a thought nearer the sound. So soft that stone, so sharp that bit, so timorous and tentative the unpractised strokes of Robert Carlton!

Every now and then he would stop, and anxiously apply a straight lath to the spreading smoothness; but he was improving, and in the end the plane was at least as true as it was smooth. The key-marks of the marbling-hammer were not always parallel or of even length, and the rows declined from left to right like the hand of a weak writer: "bad batting," Tom Ivey would have called it, a "bat" being the mark in question, and long, even bats, "straight along the stone," the mason's ideal, as the inquisitive amateur had discovered the first day Ivey worked for him. But knowledge and skill lie a gulf apart, and on the whole Carlton felt encouraged. He had done but one side of four, but the one was smooth enough to face the world as coursed rubble; let him but get and keep his angles, and the other three would matter less. So now he took the straight-edge, as the lath was called, and the bit of black slate which Tom had also left behind him; and with these and the mason's square a rectangular parallelogram with eleven-inch ends was duly ruled on the satisfactory surface. Hammer and cold-chisel again. Much use of the square, but no more play with the marbling-hammer. No need to perfect the parts doomed to mortar and eternal night; rough criss-cross work with a mason's axe is the thing for them; as Carlton knew when he rather reluctantly applied himself to the mastery of that implement, just as he was beginning to acquire some proficiency with the other. The mason's axe was the most treacherous of them all. It was a hand pickaxe with a point like a stiletto; a touch, and the steel lay buried. But it was the right tool to use, and Carlton used it to the best of his ability, stooping more and more over his work as the light began to fail him.

He was going to succeed at last! If only he had not lost so much time! Then he might have mixed some mortar and laid the first stone of his own cutting—the first stone of the new church! That would have been something like a day's work; yet he was not dissatisfied with his progress. Swish, swish, swish; he might have done much worse. He had pulled down the bad walls—swish—and what was good of them—swish—he had saved and there they were. He looked up, the perspiration standing thick upon his white forehead, his eyes all eagerness and determination. He stood upright to rest a moment in the mellow light—happy again! Happy because he had not time to think of himself, but only of what he was doing, and of what he felt certain he could do: happy in his aching limbs and soaking flannels, and all that with a happiness he was for once not destined to realise and to check. For, even as he stood, Glen barked, and Carlton turned in time to see the village constable tuck his cane under his arm while he stood still to feel in his pockets. The man was in full uniform—a strange circumstance in itself.

"Good evening, Frost," said Mr. Carlton.

"Evenin', sir."

The constable was an imposing figure of a man, with a handsome stupid face, and a stolid deliberation of word and deed which gave an impression of artless but indefatigable vigilance. In reality the fellow had few inferiors in the parish.

"For me?" and Carlton held out his hand as the other produced a paper.

"For you an' me," said the constable, winking as he kept the paper to himself. And in an impressive voice he read out a warrant for the apprehension of the Reverend Robert Carlton, Clerk in Holy Orders, on a charge of unlawfully and maliciously setting fire to the parish church of Long Stow, in the County of Suffolk, on the night of the 24th or the morning of the 25th June, in the year of grace 1882; the warrant was signed by two justices—Sir Wilton Gleed of Long Stow Hall, and Canon Wilders of Lakenhall.

"Like to see it for yourself?" inquired Frost.

"No, thank you; that's quite enough for me. Well, upon my word!"

And Carlton stood staring into space, a glitter in his eyes, a smile upon his lips, incapable of unmixed indignation: really, Sir Wilton was a better fighter than he had supposed.

"You will have to come with me to Lakenhall," said the constable's voice.

Carlton realised the situation.

"To-night?"

"At once, sir, if you please. They've sent a trap for us from Lakenhall. That's waiting at the gate."

The mason's axe was still in his hand, the unfinished stone at his feet. Carlton looked wistfully from one to the other, and thence in appeal to the officer of the law.

"I say, Frost, is there any hurry for a quarter of an hour? I'd—I'd give a sovereign to finish this stone!"

Virtue blazed in the constable's face.

"You don't bribe me, sir!" he cried. "I'm ashamed of you, I am, for tryin' that on! No, Mr. Carlton, you've got to come straight away."

"But surely I may change first?"

"You'll have to be quick, and I'll have to come with you."

"Is that necessary?" asked Carlton with some heat, as he flung his tools under cover.

"That's left to me, sir, and I don't trust no gentleman in his dressing-room. My orders are to take you alive, Mr. Carlton."

Carlton was upon him in two strides.

"Very well," said he, "you shall; and you shall come upstairs and see me change. But address another word to me at your peril!"

A small crowd had collected at the gate; a Lakenhall policeman was waiting in the trap. Carlton came down the drive with his long coat flying and his head thrown back. Somehow he was allowed to depart without a groan.

On the way he never spoke, and something kept the constables from speaking before him. They had a slow horse; it was nearly an hour before Carlton saw the inside of a police-station for the first time in his life. Here he was formally charged by a portly inspector with whom he had some slight acquaintance; the charge concluded with the usual warning that anything he said might be given in evidence against him.

"I hear," said Carlton. "And now?"

The inspector shrugged his personal regret.

"I'm afraid there's only one thing for it now, sir."

"The cells, eh?"

"That's it, Mr. Carlton."

"Till when?"

"Monday morning, sir, the magistrates sit."

"Lead the way, then," said Carlton. "I can spend my Sunday in gaol as well as in my own rectory."

His eye was stern but steady; he was filled with contempt, but without a fear. He knew who was at the bottom of this charge, and had begun by quite admiring the man's resource; but his admiration did not survive a second thought. What a fool the fellow must be! No fool like an old fool, said the proverb; and none so insanely reckless as your prudent people, once they lose their head, thought Robert Carlton in his cell. Of the charge itself he scarcely condescended to think at all; for to his mind, the more innocent on that score for his guilt upon another, the thing seemed more preposterous than it really was. He burn the church! With what object, pray? And what did they suppose he had risked his life for at the fire? Remorse, or show? He could have laughed; he was unable to imagine a shred of evidence against himself.

There was a Testament on the table, but he had brought his Bible in his pocket; and by the gas-jet in its wire guard, that striped the walls with lean shadows like the bars of some wild beast's cage, Robert Carlton forgot his own sins, persecution and imprisonment, in those of his hero St. Paul; and was in another world when the rattle of a key brought him back to this. It was the fat inspector himself, with good news on his face, and in his hand the card of Canon Wilders, Rector of Lakenhall and chairman of the local bench.

"He doesn't want to see me, does he?" said Carlton, in plain alarm.

"If you've no objection to seeing him, sir."

"But he was one of those who signed the warrant! Tell him I can't see anybody. Thank him very much. Say that I appreciate his kindness, but would prefer to be alone."

In a few minutes the man returned.

"That's a pity you won't see the canon, sir; he don't half like it. He couldn't help signing the warrant, not in his position; that seem to me to be the very reason why he come the minute he heard we had you here; and it's my opinion he'd like to see you out of custody."

"You mean on bail?"

"Yes, sir."

"Because I'm a clergyman, and it's a disgrace to the cloth!"

This explanation was a sudden idea impulsively expressed; but the inspector's face was its tacit confirmation.

"Is he here still?" demanded the prisoner.

"Yes, sir, he is."

"You can say I've been taken on a false and abominable charge," cried Carlton, "and I don't want my liberty till the falsehood's proved! But I am equally obliged to Canon Wilders," he added with less scorn, "and you will kindly tell him so with my compliments."

But he paced his cell in a curious twitter for one who had entered it without a qualm. In all his trouble this was the first word from a clerical neighbour: to a man they had stood aloof from him in his shame. His own movements were in part responsible: he had disappeared from view. Nor had he expected or coveted their sympathy; yet, now that one of them had come forward, Carlton was conscious of a wound he had not felt before. There was Preston of Linkworth—but his wife would account for him. There was Bosanquet of Bedingfield, and there were others. They might have inquired at the infirmary (Preston had), but he had never heard of it. As for Wilders, he was a worthy man of local mark, for whom Carlton had preached upon occasion; one prosperous alike in worldly welfare and in spiritual satisfaction; the last person to go into disgrace; and yet, by reason of a certain officiousness of character, the first to come forward as he had done. Carlton had no wish to be ungracious or ungrateful, or to make a personal matter of the signing of the warrant; but he could not face his fellows with this new charge hanging over him, nor was he going free by the favour of living man. On the other hand, he pondered more upon his brother clergymen that Saturday night in gaol than in all these eight weeks past. And the sense of mere social downfall, the dullest of his aches hitherto, became suddenly acute, so that for that alone he wished they had not put him in prison. But for all the rest he cared as little as before, and showed as little interest in the pending event.

His indifference quite troubled the inspector, who evinced a desire to show the prisoner every possible consideration, and was an early visitor next morning.

"That ain't no business of mine, sir; but you'll be wanting to see a solicitor during the day?"

"Why so?" asked Carlton.

"Well, sir, your case will come up to-morrow morning."

"But what do I want with a solicitor?"

"Why, sir, every pris—that is, accused—"

The inspector boggled at the word, and stood confounded by the other's density.

"Oh, I see!" cried Carlton. "So you're thinking of my defence, are you? Thanks very much, but I don't want a lawyer to defend me. I make your side a present of the lawyers, Mr. Inspector; they'll want them all. It's for them to prove me guilty, not for me to prove my innocence."

"And do you really think we have no case against you?" inquired the inspector, with a change of tone, for he happened to have charge of the case himself.

"I don't think about it," returned Carlton, with unaffected indifference. "The thing's too preposterous to be worth a thought."

"I'm glad you find it so," said the other, nettled; "let's hope you won't change your mind. I only spoke for your own good; there's plenty would blame me for speaking at all. I won't trouble you no more, sir. I might have known I'd get no thanks, after the way you served Canon Wilders last night. Defend yourself, and let's see you do it!"

The door shut with a clang, and Carlton watched the vibrations in some distress. He was sorry to hurt the feelings of his would-be friends, but he needed no man's friendship in the present crisis. God would be his friend; his faith in Him was as profound as his contempt of the false charge hanging over himself. The latter, he felt convinced, must break down as it deserved; but if not, then the meaning would be clear. It would mean that he had not been punished sufficiently for what he had done, and must accordingly be prepared to suffer something for that which he had not done, but of which his sin had indubitably caused the doing. And Robert Carlton was so prepared in his heart of hearts. Yet he was unable to carry his pious fatalism to its logical conclusion, and to abate his bitterness against the human instruments of a vengeance he was willing to think Divine.

On the contrary, he condescended at intervals of the day to give his mind to the proceedings of the next; and he did recall one or two circumstances which prejudice and malice might twist against him. To consider these was to be instantly inspired with a conclusive reply on every point; but Carlton was not sure whether the law would permit him to reply at all. So in the afternoon he begged for newspapers, and his request, though acceded to, was all over Lakenhall by nightfall. A suspended clergyman who thought so little of his notorious sins that he could ask for newspapers on a Sunday afternoon! The inference drawn by a small community, greatly excited about the case, and unconsciously anxious to believe the worst of one who was bad enough at best, will be readily imagined. The whole town shook its head.

Meanwhile the object of popular detestation was comparatively happy in the exercise of his receptive powers. By good luck his bundle of provincial newspapers contained that which can only be met with in a local press: a verbatim report of the police-court proceedings in a painful case of infinitesimal interest to the world at large. The interest, however, was all-absorbing to Robert Carlton. The accused had been represented by a solicitor. The solicitor had fought his case tooth-and-nail. There had been certain "scenes in court"; all were reported in the local paper, and no point involved was lost upon the alert brain of the imprisoned clergyman. It was with difficulty that he dismissed the subject from his mind when the church-bells rang once more through the quiet country town. It happened, however, that the parish church was quite near the police-court; and in the morning Carlton had been enabled to follow the whole service, partly through knowing it by heart, partly from the strains of hymn or psalm that reached him at due intervals through the grated window: and ever since then he had been looking forward to evensong. So now when first the bells ceased, and then the voluntary, the prisoner presently rehearsed the exhortation (in silence) on his feet, the general confession (half aloud) upon his knees; then followed the psalms, also from memory, his lips moving, his hands folded; then knelt again to pray the prayers. And his eyes were as earnest, his attitude as reverent, and even certain gestures as punctilious, as though he were back in his church that had been burnt, instead of lying in gaol for burning it.

The August evening came early to its close; a little while the new moon glimmered in the cell; then the organ pealed the people out of church, and a few steps passed that way, and a few voices floated in through the bars, before all was quiet in the little old town. And Robert Carlton thought no more that night upon his enemies, and took no further heed for the morrow.

CHAPTER XV

HIS OWN LAWYER

Canon Wilders was supported by Mr. Preston, of Linkworth, and by a youthful justice whom Robert Carlton did not know by name, but who sat like the graven image of Rhadamanthus, encased in the atrocious trousers and the excruciating collar of the year 1882.

Considering the romantic interest of the case, this was by no means "a full bench"; there were, however, some conspicuous and deliberate absentees, including Sir Wilton Gleed and Dr. Marigold. Carlton was less surprised at his enemy's abstinence than at the position voluntarily occupied by James Preston, an indolent cleric but genial gentleman, who had been his friend. His surprise deepened when Preston nodded to him, hastily enough, and with a change of colour, but yet in a way that thrilled Carlton with a doubt as to whether he had altogether lost that friend. He was in no such suspense concerning the stately chairman, who very properly looked at the prisoner as though he had never seen him before, and never addressed him without tuning his voice to the proper pitch of distant disapproval. This was not a question of losing a friend, but of having made an enemy of the most potent personage in the court.

The latter was densely crowded when the stout inspector opened the case, but the familiar faces stood out in quick succession, and they were not a few. In a doorway apart stood a Long Stow trio—the saddler, the sexton, and Tom Ivey; all three were in their Sunday clothes, and more or less visibly ill at ease; but it was only Ivey who reddened and looked away when the prisoner caught his eye. As for Carlton, he became so lost in sudden and absorbing speculation that it was some minutes before he realised that the inspector had finished a bald brief statement of his case, and that a witness was already in the box and giving evidence. The witness, however, was only Frost, the village constable, and his evidence merely that of the arrest on the Saturday at Long Stow. Carlton nevertheless whipped out his pocket-book, and the witness waited before standing down.

"May I ask him two or three questions?" said the prisoner, addressing himself with courtesy to the bench.

"As many as you please," replied the chairman, "provided they are relevant."

Carlton bowed before turning to the witness.

"How far were you responsible for the warrant on which you arrested me?"

"Re-spon-si-ble!" exclaimed the chairman in separate syllables. "What do you mean?"

"I wish to ascertain exactly in what measure the witness has been concerned in trumping up this charge against me."

"That is not the language in which to inquire!"

"Your worships may discover that it is exceedingly mild language, before the case is over."

"I shall not allow you to cross-examine witnesses unless you do so with due respect to the bench."

The clerk to the justices, who had examined the witness, was the means of averting an immediate scene.

"I think, your worship, that he wishes to know whether the witness laid the information against him."

"I thank you," said Carlton, an incredible twinkle in his eye, as he again turned to the witness. "I do desire to ask you, with due respect to the bench, whether you 'laid this information' against me, or whether you did not?"

"I did," said Frost.

"Before whom did you 'lay' it?"

"The magistrate."

"What magistrate?"

"Sir Wilton Gleed."

"And when?"

"Last Friday."

"The date, please!"

"That would be the 18th."

"The 18th of August! And the church was burnt on the morning of the 25th of June! How is it that it took you eight weeks all but two days to 'lay your information' against me?"

The witness looked confused; but the chairman was quick to interpose; he had been waiting his opportunity.

"That may or may not transpire in the evidence," said he; "it is in either event an absolutely inadmissible question, and I should strongly recommend you to employ a solicitor. If you like I will adjourn the court for half-an-hour while you instruct one; but I will not have the time of the court wasted by irrelevant and inadmissible questions such as you seem inclined to put. If you have nothing better to ask the witness I shall order him to stand down."

"Let him stand down," returned the prisoner, indifferently. "I have done with him."

Robert Carlton had surprised himself. He had come into court with the most admirable intentions that it was possible to entertain: he was to have kept cool but humble, to have curbed his contempt of proceedings conducted (if not instituted) in the best of good faith, and never for an instant to have forgotten his guilt of sin in his innocence of crime. In this spirit he had risen from his knees that morning, and with this resolve he had left his cell and been ushered into court; but the very atmosphere of the place had made the blood sing in his veins; and it needed but the chairman's voice to make it boil. He had sinned, and chosen to suffer for his sin: so no crime was too dastardly to lay at his door. He was down, and deservedly down, so friends and acquaintances alike must gather and conspire to trample him. Carlton's point of view went round like a weathercock in the wind; flesh and blood flew to the front, in despite of spirit; and all the man in him rebelled at man's injustice, in despite of his prayers.

So when the next witness was being sworn (it was his own sexton), and James Preston whispered to Canon Wilders, the man who had preached for both of them looked on grimly.

"As you seem bent upon conducting your own case," said Wilders, leaning back, "you may possibly prefer a chair at the table; if so, there is one at your disposal." And he pointed into the well of the court.

Carlton thanked him in the voice that all his will could not purge of all its scorn; he was perfectly comfortable where he was. Then he looked pointedly at Preston, and his face and tone softened together. "But I shall not forget the suggestion," he said; and again his friend changed colour.

The decrepit hero of the overweening hallucination had hobbled into the witness-box meanwhile. Carlton had not come in contact with him since the morning before the fire, and he little thought that his last conversation with the sexton was about to come up in evidence against him. Yet such was the case.

Old Busby had been responsible for the lighting of the church. He had kept the paraffin and filled the lamps. But in the month of June the lamps were rarely needed. They had not been lighted on the Sunday before the fire. There would have been even less occasion for them—by one minute—the following Sunday. And yet, on the Saturday morning, the prisoner had ordered the witness to see that the lamps were full!

So Busby deposed; and the point seemed of sinister significance. It took the prisoner plainly by surprise: the circumstance had escaped his memory. In a minute, however, he had recalled it in detail; and his cross-examination, though provocative of some mirth, and curtailed in consequence, was by no means ineffectual.

"You remember when the lamps went out, through your neglect, in the middle of even-song?"

"I'm like to remember it. That was when I swallowed the frog."

The court laughed, but not the prisoner, who was too much in earnest even to smile.

"I reminded you pretty often about the lamps after that?"

"Ay, you were for ever at me about 'em."

"Now, on the morning you mention, where was I when I told you to go and fill the lamps?"

The sexton thought.

"In your study, sir."

"And what were you doing there? Do you remember?"

"I do that! I was telling you about the frog."

This time the prisoner smiled himself.

"And did I listen to you?" he demanded, a sudden change upon his face, as though the act of smiling had put him in pain.

"No, that you didn't," the old man grumbled; "you fared as though you didn't hear."

"So I told you to go away and fill your lamps," said Carlton, sadly, "even though it was Midsummer Day! I have finished with the witness."

He was as one who had brilliantly parried a deadly thrust, and yet received a secret wound in the onset. He rested his head upon his hand to hide his pain, and only raised it at the sound of James Preston's voice putting the first question from the bench:

"As sexton, did you keep the key of the church?"

"In the old days I did, sir; but that's been open church ever since Mr. Carlton come."

"You mean that the church was open day and night?"

"To be sure it was."

"Thank you," said Preston hastily, as though glad to relapse into silence. Carlton did not add to his embarrassment by a glance, but his heart throbbed with gratitude for the goodwill he could no longer question.

"Did you fill the lamps?" asked the chairman as the witness was preparing to hobble from the box.

"Yes, sir, I did."

And, watching the chairman's face, Carlton was still more thankful to have one friend upon the bench; for it seemed to him that the young gentleman in the tall collar and the tight trousers was alone in preserving a Rhadamanthine impartiality.

What surprised him equally was the strength and the nature of the evidence produced. In his complete innocence of the crime imputed to him, he had been unable to conceive or to recall a single incriminating circumstance not susceptible of an easy and immediate explanation. Yet more than one arose during the afternoon, when first the saddler, and afterwards Tom Ivey, went into the box to bear witness against him; and more than once the explanation, so full and clear in his own mind, was incapable of confirmation or admission in the form of evidence. The more striking instances were afforded by Fuller, whose testimony, though convincing enough, and not the less so for its real or apparent reluctance, came as a complete surprise to the prisoner. It appeared that the saddler had returned to the rectory on the fatal night, more than an hour after his first visit and summary dismissal, in order to have his "say," and "not let the reverend have it all his own way." The midnight visitor had found a light in the study, but the door shut, and only the dog within. He had not entered, but had waited about the drive, till, seeing a light in the church, he had made up his mind that "the reverend" was there, and had decided not to interrupt him. So the saddler had gone home and to bed, and was fast asleep when the church-bells sounded the alarm.

"And what made you so sure that it was Mr. Carlton in the church with the light?" inquired Mr. Preston.

"Because I couldn't find him in the rectory."

"But you did not go in?"

"I knocked and called, but I only made the dog bark."

The chairman leaned forward in his turn.

"Was the barking loud?" he asked. "Loud enough to be heard all over the house?"

Carlton sprang to his feet. He had been accommodated with a chair, of which he had quietly availed himself during the examination of this witness, and the suddenness of his movement brought all eyes to his face. It was quick with impatience and sarcastic disregard.

"If you are labouring to prove that I was not at my house, but in the church," he cried, "your worship may save himself the time and trouble. I was in the church. I lit one of the lamps."

This did not strike the prisoner as the sensational statement that it was; he was therefore amazed at its effect upon the bench, where even Rhadamanthus came to life, while James Preston opened eyes of horror, and Wilders whispered to the clerk.

"That," said the chairman, "is an extremely serious statement, and one that you are surely ill-advised in making. It is not evidence, but it is being taken down in writing, and may be given in evidence against you at your trial. I should certainly advise you to refrain from further statements of the kind."

"I thought you wanted to get at the truth?"

"So we do. But I have warned you. Have you any questions to ask the witness?"

"Not one; he is equally correct in his statements and his suppositions."

Thomas Ivey was then sworn, amid the hush of deepening interest, and gave his evidence in a manly, straightforward, level-headed fashion, that added its own weight to what he said for good or ill; and his testimony told both ways. He described the scene in the church on his arrival; the character of the fire, and the attitude of Mr. Carlton; both of which, he admitted (in answer to a question from the chairman), had struck him as suspicious at the first glance.

"But did you see him do anything that you thought suspicious?" asked the well-meaning Mr. Preston.

"I did, sir."

"What was that?" from the chairman.

"He threw something into the flames. But I couldn't see what that was."

"Did you afterwards find out?"

"No, sir."

Once more the prisoner attracted every eye. It was felt that he would make another of his reckless and voluntary declarations. But this time he was silent enough; and though the evidence now took a turn in his favour, that silence left its mark.

Everybody knew how the clergyman had risked his life, when it was too late, to save the church. But the story had not yet been told as Mr. Preston contrived to elicit it from the lips of Tom Ivey. The Rector of Linkworth had been from home when the fire took place. There was nothing unnatural in his desire for details, nor did he put an improper question. The chairman, however, betrayed more than a little impatience, while the junior justice, on the other hand, displayed excitement of another kind, and actually put in his word at last.

"Do you mean to say you let him throw the water single-handed," said he, "while the rest of you stayed outside?"

"There was no stopping him, sir," said Ivey. "He would have all the danger to himself."

"Then you could not see what use he made of the water?" suggested the chairman, dryly.

"No, sir," said Tom; "I could only see the steam." And his tone was still more dry.

Wilders looked at the clock as the examination concluded. The case had not been taken till the afternoon; it was now nearly five. Wilders beckoned and spoke to the inspector, subsequently addressing the prisoner in his coldest tone.

"I understand that this is the last witness to be called against you," said he. "Do you propose to cross-examine him?"

"I do."

"And may I ask if you have any witnesses to call for your defence?"

"I may have one."

"Then it becomes my duty to adjourn the case." He whispered again to the inspector, and at greater length with his colleagues, James Preston appearing tenacious of some point upon which the chairman ultimately gave way. "As the police have completed their case," continued Wilders, "a remand of one day will be sufficient, and we shall simply adjourn until to-morrow morning. But you may, if you like, apply for bail; though the question, having due regard to the evidence which we have heard, is one that would now require our grave consideration."

"You may spare yourselves the trouble," said Carlton shortly. "I don't want bail."

And he went back to prison to lament his temper, but not to go through the form of further prayer for patience and humility; for he felt that these were beyond him in that public court, packed with prejudice from door to door.

"I told you what he'd say," grumbled Wilders in the retiring-room.

"I don't blame him," said Mr. Preston. "My dear sir, he's innocent of this!"

"I shall form my opinion to-morrow," returned the canon, with dignity. "Meanwhile I confess to some curiosity as to whom he thinks of calling as his witness."

"The chappie shows us sport," quoth Rhadamanthus, "guilty or not guilty; and I'm not giving odds either way."

CHAPTER XVI

END OF THE DUEL

Rhadamanthus reappeared without a visible garment that he had worn the day before. He came spurred and breeched from the saddle, with a horseshoe pin in his snowy tie, a more human collar, and a keener front for the proceedings withal. Carlton felt his eye upon him from the first, and returned the compliment by taking a new interest in the nameless youth; he had long read the minds of the other two; his fate was in this young fellow's keeping. He had no time, however, for idle speculation as to the result. Tom Ivey was back in the witness-box, and the accused was invited to cross-examine without delay.

Carlton soon showed that the interval had enabled him to profit by the experience of the previous day. His questions were cunningly prepared. He began with one not easy to put in an admissible form, yet he succeeded in so putting it.

"You have sworn," said he, "that your very first glimpse of me in the burning church was sufficient to create a certain suspicion in your mind. Did you mention this suspicion to anybody—that night?"

"Not that night."

"That month?"

"Nor yet that month, sir."

"And why?"

"I didn't suspect you any more, sir."

Carlton tried hard to suppress his satisfaction, as a sensation to which he was no longer entitled. He had come back to this in the night; but it was harder to abide by it during the day. He paused a little, in honest effort to rid his mind and tone of any taint of triumph; but his advantage had to be pursued.

"May I ask when this suspicion perished?"

"Before we had been five minutes together, trying to save the church!"

"You are getting upon dangerous ground," said the chairman. "What the witness thought, or when he ceased to think it, is not evidence."

"Another point, then," said Carlton: "do you remember the appearance of the lamps?"

"Yes."

"What was it?"

"They were crooked."

"Did you notice any paraffin spilt about?"

"Yes, when my attention was called to it."

"Where was this paraffin?"

"On the pews that were catching fire."

"And who called your attention to it?"

"You did yourself, sir."

"I did myself!" repeated Carlton, struggling with his tone. "That will do for that. I am going back for a moment to those suspicions of yours. Have you never mentioned them to a human being?"

"Yes, sir, I have."

"As things of the past?"

"As things of the past."

"When was it that you first spoke of them?"

"Last Friday—the eighteenth, sir."

"And did you then speak of your own accord, or were you questioned?"

"I was questioned."

"As the first man to reach the burning church?"

"Yes, sir."

"Take care!" cried Wilders. "That was a leading question."

"It is the last," replied Carlton. "I have finished with the witness. I would take this opportunity, however, of apologising to your worships for the various errors and excesses which I have committed, and may still commit, in my ignorance and inexperience of the law, and my indignation at the charge. In this respect, and this alone, I crave the indulgence of the bench, and beg leave to rectify one of my mistakes. I spoke in haste when I said, yesterday, that I had no questions to ask the witness Fuller. I desire, with your worships' permission, to have that witness recalled."

The chairman was rather sharp: subsequent evidence might make the recall of witnesses a necessity, but the lost opportunities of counsel, or of accused persons conducting their own defence, were an altogether insufficient reason. However, the man was in court, and the application would be allowed.

"I appreciate the privilege," said Carlton, "and promise that it shall not detain us many moments."

He was becoming as fluent and adroit as a past practitioner; in the pauses of the fight he felt ashamed of his facility, a haunting sense that it was indecent in him to defend himself at all. Yet he was one against many; and, in this matter, an innocent man. Fight he must, and that with all the skill and spirit in his power. His liberty, his self-respect; his one remaining chance, object, and desire in life; nay, his very life itself was at stake with these. It was no time for dwelling upon the past. The sin that he had committed was one thing; the crime that he had not committed was another. It was his duty to be just to himself. Yet this was how he treated himself, whenever he had time to think! He resolved to give himself fairer play than he seemed likely to receive at the hands of others; and his resolve declared itself in the ringing voice that shocked not a few who heard it, having found him guilty already in their hearts.

"About that very story of the empty rectory and the light in the church," he began, with Fuller—"about that perfectly true story," he added, wilfully, "which you told us yesterday. Did you tell it to anybody at the time?"

"Only Tom Ivey."

"Why only to him?"

"He asked me to keep that to myself."

"And did you?"

"I did my best, sir, but that slipped out one day when I was talking to—"

"Never mind his or her name. You did your best to keep the matter to yourself, but it slipped out one day in conversation. Now when did you last tell that true story, not counting yesterday, as fully and particularly as you told it here in court? Think. I want the exact date of the very last occasion."

"That was last Friday, sir—to-day's the 22nd—that would be the 18th of August."

"Last Friday, the 18th of August; a fatal day to me!" said Robert Carlton. "Thank you. That is all I want from you."

The justices put no question. The clerk did not re-examine. The witness was ordered to stand down. Then followed a short but heavy silence, pregnant with speculation as to the drift of all these questions and the object of so much unexplained insistence upon a date. It meant something. What could it mean? Carlton stood upright in the dock, calm, confident, inscrutable; it seemed a great many moments before the silence was broken by the formal tones of the clerk.

"Do you call any witness for the defence?" he asked.

Carlton dropped his eyes into the well of the court, and they fell upon a pair that were fastened upon his face with the glitter of fixed bayonets.

"Yes," said he. "I wish you to call Sir Wilton Gleed."

Quietly though distinctly spoken, the name clapped like thunder on the court. Amazement fell on all alike, for the issue between these two had been the common theme for days. Popular sympathy had rightly sided with morality, and its champion had lost nothing by his tactful magnanimity in refraining from sitting upon the bench; that he should be put in the box instead, and by his shameless adversary, was an audacity as hard to credit as to understand. There was a moment's hush, then a minute's buzz, to which the justices themselves contributed. Wilders muttered that the man was mad; his colleague on the right confessed himself nonplussed; his colleague on the left dropped his shaven chin upon his gold horseshoe, and his shoulders shook with joy. Meanwhile Sir Wilton had forced a grin and found his voice.

"You want me in the box, do you?"

"I do."

"Very well; you shall have me."

And he was sworn, still grinning, with an odd mixture of malevolence and deprecation for those who ran to read. "I meant to keep out of this," the florid face said; "but now I'm in it—well, you'll see! It's the fellow's own fault; his blood" etc., etc. But this was not what Sir Wilton was saying in his heart.

Carlton began at the beginning.

"You are the patron of the living of Long Stow, are you not?"

"You know I am."

"I want the bench to have it from you; kindly answer my question."

"I am the patron of the living of Long Stow," said Sir Wilton, with mock resignation.

"In the year 1880 did you, of your own free will and accord, present that living to me?"

"Yes, and I've repented it ever since!"

There was a sympathetic murmur at the back of the court. It was immediately checked. Every face was thrust forward, every ear strained, every eye absorbed between the prisoner in the dock and the witness in the box. It was no longer the uphill fight of one against many; it was single combat between man and man, and the electricity of single combat charged the air.

"You have repented it more than ever of late?" asked Carlton in steady tones. The skin upon his forehead seemed stretched with pain; the veins showed blue and swollen; but the many judged him from his voice alone.

"Naturally," sneered Sir Wilton.

"So much so that you were resolved I should resign?"

"I hoped you would have the decency to do so."

"Did you come to the rectory on the fifth of this month, and tell me it was my first duty to resign the living?"

"I don't remember the date."

"Was it the Saturday before Bank Holiday?"

"I daresay. Yes, it must have been. I didn't expect to find you there. I went to see the wreck and ruin of your home and church, not you."

"But you did come, and you did see me, and you did tell me it was my first duty to resign my living?"

"Certainly I did."

"Do you remember your words?"

"Some of them."

Carlton looked at his pocket-book—at a note made overnight.

"Do you remember making use of the following expressions: 'Law or no law, I'll have you out of this! I'll hound you out of it! I'll have you torn in pieces if you stay'?"

"I may have said something of the kind," said the witness, with assumed indifference.

"Did you, or did you not?" cried Carlton, slapping his hand on the rail of the dock; the voice, the look, the gesture were familiar to many present who had heard him preach; and thrilled them for all their new knowledge of the preacher.

"Really I can't recall my exact words. I rather fancied they were stronger."

Some one laughed at this, and the witness managed to recapture his grin; but his demeanour was unconvincing.

"I am not talking about their strength," said Carlton. "Will you swear that you did not say, 'I'll have you out of this! I'll hound you out of it'?"

"No, I will not."

"I thank you," said Carlton; and his ringing voice fell at a word to the pitch of perfect courtesy. He ticked off the note in his pocket-book, and the court breathed again; but its worthy president did more: he had forgotten his position for several minutes, and he hastened to reassert it with the first observation that entered his head.

"I don't see the point of this examination," said Canon Wilders.

"You will presently."

"If I don't I shall put a stop to it!"

Carlton raised his eyes from his notes, but not to the bench; they were only for the witness now.

"Do you remember when and where we met again?"

"You had the insolence to call at my house."

"Was it on a Monday morning, the first after the Bank Holiday?"

"I suppose it was."

"I do not ask you to recall your exact words on that occasion. I simply ask you to inform the bench whether I did, or did not, offer to resign the living then and there—on a certain condition."

"Yes; you did," said Sir Wilton, doggedly. He was very red in the face.

Carlton could not resist a moment's enjoyment of his discomfiture: it heightened the pleasure of letting him off.

"And did you decline?" he said at length.

"Stop a moment," said the chairman. "What was this condition, Sir Wilton?"

"Am I obliged to give it?"

"Oh, if you think it inexpedient—"

"I think it unnecessary," said the witness, emphatically. "I think it has nothing whatever to do with the case."

"In that case, Sir Wilton, we shall be only too happy not to press the point."

Carlton had a great mind to press it himself. He had invited his enemy to build the church out of his own pocket. The invitation had been declined. Would it also be denied? Carlton was curious to see; but he overcame his curiosity. It would not strengthen his defence, and to mere revenge he must not stoop. So one temptation was resisted, and one advantage thrown away, even in the final phase of the long duel between these good fighters. But the other saw the struggle, and felt as he had done when Carlton had returned him his stick in the ruins of the church.

"And did you decline?" repeated Carlton, in identically the same voice as before.

"I did."

"Did I then point out to you that I was not only entitled, but might be compelled, to keep my chancel, at any rate, 'in good and substantial repair, restoring and rebuilding when necessary'? I quote the Act, your worships, as I quoted it then. Do you remember, Sir Wilton?"

"I do."

"I made the point as plain as I have made it now?"

"Yes."

"And what did you say to that?"

The sudden change in the style of the question was glossed over by the single artifice which Robert Carlton permitted himself during the conduct of his case: instead of ringing triumphant, his voice dropped as though he feared the answer. Sir Wilton fell into the trap.

"I said, 'If that's the law I'll see you keep it. Go and build your church! Where there's a law there will be a penalty; go build your church or I'll enforce it.'"

"Which did you expect to enforce—the penalty or the law?"

"I didn't mind which," declared the witness, after hesitation; and his indifference was less successfully assumed than before.

"Oh!" said Carlton; "so you didn't mind my building the church after all?"

Sir Wilton appealed wildly to the Bench.

"Am I to be browbeaten and insulted, by a convicted libertine and evil liver, without one word of protest or reproof?"

The chairman coloured with confusion and indecision.

"I am afraid that you must answer his question, Sir Wilton," said Mr. Preston, mildly.

"I share your opinion," said Rhadamanthus, in a tone that went further than the words.

The chairman threw up his chin with an air, and fixed the accused with his sternest glance.

"Pray what are you endeavouring to establish by this round-about and impertinent examination?"

"In plain language?" asked Robert Carlton.

"The plainer the better."

"Then I am endeavouring to establish—and I will establish, either here or at the assizes—the fact that that man there"—pointing to Sir Wilton Gleed—"has tried by fair means and by foul to rob me of a benefice which is still mine in more than name. And I will further establish, either here or at the higher court, if you like to send me there, the patent and the blatant fact that this very charge is the last and the foulest means by which that man has attempted to get rid of me!"

His clear voice thundered through the little court; his fine eye flashed with as fine a scorn. But it was neither look nor tone that made the silence when he ceased. It was the first unrestrained expression of a personality incomparably stronger than any other there present; it was the first just and unanimous— if unconscious—appreciation of that personality in that place. There was a round clock that ticked many times and noisily before the presiding magistrate broke the spell.

"A-bom-in-able language!" cried he in the separate syllables of his most important moments. "You deserve to answer for your words alone in the other court of which you speak!"

"I intend to prove them in this one," retorted Carlton, "if you give me fair play."

"Oh, by all means let him have fair play!" exclaimed the witness, in high tones that trembled. "I can take care of myself; don't study me. Let him say what he likes, and let those who know his character and mine judge between him and me."

Carlton looked at the quivering lip between the cropped whiskers, and his jaws snapped on a smile as he returned to his pocket-book. But the whole of his examination of Sir Wilton Gleed does not call for elaborate report: its weakness and its strength will be recognised with equal readiness. With a stronger spirit on the bench, or a weaker spirit in the dock, or even a capable solicitor to prosecute for the police, much of it had never been; as the play was cast it was the accused clergyman who presided over that country court for the longest hour in his enemy's life; nor, when he had won his ascendancy, did he use his power as unsparingly as in the winning of it. The witness was allowed to come out of the corner into which he had been driven before his appeal to the bench; he had contradicted himself, and the contradiction was left to tell its own tale without being pressed home. On the other hand, some startling admissions were obtained in regard to the responsibility with which the witness had finally sought to saddle the accused; he had bade him build the church because he believed Carlton would find it an impossible task; he recklessly admitted it, with a pale bravado that imposed upon few people in court, and on but one upon the bench.

"You were still determined to get rid of me," said Carlton, "one way or another?"

"I was."

"And this struck you as another way?"

"It did—at the moment."

"Ah," murmured the chairman, "we are all subject to the impulse of the moment!"

Carlton put this point aside.

"And why did you think that I should find it an impossible task to rebuild the church?"

"I thought you would find a difficulty in getting local men to work for you."

"Your grounds for thinking that?"

"I considered your reputation in the district."

"Any other reason?"

"One or two builders and masons had spoken to me on the subject."

Carlton found a new place in his pocket-book, and read out a list of nine names.

"Were any of these local men among the number?"

"Yes."

"All of them?"

"Ye—es."

"What! You admit having discussed me, during the present month, and since I first spoke to you about rebuilding the church, with these nine local builders or stonemasons?"

"I don't deny it," said Sir Wilton, stoutly.

"And do you know of any builder or stonemason in the neighbourhood with whom you have not discussed me?"

"Can't say I do."

"That's quite enough," said Carlton. "I shall not ask you what you said. I do not purpose calling these men, at this court; time enough for that at the assizes." And without further comment he took the witness through one or two details of their last interview in the ruins; by no means all; indeed, the date was the point most insisted upon.

"And so the very next day was last Friday, the 18th of August?" concluded Carlton with apparent levity.

The witness refused to answer, appealed to the bench, and secured another reprimand for the accused.

"I harp upon that date," said Carlton, "because, as I have already remarked, it seems to have been a fatal date for me. It has arisen so many times in the course of this case! This, however, is not the precise moment for enumerating those occasions; let us first finish with each other. Did you, Sir Wilton Gleed, on the eighteenth day of this present month, have separate or collective conversation with the witnesses Busby, Fuller, and Ivey?"

"Yes, I did," said Gleed, hot, white, and glaring.

"Separate or collective? Did you speak to them one at a time or all together?"

"Both, if you like!" cried the witness, wildly. "I can't remember. Better say both!"

"You interviewed these witnesses, separately and collectively, on the very day that the other witness, Frost, laid an information against me before yourself as Justice of the Peace?"

"I said it was that day. You ask the same question again and again!"

The man was fuming, trembling, near to tears or curses of mortification and blind rage.

"I have but two more questions to ask you, and I am done," rejoined Carlton. "Did the witness Fuller tell you of the light in the church, and the witness Ivey of what he saw later on, during these conversations of the fatal eighteenth?"

"They did."

"And was this the first you had heard of those experiences?"

"It was."

"That is my last question, Sir Wilton Gleed."

The justices put none. Gleed glared at them as he left the box.

"I think," said he, "that this is the most scandalous incident—most disgraceful thing I ever heard of in my life!"

"I quite agree with you," whispered Wilders.

"And I also," said Mr. Preston, in a different tone.

But no word fell from Rhadamanthus. His small eyes did not leave Carlton's face for above one second in the sixty. But their expression was inscrutable.

"May I now claim the indulgence of the court for a very few minutes?" asked the clergyman in the dock.

The clergymen on the bench looked at the clock and at each other. It was already past the hour for luncheon.

"Better go on," urged Preston, "and get it over."

"If you mean what you say," said Wilders to the accused, "we will hear you now; if you proceed to treat us to a mere display of words, I shall adjourn the court. Meanwhile it is my duty to remind you that whatever you say will be taken down in writing, and may be given in evidence against you upon your trial."

"In the event of my committal," returned Robert Carlton, "I am prepared to stand or fall by every word that I have uttered or may utter now; and I shall not detain you long. I am well aware how I have trespassed already upon the time of this court, but I will waste none upon vain or insincere apology. I came here to answer to a very terrible charge; it was and it is my duty to do so as fully and as emphatically as I possibly can. Yet I have little to add to the evidence before you; a comment or two, and I am done.

"It seems to me that the witnesses called by the police have between them produced but three points of any weight against me, or worthy of the serious consideration of this or any other court of law. I will take these three points in their proper order, and will give my answer to each in the fewest possible words in which I can express my meaning to your worships.

"Arthur Busby has sworn that on the morning before the fire I ordered him to fill the lamps with paraffin, though it was extremely unlikely that any artificial light would be required in church next evening. But on the man's own showing he was wearying and distressing me beyond measure at the time—a more terrible time than this!" cried Carlton from his heart; and was brought to pause, not for effect (though the effect was marked) but by the very suddenness of his emotion. "And on the man's own showing," he continued in a lower key, "he had once omitted this important duty of filling the lamps, and I was 'for ever at him' on the subject. What more natural than to tell him to go away and fill his lamps, as one had told him a dozen times before, but this time without thinking and simply to get rid of the man? On the other hand, if the paraffin had been wanted for the felonious purpose suggested, could anything be more incriminating and incredible than the suggested method of obtaining it? I submit these two questions, with the highly important point involved, to the consideration of the bench; and I do so with some confidence.

"The next point, I confess, is more difficult to dismiss. I shall not attempt to dismiss it from any mind in court. I shall simply leave it to the consideration of your worships as men of the world and students of the human heart. It is near midnight. I am not to be found at the rectory, and a light is seen in the church. I admit that I was in the church, and that I lighted one of the lamps.

"Here I am forced to allude to another matter: a matter in which, God knows, I have never denied my guilt, as I do deny my guilt of the crime of arson: a matter in which I have never sought to defend myself, as I have been compelled to do in this court for a very long day and a half.

"Consider my case on the night of the fire. I will not dwell upon it; it is surely within the knowledge or the imagination of most present. . . . There was my church. I had held my last service there. I felt that I could never hold another. And, whatever I had been, I loved my church! You upon the bench . . . you Members of Christ's Church . . . I ask not for your sympathy but for your insight. Can you think that I went into the church I loved, wilfully and deliberately to burn it to the ground? Can you not conceive my going there, in the dead of that dreadful night, to look my last upon it—to bid my church good-bye?"

His emotion was piteous, but never pitiful. It shook nothing but his voice. It neither bowed his head nor dimmed the brilliance of an eye turned full upon his fellows. And so he stood silent for a space, and none other spoke; then through Tom Ivey's evidence with a lighter touch. It was evidence in his favour: he scorned to enlarge upon it. The one adverse point was lightly—perhaps too lightly—dismissed. He had been seen to throw something into the flames. Did the prosecution suggest that he had thrown fresh fuel? Other points, already made in cross-examination, were left to take care of themselves: the paraffin on the pews, to which he himself had called Ivey's attention, was one. Indeed, in the whole course of the prisoner's speech, it was never admitted that the church had been purposely set fire to at all; the suggestion had been made in the heat of cross-examination, but it was not made again. It even seemed as though Robert Carlton had grown either certain, or careless, of the result of the inquiry—and the impression was not removed by the close of his remarks.

"And now," he said, "I have to deal with the evidence of Sir Wilton Gleed. I shall endeavour to deal with that evidence as dispassionately as I can, and as summarily as it deserves. Sir Wilton Gleed is a man with a genuine grievance, which you all know and I have never denied. But I do not propose to enter into the matter at issue between Sir Wilton Gleed and myself, or to suggest for an instant that he was anything but right in determining to rid his village of one who had brought himself to bitter but merited sorrow and disgrace. I am not here to defend my sins; nor have I defended them elsewhere; nor have I shrunk from suffering from anything I have done. But here have I been brought to book for something I never did—taken prisoner and brought to you on a criminal charge and no other. And I tell you that this criminal charge is as false as another was true, but for which this one would never have been made. But enough of mere assertion; let me crystallise some of the evidence that has come before you.

"The witnesses swear to three or four suspicious circumstances between them. Yet they seem scarcely to have opened their lips—nobody seems to have heard of those circumstances—until Friday of last week. On Friday last—my fatal date—these witnesses open their mouths with one accord. And, curiously enough, it is in Sir Wilton Gleed that they are one and all led to confide!

"But there is a still more curious and informing coincidence. Sir Wilton Gleed and I have several very stormy interviews, in which he tries, first by one artifice, then by another—all frankly admitted in his evidence—to drive me from a position which I have finally refused to resign. My refusal may be just as obdurate and indefensible as you are pleased to think it; that is not the point at all. The point is this contest of tenacity on his part and on mine, culminating in a final interview between us on the eve of the day upon which all these witnesses break their more or less complete silence concerning my movements on the night of the fire, and break it in the ear of Sir Wilton Gleed!

"I invite you to consider the obvious inference. My enemy has tried every other means of dislodging me. He has threatened and insulted me. He has set every builder and mason in the neighbourhood against me. He has deprived me—as he thinks—of the means of building my church, and then he turns round and tells me to build it or take the consequences! I make a beginning in spite of him; he has to think of some new method of expulsion; so, with infinite ingenuity, he trumps up this present charge against me."

Wilders opened his lips, but the prisoner's hand flew upward in arresting gesture.

"With infinite ingenuity, your worship, but not necessarily in bad faith. I have never yet questioned the bona fides of Sir Wilton Gleed; nor do I now. On the contrary, I am convinced that he honestly and sincerely believes me capable of any crime in the calendar; but my capability, again, is not the point; and belief and proof are very different things. If your worships hold that this horrible charge has been proved against me—proved sufficiently for this court—then send me to a higher one as your duty dictates. But if you think that hatred and prejudice, however deserved, have played the part of genuine and spontaneous suspicion; that facts have been distorted to fit a preconception, and the wish, however unconsciously, allowed to father the thought; that, in short, an honest man has been quite honestly blinded and misled by very loathing of me and all my doings; then I implore your worships to dismiss this charge against me—and let me get back to the work I left to meet it!"

The last words came as an after-thought, but they came from the heart, and as no anti-climax to those who knew the nature of the work named. In absolute silence Carlton availed himself of the chair in the dock, dropping all but out of sight, and bending double, his heart throbbing, his head singing, his hot hands pressed across his eyes. It was the sudden hum of talk which told him that the justices had retired; days passed in his brain before a hush as sudden announced their return. Meanwhile there were the scraps of conversation that found their way to his ears. Hearing all, he could distinguish little; but now and then a familiar phrase leapt home, as familiar faces declare themselves afar. "The gift of the gab" was one, and "He'd argue black was white" another. But some one said, "Give the devil his due"; and with that single crumb of justice Robert Carlton had to crouch content until his present fate was sealed.

But the hush came at last, and sank to profound silence as the magistrates took their seats—Rhadamanthus keen and grim—the clergymen plainly angry with each other. Preston's honest face hid no more of his feelings than heretofore, but the chairman cloaked annoyance with the fraction of a smile, and only his voice betrayed him as he addressed the prisoner.

"After a long and patient hearing," said Wilders, "the bench find this a case of ve-ry con-sid-er-able doubt in-deed. But, upon the whole, and taking all the cir-cum-stances into care-ful con-sid-er-ation, they are of o-pin-i-on that there is not enough ev-i-dence to justify them in sending the case to the assizes. The charge is therefore dis-missed. I should like, however, to add one word in respect to a witness, who might, had he been a less chiv-al-rous opponent—a less mag-nan-i-mous man—have sat here upon the bench instead of entering the witness-box to suffer the remorseless cross-questioning of a personal enemy. I could wish, indeed"—with covert meaning—"that Sir Wilton Gleed had seen fit to take his proper place in this court! I need hardly say that he quits it without stain or slur, of any sort or kind, upon his character; and that he does so with the heartfelt sympathy of one, at all events, of his colleagues upon the bench."

Rhadamanthus turned his back to hide his face, but James Preston did not rise till he had finished as he begun. He caught Carlton's eye, and nodded once more to him, but this time unblushingly and with much vigour. There was a little hissing as the prisoner vanished, a free man; and some hooting in the street, in which he reappeared, contrary to expectation, within a minute. It was like his brazen face, so they told him as he strode through the little crowd as one who neither heard nor saw a man of them. But no hand was lifted, no missile thrown, for the deaf ear is no earnest of physical passivity, and it was notorious that this man could take care of himself with his hands as well as with his tongue. Such a very deaf ear did he turn, however, that a flyman had to follow him to the outskirts of the town, and shout till he was hoarse, before Robert Carlton paid more heed to him than to his revilers. And all the time it was a decent man from Linkworth, only begging him to jump in, as the clergyman at last discovered with instant suspicions of the truth.

"Who sent you after me?"

"Mr. Preston, sir; leastways, he told me to be here all day, in case you wanted me."

"God bless Jim Preston!" muttered Carlton, and jumped into the fly forthwith.

But presently they were at some cross-roads. And the driver drew rein with a troubled face. He wanted to go a long way round, but his reasons were wild and unintelligible. Carlton, however, divined the real reason, and whose it was, and he himself pulled the other rein.

"No, no," said he; "drive me through my own village! They drove me through it on Saturday; take me back as they took me away. But it was like Mr. Preston to think of it. Tell him I said so, and that I'll never forget his kindness as long as I live!"

It was the red-gold heart of the August afternoon, and the shrill little choir of the ruined church sang a welcome to the friend who had never sinned against them; and Glen came bounding and barking defiance at the outside world; and the unfinished stone, the first stone that Robert Carlton was to dress and to lay with his own hands, it was just as they had made him leave it on the Saturday evening. But the story of his return was still being bandied from door to door, when a new sound came with the song of birds from the ruin in the trees, and a new ending was given to the story.

The sound was the swish, swish, swish of the mason's axe, with the stiletto's point, through sandstone as soft as cheese.

CHAPTER XVII

THREE WEEKS AND A NIGHT

Carlton completed that historic stone within another hour, and actually laid it that night. Jaded in body and brain, with every nerve exhausted, he must needs do this or drop in the attempt. It was the first stone in the new church. It was finished at last. He touched it here and there with the straight-edge. He felt its angles with the square. This stone would do. He whipped out his foot-rule and measured carefully. The stone was eleven inches all ways but one. It was the exact depth for the lower courses, but it was seventeen inches long. A seventeen-inch gap must therefore be found or made for it. And Carlton went prowling round the blackened walls, with his foot-rule and his dog, before resting from his labours. The job should be finished this time, the first stone should be laid that night.

A place was found in the base of the east end, over a stable portion of the plinth; the situation was of sacred omen, and Carlton cleared away the old mortar with immense energy. Then his difficulties began. There was new mortar to make; this was an altogether new undertaking. It had been Tom Ivey's affair. Carlton had tried his hand at most branches of the masonic art, but he had never attempted to mix the mortar. He barely knew how to begin. There was a heap of sand at one end of the shed, and a load of lime under cover. These were the ingredients. That he knew; but it was not enough.

Suddenly, he remembered his Building Construction in two volumes; the bulkier of the two treated of materials. In a minute the book was found, deep in dust, and carried to the shed for consultation on the spot. And there was only too much about mortar; the subject monopolised a column of the index; its vastness oppressed Carlton, who nevertheless attacked it then and there. A great disappointment was in store: so he was to begin by "slaking" his lime. He had forgotten that step; now he had a dim recollection of the process. According to the book it took two or three hours at least; even this minimum presupposed that the lime was a "fat lime," whatever that might be. Carlton, lacking all means of deciding such a point, gave his inclination the benefit of the doubt, and left his shovelful of quicklime under water and sand for exactly two hours and a half.

This check came in the nick of time. It reminded Robert Carlton of the flesh, whose needs he had once more neglected, though now he would have cooked and eaten if only to have killed an hour. He lit a fire. He put on the kettle. He toasted some very stale bread; he boiled an egg warm from the hen-house, then another; and having eaten he rested while he must. The sun set; the new moon whitened in the sky, but as yet could not light a man at his work when it was really dark. And that was why the lantern stood so long upon the ground outside the shed, in a whirl of tiny wings, while the mortar was being mixed at last.

But the lantern stood longer still upon a salient fragment of the razed east end, while the trowel rang, and the mortar flopped, until all lay smooth and glistening in its light. Then Carlton knelt, and lifted his handiwork with bursting muscles; and the mortar spattered his waistcoat as the great stone dropped into place. A wrench, a push, a tap with the trowel; a finishing touch with its point, a word of thanksgiving before he rose; and Robert Carlton had laid the first stone of a new church, and of his own new life.

Next morning he began systematic work, rising at five, lighting his fire, making his bed, sweeping, dusting, pumping, rinsing, all before the day's work started after breakfast, with the gentler arts of scraping and re-pointing, and all in strict obedience to the schedule which Carlton had drawn up before his arrest. The working day ended, as then arranged, with a violent assault upon that black disorder which had been the nave; but this also acquired system as the days closed in; while the influence of time was not less apparent in the gradual disappearance of that tendency to morbid reaction which had been inevitable in the first days of bodily and spiritual strain, of incessant and excessive hardship, of a solitude consummate and profound. But here time was assisted by the good sense and the strong will of Carlton himself, who knew how little virtue there is in mere remorse, and who struggled against it with all his might. It was a long time, however, before even he was master of himself in this regard. One day, in the exaltation of overwork, the high excitement of nervous and of physical exhaustion, he was actually heard whistling at his walls, and it was all over the village before he caught himself in the act; but none seemed to hear how suddenly he stopped at last; none saw the raised face, the clasped hands, the lips moving in meek apology for an instant's joy. Nor did any man dream how this one would still mortify himself, after such a lapse, with deliberate dwelling on the past. There was but one link, indeed, in all the mournful chain of recent events, upon which Robert Carlton would never permit his thoughts to concentrate; that was his successful conduct of his own case before the magistrates, culminating in his final triumph over Sir Wilton Gleed. He had made the rule in the hour of his release, and he called in all his strength of mind to its rigorous observance.

It was now three weeks since he had spoken to a human being, none having come near him to his knowledge; then one morning the air was full of whispers, though the yellowing elms hung stagnant in an autumn mist; and the outcast, looking over the wall which he was scraping, beheld a bevy of school-children perched on that of the churchyard.

He bent a little lower to his work. The wall was that thirteen-foot strip, to the left of the porch, upon which he had spent the first morning of all in getting rid of the unsound upper courses. It was still his own height in most places; so the children could not watch him at his work; but the sound of them was enough. Poor little children! To grow up with such an example and such knowledge as would be theirs! His heart had seldom smitten him so hard.

"Then said He unto the disciples, It is impossible but that offences will come: but woe unto him through whom they come!

"It were better for him that a millstone were hanged about his neck, and he cast into the sea, than that he should offend one of these little ones."

The text came unbidden; it cut the deeper for that. Woe unto him, indeed! Of all men, woe unto him! Hammer and chisel slipped from his hands; he hid his face. His thumbs went to his ears, but were drawn back. The children's voices were more than he could bear, so he bore them for his sin until another aspect of the case was driven home to his intelligence. Next moment he appeared in the porch, and the children were vanishing from the wall.

"Don't run away," he called. "Come back, you bigger ones!"

It was his old voice, come unbidden like the text; he might have been using it all these weeks. The children had never disobeyed that quiet but imperious summons. They did not begin to-day.

"Why aren't you all at school?"

There was silence, broken eventually by some bold but still respectful spirit.

"Please, sir, it's a holiday."

"Not Saturday, is it?"

He was beginning to lose count of the week-days; once already the Sabbath school-bell had nipped a day's work in the bud.

"No, sir, it's an extra holiday."

"Then spend it better. Get away into the fields, or down the river. I won't have you hanging about here. There's nothing for you to see—nothing that will do you any good. Run away all, and forget who has spoken to you. But don't let me have to speak again!"

There was no need for another word. And the workman went back to his wall; but his hands had lost their cunning; his heart was as heavy as the stones themselves.

Why had he never been harassed in this way before? He had not to think very long. He was without that friend of friendless man, his dog. The good Glen, his second shadow in these days, had chosen this one to desert him; and Carlton was glad, for nothing else would have made him appreciate the dog at his true worth. Now he thought of it, how often the faithful brute had gone barking to wall or gate, and come back wagging his tail! Preoccupied with his work, he had taken no thinking heed at the time. But now he remembered and understood.

Instead of working all the afternoon, he went in search of Glen. It surprised him to find how much he missed a companion whose presence he had often ignored for hours together; he felt as though he could do no good without the animal now; its dumb sympathy seemed to have had no small share in all that he had done as yet. That wag of the tail, how well he knew it after all! It was like the grasp of a good man's hand. That wistful eye, watching over him at his work, was it a blasphemous conceit to think of it as the mild eye of the All-seeing, shining through the mask of one of His humblest creatures, upon another as humble, and countenancing the work if not the man? If this was blasphemy, then Robert Carlton blasphemed for once in his heart; and had his deserts in an unsuccessful quest.

He had searched the garden and the house; had stood whistling at the gate, and in each of the far corners of the glebe. Night fell upon him sawing a huge tie-beam through and through to shift it, and sawing with all the irritable energy of the unwilling workman, very remarkable in him. And for once he was glad to put on his coat.

What could have happened to the dog? Its master could scarcely eat for wondering. Now he sat frowning heavily. Anon his brow cleared, and a fixed purpose glittered in his eyes. A little later he was in the village street once more.

CHAPTER XVIII

THE NIGHT'S WORK

The night was as dark as it could possibly be. The day's mist still lingered, impervious to stars, and there was no moon. Carlton was not sorry, for he had no wish to be seen by more people than was absolutely necessary; neither was he allowing for the shabby tweeds he had unearthed to work in, for his cloth cap and untrimmed beard, which obliterated the clergyman and changed the man.

He had not gone far before he stopped in astonishment. He had met no one, and the village was as dark as the firmament; in the first few cottages there were no lights at all. Carlton groped his way up the path of one, and knocked twice without receiving an answer or detecting any sound within. It was as though his sin had driven his parishioners to the four winds.

He went on with increasing amazement, still without encountering a soul; then swerved of a sudden from the middle of the road, and hugged the wheatfield wall on the right-hand side while passing the Flint House on the left. Here were lights, and more. The front door stood open, pouring a broken beam of lamplight into the road. And on the single step, leaning upon his great stick, towered the silhouette of Jasper Musk, only less colossal than his shadow in the lighted slice of road.

Carlton half expected a challenge, and passed slowly and openly; instead of slinking as his shame dictated. But there was neither word nor sign of recognition from the gigantic figure on the step; and the lights ended where they had begun. There were none beneath the gabled thatch immediately beyond the wheatfield; and so for another hundred yards; not a glimmer to right or left, with the single exception of a lattice window over the post-office, where the bed-ridden Mrs. Ivey lay as she had been lying for many months. Carlton saw the shadow of a flower-pot on the widow's blind; no doubt it was the geranium he had taken her in early summer; he remembered placing it on the sill. His pace quickened. He was now at the long lane leading to the Plough and Harrow; and there at last were the missing lights. The inn was lit up in every window, and not only the unmistakable sound, but the very smell of feasting travelled to the road, where Robert Carlton hesitated longer than his wont. He might as well go home. It was quite bad enough to face his people piece-meal. On the other hand, there was the dog; a characteristic fixity of purpose in its owner; and a natural curiosity to know more of the entertainment that could empty every home.

The front of the inn revealed nothing after all. The brilliantly lighted parlour was deserted by all but a single attendant behind the bar; the scene of revelry was audibly the barn at the back. The inn itself had once been a farm-house, and this barn came in for all the festivals.

Carlton peered through the parlour window, and nodded to himself. The face within was new to him, but that might well prove an advantage. It was the florid face of a stout young man, passing the time with a newspaper and a cigar, the first of which he threw aside to answer the incomer's questions.

No, he had seen nothing of any collie dog; but he was a stranger himself, only come to lend a hand for the night. Black and tan collie, but more black than tan? No; the only dogs he had seen all day were the governor's tyke and a thoroughbred bitch belonging to the young gentleman at the hall.

"But have a drink," said the stout young man, reaching for a tankard.

Carlton declined civilly, though not without betraying some astonishment.

"That's free beer to-night, old man," explained the other.

"Indeed?"

"I'm here to serve ut. Change your mind?"

"No, thank you."

"Then I will."

And the young man drew a foaming pint, while a burst of revelry came through the inner doors, but slightly deadened by its passage through the open air.

"May I ask what is going on?" inquired Carlton.

"That's the biggest spread ever seen in Long Stow," said the stout youth, drawing his sleeve along his lips and turning a shade more florid than before.

"Not the harvest-home already?"

"No; that's a dinner given by the squire to every sowl in the parish—men, women, an' kids—all but one."

The questioner stood absorbed.

"All but one," repeated the temporary barman with knowing emphasis. And he winked as he leant across the bar.

"Ah!"

"Their reverend ain't here—not much!"

"I don't suppose he is. And why is the squire doing this sort of thing on this scale?"

"Why, in honour of the victory, to be sure."

"What victory?"

"Why, the one we've just had in Egypt. Tel-el—but here that is, in the Bury Post, and a fair jaw-breaker, too."

It was the first newspaper which Robert Carlton had seen for several weeks. His Standard subscription had run out at mid-summer; he had never renewed it. The world had renounced him utterly, and so must he renounce the world. To live as he was living, and yet to have an ear for the busy hum—he could not do it. For already he recognized the startling truth: it was its very completeness which rendered his isolation endurable.

Yet his eyes glistened as he ran them down the stirring columns, and his tanned face wore a coppery glow as he returned the paper across the bar.

"Thanks very much," he said. "I am glad to have seen that."

"Is it the first you've heard of it?"

"Yes; I don't often see a paper."

The young barman was eyeing him up and down, from the old tweed trousers to the old cloth cap.

"On the tramp, are you?"

Carlton did not choose to reply.

"Yet you seemed to know all about their reverend here!"

"Who does not?" cried the man in tweeds, with involuntary bitterness.

"Ah, you may well say that! And what do you think of him?"

"I think the same as everybody else."

"That he's the biggest blackguard unhung?"

"Indeed, one of them!"

"That's what the young gentleman from the hall say, when he was in here this afternoon. But the governor, Master Palmer—O Lord! how he do hate him! 'Unhung?' he say. 'Why, hangun's too good for him.' An' so it is, come to think of it: to go and do what he done, an' to top all by settun fire to his own church!"

"Come," said Carlton, "that wasn't proved."

"But everybody know it, bless you!"

"Though the charge was dismissed in open court?"

"Bah! 'Not guilty, but don't do that again!'"

And the stout youth nodded sagely over his tankard's rim.

"So that's the opinion of the neighbourhood, is it?"

"That is, and that's not likely to change."

Carlton was not astonished. He had foreseen this even from the prisoner's dock, in that pause of the proceedings when he had felt ashamed of his facility in self-defence, a haunting doubt of the propriety of his defending himself at all. And yet the virile instinct which had inspired him then was not yet dead in his breast; he could not let all this pass; the conversation was none of his seeking, yet he must say something more.

"I have never stuck up for him," he began; "but give even him his due! What possible object could a man have in burning down his own church?"

"What I asked the governor," replied the barman. "'Dog in the manger,' he say; 'didn't want the next man to reap where he've sowed. What's more, that give him an excuse for stoppun in the place,' he say."

Carlton was under no temptation to confute these arguments; his only difficulty was to suppress a smile.

"So his people don't think any the better of him for getting himself off, eh?"

"The better? That's made them right mad! The governor here, he say that was the gift of the gab and nothun else; all parsons have their fair share; but this here reverend, he do seem to be a holy terror, an' no mistake. A gentleman like Sir Wilton Gleed haven't a chance agen him; so they're all a-sayun, all but Sir Wilton himself. The young gent who was in here this afternoon, he was a-sayun as how the squire wouldn't have the reverend's name so much as spoken at the hall; and he's never been heard to name it himself since the day of the trial, he's that mad. But have you heard the latest?"

Carlton had heard quite enough, and his hand was on the latch, nor did he withdraw it as he turned his head.

"Against the reverend?" inquired he.

"That's it," said the young barman with renewed gusto. "And I nearly let you go without tellun you!"

"What has he been doing now?"

Carlton was curious to hear.

"That's not what he've been doün, but what keep comun o' what he've done," his informant said ominously. "The latest is that some young chap would go to the devil because the reverend had, so he 'listed, and he've been in the very battle there's all this to-do about!"

Of Mellis's enlistment Carlton had heard; the rest was news indeed; and his hand tightened on the latch.

"Has anything happened to him, then?" he faltered, sick at heart.

"Not as we know on yet," said the stout youth, hopefully. "But the lists ain't in, and, if this young chap's killed, everybody says it'll be another death at the reverend's door."

"So they want his blood!" exclaimed Carlton. "But what they say is true."

As he opened the door a burst of cheering came round from the barn.

"That's for the squire," he left the barman saying. "He've been on his legs these ten minutes."

The outcast had shut the door behind him, and was groping his way in a darkness no deeper than before, though perfectly opaque after the strong light within.

"And one cheer more!" screamed a voice from the barn.

Carlton need scarcely have left his rectory to have heard the final roar. Yet it was not the end.

"And three groans . . ."

This voice was hoarse; the name was lost in the night; but the outcast well knew whose it was. And he stopped instinctively, standing firm upon his feet while the groans were given—as though they lashed him like wind and rain. Then he turned his face to the storm. He could not help it. There was more clapping of the hands. Something further was to come; he might as well hear what.

The barn was a clash of violent lights and impenetrable shade. Its outlines were inseparable from the sky; but its great doors had been flung flush with their wall, which gaped twenty feet from jamb to jamb. This space, illumined by slung lanterns and naked candle-light, and streaked with tables, which ran the full length of the barn, stood out like the lighted stage of a darkened theatre. Outside hovered the unworthy element which the smallest community cannot escape, or the largest charity embrace; these vagabonds were absolutely invisible to those within; and were themselves too dazzled and disgusted to take note of each addition to their number.

Sir Wilton Gleed, on his legs once more, at the high table furthest from the doors, was making that preliminary pause which is a little luxury of the habitual orator and an embarrassing necessity to the novice. He was supported by the schoolmaster on one side and by his own son on the other. The former wore the shiny flush which was the badge of every reveller visible from without; but that was not many while all heads were turned towards the squire.

Sir Wilton began by observing, with sparkling eyes, that he was very sorry to hear that name: he himself would have preferred such an occasion to pass over without a reminder of the fact that they had a leper in their midst. It was many moments before the speaker was suffered to proceed; then he repeated the successful epithet at the top of his voice, and drove it home with a synonym; recovering his own composure during a second outburst, and continuing with conspicuous self-restraint. Now that the matter had come up, he would not let it drop, even upon that inappropriate occasion, without one word from himself; but, he promised them, it should be his last public utterance on the subject, in that parish at all events, as it was most certainly his first. And another deliberate pause ended in a sudden gesture and a new tone.

"What's the use of talking?" exclaimed the squire. "The law of England is against us; there's no more to be said while the law remains what it is. I'm not thinking of my brother magistrates' decision the other day; it would ill become me to pass one single syllable of comment upon that. No, gentlemen, I confine my criticism to that law which empowers a clergyman, convicted of the vilest villainy, to retain his living in the teeth of every protest, and to continue poisoning the clean air of this parish by wilfully remaining in our midst."

"Shame! Shame!"

"Shame or no shame," cried Sir Wilton, "I intend to bring the matter before Parliament itself"—a further outburst of vociferous approval—"intend to lay this very case before the House of Commons at the earliest possible opportunity. And I think that I can promise you some amendment of the law before another year is out. Meanwhile"—and Sir Wilton raised his hand to quell renewed enthusiasm—"meanwhile let us respect the law while it lasts. In signifying our detestation of this monstrous wrong, let us be careful not to drift into the wrong ourselves. There must be no more broken windows, mind!"

And it was now a single finger that Sir Wilton Gleed held up.

"But," he continued, "what we can do—what we are justified in doing—what it is our bounden duty to do—is henceforth to ignore this man's very existence in our midst."

"Don't call him a man!"

"That's a devil out of hell!"

"Man or devil," cried Sir Wilton, "let us absolutely ignore his existence among us. Don't go near him; don't even turn to look at him as you pass. There he is—pretending to rebuild the church—posing as a martyr—really laughing in his sleeve and crowing over all right-minded men. We shall see who laughs last! Meanwhile, take no notice of him, one way or the other; forbid your children the churchyard, if not that end of the village altogether; nothing that can feed the morbid appetite for notoriety which makes me sometimes think the man's a lunatic after all. But if he dares to show his nose among you, that's another thing; hunt him out of it as you would hunt a mad dog! He won't show himself twice. But for the present my advice to you is to leave the cur in his kennel, and the lazar in the lazar-house!"

The unseen listener left amid the musketry of prolonged clapping, mingled with a banging of tables, and a dancing of glass and silver, that followed him into the outer darkness as a sound of cymbals and big drums. He was not sorry to have heard what he had heard: in his position it was a distinct advantage to know the worst that was being said. Certainly he would not go into the village again without necessity— as certainly as he would do so the moment such necessity arose. It was as well, however, to go prepared. The present experience might rank as a narrow escape; but Robert Carlton would not have been without it if he could.

He began to think better of his opponent. So he was going to Parliament as the final court! That was legitimate; that he could admire. There is infinite stimulus in the man who does not know when he is beaten—to an adversary resembling him in that respect. And this seemed to be the one characteristic common to Mr. Carlton and Sir Wilton Gleed.

Yet the outcast felt a little hardened. And his critical faculty, always keen, though only of himself unsparing, went insensibly to work upon the new material, even as he strode on through the deserted village, not to give up his dog just yet.

"I believe he had that speech by heart, for all its opening. It came too pat."

That was Carlton's first conclusion. The next made him stop dead.

"I'll be shot if the whole function wasn't a peg to hang that speech on!"

And on he went with a short laugh of scornful conviction; there was no doubt whatever in his mind; but the speech was not worth a second thought. There was Glen to find, and there was George Mellis to think about, since think he must. Poor lad! Yes, that was his fault again; the people were right; he would be blood-guilty if the boy fell. One thing, however, was quite certain: if the worst news came it could be trusted to come to him; meanwhile he could pray for his friend, as his heart was praying now, a clean sky above him, and the untrammelled air of an open country all around.

The village had been left behind; the Lakenhall road followed for half a mile, then left at a tangent in its turn; and this open country, upon which Carlton of all men had the audacity to trespass, was the vast rabbit-warren of Sir Wilton Gleed. The dog might be caught in one of the traps; that was at once its master's fear and hope; for a broken leg would mend, and his one friend think twice before deserting him again. Carlton could even enjoy the prospect of the cripple's complete dependence upon himself: it would be something to be indispensable to living creature now. But meanwhile he could neither see nor hear anything of his dog, though he walked, and stopped, and whistled till he was tired, and then called, "Glen! Glen! Glen!" No sound came back to him in reply; not even the echo of his own voice; and at midnight he gave up the search.

At midnight also the Long Stow festivities culminated in the National Anthem, its secular companion, and much hoarse roystering on the way home; all this as Carlton approached the village; and for once he was deterred. To march into the middle of a tipsy crowd, freshly inflamed against himself, was to provoke a brawl at best. He would go round instead by the river that flowed parallel with the village street. So he crossed at the lock near the mill at this end of Long Stow, and recrossed by the white wood bridge on the Linkworth road at the other end. But this was an hour later; for three-quarters had been wasted opposite the Flint House, with its river frontage of trim mead and wild garden, and a very faint light in one back room.

By this time all was so still that the returning rector became the earlier aware of an erratic lantern and tell-tale voices in the road ahead; and he was walking slowly to let these people pass the rectory gate, when in the light went lurching before his eyes. He hurried softly. The intruders were half-way up the drive, whispering thickly, but leaving a continuous sound in their wake, from something or other that they had in tow. Carlton followed on the grass, a horrible suspicion already in his heart; but he recognised their voices first.

"Where shall we plant ut? Which is his winder?"

"That there near the end. O Lord, what a lark!"

"Yes—to think he come talkun to me while you was all in the barn. The cheek! But here's his answer for him."

The first and last speaker was the stout young barman from the Plough and Harrow; the other was Jim Cubitt, an unworthy character who had been turned out of the choir some months before. And Robert Carlton's "answer" was his missing dog, lying dead in the lantern's light, with particles of gravel glistening in his lacklustre coat.

At this, the climax of his long night's search, with its ironic interludes—all as honey matched with this—a very madness seized on Carlton, so that he sprang out of the dark into the lighted area where these two young ruffians stood, and fell upon them like a fiend. Not a word was said; there was no time even for a cry. But Cubitt came first, and had the muddled senses shaken out of him and new ones kicked in before his comrade could so much as attempt a rescue. This, however, the young barman did so gamely that the ex-chorister was flung in a heap and his champion sent tripping over him with a boxing crack upon the jaw. And Carlton towered breathless, his fists still doubled, waiting for the fallen youths to rise and fall again.

The one from the public-house merely sat upright, ruefully and sullenly enough, but with a sound discretion which the Long Stow lout had the wit to imitate.

"We never 'urt your dorg," the former vowed. "He was dead before I see him, and I don't know now who done ut. I never knew anything about that till after you was in to-night, when I heared who it must ha' been."

"I don't care!" cried Carlton, in a fury still. "You helped to drag it here—my poor dog! You would spite me like that, you whom I never saw before to-night! You're worse than Jim Cubitt; he at least had an old grievance against me; and you're both of you worse than the man who did this foul thing, whoever he may be, and I don't want to know. Out of my sight, both of you, and spread this as far as you please: what you got from me, and what you did to get it. You'll find yourselves the martyrs of the countryside!"

"I'm sorry," said the young barman, getting up. "I'm sorry, and I can't say no fairer, 'cept that I must ha' been an' got right tight. But I ain't tight now. I'm not a Long Stow chap, sir, and I shall tell them, where I come from, that you're a man, whatever else you are. But as to spreadun, I don't think I shall do much o' that; what do you say, mate?"

"I never killed his dog," said the former choirman.

Nor did Carlton ever actually know, or seek finally to ascertain, the author of a deed even more detestable than it had appeared at first sight. For when the study lamp had been brought out into the still night, the first thing it revealed was that the poor beast had been neither shot nor poisoned; its brains had been beaten out. And Carlton felt as though his own heart had been beaten out with them, as he fetched a spade from the shed, and dug a grave by lamplight a few yards from his study door.

CHAPTER XIX

THE FIRST WINTER

The last leaf had filtered from the elms; the horse chestnuts had long been bare. And now there was no more cover for the blackened stump of Long Stow church, in its ring of rotting leaves, and its meshes of trunk and twig, than for the guilty genius of this mournful spot. All the world could see him now, and gauge the crass pretence of his preposterous task; there was no deceiving such a wise little world; but it had been requested not to look, and was accordingly content with passing glimpses of a drama in which its interest was indeed upon the wane. There were some things, however, which even a docile and phlegmatic community could not help noticing as winter set in. It might not be honest work, but it was making a thin man thinner. And he was always at it. Yet it no longer seemed to give him any pleasure. Indeed, his face was changed. Its dominant expression was grim and dogged. There were no more lights and shadows. It was the face of a workman who has lost interest in his work. Nevertheless, the work went on.

It went on in all weathers. At first Carlton had tried devoting the wet days to indoor work. He had cleaned his house from top to bottom, emptied most of the rooms, stored furniture in the others, and covered with sheets like a careful housewife. Not that he cared greatly for his things; but his hermitage should not grow foul. The two rooms which he retained in use were the kitchen and his study (in which Carlton slept), with the flagged scullery for his bath. The rest of the house he shut up, after robbing his picture-frames to patch the broken windows, which he treated so ingeniously that they looked quite wonderful from the road; but on windy nights the constant rattle and the occasional crash were one long outcry for putty and a glazier. There was no more to be done indoors. And still it rained. So one day he marched through the village (unmolested after all), and it was duly ascertained that he had taken a return ticket to Felixstowe, of all places, apparently for change of air. But through the very next day's rain he could be seen (and heard) very busy at his walls: in a suit of oilskins and a sou'wester. Thus the work went on once more.

By Christmas every stone that was to stand had been scraped and pointed; a few sound ones had been scraped and relaid; here and there an entirely new stone had been cut to fit the place of one charred out of shape; but in the lower courses such instances were rare, too rare to suit his own creative taste, but Carlton was determined to deal with the lowest courses first, and to raise all the walls to his own height before finishing one. In the case of those which were to contain windows, it might be well to pause at the sill; the windows alone might take him a couple of years. Meanwhile these were the walls which had suffered most, and first let him reach the sills: if he did that within the next six months Carlton thought he would be lucky. For his progress was as that of the insect which builds the reef; it was often imperceptible even to himself; yet always the work was going on.

The man was all muscle now; spare at his best, he had scarcely an ounce of mere flesh left. Yet, for his work's sake, he made wonderfully regular meals, often with a relish; and twice in the autumn killed a sheep, having cold mutton for many days in the colder weather. But the preliminary tragedy and the ultimate waste were equally disgusting, and his normal needs seemed better met by predatory visits to the hen-yard. Practice made him a fair baker and a moderate cook; but, as he had never been particular about his food, and his only object was to maintain bodily strength, he sometimes defeated his end, and added the dejection of dyspepsia to all other ills. Otherwise the physical life suited Carlton; he was out all day long; and the worst discomforts rarely followed him into the open air. At his work, for instance, he was always warm; indoors, only when he went to bed. He never had a fire, except to cook by; thus he still had a few coals left, but he doubted whether anybody would sell him any more. There was, however, all the half-burnt woodwork of the church; most of this would burn again; and, with economy, might keep him in firing throughout the term of his suspension. Meanwhile, lamp, rug, and overcoat gave all the heat that Carlton would allow himself in the study. Once, when his stock of paraffin had run out, he had to tramp for fresh supplies into a town where his face was unknown; and that experience made him more than ever economical of such fuel as he had.

Unparalleled position for an endowed clergyman of the Church of England, the incumbent of an enviable living, an Oxford man, a man of family, a zealous High Churchman, an enlightened and alluring preacher, towards the latter end of the nineteenth century! Scandalous priest though he had also proved himself, his case was as pitiable as unique; a pariah in his own parish; the outcast of his own people; an inland Crusoe, driven to the traditional expedients of the castaway, and living the very life of such within sight and hail of a silent and unseeing world. It was a position which few men would have faced for an instant. This man maintained it throughout the winter. And throughout the winter his work went on. And the spring found him technically sane.

But his brain bore it better than his heart. Some vital part of him was certain to suffer. His brain escaped altogether, his body for a time; but his heart was hard within him; all his prayers could not soften it; and presently he lost the power even to pray.

This was the meaning of the changed face seen from the road, in the days and weeks succeeding the Long Stow celebration of the battle of Tel-el-Kebir. Thereafter it was the face of one in the coils of malignant despair. But the more gradual and substantial change, in such a man, was terrible beyond deduction from its mere outward shadow.

Here was no sudden and sweeping infidelity; no plucking of loose roots from a shallow soil. Shallow this man was not, nor easily shaken in the least of his convictions. His general tenets stood intact. He still believed in the efficacy, under God, of earnest and worthy prayer. But he could no longer believe in the efficacy of his own prayers. They were not worthy: that was the whole truth. They were earnest enough, but utterly unworthy, and it was better not to pray at all.

His most passionate prayers had been for his own forgiveness, for the restoration of his own peace of mind, for the blessing of God upon his own little labours; selfish prayers, one and all; and he saw the selfishness at last. It shocked him. He tried to stamp it out, this new and obtrusive egoism; but he failed. Denied all contact with his fellow-creatures, with only his own wishes to consult, his own work to do, his own heart to probe, his own life to discipline, the man was an egoist before he knew it; and it was only through his prayers that he ever discovered it at all. They were not only unanswered; they no longer brought their own momentary comfort, as heretofore. Of old it had been much more than momentary; now it was no comfort at all. There must be some reason for this; he asked himself what reason; and the answer was this revelation of the true character of his prayers. They were poisoned at the fount. He tried to purify them, but all in vain. Self would creep in. So then he prayed only for a renewal of the faculty of pure and unselfish prayer. And this was the most passionate of all his prayers. But it also was unanswered. So he prayed no more.

He was unforgiven: so Carlton explained it to himself. And a little brooding convinced him of his idea. If God had forgiven him, He would have shown some sign of His clemency through men. But what had men done? They had broken his windows; they had burnt his church; they had closed up every avenue to such poor atonement as was in his power; they had forced him into a position which he had never sought, though for a little it had consoled him; then tried, by false accusation, to force him out of it; and now they had cut him off from themselves, had set him apart as a thing eternally unclean, had even stooped to destroy the one dumb being that clung to him in his exile!

The murder of the dog was no little thing in itself; coming at the foot of such a list, at the bitter end of a night of bitterness, it was the last drop that petrified a truly humble and a strenuously contrite heart.

But it did not petrify his hand; and the work of that hand went on without ceasing, save on that day which was now the Day of Rest indeed—and nothing more. The other six, his energies were redoubled. If he was now more than ever a traitor to his Master, well, there was still this one thing that he could do for the Master's sake. And he did it with all his might.

No day was too wet for him; no day was too cold. His fingers might turn blue, his moustache might freeze; it is beside the point that the winter chanced to be too mild for the latter contingency. While five fingers could control the chisel, and the other hand strike true, no weather could have deterred him. And no weather did.

So the New Year came, and the work went on through January and February without a break. But the month of March, as it often will, made late amends for the insipidity of its predecessors. A spell of colourless humidity was broken by bright skies and a keen wind; the latter grew bitter with the day; the former darkened before it was time. And when Robert Carlton opened his study doors next morning, to air the room while he took his bath, a little snowdrift came tumbling in through the outer one.

Carlton looked forth upon a white world in dazzling contrast to the clear dark grey of a starless sky; at first there was no third tint. But every moment seemed lighter than the last, and presently the trees showed brittle and black as ever against the sky; for the drifted snow lay everywhere but on their waving branches; and the wind blew hard and bitter as before.

Carlton bathed grimly in broken ice; he was not going to be baffled by a little snow. He was very gradually rebuilding the east end, using the old stones where he could, but cutting more new ones than he had bargained for. He could not help it. This wall was going up. It was too near the lane. It should hide the builder's head before he left it for another wall. It was up to his thighs already.

So all that day he laboured with his feet in the snow, and only his legs entrenched against the cutting wind. The stones were ready; he now prepared them by the course. They had only to be carried from the shed with mortar mixed expressly overnight; but to avoid dropping them in the slush and snow, each stone was laid out of hand; and a considerable muscular exertion thus followed by a prolonged niggling with trowel and plummet and transverse string, and this in the fangs of the wind, as often as twice or thrice an hour. It was the hardest day yet. But it was also the most successful. The entire course was laid by half-past three in the afternoon.

In earlier days Carlton would undoubtedly have given way to that spontaneous elation for which he had been wont to pay so dearly; now a tired man crept back to his bed, without a thought beyond the next hour's rest (he had seldom been so tired), and the meal that he must then prepare as mere munition of war. Yet on his study threshold he paused and turned, as doomed men may at the door of the dreadful shed.

There was little in the scene itself to stamp it on the mind. Already the snow was beginning to disappear; but the sky was still hard and clean; and the east wind cut to the bone. The ridge of firs, cresting the ploughed uplands beyond the lane, notched the bleak sky with dark cockades on russet stems; white clouds floated above, a white moon hung higher. A robin hopped in the snow at Carlton's feet; he was a good friend to the birds, and had not forgotten them that morning. Somewhere a blackbird sung him indoors; somewhere a starling smacked its beak. And this was all; but Robert Carlton carried the impression to his grave.

Instead of sleeping for an hour, he slept far into the night; and spent the rest of it in misery between bouts of shivering and of intolerable heat. His throat was on fire, to quench it he coughed, and already his cough hurt queerly. In the morning the man was ill enough to know that he was going to be worse. He took characteristic measures while he could.

It was a fine instinct which had inspired him to economise his coal; now was the time when that little hoard might save his life. But he had only one scuttle, and for the moment felt baffled; then he dried his bath, and put the coals in that, thus eventually getting them to the study in one load. These exertions hurt Carlton like his cough. In both cases it was as though his body had been transfixed. His head swam with the pain. Yet next moment he was reeling back for wood; and not less than ten infernal minutes did he spend on such errands, a furious fever alone sustaining him. It was constructive suicide, yet not to have these things was certain death. Now it was all the alcohol in the house, in a bottle that had lasted nearly a year; now a basin of eggs, of which he had always a fair store indoors; now pail upon pail of water for his kettle. Carlton had been a great visitor of the sick, and seen many a death from the disease he was preparing to resist. He had therefore a rough idea of what to do for himself; he was only doubtful as to how long he might be able to do anything at all. The lightest breath had now become a pang. Already he was alarmingly ill, and must inevitably grow much worse. But he did not intend to die. He trusted the constitution of a lean and hardy race, and he trusted his own nerve.

At last the fire was alight, a full kettle mounted, and the spout trained upon the pillow, the bed itself being drawn up close to the fire. Under the bed was the bath full of coals, and within as easy reach the eggs, the whisky, a breakfast-cup, and the pails of water. But even now the sick man was not in his bed; he was lying in a heap upon the floor, where he had fallen the moment he could afford to faint.

On recovering he shook off half his clothes, crawled between the blankets, and beat up an egg with whisky. This was all he took that day. And there he lay, breathing needles and coughing daggers until he slept.

"I'm not going to die. They shan't get rid of me like that. I don't die like a rat in his hole!"

That seemed to be the burden of his thoughts for many days; in reality the time was forty-eight hours. And whenever the determination rose afresh in his heart, and the dry lips moved with its expression, the whole man would rouse himself to an effort beside which the building of the church was pastime. He would sit up and put on more coals with a hand black from the constant operation. Then he would lean as close as possible to the singing kettle, and inhale the steam until the gaunt arm supporting his weight could do so no more. Even then he would make a still longer arm before lying down, and replenish the kettle from one of the pails, using the breakfast-cup for a dipper. So the kettle would cease singing for a time, and, each occasion entirely exhausting the spent man, the chances were that he would fall into a sleep that was half a swoon. But he never slept very long. He would dream that the fire was black, and start up to mend it—often before the kettle had recovered its voice. So far from the fire going out, for sixty hours it never went down. Carlton would mend it almost in his sleep. Even on the third day, when a kind delirium destroyed sensation for some hours, he never forgot his fire; the lean black hand would still feel its way to the bath beneath the bed, and there grope weakly for the smaller coals. All lucid thought and all delirious whispers were gradually monopolised by the fire. It became the sick man's life. He would not let it out while he lived. And live he would. When the fire died out, then so would he. But he was not going to die this time.

"Their latest dodge to get rid of me, is it? Trust to Général Février—no, March! Never mind; he shan't lay his bony finger on me . . . You'll burn 'em if you try! . . . I tell you the law's on my side."

Delirium grew from the exception into the rule. The kettle sang no longer; the bottom was out and the whole thing red-hot; for the fire had never been so good. The fender was inches deep in ashes. With or without his reason Carlton knew enough to thrust the poker through and through the lower glow. It was a clear fire all the time.

And the heat of it at such a range! It singed the sheets; it flayed the face; but it also helped incalculably to keep this stricken body and this strenuous soul together.

The crisis came before its time. Carlton grew too weak to hold the poker or to lift a coal, but cruelly clear in his mind. Thus far he had never prayed. He had abandoned prayer with all deliberation and in all his vigour. It needed more than the fear of death to make him pray again, least of all for mere life. Now that the fire was going out, and recovery no longer possible, the case was changed; and this erring servant broke his long silence with God, to pray both for forgiveness and for a speedy issue out of his afflictions. And in the same hour came the seeming answer, as if to assure him that even his prayers had still some value in the eyes of the Most High. For delirium had dwindled into coma, with these few lucid minutes between, and the fever and the pain had passed away.

Yet it was in this world that Robert Carlton awoke yet again, to find his precious fire alight after all, and a dilapidated figure nodding over it to the song of a fresh kettle. It was old Busby, the sexton. The sick man could not speak; his little finger seemed to weigh a stone; it was some minutes before he achieved movement enough to attract the sexton's attention. But all this time the live coals had been warming his soul. And already he lay convinced that he also was going to live.

The sexton turned his face at last. It was a startling face for sick eyes at such a range. The toothless mouth, which never closed, had often reminded Mr. Carlton of one of his own gargoyles. It did so now.

And a continual trickle of saliva added a disgusting realism to the image, which was, however, immediately dispelled by a human grin of profound slyness.

"And have you been bad?" inquired the sexton.

"Beat—up—an egg. I—can't—speak."

Evidently he could not, for Busby was bending a horrid ear.

"Eh? eh?"

Carlton made a fresh effort with shut eyes.

"No food . . . faint for want . . . there no eggs?"

"Eggs? Why, yes, here's one."

"Beat up for me . . . too bad to speak."

The sexton looked more sententious than ever.

"Ah, I thought as how you'd been bad," said he, with all the nods of the successful seer. "I thought as how you'd been bad!"

"It's only been a cold," whispered Carlton, in sudden terror of the public pity.

"Only a cold?"

"Oh, yes—that's all."

"Then you've not been as bad as me!" cried Busby, triumphantly. "Do you mind what I had inside me last year? That's there still! I can hear that—"

"Will you do what I ask?"

It was a peremptory whisper now.

"I would, sir, but I don't fare to know the road."

"Then give me the egg, for heaven's sake, and you hold the cup."

Carlton managed to rise a few inches in his impatience; but his fingers had less power than those of the babe new-born, and the egg slipped through them. With fortuitous dexterity, the sexton caught it in the cup; there was a crack; and accident had accomplished the design.

"Look what you've gone and done," said Busby, reproachfully, displaying the yolk in the cup. Thereupon he received instructions which even he could follow; and at length the mess was down, stinging with the sexton's notion of a teaspoonful of whisky. This second accident was even happier than the first; there was instant agitation in every vein. And now Busby could hear without stooping.

"When did you find me?"

"That fare to be an hour ago, I suppose. Ah, but I thought as how you looked bad! Soon as ever I see you, I say to myself, 'The reverend's found what beat him at last,' I say; 'he do look wunnerful bad,' I say. And you see, I was right."

There was the tiniest gleam in the great bright eyes.

"You were partly right," said Carlton, "and partly wrong. I'm not done with yet, Busby. So then you lit the fire for me?"

"That wasn't wholly out."

"Ah!"

"That soon burnt up. Then I went and got another kettle."

The great eyes flashed suspicion.

"And told everybody you saw, I suppose!"

"I should be very sorry," said the sexton, significantly. "No, I come an' went by the lane, an' took wunnerful care that nobody set eyes on I. I thought as how you might fare to like a cup o' tea, an' that was a rare mess you'd made o' your kettle."

"You've done well," whispered Carlton. "You've saved my—saved my cold from getting worse. You shall never regret it, Busby; only don't you tell anybody I've had one—do you hear? Don't you tell a single soul that you found me in bed!"

"No fear," chuckled the sexton. "I should be very sorry to tell anybody I'd found you at all. They might hear o' that somewhere else!"

Carlton lay still with thought and purpose; and death itself could not have given the lower part of his face a harsher cast; but the hot eyes were fixed upon the fading diamonds of the window over the table. At last he spoke—and it was a pity there was but the sexton to hear the firm tones of so faint a voice.

"Find my keys, Busby. I'm going to give you a sovereign—"

"A what?"

"The first of several if you do what I want!"

Not much later the sexton was hobbling towards Lakenhall, for the first time in many years; and the sick man lay greatly doubting whether he should ever see him again. His weakness was terrible now. The excitement of conversation had provoked a relapse as grave as it was inevitable in one so weak. The flickering lamp was only fed by the stimulus of suspense, the glow of the fire, and the man's own indomitable will. The latter, however, never failed him for a moment.

"I will pull through," he would mutter at his worst. "I will—I will . . . Oh, is he never, never . . ."

He came at last—with corn-flour, meat-extract, a bottle of port, and such other requisites as had entered the sick man's head under the spur of his overdose of ardent spirits. And, simple and inadequate as they were, these things spelt the first syllable of recovery.

The sexton came night after night; he also was a lonely man; and he dearly loved a pound. In a week he was richer than he had ever been before. It became difficult for him to take a disinterested view of the determined progress which the patient made towards complete recovery and consequent independence. The situation, however, had its little compensations: at all events it enabled the imaginary sufferer to crow over the real one to his heart's content.

"Ah, sir, you don't fare to know what that is to be right ill, like I. You never had a fine fat frog settun in your middle an' keepun all the good out o' your stummick. That get every bite I eat, an' then that cry for more. Croap, croap, croap!"

One day brought forth an unsuspected fact. The sexton was no longer sexton at all. There had been no more burials. The school-bell was rung on Sundays, as all the week, by the schoolmaster's son. Busby had been dismissed with a present, as long ago as the month of August; but that was not all. He had thereupon left the Church in justifiable dudgeon, and thrown in his spiritual lot with the Particular Baptists in the little flint chapel between the Linkworth turning and the Flint House. He now exhorted Mr. Carlton to do the same.

"If you do, sir," said Busby, "you'll never fall no more."

Carlton winced. But the man had saved his life. Nothing should annoy him from the kind old imbecile who had come to his succour while the sound world stood aloof.

"You don't know that," he said quietly.

"But I do," declared the other. "I'm like to know. God's children can't sin, and I'm one on 'em."

Carlton opened his eyes.

"Do you mean to tell me you never sin?"

"I mean to tell you, sir," said the solemn sexton, "that, since God laid his hand on me, now seven month ago, I've never once committed the shadder of a sin."

"Then, if I were you, I should remember what St. Paul says—'Let him that thinketh he standeth take heed—lest—he—fall.'"

The text faltered; it was terribly two-edged; but Carlton had not perceived the pitfall until he was over the brink. He had forgotten himself in his scorn, and spoken impulsively as the man that he had been the year before. But the inveterate egotist was conveniently full of himself, and his pat retort quite free from offence.

"Fall?" said he, with his foolish eyes wide open. "Why, I couldn't do that if I tried; and I have tried, just to see; but I fare to have forgotten how to sin. Do you believe me, sir, I can't even raise a swear at this little varmin what's killun me inch by inch. Why, I'm grateful to it! But I do sometimes fare to cry to think I have to stay another day in this world o' sin, when I know there's a place prepared for me in heaven above."

This stupendous speech was too much for even Mr. Carlton's self-control. Its snivelling tone, its evident conviction (confirmed by a gargoyle's grin of infinite self-esteem), were aggravated by the complete surprise of this spiritual revelation; and between them they awoke a dormant nerve. Robert Carlton did not exhibit that annoyance which he had determined to conceal; he did much worse. He burst out laughing in the sexton's face. And his laughter was long, loud, high-pitched and hysterical, alike from weakness and from long disuse.

The sexton on his legs, in a perfect palsy of horror and offence, alone put a stop to it.

"I beg your pardon," gasped Carlton, his eyes full of tears; "oh, I beg—"

And again that hysterical, high-pitched laughter got the better of him, ringing weirdly enough through the empty house.

"Ah!" said the dotard, when it had stopped at last; and the monosyllable contented him for some moments. "Well," he at length continued, with a brisker manner and a brighter face; "well, thank God I pulled you through; thank God I didn't let you die in your sins and go to everlasting hell without another chance of immortal life. You wicked man! You wicked man! I'll go and I'll pray for you; but I'll never come near you no more."

So the solitary regained his solitude; when he spoke again, it was to himself.

"Well, he has his money," he reflected aloud: he had paid the sexton some seven pounds in all. "And my gratitude!" he cried later. "I must never forget that I owe my life to that egregious old man."

Yet the greater gratitude was beginning to stir within him, as the sap was even then stirring in the trees. It was a mild, bright day, one of the last in March. The invalid had not yet been out; he would go out now. In an instant he was wrapping up.

Oh, but it was wonderful! the feel and noise of the moist gravel under the soles of his boots; the green, damp grass; the watery sun; the beloved birds; the mild, beneficent air.

His steps took the old direction of their own accord. In a minute he was there, at the church, and seated on the very wall which he had been building a fortnight before, surveying his work.

Had some one been carrying it on in his absence? Or was it only that one noticed no difference from day to day, but all the difference in the world after an unaccustomed absence? Yes, this was it; and he drew the deep breath which his first idea had checked.

Still it was wonderful: one wall seemed so much higher, another so much cleaner than before; and yet there was no stone either laid or scraped which Carlton did not recognize at a glance, with sudden memories of special travail; and the string was still where he had stretched it to keep the line. He had under-estimated his progress at the time; that was all; but again it was as though the sap was rising in his heart.

The very tangle of blackened timber, which still cumbered nine-tenths of the inner area, no longer struck Carlton as the unconquerable chaos it had appeared on that bitter day which seemed so many days ago; yet, when he laid white hands upon such a beam as he had easily shouldered then, he could not lift it an inch. Ah, that day! It would take him weeks to undo its evil work. The wet feet and the cutting wind, he could feel them both again, with the sweat freezing on his body, and every pore an open door to death. There was the ridge of red-stemmed firs, too far east to blunt the cold steel of that deadly wind; and here beneath him the barrier he had been building last, and must finish now before he did another thing. How firm and true was this top course, that he had laid that day with the bony fingers at his throat! Well, he would have died with a good day's work behind him . . . It must have been a very near thing . . . he wondered how near when the sexton came, and why the sexton had come at all. The man had never given a good reason. He had only just fared to think there might be something wrong.

On the way indoors, the invalid stopped at a tree. It was one of the horse-chestnuts; and already every delicate extremity was swollen and sticky to the touch; and the birds sang of summer in the branches. Carlton passed on with the short, quick steps of a feeble person in a hurry. Rivers were running in his heart; he wanted to be where he could kneel.

CHAPTER XX

THE WAY OF PEACE

Three years later the man was still alone, and the church still growing under his unaided but untiring hand. Indeed, from one end, it looked almost ready for the roof, the west gable rising salient through the trees, with the original window intact underneath. But this window was the exception, the sole survivor from the fire, and for the past year the rest had been one long impediment. Even now, only the three single lights, in either transept and to the right of the porch respectively, had been wrought to a finish from sill to arch; a mullioned window was just begun; the remainder all yawned to the sky in ragged gaps of varying width. But the village looked daily on the one good end, flanked by the west walls of either transept, which happened not to have a window between them, and were consequently finished. And the village was softening a little towards its outcast, though no man said so above his breath; nor was a living soul known to have been near him all these years, unless it was the new sexton to dig a grave, or a Lakenhall curate to make an entry in the parish register.

There had, however, been one or two others; the first knocking at the study door on the evening of the first funeral, some months after Carlton's illness.

Carlton was reading at the time. His heart stopped at the sound. It was repeated before he could bring himself to open the door.

"Tom Ivey!"

"That's me, sir; may I come in?"

"Surely, Tom."

The hulking mason entered awkwardly, and refused a chair. His large frame bulked abnormally in a ready-made suit of stiff black cloth. He seemed to take up half the room, as he stood and glowered, a full-length figure of surly embarrassment and dark resolve.

"There was a funeral to-day," he began at last.

"I know."

"That was my poor mother, Mr. Carlton."

"Yes, I heard. Tom, I'm so sorry for you!"

Their hands flew together, and were one till Carlton winced.

"There's nothun to be sorry for," said Tom, with husky philosophy. "Her troubles are over, poor thing. So's one o' mine! You can start me to-morrow."

"Start you, Tom?"

"Yes, sir, I mean to work for you now. I'd like to see the man who'll stop me! You've shown 'em all the man you are; now that's my turn."

And the broad face beamed and darkened with alternate enthusiasm and defiance. Carlton beheld it with parted lips and startled eye; and so they stood through a long silence, till Carlton sat down with a smile. It was a singularly gentle smile, as he leant back in his worn old chair, and the lamplight fell upon his face.

"After all these months," he murmured; "after all these months!"

"I fare to hide my face when I count 'em up," admitted Ivey, bitterly. "But what was the good of comun when I couldn't come for good? And how could I in poor mother's time? It'd have meant—there's no sayun what that wouldn't have meant."

"You mean as regards Sir Wilton?"

"I do, Mr. Carlton."

"He will have been a good friend to you?"

"Oh, yes."

"Did those repairs, did he?"

"Yes," sighed Ivey, "he was better than his word about them; you would hardly know the place now. It made a lot of difference to mother. And I had the job."

"Oh!"

"He's kept me busy, I must say. I've never wanted work."

"Until now, I suppose?"

"To tell you the truth, sir, I'm at work for him still."

"For Sir Wilton Gleed?"

"Yes—odd jobs about the estate."

"Then my good fellow, what do you mean by offering yourself to me?"

"Mean?" exclaimed Ivey, his black determination leaping into flame. "I mean as I've made up my mind to give him the go-by for you. I'd have done that long ago if it hadn't been for mother; but better late than never. You've shown 'em the man you are, and now that's my turn. Look at what you've done with your own two hands—there'll be other two from to-morrow! You shan't work yourself right to death before my eyes. Why, your hair's white with it already!"

Carlton wheeled further from the lamp.

"Not white," he murmured.

"But that is, sir. When did you look in a glass?"

"I don't know."

"Then do you look to-morrow. That's white as snow. And your beard's grey."

"It's certainly too long," said Carlton, covering half with his hand.

"And your hand—your hand!"

It was scarred and horny as the mason's own. Carlton removed it from the light, but said nothing.

"That's done its last day's work alone," cried Tom. "I start with you to-morrow, whether you want me or not. I'll show 'em! I'll show 'em!"

And he stood nodding savagely to himself.

"My dear fellow, you can't behave like that."

The words fell softly after a long silence.

"Why can't I?"

Carlton gave innumerable reasons.

"It would put us both in the wrong," was the last. "Go on working for Sir Wilton—at any rate for another year. You owe it to him, Tom. And don't you fret about me; I am a happier man than I ever deserved to be again. Last winter it was different; but God has shown me infinite mercy and compassion. And now He has sent you to me, as a sign that even man may forgive me in the end! That is enough for me, Tom. You cannot do more for me than you have done to-night. But your duty you must do, by God's help, as long as it is as clear as it is now. Don't bother your head about me! I am getting into the knack. Perhaps by the time I come to the roof—if I ever do—the want of a church may induce others to help me finish mine. Then, if you like, you shall come back; but I won't have you made an outcast on my account; one is enough."

There were no more visits from Tom Ivey. This one came to the ears of Sir Wilton; and that diplomatist instead of playing into the enemy's hands by discharging his man, capped all his kindness to the mason by getting him the offer of an irresistible berth in that London district for which he himself sat. Thus Sir Wilton removed a wavering ally, and at the same time renewed the lease of his allegiance.

Carlton heard of it some months later, when there was another funeral, and the Lakenhall curate came in again to make the entry. This curate was a gentleman. He had a good heart and better tact. He not only conversed with Carlton as with the perfectly normal clergyman, in perfectly normal circumstances, but he would prolong these conversations as far as he deemed possible without exciting a suspicion of the profound pity which inspired him. He would bring bits of local gossip, or the latest national event; once he let fall that Sidney Gleed was up at Cambridge, and said to stand a chance of "coxing the eight," while Lydia was now a Mrs. Goldstein, the mistress of a splendid mansion in Holland Park, and another up the Thames. It was from the same source that Carlton obtained belated news of George Mellis, who had come through two campaigns without a scratch, yet never been back to play the hero on his native heath. In a word this curate, who was a very young and rather commonplace fellow, came soon to stand for the outside world, the world of newspapers and talk, to Robert Carlton, who liked him none the less because his older eye saw through the artless arts with which the lad sought to mask his charity.

The visitations of this curate, who also conducted the one weekly service in the village school, was a little arrangement between those fast friends, Sir Wilton Gleed and Canon Wilders, who would have been interested to learn the way in which their delegate improved the rare occasion of a funeral. For marriages and baptisms the Long Stow folk had taken to walking across the heath to Linkworth.

Early in the second year there came a visitor whom Robert Carlton knew at a glance, though he had never before seen him in the flesh. This was a person with the appearance of a rather dissipated sporting man, who tooled tandem through the village, and pulled up at the ruins in broad daylight. The thing was thus a scandal from the first moment of its occurrence, and the cockaded groom was beset by horrified rustics before his master's red neck had disappeared among the low and ragged walls.

Carlton had withdrawn into the invisible seclusion of the west end, where he was nervously scraping at the nearest stone when the visitor appeared, only to stop short with a whistle.

"I thought this was the church the parson was building with his own hands?"

"So it is, my lord."

"And you are what he calls his own hands!"

"No, I am he."

The visitor stared.

"You the parson?"

"I know I don't look like one," admitted Carlton, glancing from his ruined hands to the shabby clothes in which he worked; "nor can I fairly consider myself one at present. Yet I am still the only rector of this parish, and it was I who wrote to your lordship about the stone. Yours are the only quarries in this part of the country. The stone I am now using came from them. But it is just finished, and unless you will let me have some more I may have to stop; otherwise I believe that I could build up to the roof, in time, without assistance."

"And why should you?"

"My church was burnt down through my own—fault."

"I know all about that," said his lordship. "What I ask is, why should you insist upon building it up single-handed?"

"I didn't insist originally," sighed Carlton. "It is a very long story."

The earl regarded him with a pair of very penetrating little eyes; he was an ugly man with an ugly reputation, but one of those who take as little trouble to conceal their worst characteristics as to display their best.

"To be quite frank with you," said he, "I happen to know something of your story; and I consider it a jolly sight more discreditable to others than to you. That's my opinion, and I don't care who knows it. So you are really and literally doing this thing with your own two hands?"

"Literally—as yet."

"And who looks after you?"

"Oh, no one comes near me; but I am bound to say that I have learnt to look pretty well after myself. I have found it absolutely necessary for my work."

"Cookin' for yourself, and all that sort of thing?"

"Cooking and even killing when necessary."

"Is the boycott as wide and as bad as all that?"

"It is no worse than I deserve."

The visitor, looking sharply to see whether this was cant, was convinced of its sincerity at a glance, though he loudly disagreed with the opinion.

"I call it a jolly shame," said he; "but I'm not going to hurt your feelings by expressing mine. I'm the last man to rake up the past. But it would be a different thing if you had really fired the church; that was the last iniquity, charging you with that! How do I know you didn't? There was a young friend of mine on the bench, and I had it from him as a fact, with a jolly lot more besides. Now show me what you've done before I go."

This did not take a minute; there was so little to show for the first long year and more of scraping, re-pointing, or rebuilding from the ground. Save at the end where they had stood talking, there was scarcely a wall that reached to their shoulders, and their tour of inspection was closely followed from the road. It was conducted with few words on either side, though the noble Earl muttered several which would not have been muttered in other company. In the end he made a startling undertaking. He would not only send as much more stone as was required, but neither the stuff nor its delivery should cost Mr. Carlton a penny.

Carlton turned a deeper bronze, but begged as a favour to be allowed to pay. The new church was his debt to the parish. It was the one debt that he would pay. The uttermost farthing and the least last stone were to have come out of his own pocket. That had been his undertaking; it was still his heart's ambition; but as such he saw its unworthy side; and would place himself in his lordship's hands, sooner than be swayed by false pride in such a matter.

"Then you shall pay through the nose!" the other promised him; "and I'm damned if I don't think all the more of you. I beg your pardon. I was trying not to swear. But I never could stand parsons, and I suppose it'll shock you when I tell you straight that you're the best I've struck! You're a man, you are, and I take off my hat to you."

He did so openly before the wide eyes and wider mouths of those watching from the road; and so ended an incident which Sir Wilton Gleed described as one of the most scandalous in all his experience. "Birds of a feather," was, however, his ready and untiring comment; and the saying went from door to door, as "not guilty but don't do it again," had gone before it; for there is nothing like a timeworn saying to crystallise a widespread sentiment.

This one did not come to Robert Carlton's ears, but he was perhaps the first to whom the obvious comment had occurred, and its easy justification did a little damp the glow in which his latest champion had left him. It were better to have won the allegiance of a better man. Yet who was he to judge his fellows? He had forfeited the right to criticise another. Let him then be truly and duly thankful; for with each waning year he had more and more occasion. Surely the heart of man was beginning at last to soften towards an erring brother, who repented very bitterly of his sin, and who was doing faithfully the little that he could to undo the least of his sin's results. Ah, that he could have done more! Ah, that by dying he could bring the dead to life!

He was only a man; he could only suffer in his turn. That he had done, was doing, and was still to do. And he thanked God for it again; so much of the old spirit still endured. Yet was he none the less thankful for every token of pardon or of pity from mere men. He knew that many would justly execrate his name until the end. He knew of one at least who would never forgive him in this life.

This one came on a moonlight night in the spring of this fourth year; came limping into the churchyard, leaning on his great stick, and growling savagely to himself; little suspecting that he had Carlton caught in the ruins, listening, watching, fascinated, from one of those ragged interstices with which even his perseverance and even his ingenuity could scarcely cope. To be exact, it was, or was to be, the mullioned window in the south transept; and as Musk advanced past this angle of the building, the clergyman first leant, then crept, over the sill to watch him.

He stole into the open. Musk had his back turned; his shoulders were very round. Carlton knew well at what grave the other stood staring, and his heart stirred heavily within him. Oh, his wickedness! Oh, his sin! How could there be any forgiveness, in heaven or on earth, for him a clergyman? The poor old man, so old, so bent! He must speak to him; he must throw himself at his feet; so bent, so lame! Oh, that that stick might strike the life out of him then and there!

He was creeping forward; suddenly he stopped. Musk was stooping, moving his stick to and fro across the grave, with a sweeping movement, as of a scythe. What was he doing? Carlton remembered—divined—and his blood ran cold. The snowdrops were out; he had put some on the grave. It had no stone, no name. It was only the tidiest and the greenest mound in all the churchyard. He saw to that. And yet his flowers desecrated it; must be swept to the winds . . .

Musk had come away. He was looking at the south wall where it had obviously been rebuilt. Carlton was skulking in the porch. The high moon fell heavily on the upturned face, covering it with white patches and black wrinkles; and these were working like a seething mass; but for a long time the great frame stood motionless. Then, in a flash, a huge fist flew from the huge shoulder, struck the sandstone a sickening blow, swung round and was shaken at the rectory through the trees until the blood dripped from the mangled knuckles. Carlton was so near that he could both see and hear the heavy drops. He drew further within the porch: he had also seen his enemy's face.

Carlton had the fair mind and the true eye of the exceptional man. He saw most things immediately as they really were, not as he wished to see them, still less as they affected himself. He saw the moonlit face of Jasper Musk for many a day. It did not haunt him. He could have dismissed the vision from his mind at will; he preferred to consider it calmly in a white light. There was hate undying and invincible. There was something to respect. Carlton compared the petty though persistent enmity of Sir Wilton Gleed with the great dumb hatred of Jasper Musk; the last was inexorable as it was just; the first not wholly one or the other, or Carlton was mistaken in the smaller man. Sir Wilton might be the last man on earth to forgive him, yet in the very end he would follow the world, supposing for a moment that the world ever led. But Jasper Musk would hate the harder as the hate of others dwindled and died.

This conviction cast no new shadow across Carlton's life, but it brought a new name into his prayers, and put the fine edge on an old anxiety. He had always been anxious about his child, though in the beginning that sense had been overborne by others. Now, however, it was acute enough. What was becoming of the boy? Did he live? Was Musk bringing him up? Was he kindly treated? Yes, yes, they would be kind enough! Carlton trusted his enemy there; but his own position was none the less grieving as he came to realise what it was. He had no position at all towards the child—no rights, no control, no voice, no locus standi whatsoever. Was it better so, or worse? What were they teaching the child? Would he also grow up to deny God, and to execrate the name of his unworthy minister?

Yes, it was a shadow; but no new one; it only fell heavier and stretched further than before. And gradually Carlton became obsessed with the idea that he must do something, take some step, give some earnest of voluntary responsibility, no matter what new humiliation awaited him. But what to do, what step to take, for the best! As life grew a very little easier in other ways that have been shown, this problem came upon Carlton as a fresh complication, and as a poignant reminder of his original wickedness. It was not, however, a problem to be solved out of hand. It required infinite thought, and ceaseless prayer for that right judgment for which Robert Carlton now again looked upward as well as within. But while he thought, and even while he prayed, the walls were still growing under his hands.

And in his work he was strangely and serenely happy; there were no more spasmodic joys and qualms. Enormous difficulties lay between him and the impossible roof. He was at once artist and man enough to be stimulated by these. He drew in chalk, upon the bare floors of his disused rooms, full-size diagrams of all his arches, divided into as many parts as there were to be stones, according to the easy rule set forth in his precious book. Then he collected all the boxes, tin, wood, and cardboard, that he could find upon the premises, and cut these up into numbered patterns coinciding exactly with the diagrams on the floor, thus providing himself with evening occupation for a whole winter, and having all in readiness by the spring. Summer, however, found him still in travail with the mullioned window in the north transept; and the mullion and the tracery he was omitting altogether; the bare arch beat him long enough.

Prolonged solitude may debase a man to the savage or exalt him to the saint; it never leaves him the mere man he was. Robert Carlton was still too human to merit for a moment the hyperbole of saint; nevertheless he developed in his loneliness several of those traits which are less of this world than of a better. His mind dwelt continuously upon holy things; it had ceased altogether to feed upon itself. He had suffered no more sickness, either of body or of soul, such as that which had threatened to destroy both in the first awful winter. The whole man was chastened, purified, simplified and refined, by the consuming fires through which he had passed. His faith had never been stronger than it was now; it had never, never been so near in sheer simplicity to the faith of a little child. In a word, and little as he knew it, this great sinner, proven libertine, suspected incendiary, was now living in the very sight and smile of God; and even His humblest creatures loved and trusted him as never in the days of prosperity and good report; for now he loved them first. Nature, indeed, had not endowed him with that sympathetic insight into inferior life—that genius for herself—which is born in most people who are to have it at all. To Robert Carlton the talent only came in his lonely and dishonoured prime, as the solace of his exile, as a new interest and occupation for his mind, and surely also as a sign of grace returning. There grew upon him in these years the knowledge and love of very little things, trodden under foot or brushed aside until now; a larger passion for nature in all her moods, and all their manifestations; and, above all, the equal peace and independence of him to whom the grasses whisper and the elements sing.

So one wind braced him to titanic effort, and another confirmed him in patient toil, and another relaxed both mind and members in merited ease; so he came to know the birds about him, almost as a shepherd knows his sheep, and even to discover some individuality beneath the feathers. There was one huge sparrow, a perfect demon for the crumbs which Carlton strewed every morning near the scene of his day's work, so that he might not be quite alone. The lowest human qualities came out in this small bird until finally, and with infinite ingenuity, it was trapped, rationed, and compelled to watch a feast of the smaller fry through the wires of a cage. Then there was a robin which in time came to perch upon the solitary's hat while he worked; only in the beginning were there crumbs in the brim. And again there was a starling that entertained him by the hour together, and all for love, from an elder-bush close to the shed.

But each of these years brought riper knowledge, until God's leafy acre, with its canopy of changing sky, both teeming with life to his quickened vision, became not only the outcast's second Bible, but all the almanac he needed or possessed. With no newspaper to distract his mind, and perhaps not a letter or a human voice for months, it was on bird and leaf that he came to rely for the time of year; while the field of his research was greatly extended by nocturnal exercise upon the pine-serrated plateau beyond the church. Now the tips of the chestnut twigs might bulge and bud, but spring was not spring until the plover paraded his new black breast, or a peewit rose screaming at the midnight intruder. All summer the small bird was king; hedgerows twittered; crumbs were scorned; man was jilted for slug and worm. But the end came in sight with the homebred mallard, flying feebly in his summer feathers; and the flight of the wild duck was the end of all. The third year found Carlton watching for the mallard as his bird of ill-omen, and redoubling his efforts while his ear prepared for the shrill music of the full-grown quills in final flight. Harsh experience had taught him how little he could do, with any certainty or any continuity, in the season when the little birds and he were best friends.

It was late in May, and the church would soon be hidden for another summer; meanwhile Carlton was still at work upon his transept window, in a corner which a great stack of undressed sandstone made invisible from the lane, as it already was from the road. The folk from other villages were beginning to stop and watch him longer than he liked, and he did not care to be a cynosure at all. He only asked to build his church in peace, and with it an example which should do at least a little to counteract the one he had already set; and he meant both for his own people, not for the outlying world. He really feared a reaction in his favour on the part of the sentimental outsider. It would do him fresh injury in the eyes of many of whom he honestly longed to win back in the end. Moreover, his head was very level in these days. He saw nothing heroic in his own conduct. With all his wish to undo a little of the harm that he had done to others, there was a very human eagerness to redeem his own past, so far as that was possible upon earth. Carlton was never unaware of this incentive. He entertained no illusions about himself, nor did he wish to create any in others. For example, there was his work. It was never easy, sometimes hopeless, always fascinating. But the man himself desired no credit for devotion to labour which he loved for its own sake, and in which he was still capable (but no longer ashamed) of forgetting the past.

The transept window engrossed him to the last degree; mullion or no mullion, it involved the largest arch that Carlton had yet attempted; and already it alone had occupied many weeks. The patterns had been the easy recreation of his winter evenings, but it had taken him all the spring to reproduce a score of these in solid stone; for though the walls were coursed rubble, the windows must have ashlar facings, to be as they had been before; and ashlar is to coursed rubble what broadcloth is to Harris tweed. What with indefatigable labour, however, and the general proficiency which he had now attained in his self-taught craft, Carlton had his jambs up by the end of May, and his arched framework fixed between them, all ready to support the arch itself. He was now engaged upon the nine wedge-shaped stones to form the latter, working each to the fine ashlar finish, as also to the exact dimensions of its fellow in tin, wood, or cardboard, and laying them in couples on alternate sides of the wooden centre, so as to weight it evenly as the book ordained.

It was the middle of the afternoon, and the quiet corner was already in shadow; beyond, the wet grass glistened, for the day was a duel between sun and rain. Carlton was taking the busier advantage of a brilliant interval, and roughing out a new voussoir with the bold precision of the expert mason. Ting, ting, ting, fell the hammer on the cold-chisel; the soft, wet sandstone peeled off in curling flakes; the quick strokes rang like a bell through the cool and cleanly air. It had been honest rain, and it was honest sunshine. The green world broke freshly upon all the senses. Every colour was more vivid than its wont, from the reddish yellow of the rain-soaked stone to lilac and laburnum in the rectory garden; from the creamy castles of the full-blown chestnuts to the emerald sprays which were all that the slower elms had as yet to show against an uncertain sky. Every inch of earth, every blade and petal, was contributing its quota to the sweet summer smell. The birds sang; the bees hummed; the hammer rang. And Carlton was so intent upon his task, so bent upon making up for time lost that day, that it might have been mid-winter for the little he looked and listened; yet he heard and saw none the less; and his face was filled with quiet peace.

In appearance he was many years older; at a distance he might have passed for the father of the man who had drawn a larger congregation than the old church would hold. His hair was grey; his beard was grizzled. Incessant manual toil had aged him even more by giving his body a constant stoop. And the hands were the hands of a labouring man. But the brown eye, once inflammable, was now all gentleness and humility; the whole face was sweetened and exalted by solitude and suffering; in expression more patient, less austere; though the untrained beard and moustache, hiding mouth and jaw, had something to do with this.

To his gentleness, however, there was striking testimony even now, as his hammer rained ringing blows upon the cold-chisel; for within easy reach of it perched the tame robin on another stone, quizzically watching the performance. Then, in the same moment, three things happened. The robin flew away, Carlton turned his head, and the ringing blows broke off.

CHAPTER XXI

AT THE FLINT HOUSE

"The child must have a name, Jasper."

"All right, you give it one. That's nothun to me."

"But he must be christened properly."

"Why must he?"

"Oh, Jasper, if you don't fare to believe, his mother did, poor thing!"

"And a lot of good that did her . . . but do you have your way. Make a canting little Christian of him if you like. Do you think I care what you do with the brat? I know what I'd do with it, if that wasn't for the law!"

So, in the early days, while Robert Carlton was still learning to live alone, his son was trundled across the heath to Linkworth, and there christened George after no one in particular. Followed the remaining period of extreme infancy, during which Jasper Musk seldom set eyes upon the child, and was more or less oblivious to its concrete existence. Then one afternoon, the second summer, as Jasper sat smoking at a back window, in the big chair to which his sciatica would bind him from morning till night, there was a shuffling and a grunting in the passage, and in came the child on all fours, with the lamp of adventure alight and shining in grimy cheeks and great grey eyes.

Musk took the pipe from his mouth, and met the small intruder with an expressionless stare. Had his wife been by, no doubt he would have bidden her take the little devil out of his sight; he had done so before, using a harsher and more literal epithet for choice. But this afternoon he was alone, and very weary of his solitary confinement. So for the moment Musk sat stolidly intent; and the child, after a halt induced by the creaking of the open door and the austere apparition within, advanced once more, with the infantile equivalent for a cheer.

"Well, you've got a cheek!" said Jasper, grimly.

The boy had reached his legs, and was pulling himself up by the particularly lame one, chattering the while in the foreign tongue of one year old. Musk winced and muttered, then suddenly encircled the small body with his mighty hands, and set the child high and dry upon his knee.

"And now what?" said he. "And now what?"

For answer a chubby hand flew straight at his whiskers, grabbed them unerringly, and pulled without mercy, but with yells of delight that brought Musk's wife in hot haste from a far corner of the rambling house. In the doorway she threw up her arms.

"Oh, Georgie!" she cried aghast. "You naughty boy—you naughty boy!"

Jasper had already created a diversion in favour of his whiskers, and was in the act of blowing open an enormous watch when his wife appeared.

"Now you take and mind your own business," snapped he, "and we'll mind ours . . . Blow—can't you blow? Like this, then—p-f-f-f—and there you are! Now you try; blow, and that'll open again."

Georgie walked before the summer was over; and this was the year in which Jasper scarcely set foot to the ground, so he made use of the child from the first. Now it was his pipe, now his spectacles, now the newspaper; these were the first familiar objects which the child came to know by name before he could speak; and he never saw any one of the three without taking it as straight as he could toddle to the great grey man in the chair.

Mrs. Musk suddenly found half her work with Georgie taken entirely off her hands. She was even quicker over another discovery. Jasper would not own that he had taken to the child; in her presence, on the contrary, he ignored its very existence as utterly as heretofore. Yet now every day she could have found them together at most hours; only she knew better.

Cheerless environment for this new life—a gloomy old house—a grim old couple. Nevertheless, and in very spite of all the circumstances of his birth, Georgie from the first evinced that temperament which is a sun unto itself. An expansive gaiety was his normal mood, and for years the only variant was a terrible and overwhelming indignation with all his world. He was, in fact, an entirely healthy little savage, with all the wild spirits and facile affections of his age, and no exemption from its traditional ills. Once he had croup so severely that two doctors came in the middle of the night, and Georgie never forgot their grave faces and his grandfather's grim one at the foot of the bed. Indeed, the scene formed his first permanent impression, though the sequel was more memorable in itself. Georgie seemed to go to sleep for days and days, and to awake in another world, though the bed was the same, and the medicine-bottles, and the singing kettle; for it was day-time, and the room full of sun, and the doctors gone; but in the sunlight there stood instead the loveliest lady whom Georgie had beheld in his three or four years of earthly experience. Thereupon he lay with his firm little mouth pursed up, his grey eyes greater than even their wont, and his mind at work upon some surreptitious teaching of his grandmother. It was a very simple question that he asked in the end, but it made the lady kiss him and cry over him in a way he never could understand.

"Are you a angel?" Georgie had said.

Gwynneth happened to be somewhat morbidly aware of her own poverty in angelic qualities, though it was not this that made her cry. She was alone at the hall for the winter, which Sir Wilton and Lady Gleed were spending upon a well-beaten track abroad, while Sidney was still at Cambridge. Gwynneth also might have drifted from Cannes to Nice, and from Nice to Mentone, for she had been taken from school on Lydia's marriage, and assigned a permanent position at the side of Lady Gleed. In this capacity the girl had not shone, though her peculiar character had lost nothing by the duty and faithful practice of consistent self-suppression. On the other hand, there was the demoralising sense of personal superiority, which was thrust upon Gwynneth at every turn of this companionship, causing her to take an unhealthy interest in her own faults, in order to preserve any humility at all; for she was full of mental and of bodily vigour, and her aunt was signally devoid of both. Consequently when Lydia petitioned to go instead (having become a mother to her great disgust, and demanding an immediate separation from her infant), the proposal was adopted to the equal satisfaction of all concerned. Gwynneth, for her part, was very sorry not to travel and see the world; but she knew, from a tantalising experience, that hotel life was all that one could count upon seeing with Lady Gleed; and from every other point of view it was infinite relief to be alone. Literally alone she was not, since the little German housekeeper never left the hall. But Fraulein Hentig was a self-contained and entirely tactful companion, with whom it was possible to enjoy the delights of solitude while escaping the disadvantages. The two were very good friends.

Gwynneth was now in her twentieth year, a tall and graceful girl, albeit with the slight stoop of the natural student that she was. At her school she had won all available honours, but it was not a modern school, and in those days such as Gwynneth had no definite knowledge of any wider arena. So she left her school without great regret. She had learnt all that they could teach her there. And she taught herself twice as much in stolen hours spent in the hall library, which had been bought with the place, and hitherto only used by Sidney on wet days. But now there was no need to steal an hour; the girl's time was all her own, and she held high revel among the books. Moreover, it was the dawn of the University Extension system, and Gwynneth heard of a course of lectures upon English literature, only eight miles from Long Stow, just in time to attend. To do so she had to fight a weekly battle with the coachman, but Fraulein Hentig took her side, and the opposition did not endure. Gwynneth took voluminous notes and wrote elaborate essays, bringing to the whole interest that energy, thoroughness and enthusiasm, to which, though each was an essential characteristic, she was only now enabled to give free play. Yet the young girl was no mere bookworm, though at this stage of her career she seemed little else. It was a phase of intellectual absorption, but all the while it needed but a touch of human interest in her life to awake the deeper nature of the eternal woman. Such awakening had come with the most alarming period of Georgie's illness. Gwynneth was starting for her lecture, primed with sharp pencils and her new essay, when she heard in the village that two doctors had been at the Flint House in the night. She did not go to that lecture at all, but for two days and nights was scarcely an hour absent from the bedside of a little boy whom she had barely known by sight before. And his first comprehensible words formed the question which Gwynneth, worn out by watching, had answered in the fashion he could never understand.

Well, she was destined to be the boy's good angel, though he never mistook her for one again; and sometimes she looked the part. The dark eyes, so ardent in the pursuit of knowledge, or of any other of her heart's desires, could yet sparkle with childish glee, or soften with the tenderness of the ideal Madonna. The self-willed mouth and nose were only sweet as Georgie saw them; and none but he knew the warmth of the pale brown cheek or the crisp electric touch of the dark brown hair. Little knowing it before, and never dreaming of it now, Gwynneth had long been hankering for all that the little child gave her out of the fulness and purity of his tiny heart. She supposed that she was happy because at last she was being of some trifling use to somebody; it made her think more of herself. Looking deeper (as she thought), through the deceptive lenses of her inner consciousness, Gwynneth took a still less favourable view of her latest interest in life. It was that and not much more to the imperfect introspection of her morbid mood.

Nevertheless, this was the happiest time that she had ever known. Georgie and she became inseparable, even when the boy was well again; and on him Gwynneth was really lavishing all the love and tenderness which had been gathering in her heart since the hour when she had kissed a dead forehead for the last time. The fact was that the girl had an inborn capacity for passionate devotion, and was now once more enabled to indulge this sweet instinct to the full. She still went to her weekly lecture, read every book in the syllabus, and wrote her essay with as much care for detail as her innate energy would permit. Nor was her work the worse for the counter-attraction which now filled her young life to the brim. Georgie spoke of Gwynneth as his "lady," with a sufficient emphasis upon the possessive pronoun, and to her by a succession of pet names of their joint invention.

Croup is an enemy that lives to fight another day, as Dr. Marigold said when he paid his last visit; and that word was sufficient for the Musks. Thenceforward Georgie had only to sneeze to be put to bed, where he wasted many days before the winter was over. But Georgie was not to be depressed, and as Gwynneth would come and play with him for hours it was perhaps no wonder. They both had some imagination; one showed it by extemporary flights of downright romance, and the other by following these with immense eyes and not a syllable of his own from beginning to end. Then and there they would dramatise the story, for it was usually one of adventure, and Georgie had a clockwork paddle-steamer called the Dover, which sailed the bed manned by cardboard sailors of Gwynneth's making. In these seas the roughest weather was experienced in crossing Georgie's legs, but the best fun was in the polar regions, where the vessel lay wedged for months between two pillows, while the crew hunted bear and walrus over Georgie's person, and dug winter quarters under the clothes.

One day, when he really had a cold, and had fallen asleep upon the icebergs, Gwynneth took upon herself to search the cupboard for some picture-book which he might not have seen before; and in so doing she came across the photograph of a comely young woman, not much older than herself, which compelled her attention rather than her curiosity, for she guessed at once who it was. Moreover, the face was striking and interesting in itself. The eyes had a strange look, half reckless, half defiant, but, even in a faded and inartistic photograph, of a subtle fascination. There was some slight coarseness of eyelid and nostril; but for all that it was a fine expression, full of courage and full of will. The will was obvious in the mouth. It had the strength of Musk himself. Yet there was something about the mouth—so firm—so full—that Gwynneth did not like. She could not have said what it was, but she preferred looking into the eyes. They fascinated her, and she did not lift her own eyes from them till Mrs. Musk entered and caught her thus engaged.

"Oh, where did you find that? Give it to me—give it to me!" and the poor soul held out hands that trembled with her voice. "That's Georgie's poor mother," she sobbed, "and I didn't know there was another left. I thought he'd taken and burnt them every one!"

And she slipped the photograph inside her bodice, and pressed her lean hands upon it, as though it were the babe itself at her breast once more. Next instant Gwynneth's arms were about the old woman's neck, and her fresh lips had touched the wet and shrivelled cheek of Georgie's grandmother.

"Ah! but you are good to us," said Mrs. Musk. "I never would have believed a young lady could be so sweet and kind as you!"

Not that Gwynneth was in the habit of going among the people; that was a practice which Lady Gleed would not permit in a young lady over whom she exercised any sort of control. Consequently there was some talk in the village at this time, and a little scene at the hall soon after Sir Wilton and his wife arrived for the Easter recess. But Gwynneth argued that in no sense could the Musks be accounted ordinary villagers; and the squire himself took her side very firmly in the matter.

"I won't have you rate Musk among the yokels," said Sir Wilton afterwards. "He is the one substantial man in the place, and a very good friend of mine."

"Well, I don't consider it nice for Gwynneth to be always with that child."

"She doesn't know the child's history; you have only to hear her talk about him to see that."

"I don't think it nice, all the same," Lady Gleed repeated.

"Then take her back to town with you."

"No, she is out now, and I can't be bothered with her this season. She is not like other girls. I've a good mind to send her abroad for a year."

"You can do as you like about that. It might be a very good thing. Meanwhile I'm not going to have Musk's feelings hurt; only yesterday, when I went to see him, he was telling me all Gwynneth has done for them during the winter. I'm not going to break with a man like that by suddenly forbidding her to do any more."

So it was decided that Gwynneth should go for a year to a relation of Fraulein Hentig's at Leipzig, for the sake of her music, which the girl had neglected rather disgracefully since leaving school, but of which she was none the less fond, given the proper stimulus. Gwynneth herself acclaimed the plan, and indeed had a voice in it; there was only one reason why she was not entirely glad to go; and her devotion to Georgie was more constant than ever during the few weeks which were left to her.

Summer was beginning, and the boy was well and strong, with chubby cheeks and sturdy bare legs. Often Gwynneth had him to play in the hall garden—this on Sir Wilton's own suggestion—but more often she took him for a walk. There were beautiful walks all round Long Stow. There was the windy walk across the heather towards Linkworth; there were cool walks by the tiny river that ran parallel with the village street, bounding the hall meadow and both meadow and garden of the Flint House; there was a fascinating expedition, with spade and pail, to the sand-hills off the road to Lakenhall. Yet it was on none of these excursions that Gwynneth lost Georgie, but while leaving some papers at the saddler's workshop, in Long Stow itself.

Fuller would keep her to talk politics, or rather to listen to his own: it was the year of the first Home Rule Bill, and even Mr. Gladstone had never stirred the saddler's anger, hatred and contempt to such a pitch as they reached in this connection. Gwynneth, on her side, had an insufficient grasp of the measure, but an instinctive veneration for the man; and she was young enough to grow heated in argument, even with the saddler. When at length she turned away, more flushed than victorious, there was no vestige of the child.

"Georgie! Georgie!"

Neither was there any answer. Gwynneth turned upon the politician.

"Didn't you see him, Mr. Fuller?"

"Gord love you, miss, I thought you come alone!"

And the saddler leant across his bench until his spectacles were flush with the open window at which Gwynneth stood.

"Alone? Georgie Musk was with me; and I've lost him through arguing with you."

She inquired at the next cottage. Yes, they had seen him pass "with you, miss," but that was all. There were no cottages further on; the saddler's was the last on that side and at that end of the village. Opposite was the rectory gate, with the low flint wall running far to the right, overhung at present by the great leaves and heavy blossoms of the chestnuts. And all at once Gwynneth noticed that the chestnut leaves were very dark, the sky overcast, and another shower even then beginning.

"He will get wet—it may kill him!"

And the girl ran wildly on along the road; but it was a straight road, and she could see further than Georgie could possibly have travelled. So now there was only the lane running up by the church.

Gwynneth took it at top speed; an instant brought her abreast of the east end, gaping wide and deep for the east window, yet built like a rock on either side to the height of the eaves. Another step, and Gwynneth was standing still.

Already her sub-consciousness had remarked the silence of hammer and chisel, which had tinkled in her ears as she brought Georgie up the village, ringing more distinctly at every step, and quite loud when first they had stopped at the saddler's window. Then it must have ceased altogether. But now Gwynneth heard another sound instead.

CHAPTER XXII

A LITTLE CHILD

Georgie stood beyond the mason's litter, his firm legs planted in the wet grass, his holland pinafore less brown than his knees. A sailor hat, with the brim turned down, threw the roguish face into shadow; but the flush of successful flight was not extinguished; and the great eyes fixed on Carlton were nowise abashed. Shyness had never been a feature of Georgie's character.

"Hallo!" said he.

Carlton stood like his own walls.

So this was the child.

A new instinct was awake in the man's breast; he had never an instant's doubt.

And it struck him dumb.

"I say," said Georgie, "are you angry?"

But he showed no anxiety on the point, merely beaming while the grown man fought for words.

"Angry? No—no—"

And now he was fighting for the power of speech—fighting hot eyes and twitching lips for his own manhood—and for the little impudent face that would fill with fear if he lost. But he won.

"Of course I'm not angry; but"—for he must know for certain—"what's your name?"

"Georgie."

"That's not all."

"Georgie Musk."

Carlton filled his lungs.

"And who sent you here, Georgie?"

"Nobody di'n't."

"Then how have you come?"

"By my own self, course."

"What! all the way from the Flint House? That's where you live, isn't it?"

Carlton put the second question with sudden misgiving. The name was not unique in that country; he might be mistaken after all. And already—in these few moments—he could not bear the idea of being thus mistaken in this sturdy, friendly, independent boy.

"Yes, that's where," said Georgie, nodding.

"Then what can have brought him here!"

"Well, you see," said Georgie, confidentially, "my lady taked me for a walk—"

"Your lady?"

"And I wunned away."

"But who do you mean by your lady?"

"My lady," said Georgie, turning dense.

"Your governess?" guessed Carlton.

"Oh, my governess, my governess!" cried Georgie, roaring with laughter because the word was new to him, but made a splendid expletive: "oh, my governess, gwacious me!"

"Well, whoever it is," muttered Carlton, "she oughtn't to have lost you; and you stay with me until she finds you."

"That's good," said Georgie, with conviction. "I liker stay wif you."

Carlton caught the child up suddenly, and swung him shoulder-high. What a laugh he had! And what a firm boy, so heavy and straight and strong! Carlton sat down in his barrow, taking the little fellow on his knee, yet holding him at arm's length for self-control.

"How can you like being with a person you've never seen before?" asked Carlton, tremulous again, for all his strength.

"'Cos I heard you makin' somekin," said Georgie, who was looking about him. "What are you makin', I say?"

It was here that, without any particular provocation, Robert Carlton's resolution suddenly failed him, so that he hugged and kissed the child, in a sudden access of uncontrollable emotion. This, however, was as suddenly suppressed. Georgie had wriggled from his knee; but instead of running away (as the other feared for one breathless moment), he continued looking about him as before, bored a little, but nothing more.

"What are you buildin', I say?" he now inquired.

"A church."

"What's a church?"

Carlton came straight to his feet.

"Do you never go to one?" he asked; but his tone was nearly all remorse.

"No, I never."

"Then have you never heard of God?"

And now the tone was his most determined one.

"Yes," said Georgie, subdued but not frightened.

"You are sure that you have been told about God?"

"Yes, sure."

"Who has taught you?"

"My lady and granny—not grand-daddy."

"You say your prayers to Him?"

"Yes, I always."

"Sure?"

"Yes, sure."

Carlton stood with heaving chest. He was spared something at last; his cup was not to overflow after all. And, as he stood, the grass whispered, and the rain came down.

Again Georgie was caught up, to be set down next instant in the shed; but this time he was really offended.

"I don't want to come in," he whimpered. "I want to build wif your bwicks. They're much, much bigger'n mine!"

"But it's raining, don't you see? It would never do for Georgie to get wet."

"Oh, I wish I would play wif your bwicks!"

"Why, Georgie, you couldn't lift them; you're not strong enough."

"But I are, I tell you. I really are!"

"Here's one, then," said Carlton, who kept his misfits in the shed. "You try."

Georgie did try. He rolled the stone over, though it was no small one; lift it he could not.

"You see, it was heavier than you thought."

"'Cos never mind," coaxed Georgie, in another formula of his own; "you carry it for me!"

"But it's raining, and we should both be wet through."

"'Cos never mind!"

"But I do mind; and, what's more, everybody else would mind as well."

"Then what shall we do?" cried Georgie, from his depths.

Carlton had no idea. But the boy was weary, and must be amused; that was the first necessity; and he who had never laid himself out to conciliate men must strain every nerve to please this little child. His eyes flew round the shed. And there upon the shelf stood his gargoyles deep in dust.

"Oh, what a funny old man!" cried Georgie. "Oh, ho, ho!"

But Carlton, in his ignorance of children, had over-estimated a strong child's strength; the stone head slipped through the tiny hands, narrowly missing the tiny toes; and when Georgie stooped and rolled it over, it was seen that a terrible accident had really occurred.

"Oh, oh, oh!" cried an alarming little voice, "Oh, he's broken his nose, he's broken it to bits; oh, oh!"

Carlton made a dive for the other gargoyle; but this was a peculiarly sinister face; and Georgie's tears only ran the faster.

"Oh, I don't like that one. It's a ho'ble face. I don't like it."

Carlton cast the thing from him, and at the same moment became and looked inspired.

"Shall I make you a new face, Georgie? A better one than either of the others?"

"Yes, do, I say! A new face! A new face!"

And shouts of delight came from the tear-stained one: such was the sound that Gwynneth heard in the lane.

A very inspiration it proved. All unpractised in their earliest accomplishment, the hard-worked hands had never been so deft before; nor ever stone softer or chisel sharper than the first of each that could be found. They were trembling, those tanned and twisted fingers, but that only seemed to impart a nervous vigour to their touch. When the thing had taken rough shape, and a deep curve or two suggested a whole head of hair; when eyes and nose had come from the same sure delving, and the mouth almost at a touch; then the mouth of Georgie, long open in mere fascination, recovered its primary function, and yelled approval in surprising terms.

"Oh, my Jove, my Jove!" he roared. "What a lovely, lovely, lovely face! Oh, my Jove, I must show it to my lady!"

Carlton looked upon a baby face on fire with rapture; and for once no dissimilar light shone upon his own.

"Will you—give me a kiss for it, Georgie?"

Without a word the little arms flew round a weatherbeaten neck that bent to meet them, and the glowing cheeks buried themselves, voluntarily, in the beard that had only hurt before; and not one kiss, but countless kisses, were Georgie's thanks for the lump of sandstone that had grown into a face before his eyes. And such was the scene whereon Gwynneth Gleed arrived.

At first she drew back, hesitating in the rain, because neither of them saw her, and she could not, could not understand! But her hesitation was short-lived, or, rather, it had to be conquered and it was. So with flaming cheeks—because they would not see her—and dark hair limp from the rain—eyes sparkling, lips parted, teeth peeping—came Gwynneth to the shed at last.

And the child ran to her, while the man's eyes followed him hungrily, climbing no higher than Georgie's height.

"Oh, look what a lovely, lovely face the workman made me; do look, I say! Is it wery kind of him to make me such a lovely thing?"

Gwynneth had been dragged to where the new head stood mounted upon a misfit; and Carlton had been obliged to rise. But his eyes had not risen from the child.

"Is it kind of him, I tell you?" persisted Georgie.

"Very kind," said Gwynneth, "indeed."

And civility compelled Carlton to look up at last.

"It was only to pass the time," he said. "I was obliged to bring him in out of the rain."

"It was so good of you," murmured Gwynneth. "But it was not good of Georgie to run away as soon as my back was turned!"

Georgie paid no heed to this reproach; he was busy playing with the uncouth head.

"Oh, don't say that," said Carlton, quickly; "I don't get so many visitors! Are you the little chap's governess?" he added, yet more quickly, to undo the visible effects of his words.

"No, I'm—from the hall, you know."

He could not but start at this. But now he was guarding his tongue. And, as he reflected, there came back to him the vague memory of a face in church, followed by the sharper picture of a very young girl at the piano in a pleasant room—the last that he had ever been in.

Gwynneth had recalled the same scene, and could see him as he had been, while she gazed upon him as he was.

"I remember," he said, gravely. "So you take an interest in this little chap, Miss Gleed?"

"Rather more than that," replied Gwynneth, taken out of herself in an instant, and declaring her innocence by her sudden and unconscious enthusiasm. "I love him dearly," she said from her heart: and together their eyes returned to the round sailor hat, the brown pinafore and the browner legs which were all that was now to be seen of Georgie the engrossed.

"He is indeed a dear little fellow," said Carlton, smothering his sighs.

"And so affectionate!" added Gwynneth, thinking of the strange pair together as she had found them.

"Marvellously independent, too, for his age."

"He is not quite four. You would think him older."

"Indeed I would . . . And so you are his 'lady'!"

"So he insists on calling me."

"You seem to be very much to him," said Robert Carlton, jealously enough at heart, as he looked for once into the fine, kind, enthusiastic eyes of Gwynneth; but they fell embarrassed, and his own were quick enough to wander back to the boy.

"I have been more or less alone since last autumn," said Gwynneth. "Georgie has been as much to me as I can possibly have been to him."

"But he lives at the Flint House, does he not? I—I gathered he was a grandchild of the Musks."

"So he is."

"Are they bringing him up?"

"Yes."

"Kindly?"

"Oh, yes—kindly. But—"

"Are they fond of him?"

"Touchingly so; but, of course, they are two old people."

"And so you stepped in to lighten and brighten a little child's life!"

Gwynneth blushed unseen; for all this time he was looking at Georgie and not at her.

"You mustn't put it like that," she said, "for it isn't the case. It was quite a selfish pleasure. I was all alone. And it began by his being dreadfully ill."

"What—Georgie?"

"Yes, and I was able to nurse him a little. And after that we couldn't do without each other. But now we shall have to try."

He had looked at her with the last quick question, and was looking still, a new anxiety in his eyes.

"Do you mean that you are going away?" he said; and his tone did not conceal his disappointment.

"I am sorry to say I am," replied Gwynneth, feeling all she said.

"Soon?"

"To-morrow."

"Far?"

"Abroad."

"But not for long!"

"A year."

Her eyes fell at last before the frank trouble in his; and he ended the pause with a sigh. "I am very sorry," he said. "I was hoping that you would often bring him here to see me." Nor was any compliment taken or intended in a speech which rang with the primitive sincerity of one who had spoken very little for a very long time.

Gwynneth took the short step that brought her to the opening of the shed. She had suddenly discovered that the rain had never ceased pattering on the corrugated roof, and was wondering when the shower would stop. She wished it was fair, for more reasons than one. It was high time she took Georgie away; and she did not know what Musk would say when he heard where they had been. She only knew his opinion of parsons generally, and of all that they professed, though she had once heard him allow that they were not all as bad as this one. Besides, even Gwynneth felt natural qualms in the society of an outcast whom no one else went near, quite apart from the popular conviction that he had burnt his own church to the ground. That she had never believed. And now, when she found him all but at his work; when she saw him at close quarters, aged and bent, with tattered clothes and battered hands, yet handsome as ever, and now picturesque; and when she looked upon the gigantic work that had aged him, the finished wall here, the deliberate preparations there; then that old calumny was blown to final shreds for Gwynneth. He might have done worse, as she had sometimes heard said, but he had not done that. And the woman went to work within her: was there nothing she could do for him? Was there no little luxury she could get and send him? His clothes were torn—if only she could mend them! Alas! that she was going abroad next day.

Another moment and she was glad: how could she do anything, a young girl, when all the rest of the world held aloof? Anything that she did, or tried to do, would inevitably, if not rightly and properly, be misconstrued. Yet, after this, it would be too painful to live so near and to go on doing nothing. She had felt that long ago; and the memory of their last encounter reoccupied her thoughts. No, she could do no more now than she had been able to do then. Therefore she was glad to be going away. And all this passed through her mind in the mere minute that elapsed before the rain stopped as suddenly as it had begun.

Yet in that minute Robert Carlton had got Georgie back upon his knee, and Gwynneth caught him trying to extract a promise from the child; in another he had risen, a duskier bronze than before, and was telling her honestly what the promise was to have been.

"I wanted him to come again to see me finish that head, but not to tell his grandparents where he was going, or they would not let him. You see, I am ashamed of it already! Make allowances for one who has not spoken to either woman or child for very nearly four years."

Gwynneth was deeply moved.

"Allowances," she could but repeat; "allowances!"

"Allow'nces, allow'nces!" chimed Georgie, to whom a new word was necessarily humorous.

Carlton picked him up, and kissed him lightly for the last time. To Gwynneth he only bowed. And she was longing to take his hand.

"Good-bye, Miss Gleed; a good journey and a happy time to you."

Gwynneth had to say something, since she could do nothing, to show her sympathy. "I think it's all wonderful—wonderful!" was all she did say, with a little wave towards the sandstone walls. And yet her small speech haunted her for weeks, seeming in turns so many things that she had never meant it to be.

Georgie also waved with energy. "Good-bye, good-bye, I'll see you in the mornin'!" was his irresponsible farewell.

And so they disappeared together, as the sun shone again through the trees with the emerald tips, now dripping diamonds too; but to Robert Carlton that little scene of his endless labours, the shed, the strewed stones, the barrow, the rising walls, the blossoming chestnuts, the jewelled elms, had never looked so drab and desolate before.

Yet, long after it was really dark, the lonely man still hovered about the spot, now standing where the child had stood with his brown pinafore and his browner legs; now sitting empty-kneed in the empty barrow; now handling the rough stone head that he had hewn in a few minutes for little Georgie.

CHAPTER XXIII

DESIGN AND ACCIDENT

Next morning he was early at his arch, and had soon finished the voussoir which he had been roughing out when this vital interruption occurred. But he was not satisfied with the stone, and wasted much time in turning it over and over and wondering whether it would do or not. Now this was a point upon which Carlton usually knew his mind in a twinkling. Indecision of any sort was, indeed, among the last of his failings; but that man is not himself who has not closed an eye all night; and Robert Carlton had only closed his in prayer.

Later in the morning his case was worse. He would think of the boy until the chisel went too deep and spoilt another stone. Or, just when he was beginning to get on, he would drop his tools and wheel round suddenly, half hoping to see a second little apparition in a sailor hat with the brim turned down. But these things do not happen twice, much less when looked and longed for, as Carlton knew very well. And yet his knowledge did not help him in the matter; on the other hand, it drove him again and again to his gate, to gaze wistfully up and down the road he never traversed; and this was the most disastrous habit of all.

Once more the work stood still; for the first time in three whole years, it stood practically still for days.

Meanwhile, at the Flint House, there had never been any secret as to what had happened between showers at the church. Gwynneth had told Mrs. Musk, and Mrs. Musk had deemed it better to tell Jasper himself than to let him gather the truth from Georgie's prattle. And in the event Musk took it better than his wife had dared to hope, merely vilifying quick and dead with renewed rancour, and grimly undertaking that the incident should not occur again.

So Georgie saw more of his grandfather than he had ever seen before, and rather more than he cared to see after his close association with Gwynneth, whose wonderful letter from Leipzig was small comfort to so small a soul, though Mrs. Musk had to read it to Georgie many times a day.

"Oh! I wish I would go and see workman," the boy would exclaim without fear. "I wish I would! I wish I would!"

"I daresay you do," Jasper would growl from his chair.

"Then can I; can I, I say, grand-daddy?"

"No, you can't."

"Oh! why can't I?"

"Because I tell you."

"But, you see, grand-daddy, he was making me such a lovely, lovely face. I must go back for it. Really I must. He did say he finish fen I go back. So of course I must go. See? See? See?"

Thus pestered, Jasper once thundered:

"Oh, yes, I see! I know him—I know him. I see hard enough! But if ever you do go I'll—I'll—I'll give ye what ye never had afore and'll never want again!"

"Oh, don't be angry wif me," Georgie whimpered. "Oh, I wish my lady would come back!"

"I daresay you do," said Jasper, calming. "And I don't."

But a child forgets; at all events Georgie did; and so surely as his ennui in the garden, within strict sight of the terrible old man in the chair, reached a certain pitch, so surely did the treasonable aspiration rise to his innocent lips.

"I wish I would go and see workman. I wish I would!"

But at last one day the old man rose, stick and all; and at this even Georgie trembled; for it was long since he had seen his grandfather on his feet. Over the grass he came hobbling, ungainly, abnormal, frowning down upon the buttercups. Georgie crept aside. But Musk passed him without a word. Three times he limped the length of the overgrown lawn, muttering, frowning; and the third time his lameness was palpably less.

"Why, Jasper," cried Mrs. Musk, running out, "you're getting better!"

"No, I ain't," he roared. "You mind your own business and get away indoors."

Mrs. Musk was meekly obeying, and Georgie escaping at her skirt, when a second roar recalled the child. Jasper was leaning with both hands on the stick before him, his frown gone, but in its place a surely devilish smile, since the child mistook it for the real thing.

"So you're still longun to go back and see the workman, as you call him, at the church?"

"Oh, yes, I are!"

And round eyes kindled at the thought.

"Very well. You may."

Georgie could scarcely believe his ears.

"Fen may I? Now? Now, I say?"

"When you like, so long as you don't bother me."

Georgie jumped and shouted in his joy.

"Goin' to see workman, goin' to see workman! Oh, my Jove, my Jove! Goin' to see workman makin' lovely, lovely faces all for me—every bit!"

"Hold your noise," said Jasper, roughly; "and go, if you're going."

Carlton had given up expecting him, divining at last that Musk knew of their one interview, and would never let them have another. So once more Georgie surprised him at his work; but this time he had to hail his friend; for now Carlton was making up for lost time, and at the moment, up on a scaffolding, was all absorbed in the exciting task of fitting the finished voussoirs over the wooden centre which supported the arch until the keystone should complete it. And the keystone was actually in one hand, a trowel full of mortar in the other, when the first sound of Georgie's voice drove all else from his mind.

"I say, I say, I say!" he ran up shouting. "Workman, workman!"

But now the workman was only collecting himself, and thanking God with quivering lips, before he could trust himself upon his ladder.

"So here you are at last," he said, swinging the child off his legs without endearment. Yet all his being yearned towards the merry independent little boy. The straight strong legs seemed browner and rounder already. It might have been the same holland pinafore; it was the same sailor hat.

"Yes, here I are," said Georgie, "and I wish you would make lovely, lovely faces out of bwick."

"Not run away again, I hope?"

"No, 'cos I came by my own self."

Carlton asked no more questions. Any minute the child might be missed and sent for; every moment was precious meanwhile. It was a heavenly day in early June, the elms in full leaf at last against the blue, the churchyard dappled with light and shade, the fresh sandstone yellow as gold where the sun caught it fairly. And in the sunlight stood its own incarnation—sturdy champion of the golden age—laughing child of June.

Carlton could see nothing else.

"Come on, I say," urged Georgie; "come an' make faces, quick, sharp!"

And he dragged the sculptor to his rude studio.

"There it is, there it is," shouted Georgie, spying the unfinished head high up on the shelf. "You did say you finish fen I come back. Finish—finish—quick, sharp!"

Carlton brought the thing outside, for the shed was close, and went to work at the foot of his ladder, with Georgie sitting on the lowest rung. And any merit which the rough attempt had possessed was speedily removed by an over-elaboration on which Georgie insisted, and which certainly served its purpose by earning his vociferous applause.

"Oh, his eyes! What funny eyes! Make them open and shut, I say—can you?"

A doll, which Gwynneth had unearthed, before she knew her Georgie very well, had retained this accomplishment even when the head was off its body.

"I'm afraid I can't do that," said Carlton.

"Try—try."

So Carlton gouged in the soft stone till the holes for the eyeballs had disappeared.

"Now open them again!"

And fresh holes were made: they were the most sunken eyes ever seen before Georgie was tired of the game. Next he must have ears, which were supposed to be concealed by the very heavy head of hair; and when the ears arrived, they were not worth having without ear-rings; but there the sculptor was nonplussed, and struck.

"All right," said Georgie, cheerfully; "then I'll carry it home without."

"What, run away directly it's done?"

The cold-blooded ingratitude of infancy was new to Carlton, as his hurt face was to Georgie, who eyed it with some compassion.

"All right," said he; "I'll stay a little bit if you like."

"And sit on my knee, Georgie."

"All right."

But there was no sentiment about Georgie to-day; it was mere magnanimity, and he showed it.

"Quite comfy, Georgie?"

"No," sighed the boy, screwing about on the one thin thigh; "I think it's only a little comfy."

"That better?"

And, the other leg being slipped under his small person, Georgie said it was.

"Are you sure, Georgie, that you want to take that head home at all?"

"Course I are," said Georgie, decidedly. "I must take it, you see; course I must."

Carlton was again tormented by the ignoble inclination which he had overcome by impulse rather than by will at the last interview. Was a child of four too young to keep a secret? If only this one could be induced to go and come back, and back, and back, without ever saying a word to anybody! The proposition had shamed him before; and did now; but the new love within him was stronger than his shame.

"You wouldn't show it," suggested Carlton, "to your grandfather, would you?"

"Course I'll show it to him," said Georgie, for whom the stipulation was too oblique.

"But he'll be angry!"

"Course he won't," said Georgie, more superior than ever, and with the air of one who does not care to argue any more.

"But you know he was before," said Carlton, drawing his bow.

"Oh, bovver!" exclaimed Georgie, losing patience. "Well, then, he won't be angry to-day, I know he won't."

"How do you know, Georgie?"

"'Cos he did tell me I could come."

"Not here?"

Georgie nodded solemnly.

"Yes, he did. I know he did."

What could it mean? The child was strangely dependable for his years; indeed, it was impossible to look in those great and candid eyes and to doubt the testimony of the equally candid little tongue. Then what could it mean? Had Musk relented? Was he relenting? Carlton's heart leapt at the thought, and with his heart his eyes; and in the same second he had his answer.

Close at hand in the sunlight, where Georgie had stood last, brimming over with delight, there now stood Jasper Musk himself, huge with hate, livid with rage, vindictive, remorseless—but not surprised. Carlton saw this at the first glance, in the triumphant lightning flashing from the fixed eyes, and playing over the heavy, grim, inexorable face. And that was his answer; furthermore it prepared him for all, and more than all, that was to come.

"Put the boy down," said Jasper Musk, with sinister self-control.

Instinctively the child slipped to the ground; but there his courage failed him, so that he turned his back upon the terrible old man, and hid his face in the lap that he had left.

"Come here, George!"

But Carlton held him firmly with both hands.

Musk bore down on them in a series of little shuffling steps, his great face wincing with the pain of each. His voice had already risen; now it was so terrible to hear, so hoarse and high with passion, that in an instant Carlton had his thumbs in the small boy's ears.

"Snivelling hypocrite! Whited sepulchre! Do you hand the child over to me, or I'll break this stick across your back. So I've caught ye, temptun him here to make up to him behind my back! But you don't—no, you don't—not while I'm alive to stop that. He's nothun to you and you're nothun to him, and do you meddle with him again at your peril. I've taken the trouble to learn the law of it, so I know. God damn ye! will you take your hands off him, or am I to break your blasted head?"

"You can do what you like," said Carlton; "but the boy shall not hear you using that language to me. So you will never get a better opportunity than you have." And his nostrils curled as he bent his defenceless head over that of the boy, and pressed a little harder with his thumbs.

The other gnashed his teeth, and his great hand tightened on his stick. But he could not strike like that. And his enemy knew it; trust him to know when he was safe!

"I'm not going to prison for ye," said Musk, "if that's what you want. I daresay you'd think that worth a crack on the head to get me locked up for a bit; well, then, you shan't. Do you leave go o' the kid, and I won't swear no more."

The effort at self-control was plain enough, as Carlton looked up, without complying all at once.

"One moment," he said. "You sent him here yourself, I think?"

"What, the child?"

"Yes."

"I didn't send him. He was pestering me to come. So at last I gave him leave to do as he liked."

"In order that you might follow and abuse me in front of him!"

"I'll tell no lies," said Musk, sturdily. "I meant to let him hear what I thought of you, and I won't deny it."

Carlton looked a little longer upon the broad face between the steely bristles and the silvery hair; it had aged nothing in these years which had been as twenty to himself; and for the moment there was all the old rugged dignity in its independent purpose and honest unrelenting hate. A bargain had been in Carlton's mind, but at the last he decided to trust his enemy instead.

"It's all right, Georgie," he whispered: "we are not really angry with each other. Run away and play."

"But I don't want to!"

"You must," said Carlton, and rose without taking further notice of the child. "Mr. Musk," he said, in a low voice but firm, "is it to be like this between us to the bitter end?"

"That is."

"I do not ask your forgiveness—"

"Glad to hear it."

"I only ask—in pity's name—to be allowed to do something for the boy!"

Musk moved a muscle at last, and his eyes came close together with a gleam. "I daresay you do," said he.

"But will you not listen—"

"I'm listening now, ain't I?"

"Ah, but not to my prayer! I see it in your face; you have no pity. God knows how little I deserve! Yet it's little enough that I ask: only to see him sometimes, and not even to see him if you set your face against it. I would be content—at least I would try to be—if I knew he was going to good schools, if—if I might have hand or voice in his life. You say I have no rights. That is my punishment; a new one, that I never felt until I saw the boy for the first time the other day; but if you knew how I have felt it since! If you knew what it would be to me to do anything—give anything—"

"I knew that were comun," said Musk, nodding to himself . . . "So you'd like to do the handsome, would you?" His whole face became suddenly suffused, as with walnut-juice; the very whites of his eyes seemed white no longer, while the pupils shrank to steel points in their midst. "I know you!" he cried, beside himself again; "but don't you try them games with me. That's your line, that is—buy your way back! You'd buy it with the parish, by making them a church; and you'd buy it with the boy, by making things for him; but that's what you never shall do, not while I live to prevent it . . . What you got there, George? You give that here!"

It was the sandstone head with the sunken eyes, and Georgie was clinging to it in his trouble underneath the scaffolding; in an instant Musk had seized it from him, and dashed it with all his might against the wall, so that the soft stone flew into a dozen pieces. It was like blood to a wild beast: the demon of destruction broke loose in Jasper Musk.

"And that's how I'd treat the rest of your damned handiwork," he roared, "if I was the village! I'd have no church of your building; I'd bring that down about your ears right quick!" His wild eye lit upon the wooden centre of the unfinished arch, and "This is what I'd do," he shouted, lunging at the woodwork with his heavy stick. "Hypocrite! Pharisee! Disgrace to God and man! Leper as—"

But the centre had been dealt a heavy thrust, as from a battering ram, with each expression; with each it had bulged a little; but the last lunge drove the whole framework from under the unfinished arch, which came crashing down amid a yellow cloud. Musk shuffled backward in time to save his toes; for an instant then both he and Carlton stood aghast.

Robbed of his latest treasure, and moreover having seen it smashed to atoms before his eyes, Georgie had been howling lustily when the crash came: when the yellow cloud lifted he lay silent enough, in a little brown heap below the scaffolding, and already the blood was through his hair.

Carlton had him in his arms that instant.

"He's insensible," he said quietly. "A nasty scalp wound, and may be more. What day is this?"

"Wednesday."

Musk did not know what he was saying, but the cool question had elicited a correct though unconscious reply.

"Wednesday used to be the doctor's day at the dispensary—"

"And is still," cried Musk, coming to his senses.

"Then one of us must run for him."

"I can't run!"

"Then you must hold him while I do. Stop! I'll take him to the house; you must bathe his head while I'm gone."

Another minute and the boy lay in the rectory study, upon the little bed in which Carlton had fought death and won three years before; yet another, and up limped Jasper, crooked with pain, out of breath, but gasping for news of Georgie as though he had been a week on the way.

"Has he come to yet?"

"No, and there's a lot of blood. We must stop it if we can. Wait till I get a sponge and some water."

Jasper Musk was bending over the boy, looking huger than ever upon his knees, when Carlton returned to the room.

"What have I done?" he was muttering. "What have I done? What have I done?"

"Nothing that you could help," replied Carlton, briskly. "Now you keep squeezing this sponge out over his head—never mind the bed—till I get back."

Georgie lay insensible for hours. It was not the loss of blood, which looked much worse than it was, and ceased altogether with the dressing of the wound. There was, however, somewhat serious concussion underneath; and Dr. Marigold bluntly refused to guarantee the event.

"The pity is to move him," he grumbled towards night. "But is there anybody here who could nurse the boy?"

"Only myself," said Carlton, who had been quiet and quick to help all the afternoon.

The doctor shot an upward glance through his shaggy white eyebrows.

"Well, you're handy enough, I must say; and, as we know, the very devil to do things single-handed; but this you couldn't do. No, I'd like to take him straight to the infirmary, only I'm on horseback."

"There are traps in the village."

"They would jolt too much."

"Then let me carry him."

"It's five miles."

"Never mind. I could do it. And he shouldn't jolt—he shouldn't jolt!"

The mellow voice that had charmed the countryside in bygone years, it fell and quivered with infinite tenderness and love, and it sped to the heart of the gaunt old doctor. So this time Marigold raised his whole head, and his look was open, prolonged, and penetrating.

"No, no, Mr. Carlton," he said at length, and in the tone of old times. "It might do no good, after all. But I'll tell you what you shall do: you shall carry him to the Flint House, and I'll spend the night there if I must."

All this while Jasper Musk was sitting stunned and staring in the rector's chair. He had not moved for an hour, nor did he now until Carlton touched him on the shoulder.

"We are going, Mr. Musk. I am carrying Georgie to your house."

Musk raised a ghastly face.

"He isn't dead?"

"No."

"Nor going to die?"

"God forbid! But the danger is great. The doctor is going to stay with him all night."

And there was a touch of jealousy in his tone, lost upon Jasper Musk, but not on him who inspired it. Silently they left the house, and stole down the drive in the blue twilight. Carlton led, treading almost on tip-toe, as if not to wake a child that only slept in his arms. And so they came to the Flint House, its master limping on the doctor's arm.

"Go in, Mr. Carlton," said Marigold. "There's no one else to carry him upstairs."

And he detained Jasper below.

"You must let that man stay till he is out of danger," the doctor said.

"Why must I?"

"Because I am not justified in staying all night; and he will look after the boy as you and your wife cannot, and as no one else will, now that Miss Gleed is away."

Jasper bowed sullenly to his fate. But the doctor was not done.

"Besides," said he, his kind hand on the other's arm; "besides, he feels this as much as you do, and God knows he's gone through enough! To-day, I tell you candidly, but for him your little lad would be in a worse way than he is. Now don't you think after this that all of us—even you—might begin to be just a little less hard—even on him?"

CHAPTER XXIV

GLAMOUR AND RUE

Georgie's lady was meanwhile enjoying her life in Leipzig, and the more keenly since she had gone abroad without any thought of pleasure, but only to work. This was characteristic of Gwynneth Gleed. She was not light-hearted enough for a young girl; there had been too much sorrow in her early years, too little sympathy in those that came after; natural joy she had never known. A born delight in books, a blind appreciation of the country, a passion for music, and the love of one little child; these were the pleasures of Gwynneth in her twentieth year; nor as yet did they include that zest in the present, that joy of merely living, that healthy appetite for admiration, that proper pride in one's own person, that catholicity of liking for one's fellow-creatures, which are of the very spirit and essence of youth. And to youth Gwynneth added something at least akin to beauty; but never knew it until she came to live among strangers in a strange land.

These strangers, who were mostly English, and many of them young students like herself at the Conservatoire, were singularly kind to Gwynneth from the first. In some ways they were the best friends the girl ever had. They taught her the duty of gaiety at her time of life, and the absolute necessity of a certain amount of vanity in every human being. Gwynneth was given to understand that she had more to be vain about than most. Attracted themselves by the uncommon girl with the fine eyes and the shy manner, her new friends did much to mitigate the latter by making the very most of her looks and accomplishments, and seeing to it that Gwynneth did the same. She was not allowed to dress as she liked in Leipzig, nor to spend the whole of a fine afternoon at her piano, nor to be out of anything that was going on. The gaieties of the English colony were of a simple character in themselves, but they were Gwynneth's high-water-mark in dissipation, and ere long she was throwing herself into them with that enthusiasm which she brought to every pursuit. She had learnt to waltz remarkably well, and to talk brightly about nothing in particular to the acquaintance of a minute's standing. She was none the less assiduous at her practising and her harmony, and was still capable of immediate and immense excitement over this poet or that composer; but these were no longer her only topics. Nor was a holland pinafore and the small urchin it contained entirely forgotten in these days. Gwynneth wrote to Georgie oftener than to anybody else in England. And yet it was to the theatres and a real ball or so that she first looked forward upon her return.

Lady Gleed was much more than agreeably disappointed in the new Gwynneth; herself incapable of seeing beneath the thinnest surface, she could scarcely believe it was the same girl. Gwynneth was better-looking and had more to say for herself than had ever appeared possible to Lady Gleed, who decided to keep her niece in town for the rest of the season, if not to present so creditable a débutante at the next drawing-room. And a much more critical person, her son Sidney, coming up from Cambridge for a night, was not less favourably impressed.

Gleed of Trinity, a third-year man, was in his turn a vast improvement upon the private scholar who had seldom addressed a syllable to Gwynneth in his holidays, but had gone past whistling with his dogs. He was now a really handsome little man, with a clear brown skin and a moustache as mature as his manner; looked and spoke like a man of thirty; and could be amusing enough with his sly satire and his ready repartee. Cynical this youth must always be, but the cynicism was more good-humoured and less ill-natured than formerly, and not abhorrent in the man as it had been in the boy. At all events it amused Gwynneth, who was furthermore surprised and excited to find that Sidney had read quite a number of great books, and rather entertained than otherwise by his blasphemous opinions of many of them. So they had something in common after all; and Sidney was certainly very attentive and gay and nice-looking.

It was in the drawing-room in Hyde Park Place, during an hour which went very quickly, that Gwynneth made these discoveries; she was still too simple to remark, much less read, the calculating droop of Sidney's eyelids or the veiled preoccupation of the hereditary stare.

"I wonder if you'd care to have a look at Cambridge," at last said Sidney, in the purely speculative tone.

"Like to? I'd love it!" cried Gwynneth at once.

Sidney paused, without relaxing his stare. She was certainly very animated. Sidney was not sure that he cared for quite so much animation with so little cause.

"I shouldn't wonder if you did rather like it," he proceeded, "in May-week—which never is in May, you know."

"Oh? When is it?"

"The week after next. There'll be heaps going on. Races every afternoon—"

"And don't you steer your boat?" interrupted Gwynneth, a partisan on the spot.

Sidney smiled.

"I cox it, Gwynneth; and if we aren't head of the river we shall not be very far off. But it isn't only the races; there are all sorts of other things, a good match, garden-parties galore, and a dance every night."

"You dance there!"

"Yes," said Sidney; "do you?"

"Rather!"

"Get some in Leipzig?"

"All that there was to get."

"They dance well out there?"

"I don't know."

"But you do, of course?"

Gwynneth saw the drift of this examination, and showed that she saw it, but Sidney liked her the better for her dry reply:

"You'd better try me."

"You'd better try me," he rejoined adroitly.

"Very well," said Gwynneth. "Here?"

"Come on," said Sidney, his eyes sparkling, his brown skin a warmer hue; and in an instant they were threading their way between the cumbrous chairs and tiny tables of the big room, ploughing through its heavy pile, he in patent leather boots, she in her walking shoes, and not so much as a piano-organ in the street to set the time. Yet, even under these conditions, a turn was enough for Sidney, though he did not want to stop, and was very quick in asking whether he would do.

"You know you will," said Gwynneth, forgetting everything in the prospect of so excellent a partner.

"And you dance rippingly," declared her cousin; "by Jove, I wish we could have you at the First Trinity ball!"

So did Gwynneth; but, instead of betraying further eagerness, sat down at the piano, and, saying it was nothing without the music, forthwith treated Sidney to snatch after snatch of the waltzes of the hour, rendering each with a brilliance of touch and a delicacy of execution alike worthy of a better cause. A year ago Gwynneth would not have done this.

Sidney, his hands in his pockets, but a sparkle still in his eyes, stood watching her without a word until the end.

"Look here," he then announced, "you've simply got to come, and that's all about it. Of course the mater couldn't get away, but Lydia isn't so full up, and I should think she'd jump at it. I'll write to her and fix it up. There's a piano in our rooms, and we'll have it tuned for you; no, we'll get a grand in for the week; and the whole court will be full of men listening."

"Who are 'we'?" inquired Gwynneth.

"Oh, I share rooms with another fellow; an Eton man; you'll like him."

And once more Sidney looked a little critically at his cousin, as though he wanted to be quite sure that the Eton man would like her. But at this moment the dressing-gong threw him into consternation. It appeared that he was dining out at some club, had come up for this dinner, was only sleeping in the house, and would be gone first thing in the morning. So he had better say good-bye; and did so with rather unnecessary warmth, Gwynneth thought; nevertheless, it was the dullest evening she had yet spent in Hyde Park Place, though there was a little dinner-party there also, after which the inevitable performance by Gwynneth was received with the customary acclamation.

It may be supposed that the girl was not enchanted with the prospect of Lydia for chaperone; but she determined thus early to allow nothing to interfere with her enjoyment of the Cambridge festivities. So when Mrs. Goldstein came in her carriage on the next day but one, to say that she supposed they must go, not that she was keen upon it herself, but to please Sidney, and also because she thought it only right for young girls like Gwynneth to have a good time while they could, the latter tried to seem as grateful as though every word of Lydia's did not irritate or repel her. She there and then received dictatorial instructions as to dresses requisite for the week, and undertook to follow them to the letter. It was not a congenial attitude for Gwynneth to assume, but she also was at present bent upon that "good time" which her cousin recommended. Lydia, on the other hand, cultivated the air of one who is personally past all that. She seldom smiled, but yet had a certain secret fondness for excitement. Gwynneth feared that she was far from happy; she seemed dissatisfied with her position in society, and spoke disrespectfully (when she did speak) of the dark, dapper, capable man of business, her indulgent husband.

There came a time when Gwynneth Gleed would have given much to forget the merriest week of her life, but the memory of the next few days was not to be destroyed. The girl never forgot the narrow streets teeming with exuberant youth, the narrow river in similar case, the crush and rush and uproar on the banks, the procession of boats flashing past, each with an eight in which Gwynneth took no interest, but a ninth who had always the same calm, brown, clean-cut face in her mind's eye. How well he looked, swinging with his crew, he in his blazer, cool and malicious, doing his part with splendid precision if only they did theirs! One night they made their bump right opposite the boat in which Gwynneth stood on tiptoe; and Sidney's smile at the supreme moment was one of her vivid recollections; and her little scene with Lydia another, which she brought upon herself by cheering as loud as any of the men. Sidney seemed very popular. Gwynneth was so proud to be seen with him, especially when he wore his battered mortar-board and blue gown, which appealed in some foolish way to her own vague intellectual aspirations. And she looked down upon all the gowns that were not blue.

But everything in Cambridge did appeal to Gwynneth, from the anthem and the chancel-roof in King's Chapel to luncheon with Sidney and the Eton man in Old Court. Lydia was for ever reproving her cousin's enthusiasm; but Gwynneth was enjoying herself too much to resent anything that Mrs. Goldstein could say. At the outset, however, a close observer might have caught even Sidney with a cocked eyebrow, and the eye beneath upon the Eton man; the girl was so frank and unsophisticated in the display of her delight; but the Eton man seemed to admire it in her, and Sidney gave up looking like that. The Eton man was twice his height, could sing, and swore that nobody had ever played his accompaniments as Gwynneth did; but he was not in any boat, and he could not compare with Sidney as a partner. Nevertheless, his attentions and attractions had more to answer for than anybody knew.

Gwynneth had thought Sidney very nice in town, but at Cambridge he was perfect. He was a thorough little man of the world, unconscious, unconcerned, whereas many of the men whom Gwynneth met were scarcely worthy of the name. Sidney did things like a prince, having an enviable allowance, and a very good idea of the way in which things should be done. And his arrangements were masterly; no day like the last, or next; and the whole a whirl of gaiety and excitement literally intoxicating to one whose experience of this kind was so limited as poor Gwynneth's. It all ended with the First Trinity ball. There is no need to dilate on the astonishing magnificence of this revel; it was the most memorable and splendid of them all; and the Backs by night, with a moon in the heaven above and another in the water below, and grey old gables salient in its light, and the Guards' Band in the faint distance, that ought to have been so loud and near; all this was even more entrancing than the ball itself, and Gwynneth moved as in a dream. She had had the audacity to divide her dances between Sidney and the Eton man; but one of them was given cause to complain towards the end, and the more so since the girl had never looked so radiant in her life. The next day Gwynneth and Lydia (who would not speak to her) were to return to town. It had never been arranged that Sidney was to accompany them; yet he did; and before evening there was trouble in Hyde Park Place.

Sir Wilton would not hear of it at first; he was soon obliged to do that. But he stood firm in refusing his consent to a formal engagement between Sidney and his first cousin, and found an unexpected ally in Gwynneth herself. The girl was paying for her week's delirium by a deeper depression than her face betrayed or her heart admitted. Already she was beginning to disappoint her cousin. But this was too much.

"You agree with him?" gasped Sidney. "You'd rather not be engaged? Then why, my darling, did you ever say 'yes'?"

"It wasn't to that question, dear," said Gwynneth, colouring.

"It amounted to the same thing."

"It will amount to the same thing," Gwynneth said earnestly; "at least I hope and pray that it may. But, of course, it's quite true that we're both very young; and at least it's within the bounds of possibility that—one or other of us might—some day—change."

"Speak for yourself," said Sidney, with a taunting bitterness.

"Dear, if you'll believe me, I'm thinking quite as much of you. At twenty-two you would tie yourself for life!"

"That's my look-out," said Sidney, grandly. "Age isn't everything, and I'm not a boy; anyhow I know my own mind, if you don't know yours."

Gwynneth's eyes filled with tears.

"Oh, why did you tell me you cared for me?" she exclaimed. "Why did you make me say I cared for you? It was true—it was true—but we seem to have spoilt it by putting it into words. Oh, I was so happy before you spoke! I never was so happy as all last week. I could have gone on like that—I was so happy. And now it's all different already; you are, and I am . . ."

Sidney was watching her tears unmoved, for she had made him reflect. All at once he saw his heartlessness, and next moment he was kissing her tears away; vowing there was no difference in him; but, if it was otherwise with her, well, then, let them consider everything unsaid, and start afresh.

Gwynneth shook her head. Her eyes were dry again and full of thought.

"No, dear, we can't do that; and you mustn't think I am not happy in your love, because I am. Only, there seemed to be such a spell between us before we were sure of each other. But perhaps it's always like that."

In the end they were engaged, but it was not to be a public engagement for six months. Meanwhile Sidney returned to Cambridge for the Long, having taken only a part of his degree; and Gwynneth quickly recovered her reputation as a reformed character in the eyes of Lady Gleed, who was less against the match than her husband, and who took the girl to innumerable parties, each of which Gwynneth made a determined effort to enjoy as thoroughly as the first half of the First Trinity ball.

She seemed always in the highest spirits; and there was no one about her who knew her well enough to know also that this perpetual brightness was hard and unnatural in Gwynneth. Closer observers than Sir Wilton and his wife might indeed have suspected as much; but there was only one occasion upon which Gwynneth betrayed the livelier symptoms of a troubled spirit. This was on her birthday at the beginning of July; upon the breakfast table was a registered packet with the Cambridge post-mark, and in its morocco case Gwynneth presently beheld a richer necklace than she had ever dreamt of possessing as her own. Yet the look in her face was so strange that Lady Gleed was obliged to speak.

"Don't you like pearls, my dear?"

"Oh! yes, oh! yes."

"But you don't look pleased."

"No more I am!"

And she rushed from the room in unaccountable tears, and upstairs to her own, where she was presently discovered writing a letter at top speed, and crying bitterly as she wrote; it was Lady Gleed herself who discovered her.

"What is the matter, Gwynneth?"

"I am writing to Sidney. I cannot take such presents from him. I am writing to tell him why."

"I think you are very silly," said Lady Gleed. "But your uncle wants to see you in his study; that is really why I came up; and I don't think you'll be so silly when you have heard what he has to tell you."

There was an air of mystery about Lady Gleed, who furthermore kissed Gwynneth before they separated on the landing. The girl went downstairs with chill forebodings. Sir Wilton was seated at his massive desk, but rose fussily as she entered, and wheeled up a chair with almost excessive courtesy. Gwynneth had seldom seen him looking so benign.

"I sent for you," said Sir Wilton, resuming his own seat, "because I have some news for you, Gwynneth, which I am sure you will be as glad to hear as I am to communicate it. It is against the law to dwell upon a lady's age, but at yours I think you can afford to forgive me. I believe that you are twenty-one to-day?"

Gwynneth had not thought of that before, and at the present moment she could scarcely believe she was no more. She made her admission with a sigh.

"Then for twenty-one years," pursued Sir Wilton, beaming, "or let us say for as many of them as you can remember, you have, I presume, looked upon yourself as an entirely penniless young lady? That has not been the case; at least it is the case no longer. I—I hope I am not giving you bad news?"

Gwynneth was trembling all over. She had lost every vestige of colour.

"My mother!" she gasped. "Why did she never know?"

"Because, under the terms of your grandfather's will, nobody but myself was to know anything at all about it until to-day."

"It was cruel," cried the girl, in a breaking voice; "it might have kept her here! It makes me not want to hear anything now . . . but of course I must . . . forgive me, please."

"My dear child," said Sir Wilton, kindly, "it is natural enough that you should feel that. I can only ask you to believe that I at least had no choice in the matter. And there were reasons; it is too painful to go into them; your father was my brother, and I had rather say no more. I, for my part, was obliged to fulfil the conditions. I have tried to do my duty. I would gladly have done more, but your dear mother was the most independent woman I ever met. I honoured her for it. But what could I do? I must beg of you, my dear, to look upon the bright side; and, believe me, this business has the very brightest side it is possible to imagine."

Gwynneth did her best. It was fine to be independent in her turn. But the thought of her mother made her ashamed to touch a penny. And it was a matter of several thousand pounds, invested all these years at compound interest, yet with that absolute safety which distinguished the financial operations of Sir Wilton Gleed.

Sir Wilton could not say off-hand what the present capital would yield if left where it was at simple interest, but he fancied it would work out at seven or eight hundred a year at the very least. And these figures, which sounded fabulous to poor Gwynneth, were obviously in themselves the bright side upon which her uncle had harped. Yet he continued to beam as though there was something more to come, and looked so knowing that Gwynneth was obliged to ask him what it was.

"Can't you see?" he said. "Can't you see?"

"It is an immense amount of money. I can't see beyond that."

"You heard me say that nobody knew anything at all about it except myself, and, of course, my solicitors?"

"Yes."

"Even your aunt did not know until I told her just now."

"Indeed."

"And Sidney won't know until you tell him!"

Then Gwynneth saw. Sir Wilton took care that she should. He did not on principle approve of marriages between cousins; he said so frankly; he might be wrong. But there was one thing which made him very proud of his son's choice. And this was that thing; there were others also upon which Sir Wilton touched with much playful gallantry.

"But perhaps," said he, "you won't have anything more to say to the poor lad now!"

CHAPTER XXV

SIGNS OF CHANGE

Georgie was a short head taller, and no pinafore concealed the glories of his sailor suit; but it was still the same baby face, round as the eyes that greeted all comers with the same friendly gaze. His sentences were longer and more ambitiously constructed; but he still said "somekin" and "I wish I would," and, when excited, "my Jove!" And his lady once more danced attendance by the hour and day together; for Sir Wilton and Lady Gleed were paying visits until September; and Sidney was still understood to be making up for lost time at Cambridge.

Gwynneth had enjoyed the child's society the year before; now she seemed dependent upon it. She would have him with her daily on one pretext or another, sometimes upon none at all. She said she liked to hear him talk, and that was well, for Georgie's tongue only rested in his sleep. But now there was often an intrinsic interest in his conversation. He gave Gwynneth many an item of village news which was real news to her. Thus it was from his own lips that she first heard of his accident, on seeing the scar through his hair.

"Course I was in bed," swaggered Georgie; "I was in bed for years an' years an' years—in bed and sensible."

"Oh, Georgie, do you mean insensible?"

"No, sensible, I tell you."

"Did you know what was going on?"

"Course I di'n't, not a bit. How could I fen I was sensible?"

"My poor darling, it might have killed you! How ever did you do it?"

But, as so often happens in such cases, that was what Georgie had never been able to remember. So Gwynneth turned to Jasper Musk, who sat within earshot; it was in the Flint House garden, on the very afternoon of her return.

"That was my fault," said Jasper, gruffly enough, yet with such a glance at Georgie that Gwynneth was sorry she had broached the subject, and changed it at once.

But she reverted to it as soon as she had Georgie to herself. Who had looked after him when he was ill? She was feeling very jealous of somebody.

"Granny did."

"No one else?"

"An' grand-daddy."

"Was that all, Georgie?"

Gwynneth was very sorry she had ever gone abroad.

"Course it wasn't all," said Georgie, remembering. "There was the funny old man from the church."

"Mr. Carlton?"

"Yes."

"So he came to see you?"

"Yes, he often. I love him," Georgie announced with emphasis; "he makes lovely, lovely, lovely faces!"

"And does he ever come now?"

"No, not now, course he doesn't; he's too busy buildin' his church."

"So he's building still!"

"Yes, 'cos he builds wery nicely," Georgie was pleased to say; "better'n me, he builds, far better'n me."

"And is he still alone?"

"All alone," said Georgie; "all alonypony by his own little self!"

And the inconsequent nonsense sent him off into untimely laughter, louder and more uproarious than ever, quite a virile guffaw. But Gwynneth could not even smile. And now when neither listening to Georgie nor haunted by her engagement, Gwynneth began to think of the lonely outcast behind those trees, as she had begun indeed to think of him the spring before last, while her mind and life were yet unfilled by the motley interests which this last year had brought into both.

The thought afflicted her with a sense of personal hardness and cruelty; there was this lonely man, doing the work of ten, not spasmodically, but day after day, and year after year, still unaided and unforgiven by the very people in whose midst and for whose benefit those prodigies of labour were being performed. Gwynneth knew now that there had been some mysterious wickedness before the burning of the church. It was all she cared to know. What crime could warrant such hardness of heart in the face of such devotion, skill, patience, consummate endurance, and invincible determination? These were heroic qualities, no matter what vileness lay beneath or behind them; and the generous capacity for hero-worship was very strong in Gwynneth. She would have honoured this man for his splendid pertinacity, and have wiped all else from the slate. That his own parishioners continued to dishonour him, and that she perforce had to do as they did, made her indignant with them and dissatisfied with herself. So far as Gwynneth was honestly aware, this feeling was a purely impersonal one. It would have been excited by any other being who had achieved the like and been thus rewarded. It is noteworthy, however, that Gwynneth found it necessary to explain the position to herself.

It was strange, too, how her life had impinged upon his, strange because the points of contact had in each case left a disproportionate impression upon her mind. She often thought of them. There was once in the very beginning, when she had actually stopped him in the village to ask the name of the poem from which he had quoted on Sunday. Gwynneth had never told a soul about this, she was so ashamed of her unmaidenly impulse; but she still remembered the look of pleasure that had flashed through his pain, and the kind sad voice which both answered her question and thanked her for asking it. That must have been only a day or two before the fire; the same summer there was the silent scene between them in the drawing-room, when she longed to shake hands with him, to show him her sympathy, but did not dare. Then came the finding of Georgie in the stonemason's shed, only the spring before last; but Gwynneth found that she had been gauche as usual even then, that she had never risen to any of these occasions, but that her one small attempt to express her sympathy had been nothing less than a piece of tactless presumption on her part. And yet she felt so much!

Well, it was something that Musk had opened his doors to him, if only under pressure of a harrowing occasion; even then it was much, very much, in the prime infidel of the parish. It was a beginning, an example; it might show others the way. Gwynneth presently discovered that it had.

She had not brought Georgie to see the saddler this time, and she was trying to follow that thinker's harangue as though she had really come to him for political instruction; but all the while the sound from among the trees distracted her attention and mystified her mind. It was neither the ringing impact of iron upon iron, nor the swish of a sharp steel point through the soft sandstone. It was the drone of a saw, as Gwynneth knew well enough when she asked what the sound was in the first opportunity afforded her.

"That's the reverend," said the saddler, dryly.

"It sounds like sawing," said disingenuous Gwynneth. "Has he reached the roof?"

"Gord love yer, miss, not he!"

Gwynneth was consumed with an interest that she feared to show, especially with the saddler looking at her through his spectacles as others had done when Mr. Carlton supplied the topic of conversation. It was a look that seemed to ask her how much she knew, and it always offended her. She did not want to know what he had done; all her interest was in what he was doing, alone there behind the trees. Yet now she felt that speak she must, if it was only to soften a single heart, in the very slightest degree, towards that unhappy man; and she had come to the saddler with no other purpose.

"Does no one go near him yet?" she asked point-blank.

The saddler leant across his bench; the girl had refused the only chair in the little workshop, and was standing outside at the open window, as all his visitors did.

"You won't tell Sir Wilton, miss?"

"I shan't go out of my way to make mischief, Mr. Fuller, if that's what you mean. But you had better not tell me any secrets," said Gwynneth, with a coldness that cost her an effort; however, the saddler's skin was in keeping with his calling.

"Then you can keep that or not," said he, "as you think fit; but I go and see him now and then, and, what's more, I'm not ashamed of it."

"I should think not!" the girl broke out; and Fuller sunned himself in the warmth of fine eyes on fire. "I mean," stammered Gwynneth, "after all this time, and all he has done!"

"What I said to myself last Christmas, miss; and I'm the only man that say it to-day, in this here village full of old women and hypocrites; if you'll excuse my blunt way o' speaking to a young lady like you. 'This here's gone on long enough,' thinks I; 'an' it's the season of peace an' good-will,' I says to myself; 'darned if I don't step across the road to cheer up the poor old reverend, an' Sir Wilton can turn me out of house an' home if he find out an' think proper.' Don't you mistake me, miss; I wasn't thinking of Sir Wilton in what I said just now, and ought not to have said to a young lady like you. No, miss, Sir Wilton has his own quarrel with the reverend; and I had my quarrel, as far as that go; but, Gord love yer, a man of my experience can afford to forgive an' forget, an' be generous as well as just. There isn't a juster man alive than me, Miss Gwynneth; and not a soul in this parish, or out of it, that can say I'm not generous too."

"I'm sure of it, Mr. Fuller. But did you go over to the rectory?"

"There and then," cried Fuller; "there—and—then. And I told him straight that I for one—but that's no use to go over what I said and he said," observed the saddler, hastily. "I can only tell you that in ten minutes we were chattun away as though nothun had ever come between us. And what do you suppose, miss? What do you suppose?"

Gwynneth shook her head, unable to imagine what was coming, and anxious to hear.

"He hadn't seen a newspaper in all these years! Hadn't so much as heard of that there Home Rule Bill of old Gladstone's, and didn't even know there'd been a war in the Sowd'n!" Gwynneth looked equally ignorant of this. "You know, miss? The Sowd'n, where General Gordon was betrayed and deserted by them varmin you'd stick up for. But we won't quarrel no more about that: only to think of the poor old reverend knowun no more about it than the man in the moon until I told him! Why, I had to tell him one of the Royal Family was dead an' buried; it would have been just the same if it had been the Queen herself, God bless her!"

"So he has been absolutely shut off from the world," Gwynneth murmured.

"There you've hit it, miss! 'Shut off from the world,' there you've put it into better language than I did," said the saddler, with his most complimentary air. "Gord love yer, miss, it used to be the reverend that passed his Standard on to me; but ever since last Christmas it's been me that's taken my East Anglian over to him; so the boot's been on the other leg properly; and right glad I've been to do anything for him, and to take my pipe across now and then as though nothun had ever happened. Not that he fare to care much for that, neither; he've been so long alone, I do believe he've got to like his own society as well as any. Yes, miss, shut off from the world he have been and he is; but he won't be shut off from the world much longer!"

"Oh?"

Gwynneth's interest was re-awakened.

"No," said Fuller, with the air of mystery in which his class delights; "no, miss, he's not one to be shut off longer than he can help. Hear that sound?"

"I do indeed."

Latterly she had been listening to nothing else.

"That's a saw!"

"Well?"

"Do you know what he's sawun?"

"No."

"Planks for benches!"

Gwynneth repeated the last word in a puzzled whisper; and so stood staring until the obvious explanation had become obvious to her. It remained inexplicable.

"I don't see the good of benches before the church is finished, Mr. Fuller."

"He mean to hold his services whether that's finished or not. And I mean to attend 'em," the saddler said with an air.

"But—I thought—"

"He was suspended for five year, and the bishop has given him leave to get to work directly the five year is up. That I happen to know."

"It must be nearly up now!"

"That's up next Sunday as ever is, and you'll know it when you hear the bell ring. He's got one of the old uns slung to a tree, for I helped him to sling it, and it's the first help he's had all this time. I wouldn't mention it, miss, for the reverend doesn't want a crowd; there'll be quite enough come when they hear the bell, if it's only to see what happens; but the whole neighbourhood 'll be there if that get about."

"And there's really going to be service in the church—just as it is—without a roof—this very next Sunday!"

It sounded incredible to Gwynneth, and yet it thrilled her as the incredible does not. The very drone of the saw was thrilling now.

"There is, miss, and I mean to be there," said the village Hampden, with inflated chest. "I can't help it if that cost me Sir Wilton's custom, the reverend and me are good friends again, and I mean to be there."

CHAPTER XXVI

A VERY FEW WORDS

It had been in the air all Saturday, but few believed the rumour until ten minutes to eleven next morning. At that hour and at that minute Long Stow was electrified by the measured ringing of a single bell—a bell hoarse with five years' rest and rust—a bell no ear had heard since the night of the fire.

Gwynneth was afield upon the upland, far beyond the church, a pitiful waverer between desire and indecision. Now she must go; and now she must not think of it. It was unnecessary, gratuitous, provocative, ostentatious, unmaidenly, immodest—and yet—both her duty and her desire. So the string of adjectives might be applied to her; they were no deterrent to a nature which hesitated often, but seldom was afraid. Gwynneth treated more respectfully the poignant query of her own consciousness: was she absolutely certain that she did not at all desire to show off like the saddler? She was not.

She did desire to show off, if it was showing off to honour openly the man whom she admired and wished others to admire. She gloried in the man's achievement, and possibly also in her own appreciation of it and him. That was her real point of contact with the saddler. But for Fuller there was the excuse of unconsciousness, and for Gwynneth there was not. So she read herself that Sunday morning, under an August sky without a fleck and a sun that drew the resin from those very pine-trees upon which the outcast had so often gazed. It was thereabouts that Gwynneth lingered, of self-analysis all compact. Then the hoarse bell began—came calling up to her from the clump of chestnuts and of elms—calling like a friend in pain . . .

Gwynneth reached church by way of the strip of glebe behind it and the gate into this from the lane, thus escaping the throng already gathered at the other gate. She saw nothing but the rude benches as she entered in; the last of these was too near for her; she shrank to the far end of it, close against the wall, and the bell stopped as she sank upon her knees. The beating of her heart seemed to take its place. Then there came a light yet measured step. It passed very near, with a subdued and subtle rustle, that might yet have meant one other woman. But Gwynneth knew better, though she never looked.

"I will arise, and go to my father, and will say unto him, Father, I have sinned against heaven, and before thee, and am no more worthy to be called thy son."

Already the girl could not see; all her being was involved in an effort to suppress a sob. It was suppressed. There were no tears in the voice that so moved Gwynneth. How serene it was, though sad! It began to soothe her, as she remembered that it had done when she was quite a little girl. She was a little girl again: these five years fled . . . But oh, why had he chosen that sentence of the scriptures? Gwynneth looked at her book (for now she could see) and found that some of the others would have been worse.

At last she could raise her eyes; and there was Fuller in the very front; and not another soul.

But Gwynneth cared for nothing any more except the gentle voice that it was her pride to follow in the general confession, kneeling indeed, yet kneeling bolt upright in her proud allegiance.

A strange picture, the rude benches, the ragged walls; the east window still a chasm, the hot sun streaming through it down the aisle; and over all the blue cruciform of sky, broken only by the nodding plumes of the taller elms. And a congregation yet more strange—only Gwynneth and the saddler. But this did not continue. Gwynneth heard movements in the porch behind her, and presently a stumble on the part of one driven in by the press; but no voices; not a whisper; and ere-long he who had been forced in, tired of standing, came on tiptoe and occupied the end of Gwynneth's bench.

Now it was the second lesson. The rector was reading it in the same sweet voice, with all his old precision and knowledge of his mother tongue, and never a trip or an undue emphasis. No one would have believed that that voice had been all but silent for five whole years. And yet some change there was, something different in the reading, something even in the voice; the clerical monotone was abandoned, the reading was more human, natural, and sympathetic. The change was in keeping with others. The rector wore no vestments in the naked eye of heaven, but only his cassock, his surplice, and his Oxford hood. There were flowers upon the simple table behind him, such roses as still grew wild in his tangled garden, but no candle to melt double in the sun. The lectern he had done his best to burnish; but it was still a cripple from the fire. Above, the rector's hair shone like silver, for the sun swept over it, but the lean dark face was all in shadow. Gwynneth only saw the fresh trim cut of the grizzled beard, and the walnut colour of the gnarled hand drooping over the book. That speaking hand!

Now it was the first hymn—actually! So he dared to have hymns, and to sing them if necessary by himself! But it was not necessary, and not only Gwynneth joined in with all the little voice she possessed, but presently there were false notes from the other end of the bench, and the saddler was not silent. But Robert Carlton's voice rang sweet and clear above the rest:—

"Jesu, Lover of my soul, Let me to Thy Bosom fly,
While the gathering waters roll, While the tempest still is high:
Hide me, O my Saviour, hide, Till the storm of life is past:
Safe into the haven guide, O receive my soul at last . . ."

The hymn haunted Gwynneth upon her knees, taking her mind from the remaining prayers. It was a hymn that she had loved as a little child, and now it seemed so simple and so whole-hearted to one who longed always to be both. But it was the passionate humility of it that touched and filled the heart; and yet there had been neither tremor nor appeal in the voice that led; and the humility was only in accord with one of the simplest services ever held.

The second hymn was another of Gwynneth's favourites; she could not afterwards have said which, for in the middle Mr. Carlton knelt, and then came forward to the twisted lectern at the head of the aisle.

It was not a sermon; it was only a very few words. Yet in Long Stow nothing else was talked of that day, nor for many a day to follow.

The few words were these:—

"The first verse of the nineteenth psalm:

"The heavens declare the glory of God; and the firmament sheweth his handywork.

"Though I have given you a text, my brethren, I do not intend this morning to preach any sermon. If you care to hear me again—if you choose to give me another trial—if you are willing to help me to start afresh—then come again next Sunday, only come in properly, and make the best of the poor benches which are all I have to offer you as yet. There will only be one weekly service at present. I believe that you could nearly all come to that—if you would! But I am afraid that many would have to stand.

"I cannot tell you how grieved I am that your church is not ready for you; but I hope and believe, as I stand before you here, that it will be ready soon, much sooner than you suppose. Then one great wrong will be righted, though only one.

"Meanwhile, so long as we are blessed with days like these—and I pray that many may be in store for us—meanwhile, could there be a fitter or a lovelier roof to the House of God than His own sky as we see it above us to-day? Though at present we can have no music worthy the name, have you not noticed, during all this our service, the constant song and twitter of those friends of man, as I know them to be, of whom Jesus said, 'Not one of them is forgotten before God'? And for incense, what fragrance have we not, in our unfinished church, that is the House of God all the more because it is also His open air.

"My brethren, you need be no farther from heaven, here in this place, unfinished as it is, than when the roof is up, and the windows are in, and proper seats, and when a new organ peals . . . and one whom you can respect stands where I am standing now . . .

"My brethren—once my friends—will you never, never be my friends again?

"Oh spare me a little that I may recover my strength: before I go hence, and be no more seen . . .

"Dear friends, I have said far more than I ever meant to say. But it is your own fault; you have been so good to me; so many of you have come in; and you are listening to me—to me! If you never listen to me again, if you never come near me any more, I shall still thank you—thank you—to my dying hour!

"But let no eye be dim for me. I do not deserve it. I do not want it. If you ever cared for me—any of you—be strong now and help me . . .

"And remember—never, never forget—that a just God sits in yonder blue heaven above us—that He is not hard—that I told you . . . He is merciful . . . merciful . . . merciful . . .

"O look above once more before we part, and see again how 'The heavens declare the glory of God; and the firmament sheweth his handywork.'

"And now to God the Father, God the Son, and God the
Holy Ghost, be ascribed all honour, power, dominion,
Might, henceforth and for ever. Amen."

He had controlled himself by a superb effort. The end was as calm as the beginning; but the rather hard, almost defiant note, that might have marred the latter in ears less eager than Gwynneth's and more sensitive than those of the people in the porch, that note had passed out of Robert Carlton's voice for ever.

And there no longer were any people in the porch; one by one they had all crept in to listen, some stealing to the rude seats, more standing behind, none remaining outside. Thus had they melted the heart they could not daunt, until all at once it was speaking to their hearts out of its own exceeding fulness, in a way undreamed of when the preacher delivered his text.

And this was to be seen as he came down the aisle, white head erect, pale face averted, and so through the midst of his people—his once more—without catching the eye of one.

CHAPTER XXVII

AN ESCAPE

Mr. Fuller had made a hasty exit; but he waylaid Gwynneth on the road. "Excuse me, miss," he cried, and the girl felt bound to do so. Next moment she was trying to sort the mixed emotions in the saddler's face, for a few steps had brought them to his house, and he had halted at the workshop window.

"Well, miss, and what do you think of it?"

"Oh, Mr. Fuller, please don't ask me."

"I don't mean the sermon, miss; I mean the flock of sheep that come and listened to the sermon," said the saddler, with a bitterness that astonished Gwynneth.

"But, surely, Mr. Fuller, you were glad they did come? I was so thankful!" declared the girl.

"So was I, miss; so was I," said the saddler, grimly; "but, Gord love yer, do you suppose they ever would have shown their noses if you an' me hadn't given 'em the lead?"

"Then we ought to be very proud, Mr. Fuller; at least you ought, since but for you I never should have known in time."

"But do you think a man of 'em 'll admit it?" continued Fuller fiercely. "Not they—I know 'em. They'll take the credit, the moment there's any credit to take—them that hasn't given him a word or a look in all these years. But the reverend, he know—he know!"

"I'm sure he does," said Gwynneth, kindly; and left the forerunner to his ignoble jealousy, only hoping there was some foundation for it, and that a real reaction was already in the air.

Even on her way home there were further signs. Jones the schoolmaster, an implacable enemy these five years, but an emotional man all his life, was still dabbing his eyes as he held unguarded converse with the phlegmatic owner of the mill on the lock, who had been his fellow churchwarden in the days before the fire.

"I'll be his churchwarden again," declared the schoolmaster, "and Sir Wilton can say what he likes. We know who ruled the roast before, and we know—"

Gwynneth caught no more as she hurried on, her first desire a quiet hour without a whisper from the world. She wished to recall every word of the sermon, while every syllable remained in her mind, and then to write it all down and to possess it for ever. Such was her first feverish resolve; nor, analytical as she was, did she stop to analyse this. The stable gates were open; it never occurred to Gwynneth to wonder why. There was a good way through the stable-yard to the garden, whose uttermost end she might thus reach without being seen from the house. And Fraulein Hentig had known where she was thinking of going, had shaken Gwynneth not a little with her remonstrances, but would be none the less certain to ask questions when next they met.

Near the Italian garden was a certain walk, with stark yew hedges on either hand, and fine grass stretched like a drugget from end to end. Across this strip the old English flowers, poppies and peonies, hollyhocks and larkspur, faced each other in serried lines as in a country dance; and the vista ended in a thatched summer-house where it was always cool. The spot was a favourite haunt of Gwynneth, who would catch herself humming the old English songs there, and thinking of patches and powder and the minuet. It had not that effect this morning; she neither saw nor smelt the flowers, nor heard the thrush which was singing to her with persistent sweetness from the stately trees upon the lawn beyond. Gwynneth was in that other world which had existed all these years within half-a-mile of this one. What she heard was the virile cadence of the voice which had always thrilled her; strong and masterful in the beginning; softening all at once, as the people pressed in to hear; then for a little high-pitched and hoarse, spasmodic, tremulous, too touching even to remember with dry eyes; then that last pause, and the silver clarion of his proper voice once more and to the end. And what Gwynneth saw, through her tears, was the sunlight resting on that stricken head, as though God had stretched out His hand in final mercy and forgiveness.

But what she was to see, before many minutes were past, or the sermon over in her mind, was a dapper figure approaching between the old flowers and the spruce hedges, a figure in riding breeches, swinging a cutaway coat in his walk.

It was Sidney, ridden over from Cambridge on a hired horse. Gwynneth had time to come out of the summer-house to meet him, but none to think. So he had given her a kiss before she realised what that meant—and knew in her heart that it must be the last. And the next moment she saw that he was displeased.

"So here you are!" was his verbal greeting: "I've been looking for you all over the shop."

"I'm so sorry," said poor Gwynneth. "If you had only let us know—"

"Oh, that's all right; I took my risk, of course."

He looked her up and down, as she stood in the sunlight, tall and comely, her state of mind instinctively and successfully concealed; and the brown tinge came upon his handsome face as the annoyance vanished. Endearments fell from his lips, but now she made him keep his distance, though so tactfully that he obviously did not realise his repulse. Gwynneth looked at him for an instant with great compassion; then she led the way into the summer-house, her mind made up.

"You haven't been here all the morning, have you?" he went on. "No, I see you haven't; there are your gloves."

"Yes."

"Been for a walk?"

"Well, I did go for one."

"What do you mean?" demanded Sidney, struck at last by her manner.

"I've been to church!"

"What! Over to Linkworth and back?"

"No."

Her tone trembled; he was not helping her at all.

"Then what church did you go to, and what on earth's up with you, darling?"

"I went to our own church."

"But I thought that Lakenhall chap only came in the afternoon?"

"He doesn't go to the church."

Sidney stared an instant, and was on his feet the next. "You don't mean to say you've been up to the church talking to—to Carlton?" he cried.

"No, not talking to him."

"Then do you mind telling me what you do mean?"

Gwynneth did her best to explain the occasion and to describe the service, but found herself unable to do the subject justice in a few words, and drifted into a nervous enthusiasm as she went. Sidney's eyes seemed smaller than when she began; she had never known he had so sharp a chin. But he heard her out, standing in the doorway, and not always looking her way; it was when averted that his face looked so hard. When she had finished he gave her his whole attention, and was some time regarding her, his hands in his pockets, without a word.

"So you deliberately went to hear that blackguard!"

"You needn't call him that," said Gwynneth, hotly.

"But I do."

"I should be ashamed to abuse him after all he has done!"

"That doesn't alter what—what you apparently and very properly know nothing about, Gwynneth."

"And I don't want to know!" cried the girl, indignant at his tone. "I only say, whatever he has done, he has paid very bitterly for it, and made such amends as were never made by anybody I ever heard of. He may have been all you say. He is more than all that I can say now!"

"And what do you say?" inquired Sidney, with polite contempt.

"That we shall honour ourselves in future by honouring him, and dishonour ourselves by continuing to dishonour him. He has had his punishment, and look how he has borne it! Why, he has done what was never done in the world before by one solitary man."

Gwynneth stopped breathless. Sidney eyed her coolly, his nostrils curling. "So that's your opinion," he sneered.

"It's a good deal more than that," cried Gwynneth. "It's my fixed conviction and personal resolve."

"To honour that fellow, eh?"

Gwynneth coloured.

"To the extent of attending his services when I happen to be here," she said. And Sidney gave her a pregnant look—a more honest look—angry and determined as her own.

"And what about me?" he said. "What if I object?"

Gwynneth was slow to answer, to tell him the sharp truth outright.

"Do you mean to go your own way in spite of me, in spite of the governor, in spite of all of us?"

Gwynneth saw that she could not remain at the hall and follow such a course. So this question went unanswered like the last, though for a different reason. Meanwhile Sidney was accounting for her silence to his own satisfaction, and he now conceived that the moment had arrived for him to play the strong man.

"Look here, Gwynneth," said he, "this is all rot and bosh, and worse—if you'll take my word for it. And you must take my word, and take it on trust in a thing like this, or you never will in anything. I tell you this fellow Carlton is the most unspeakable skunk. But it isn't a thing we can discuss together. Isn't that enough for you? Isn't my wish enough, in a thing like this, which I know all about and you don't? Have I got to enforce it while we're still engaged? If so—"

Gwynneth had raised her head slowly, and at last she spoke.

"We are not engaged, Sidney," she said quietly.

"Not—engaged?"

"It has never been a proper engagement."

"A proper engagement!" Sidney gasped. "Not a public one, if you like! What difference does that make?"

"No difference. It only makes it—easier—"

"What does it make easier?" he demanded fiercely.

Gwynneth was choking with humiliation. It was some moments before she could command her voice. Her distress was pitiful; but the young man was already busy pitying himself. A sudden change had come over Sidney. It was not in all respects a change for the worse. His cynical aplomb had already disappeared, leaving a tremulous, an angry, but a human being behind. So Gwynneth felt a leaning to him even at the last; but this time she knew her mind.

And she spoke it with equal candour and humility: it was all her fault: she could never forgive herself; but he would forgive her, when he saw for himself what the woman will always see quicker than the man. She liked him better than anybody she knew; that week at Cambridge had been the happiest week in her life; one day they would, they must, be good friends again. Meanwhile they had both made a miserable mistake. This was not love.

"Speak for yourself," cried Sidney, all bitterness and mortification. "And I never believed in a woman before," he groaned; "my God, I never shall again!"

And he strode out savagely into the sun; but a different Sidney was back next moment, one that reminded Gwynneth of the very old days, when he would pass her whistling with his dog. A sneer was on his lips, and his dry eyes glittered.

"I beg your pardon for making a scene, Gwynneth; it isn't in my line, as you know, and I apologise. But do you mind telling me when you discovered that you had—changed?"

"I have not changed, Sidney. That is my shame."

"Do you mean that you never did care about me?"

"Never in that way. I am ashamed to say it—more humiliated and ashamed than you can ever know. But it's the truth."

"Yet at the First Trinity ball, I remember, if you don't—"

His tone was more than Gwynneth could endure.

"Yes, I remember," she cried; "and I can explain it, though explanations are no excuse. Sidney, you know what my life was until the last few months? Happy enough in heaps of ways, but not the least gaiety in it; and suddenly I felt the want of it. I felt it first abroad, and you met that want in your May-week in a way beyond my dreams. You may sneer at me now, but you were awfully nice to me then, and I shall never, never forget it. You were so nice that I honestly did think for a little that you met every other want as well! Yet I tell you now, what I tried to tell you once before, that when once you had spoken nothing was the same. It was like touching a bubble. The bubble had burst."

"You felt like that from the first?"

Gwynneth turned away, for now they were both upon their feet, restlessly hovering between the summer-house and the sunlight.

"And yet it has taken you two months to tell me," pursued Sidney without remorse.

"I know; it was dreadful of me; yet I could not tell you till I was absolutely certain, and it is not so easy to be certain of oneself in such things. If you find no difficulty, Sidney, then you might pity those who do. Nevertheless, I did write, on my birthday, when you sent me those beautiful pearls. Sidney, you must take them back—for my sake. I meant to send them back at once, but you know what I heard that very morning! It may have been cowardly and weak, but how could I tell you I did not love you the moment I knew I was to have a little money of my own? It's hard enough as it is; but I had not the pluck for that. Yet it is hard enough now," repeated Gwynneth, with great feeling; "and you haven't made it easier, Sidney. No, I don't mean anything you may have said; you have not said more than I deserve. But you tempted me—you little know how you have tempted me—to be dishonest with you to the end. It would have been so easy to make poor Mr. Carlton the whole cause, and not to have told you the truth at all!"

"Then I wish to God you had done so!" Sidney cried out, revealing the character of his wound unawares, yet once more human, young, and vain. Moreover there was passion enough in his eyes and voice, as there had been in his wooing. "Besides," he continued, "poor Mr. Carlton, as you call him, is the cause, I don't care what you say. Curse him! Curse him, body and soul!"

Gwynneth was outside in the sun, doubly adorable now that he had lost her, and for other reasons too. Her sweet skin was flushed, and even her tears inflamed the unhappy young man. He looked at her long and passionately, then muttered venom through his teeth.

"What did you say?"

"I said it was like him, too, the blackguard!"

"I don't know what you mean, and I don't want to."

"It's as well," jeered Sidney, with exceeding malice; but already she was turning away. She was turning away without one word. In an instant he had her by both wrists, as the devil possessed himself.

"Let me go," cried Gwynneth. "You're hurting me!"

"I'm not. I'm not. I'm only going to let you know the kind of beast that's come between us."

Gwynneth stood with unresisting wrists. Her scorn was splendid.

"I am not sorry to have seen you in your true colours, Sidney."

"You are going to see some one else in his."

Her scorn had destroyed his last scruple. His eyes were devilish now.

"Let me go, you brute!"

"There are worse, Gwynneth, there are worse. It isn't a thing we can discuss, as I told you. But did you never notice the likeness?"

Her blank face put the involuntary question he desired.

"Only between the one big villain in this parish—and the one rather jolly little boy!"

At last her wrists were released. But Gwynneth remained standing in the sun. She was not looking at Sidney; on the contrary, her face declared her oblivious to his continued presence. It was white with several kinds of horror; it was pinched with many separate pangs. So she stood a few moments, then went her way slowly, only turning with a shudder. As for him, his fever subsided as he watched; and, before the diminishing figure had passed out of the vista of cropped hedges and crude flowers, even Sidney Gleed knew himself, for once in his life, for what he was and would be to its end.

CHAPTER XXVIII

THE TURNING TIDE

Next Sunday there was a real congregation. Yet the benches were almost as empty as before, the people herding near the porch until entreated either to occupy such seats as there were, or to leave the church. "Curiosity may have brought some of you here," said Mr. Carlton; "but I earnestly hope that none will remain in that spirit." The benches were full in a minute, and many had still to stand. All the next week Robert Carlton spent in sawing more planks to one length, and more props to one height for their support. And on the third Sunday his church was packed.

The summer of 1887 was, however, a remarkable one. And the month of August was an ideal month for the inauguration of open-air services, where there were trees.

In those hot still days came visitors of every type, and in greater numbers than Robert Carlton desired. The tide had turned; he was early aware of his danger now. Again and again it became his own sore duty to remind this one or the other, distantly perhaps, yet none the less unmistakably, of that which they might forget, but he never. Their open admiration tried him acutely. He did like it a little for its own sake, after five years' ostracism; more for the fresh purchase it gave him over simple hearts; but he was very hard on himself for liking it at all. On the other hand, he knew that it must put many a mind, the subtler minds, more than ever against him. It also renewed his own shame. So it was not admiration that he wanted at all; it was confidence, forgiveness, love; and these if possible by degrees. It was not possible, and Robert Carlton had to suffer in turn from the saddler, the schoolmaster, and the rest. The first would come to hedge and hedge with a view to Sir Wilton's imminent return; the next would intercept him as he came away, learn what he had been saying, and forthwith step across to the church to let the reverend know how the schoolmaster's character impressed itself upon a man of his experience. It was an unattractive trait in Fuller that he questioned everybody's sincerity but his own, albeit his strictures were not seldom justifiable. He talked, however, as though for years he had been the one and only philanthropist to hold any dealings with the rector; at last it became necessary to set him right on the point, which Mr. Carlton did with a mild account of his illness and the sexton's aid.

"I do wish I'd ha' known," said Fuller, with perfect truth; "I do wish I'd ha' known an' had the nursun of yer, reverend, instead o' him. And he never come near you no more; so I should expect."

"But you tell me he's very ailing, Fuller."

"He haven't been ailun all these years."

"We—we had a little tiff in the end. It was my fault. I wonder if he'd see me now?"

"I'll make him, reverend, I'll tell him he's got to."

"No, Fuller, I can't allow that. Besides, he has not got to do anything of the sort; he has turned dissenter, and may prefer me to stop away. Nevertheless I shall call, if only to ask how he is."

There was no need to ask, in the event. The old sexton was failing fast, and "not long for this world," as his daughter announced in front of him. The poor man was in bed, and very dirty, but as sensible as he ever had been; and he welcomed the rector with cadaverous grins.

"They tell me," he whispered, "you fare to finish the church with your own two hands. You're a wonderful man, sir—and I'm another."

"You are, indeed. Why, you must be nearly ninety, Busby?"

"Eighty-eight, sir, come next September. But I wasn't thinkun o' my age, sir. Do you remember that little varmin I swallered out 'f a pond?"

"I remember."

"I've killed that, sir!"

And the sunken eyes shone like lamps.

"I congratulate you, Busby."

"I killed that two year ago; and you'll never guess how!" The ex-sexton proceeded to rehearse the various remedies he had tried in vain. "I killed that with bacca-smoke," he concluded in sepulchral triumph. "It was the minister's idea. I had to swaller the bacca-smoke instead o' puffun that out, an' that choked that in three pipes!"

The rector said it must be a great relief to be rid of such an incubus. Busby, however, with a sick man's reluctance to admit any alleviating circumstance in his case, was not so sure about that. He sometimes fared to wish he had the little varmin back. Croap, croap, croap! That had been wonderful good company after all. The ex-sexton was not too ill to wax eloquent upon his favourite topic. And the tenor of his talk was that mankind had been building churches since the world began, but what other man had lived for years with a live frog on his chest?

Their religious dispute was evidently forgotten, and Mr. Carlton did not feel it incumbent upon him to risk another in the circumstances of the case. On the way home the other egotist waylaid him, with his opinion of old Busby's hallucination and general sanity since the saddler could remember him.

"But half the village and half the county is the same, reverend. Silly Suffolk!"

"Yet you're a Suffolk man yourself, Fuller," observed Mr. Carlton, mildly.

"Yes, reverend, but there was corn in Egypt, if you recollect."

Meanwhile the building still went on, and was rapidly nearing a point beyond which Carlton himself could not proceed unaided. That point was the last window; the others were all finished. He had left out the single mullions and all the tracery. They might be added afterwards by an expert hand. They were not essential to the windows, which were ready for glazing as they were. But the east window was another affair. It must have its two mullions as before, with the quatrefoil tracery which had remained undamaged in the west window opposite. All this was beyond the self-taught hewer of coursed rubble and of gargoyles; the arch itself must be two feet wider than any he had yet attempted; but on a worthy east window he had set his heart.

Such was the dilemma in which Robert Carlton found himself at the end of August, and there seemed only one thing to be done. He must call for aid at last, and now he knew that aid would come, for he had received various offers of assistance since the beginning of the month. Some of these were from local firms which had refused his work in the beginning; Carlton had promised that if he called for tenders he would consider theirs; and now call he must. Yet he could not bring himself to do so all at once.

To call in the world after all! To open his leafy solitude to the British workmen in gangs, to hear their chaff, to smell their tobacco, where he had laboured in quiet and alone through so many, many seasons!

But it had to come. A tinge of autumn was on the trees. Any Sunday now the open-air service might prove a discomfort and a peril to all; in a few weeks at most it would become impossible. But the people must have their church. They had waited long enough. Therefore any further reluctance in him was little and unworthy, as Carlton saw at once for himself. Yet there was now so much else to do, so many poor folks to see, so many old threads to take up, that for once he temporised. And even as he temporised, his mind made up, and a competition pending between the masons of the neighbourhood, Sir Wilton Gleed arrived in Long Stow for the shooting.

Sir Wilton arrived with a frown. It deepened but little at what he heard. He was prepared for everything; and about Gwynneth he knew. She had left his house, she had gone her own way, he washed his hands of her, and only congratulated Sidney on his escape. That chapter was closed. It was the older matter that harassed Sir Wilton Gleed.

So that devil had reinstated himself after all! The fact might not be finally accomplished; it was none the less inevitable, imminent. And Sir Wilton had long been prepared for it; for the last two years he had been unable to move without hearing the name he abhorred; it dogged him in town, it followed him to Scotland, it awaited him in every hole and corner of the Continent. Once he had been fond of speaking of his property; but in two senses it was hard to do this without giving the place a name. Sir Wilton was learning to deny himself the boast altogether.

Long Stow? Could there be two Long Stows? Then that must be the place where the parson was building up his church. What a romance! And what a man! Oh, no doubt he was a very dreadful person also; but there, in any case, was a Man.

Sir Wilton could not deny it; and by degrees he wearied of insisting upon the deplorable side of the man's character. The task was ungrateful; it put himself in an ungenerous light, which was the harder upon one who was by no means ill-natured in grain. Gradually he took to admitting his adversary's good points; even admitted them to himself; but that did not remove the chronic irritation of infallible defeat. And defeated Sir Wilton already was, with the people flocking to that man again, and doubtless willing to help him finish his church. His own parishioners had forgiven him—and well they might, said Sir Wilton's friends in every country-house. Besides, the suspended parson was a figure of the past; the law was done with him; he was absolutely free to begin afresh. Henceforth the vindictiveness of the individual must recoil deservedly upon the individual's head.

Sir Wilton saw all this before his actual return; and he realised the madness of either urging or attempting to coerce his tenantry to harden their hearts, a second time, against one who had committed no second sin. If he failed it would destroy his influence in the neighbourhood; even if he succeeded it would damage his popularity elsewhere. And a chat with the schoolmaster, a call upon one or two of the neighbouring clergy, a word with old Marigold in his gig, all served but to convince him finally of these facts.

Sir Wilton's mind was made up. He had come back primed with a desperate measure for the last of all. Once it was resolved upon, his spirits rose.

He told his wife and took her breath away; but a very little reasoning brought the lady round the compass to his view. This was after breakfast on the second day. The same forenoon Sir Wilton went up the village, brisk and rosy, a flower in his coat, and a word for all. Past the Flint House he began to walk slowly, took no notice of a courtesy, swung round suddenly himself, and was knocking at Jasper Musk's door that minute, still a thought less confident than he had been.

Musk was in his garden, fast as usual to his chair. Mrs. Musk brought out another chair for Sir Wilton, and drove Georgie indoors on her way back. Sir Wilton watched the child out of sight, and then favoured Jasper with his peculiarly fixed stare. There was unusual meaning in it this morning.

"So the world has forgiven him," said Sir Wilton Gleed.

Musk stared in his turn, his great face glowing with contempt. "Have you?" said he at last.

"Not yet," replied Sir Wilton, a shade more pink in the face. He had meant to lead up to his intention. He was taken aback.

"But you mean to, do you?" pursued Musk, pressing his point in no respectful tone: in all their relations this one had never pandered to the other.

"I don't say that, either," replied Sir Wilton, in studied tones.

"Then what do you say?"

"Less than anybody else, a good deal less," declared the squire. "I—I don't quite understand your tone, Musk, I must say; but I can well understand your position in this matter. It is unique, of course. So is mine, in a sense. But I must beg of you not to jump to conclusions. I am the last person to make a hero of the man I did my best to kick out of the parish five years ago; next to yourself, no one has reason to love the fellow less. I thought it a public scandal that he should be empowered to stay here against all our wills. My opinion of that whole black matter is absolutely and totally unchanged. But I do confess to you, Musk, that this last year or two have somewhat modified my opinion of the man himself."

Musk's eyes had never dropped or lifted from his visitor's face. Their expression was inscrutable. The iron cast of that massive countenance was the only key to the workings of the mind within: the lines seemed subtly emphasised, as in the faces of the dead. And his gigantic body was the same; only the eyes seemed alive; and they were as still as the rest of him.

"What if I've modified mine?"

Sir Wilton looked up quickly; for the habitual starer had been for once outstared. "Do you mean that you have?" cried he.

"I don't say as I have or I haven't. But that's a man, Sir Wilton, and I won't deny it."

"Exactly what everybody is saying. I say no more myself."

"And I won't say no less . . . Suppose you was to patch it up with him, Sir Wilton?"

"I should help him finish his church."

Musk sat silent for some time. His eyes seemed smaller. But they had not moved.

"That would be a wonderful good action on your part, Sir Wilton," he said at last.

"Not at all, Musk. I should be doing it for the people, not for Mr. Carlton."

Another pause.

"And yet, Sir Wilton, in a manner o' speaking, you might say as he deserved it, too?"

Sir Wilton was quite himself again—a gentleman in keeping with the flower in his coat.

"I certainly never expected to hear you say so, Musk," said he frankly; "though it's what I've sometimes thought myself."

"I haven't said as I forgave him, have I?"

"No, no, Musk, you haven't; it is not in human nature that you could."

It was a strange tongue that had spoken in the massive head; there was no forgiveness in that voice. Yet in the next breath the note of hate was hushed as suddenly as it had been struck.

"That may be in human natur'," said Musk, "but that ain't in mine. I'm not a religious man, Sir Wilton. That may be the reason. But I do have enough respect for religion to wish to see that church up again before I die."

"I consider it very generous of you to say so, Musk," declared the other, with enthusiasm.

"But I do say it, Sir Wilton, and I never said a truer word."

"So I hear; and that decides me!" cried Sir Wilton, jumping up. "I really had decided—for the sake of the parish—and was actually on my way to the church to take the whole job over. A gang of competent workmen could polish it off in a couple of months; and it ought to be polished off. But it's really wonderful what he has done!"

"I don't deny it," said Musk; and waited for the squire to recover his point, his own set face unchanged.

"Yes," resumed Sir Wilton, suddenly, "I was on my way up to make him that proposal just now; but as I passed your door I could not resist coming in. I thought I would like to tell you what I intended to do, and to give you my reasons for doing it."

"There was no need to do that," said Musk, with an upward movement of the lips, hardly to be called a smile; for once also his great head moved slowly from side to side.

"And now I shall be going on," announced Sir Wilton, who did not like this look, and was now less inclined to suffer disrespect.

"Hold on a bit, Sir Wilton. I'm glued tight to this here chair by my old enemy; that seem to get worse and worse, and I'm jealous I shall soon set foot to the ground for the last time. That take me ten minutes to mount upstairs to bed. I haven't been further'n this here lawn these twelve months. So I can't come and see you, Sir Wilton; and I should like another word or two now we're on the subject. You see, he was here a good bit when the boy was bad, and even I don't feel all I did about him, though forgive him I never shall on earth. At the same time I'd like to see him have his church. That'd want consecrating again, sir, I suppose?"

"I suppose it would."

"Would the bishop do it, think you?"

"Like a shot," said Sir Wilton, a touch of pique in his tone. "I had some correspondence with him years ago about this matter, and I was surprised at the view the bishop took. He will come, if he is alive."

Jasper had taken his eyes from Sir Wilton's face at last; they were resting on the level sunlit land beyond the river. "That'll be a great day for Long Stow," he murmured almost to himself; and suddenly his lips came tight together at the corners.

"It should be a very interesting ceremony," said Sir Wilton, foreseeing his part in it. He had forgiven his enemy, the scandalous clergyman who had lived down a scandal and a tragedy; it was Sir Wilton who had helped him to live them down. Not at first; then he had been adamant; but his justice in the beginning was only equalled by his generosity in the end, when the man had proved his manhood, and the sinner had atoned for his sin, so far as atonement was possible in this world. That poor pertinacious devil had been five years running up the walls. Sir Wilton Gleed had thrown his money and his influence into the scale, and finished the whole thing in less than five months. They were saying all this at the opening ceremony; everybody was there. His magnanimity was being talked of in the same breath with the parson's pluck. The bishop was his guest.

"A very interesting ceremony," repeated Sir Wilton. "We could have it at Christmas, if not before."

"That won't see me," said Jasper Musk. "I couldn't get, even if I wanted to. But sciatica that don't kill, and I hope to live to see the day." And again the corners of his mouth were much compressed.

"Yet you think you can never forgive him?"

Sir Wilton felt that he could not be the bearer of too much good-will, now that he was about it; but Musk turned his eyes full upon him, and there was a queer hard light in them.

"I don't think," said he. "I know."

And so it fell out that in an hour of unusual depression, and of natural hesitation which was yet not natural in Robert Carlton, he looked up suddenly and once more saw his enemy in the sanctuary which would soon be his very own leafy sanctuary no longer. Carlton had come there to meditate and to pray, but not to work. That sort of work was not for him any more. Others must take it up; the time was ripe; only the beginning was hard. And here was Sir Wilton Gleed advancing towards him.

And Sir Wilton was holding out his hand.

CHAPTER XXIX

A HAVEN OF HEARTS

Slower to decide than most young persons of her independent character, Gwynneth was one of those who are none the less capable of decisive conduct in a definite emergency. She behaved with spirit in the predicament in which her weakness and her strength had combined to place her. She had jilted Sidney; outsiders might not know it; but she had treated him in a way which he and his were never likely to forgive. After that, and that alone, his home could not have been her home any more; but Gwynneth had other and even stronger reasons for determining to leave Long Stow; and there were none why she should not. She had her money. She was of age. She would be a good riddance now. It was her first thought in the garden. The thought hardened to resolve while Sidney, full of bitterness and champagne, was still galling his hired horse back to Cambridge. Gwynneth also was gone within the week.

It was a chance acquaintance to whom the girl had written in her need. She had met in Leipzig a strangely interesting woman: commanding, mysterious, self-contained. This lady, a Mrs. Molyneux by name, had taken notice of Gwynneth, and, at the close of their short acquaintance, had given her a card inscribed in pencil with the name of St. Hilda's Hospital, Campden Hill.

"You have never heard of it," Mrs. Molyneux had said with a smile; "but I shall be very glad if you will come and see me and my hospital some day when you are in town."

Gwynneth had felt honoured, she could scarcely have said why, for she knew no more of this lady than she had seen for herself, which was really very little. But there is a kind of distinction which appeals to the instinct rather than to the conscious perceptions, and Gwynneth had felt both awed and flattered by an invitation which was obviously sincere. She had said that she should love to see the hospital—and had never been near it yet.

"I don't know whether you have ever thought of being a nurse," Mrs. Molyneux had added with Gwynneth's hand in hers; "but if you ever should—or if ever you want to do something, and don't know what else to do—I wish you would write to me, and let me be your friend."

The second invitation had been given with a wonderfully understanding look—a look which seemed to sift the secrets of Gwynneth's heart—a look she would not have cared to meet during the late season. She had promised again, however, very gratefully indeed; and it was her second promise that Gwynneth eventually kept.

"I had such a strong feeling about you," Mrs. Molyneux wrote by return. "I knew that I should hear from you sooner or later . . . I like your frankness in saying that it is no fine impulse, or love of nursing for its own sake, that makes you wish to come. I do not seek to know what it is. Even if you are no nurse you can play the organ in our little chapel as it has not been played yet; and that would be very much to me. So come any day and make your home with us at least for a time." The writer contrived to refer to herself as "Reverend Mother," in emphatic capitals, and her letter was signed "Constance Molyneux, Mother in God."

It happened that Gwynneth had spoken of Mrs. Molyneux to her aunt, who knew a good name when she heard it, and had often asked Gwynneth if she was not going to pay that call on Campden Hill; thus her recklessness in casting herself among strangers was more apparent than real, and little likely to aggravate her prime offence against kith and kin. Nor did it; nevertheless it was a plunge into all but unknown waters. The hospital was a private one, and Mrs. Molyneux both spoke and wrote of it as her own. It was a cancer hospital for women, evidently run upon religious lines, and those not easy to define, since Gwynneth happened to know that the Reverend Mother was not a Roman Catholic. And these things were all she did know when her hansom drew up before a red-brick building with ecclesiastical windows, and a cross over the door, in a leafy road not five minutes' climb from Kensington High Street.

Gwynneth pulled the wrought-iron bell-handle, and next moment caught her breath. The door had been opened by a portress in austere but becoming garb, a young girl like herself, and the pretty face between the quaint cap and collar was smiling a sweet greeting to the newcomer. A few worn steps of snowy stone, and a Gothic doorway, with the oak door standing open, showed more girls within against the wainscot; all were pretty; and all wore blue serge, with white aprons and long cambric cuffs, square bib-collars trimmed with lace, and Normandy caps with streamers of fine lawn. Gwynneth blushed for her own conventional attire, as she was ushered through this hall, past a dispensary where another of the uniformed girls was busy among the bottles, and so into the presence of the Reverend Mother.

Mrs. Molyneux, the well-dressed woman of the world whom Gwynneth had known in Leipzig, was a lost identity in a habit which marked her sway only by its supreme severity; an order of St. John of Jerusalem hung upon her bosom, and a crucifix dangled at her side. Her hands were hidden beneath some short and shapeless garment reaching to the waist, but one emerged for a moment to greet Gwynneth warmly. "Do you feel as if you had come into a convent?" the Reverend Mother asked, a gentle humour in her lowered voice. It was exactly what Gwynneth did feel, and the sensation was by no means displeasing to her. The Mother herself then showed Gwynneth over the establishment, which was indeed a singular amalgam of the hospital and the nunnery. The dining-room was termed the "refectory"; a cross hung over every bed in the wards upstairs, and in the nurses' cubicles below the wards. Cap and apron, bib-collar and cuffs, were laid out on Gwynneth's bed, and these she found herself expected to don then and there. The Mother returned when she was ready, and showed her the chapel last of all. It was a tiny chapel, but as beautiful as antique carving, rich embroidery, much stained glass, and hanging lights could make it. In her innocence Gwynneth wondered why these lights were burning while the summer sun, shining through the stained glass, filled the chapel with vivid beams of purple and red. She was even puzzled by the unmistakable odour of recent incense; but she said, with truth, that the chapel delighted her.

"I knew it would," the Mother whispered with her penetrating smile.

"How could you know?" Gwynneth asked, smiling also, because she had never touched on religion with Mrs. Molyneux.

"I saw you once in the English church," the Mother said. "It was before I knew you; and yet, you see, I did know you, even then!"

In this chapel there were daily matins, vespers, nones; and at each of the three services attendance was compulsory on the part of all nurses not required at an actual deathbed, and of all patients who were still up and about. French-capped, pink-frocked maid-servants and ward-maids filled the front rows of chairs; the patients sat behind; and on either hand, in the carved oak stalls, were the pretty nurses, the Reverend Mother near the entrance in their midst. The services, conducted by an attendant Anglican of small account, were punctuated by genuflexions and the sacred sign; and it was impossible to follow them in the Book of Common Prayer.

Gwynneth tried hard to lift up her heart in this strange sanctuary. She longed for real religion as she had longed for little in her life before. At the first blush, it seemed as though Providence alone could have led her into so unique a haven of equal sanctity and usefulness; and yet, also from the first, the girl was repelled a little if attracted more. She liked her work; she was a natural nurse, and soon grew used, but never hardened, to hopeless suffering and slow death. There were patients who loved Gwynneth, and not a nurse who was not fond of her, before she had been at St. Hilda's a month. Already she was playing the organ at all three services, and her own music, and the voices floating up to her, at these set times, filled her heart with peace; but she wondered if it was the right kind of peace; she wondered whether this was religion at all. Sometimes the sweet little chapel—for it was all that to Gwynneth's mind—struck her also as a stage of studied effects. The nurses were so pretty, their garb so becoming, and the blue of it had such a perfect foil in the maid-servants' pink. But then the Reverend Mother, in her sombre supremacy, gradually revealed herself as the superb mistress of deliberate effect; and a strange study Gwynneth found her; of foibles and fascination all compact; at once subtle, simple, vain, and noble. It appeared that Mrs. Molyneux was an extremely wealthy widow, whose one consoling hobby was this anomalous retreat upon Campden Hill.

The patients paid nothing; the nurses received nothing; it was a retreat for both, and Gwynneth was not the only one who had sought it primarily, and frankly, for peace of mind and salvation from self. Her hands at least were not the less tender and untiring on that account. Some of her capped and cuffed comrades were no older than herself; many were refreshingly frivolous, and properly free from care. Gwynneth's chief crony was Nurse Ella, a bright young widow, who wore spectacles, and declared herself unable to understand what the Reverend Mother had ever seen in her, as she was neither pretty nor religious, nor as young as the rest.

Nurse Ella had, however, a shrewd wit and a sharp tongue; made wicked fun of the Mother's sacerdotal pretensions when alone with Gwynneth; and thus stimulated the latter to think for herself, if only to refute her friend's arguments. Nurse Ella was above all things an extraordinarily decided character, aggressively so in immaterial issues, but good for Gwynneth by that very fact.

These opposites became fast friends. Often they would talk over the refectory fire—a wood fire in an ancient grate, which cast the right mediæval glow over the polished floor and the dark wainscotting—long after the others were in their cubicles. Nurse Ella had the greatest scorn for the conventual side of St. Hilda's, which Gwynneth would defend warmly, while her heart admitted more than her lips; the discussion would ramify, and become animated on both sides; then all at once Nurse Ella would look at her watch, and no persuasion would induce her to stay another minute. Gwynneth could have sat up half the night, and would plead in vain for ten minutes more; it seldom took Nurse Ella as many seconds to suit her action to her word. She said she would do a thing, and did it; that was Nurse Ella's principle in life.

So there was no exchange of confidences between these two, both reticent natures, and neither unduly inquisitive about the other's affairs. Gwynneth only knew that her friend's married life had been a very short one; for her own part, she had said nothing to let Nurse Ella suppose that she had herself been even asked in marriage. But one night they were speaking of another nurse, who had left St. Hilda's that day, in floods of tears, to be married the following week.

"If I felt like that," Gwynneth had declared, "I wouldn't be married at all."

Nurse Ella looked up quickly, her glasses flaming in the firelight. "What, not after you had given your word?" said she.

"Certainly not, if I felt I had made a mistake." Gwynneth was staring into the fire.

"You would break your solemn promise in a thing like that?" the other persisted.

"Better one promise than two lives," replied Gwynneth, with oracular brevity. Nurse Ella watched her in sidelong astonishment.

"It's easy to talk, my dear! I believe you are the last person who would do anything so dishonourable."

"I don't call it dishonourable."

"But it is, to break your word."

"Suppose you have changed?"

"You have no business to change. Say you'll do a thing, and do it."

The spectacled face had assumed a rigid cast which Gwynneth knew well, and for which Nurse Ella had just the chin.

"But supposing you never really loved—"

"Love is an inexact term; it's not always easy to tell when it applies to your feelings, and when it does not. But when you say you'll marry anybody, that's a definite promise, and nothing in the world should make you break it, unless it's been extracted under false pretences. We are both very positive, aren't we?" and Nurse Ella smiled. "I wonder why you are, Gwynneth?"

"Because," said the girl, impelled to frankness, yet hanging her head, "as a matter of fact, I've been more or less engaged myself."

"And you got out of it?"

"I broke it off."

"Simply because you had changed?"

"No—it was a mistake from the beginning. I had never really cared. That was my shame."

"And you broke your word—you had the courage!"

The tone was a low one of mere surprise. There was more in the look which accompanied the tone. But Gwynneth had her eyes turned inward, and her wonder was not yet.

"It had to be done," she said simply. "It was humiliating enough, but it was not so bad as going on . . . Can anything be so bad as marrying a man you do not love, just because you have made a mistake, and are too proud to admit it?"

"No . . . you are right . . . that is the worst of all."

It might have been a studied picture that the two young women made, in the old oak room, with the firelight falling on their quaint sweet garb, and reddening their pensive faces, only conscious of the inner self. Nurse Ella was standing up, gazing down into the fire, her back turned to Gwynneth; but now her tone was enough. It was neither wistful nor bitter, but only heavy with conviction; and in another moment Nurse Ella was gone, not more abruptly than usual, but without letting Gwynneth see her face again. Then Gwynneth recalled the look with which the other had exclaimed upon her courage, and either she flattered herself, or that look had been one of envy pure and simple. Could it be that her friend's decided character was all self-conscious and acquired? Was her intolerance of the slightest hesitation, in matters of no account, a life's reaction from a fatal irresolution in some crisis of her own career?

Gwynneth never knew; for a fine mutual reserve distinguished the intimacy of this pair, and even drew them together, opposite as they were in so many other respects, more than impulsive confidences on either side. One had suffered; the other was suffering now; each was a little mystery to her friend. And there was one more reason for this: neither was sure of the other's sympathy: at every point of contact they diverged.

So Gwynneth used to wonder whether Nurse Ella was in reality a widow at all, and Nurse Ella was quite sure that Gwynneth was still in love, probably with the man she had jilted, according to the wise way of women; she was so ready to speak of love in the abstract; and once she spoke so passionately. This was in Kensington Gardens, one foggy Sunday, when the two nurses were on their way to church; for they were allowed to worship where they listed after matins at St. Hilda's. Nurse Ella rented a sitting under a fashionable preacher who discoursed with much wisdom and some acidity on topics of the hour; but Gwynneth was still seeking her spiritual ideal. They would walk together as far as the Bayswater Road, where their ways diverged, unless Nurse Ella could induce Gwynneth to go with her; on this particular morning they were arguing about a novel when the houses loomed upon them through the bare trees and the fog.

"She never would have forgiven him," Nurse Ella had declared, in crisp settlement of the point at issue. "No young wife would forgive a young husband who behaved like that. So it may be the cleverest novel in the language, but it isn't true to life." Whereupon Gwynneth, who had been defending a masterpiece with laudable spirit, walked some yards in silence. "Are you sure that it matters how people behave," she then inquired, "if you really love them?"

"How they behave?" echoed her friend. "Why, Gwynneth, of course! Nothing does matter except behaviour."

"It wouldn't to me," Gwynneth exclaimed, almost through her teeth.

"But surely what one does is everything!"

"Not in love," averred Gwynneth, whose convictions were few but firm; "and those two are more in love than any other couple I know in fiction or real life. No; you love people for what they are, not for what they do."

Nurse Ella laughed outright.

"That may be good metaphysics," said she, "but it's shocking common-sense! Our actions are the only possible test of our character, as its fruit is the only test of a tree."

In Gwynneth's eyes burnt wondrous fires, and on her cheeks; and her breath was coming very quickly. But most persons look straight ahead as they walk and talk, and between these two fell the kindly fog besides.

"Suppose you loved somebody," the young girl cried at last; "and suppose you suddenly discovered he had once done something dreadful—unspeakable. Would that alter your feeling towards him?"

"It could never fail to do so, Gwynneth."

"It would not alter mine!"

Nurse Ella turned her head. But in the road the fog seemed thicker than in the gardens. And, apart from its vigour, Gwynneth's tone had sounded impersonal enough.

"I believe it would," her friend persisted, "when the time came."

"And I know that it would not," said Gwynneth, half under her breath and half through her teeth.

"Well, Gwynneth," said Nurse Ella, with a laugh, "we were evidently born to differ. In my view that would be the one sort of excuse for changing one's mind about a man—whereas you see others!"

"But I am not talking about one's mind," cried Gwynneth; "the feeling I mean, the feeling those two have in the book, lies infinitely deeper than the mind."

"And no crime could alter it?"

"Not if he atoned—not if the rest of his life were one long atonement."

"But, Gwynneth, that would make all the difference."

Gwynneth walked on in silence. She was reconsidering her own last words.

"Atonement or no atonement," she exclaimed at length, "it would make no difference—if I loved the man. Atonement or no atonement!" repeated Gwynneth defiantly.

Nurse Ella had a passion for the last word, but they were come to her corner, and there was Gwynneth glowing through the fog, her eyes alight, her cheeks flaming, a new being in the puzzled eyes of her friend.

"Come with me, Gwynneth," begged Nurse Ella, at length; "don't go off by yourself. Come, dear, and hear a shrewd, hard-headed sermon, without sentiment or superstition!"

Gwynneth smiled. That was the last thing to meet her mood.

"Then where shall you go?"

"Either St. Simeon's or All Souls'," said Gwynneth. "I haven't made up my mind."

Nurse Ella shook her head over an admission as characteristic as her disapproval. This was the Gwynneth that she knew.

"When do you make it up!" exclaimed Nurse Ella without inquiry.

"When it's a matter of the least importance," said Gwynneth, choosing to reply. "What can it signify which church I go to, what difference can it possibly make? As a matter of fact I rather think of going to All Souls'."

"I thought you didn't care about music and nothing else?"

"I don't know that there is nothing else. I think of going to see. I have often thought of it before, but St. Simeon's is rather nearer, and I generally end by going there. I shall decide on the way."

"What a girl you are, Gwynneth!" exclaimed Nurse Ella, with frank impatience. "You never seem to know your own mind—never!"

Gwynneth made no reply; but she kindled afresh, and this time very tenderly, as she went her own way through the fog.

CHAPTER XXX

THE WOMAN'S HOUR

All Souls' was dark and hazy with its share of the ubiquitous fog, here a little aggravated by the subtle fumes of incense newly burnt. In the haze hung quivering constellations of sallow gaslight, and through it gleamed an embroidered frontal, and the silken backs of praying priests, lit by candles four. Delicate strains came from an invisible organ; a light patter and a rich rustling from the feet and garments of some departing after matins, some taking their places for choral eucharist, women to the left, men to the right. Men and women, goers and comers alike, with few exceptions, bowed the knee with Romish humility at the first or the last glimpse of that shimmering frontal with the four candles above and the motionless vestments below.

The congregation was one of well-dressed women and well-to-do men; their quiet devotion was not the less noteworthy on that account. A fine reverence animated every face: the stray observer would have missed the passive countenance of the merely pious, as Gwynneth did, and discovered in its stead the happy ardour of those whose religion was a delight rather than a duty. Yet the congregation took scarcely any part in the actual service. Few untrained voices joined in the exquisite singing; few, in the body of the church, left their places to take part in the sacred climax. The congregation might have been only an audience; yet somehow it was not. Somehow also there was nothing spectacular in an office of equal dignity, distinction, and fervour.

Yet the yellow lights in a yellow fog, the perfect organ, trained voices, rich embroideries, incense, genuflexions, all these seemed at one religious pole; and Long Stow church on a summer's day, with the sky above and the birds singing, and Mr. Carlton in his surplice in the sun, surely that was at the other! It was Gwynneth's fate, at all events, to carry that single service in her heart and mind for ever, and to put every other one against it. She did so now, involuntarily at first, and then unwillingly, as she knelt or stood at the end of her row—her cambric cuffs and fine lawn streamers in high relief against the rich furs and the sombre feathers of those about her.

On the other side of the nave, far back and close to the wall, a grizzled gentleman stood and knelt by turns, in much obscurity; and his attention never flagged. No detail of the elaborate ritual appeared unfamiliar to this worshipper, and yet for a time his expression was rather that of the alien critic. Gradually, however, the lines disappeared from his forehead, his eyes opened wider, and brightened with the peaceful ardour which he himself had already remarked in the eyes of others. He was a tall thin man, very weather-beaten and rather bent, wearing a new overcoat and a soft muffler; there was nothing in his appearance to declare him of the cloth himself. His grey beard was close trimmed. He wore gloves and carried a tall hat shoulder high in the press going out. He was no more readily recognisable as the lonely builder of Long Stow church, than Gwynneth in her nurse's garb as the niece of Sir Wilton Gleed. But their separate fates brought them face to face in the porch, and recognition was immediate on both sides.

"Miss Gleed?" said Robert Carlton, raising his hat before it covered his grey hairs.

"Mr. Carlton!" she exclaimed in turn. There had been no time to think, and her voice told only of her surprise; her own ear noticed it, and she had time to marvel at herself.

"I thought I could not be mistaken," Carlton was saying. And they were shaking hands.

"I never expected to see you here," said Gwynneth, with a strange emphasis, as though the declaration were due to herself.

"I never thought of coming until an hour or two ago."

No more had Gwynneth: then the miracle was twofold. Her heart gave thanks. It was not afraid.

Meanwhile the crowd was carrying them gently, insensibly, but side by side, across the flagged yard to the gate.

"It's the first Sunday I've spent in town for years," observed Carlton; "you are here altogether, I believe?"

"Well, for some years, at least. I am learning to be a nurse."

And Gwynneth blushed for her conspicuous attire, just as Carlton gave a downward glance at the quaint cap on a level with his shoulder.

"So I heard," he said. "May I ask which hospital you are at?" He could recall none where the uniform was so picturesque.

"You would not know it, Mr. Carlton; it is a private hospital on Campden Hill."

They had passed through the gate, and they paused with one consent.

"Are you returning there now, Miss Gleed?"

"Yes—through the gardens."

"Then so far our way is the same." He did not ask whether he might accompany her, but took the outer edge of the pavement as a matter of course. "I am staying at Charing Cross," he explained as they walked; "early this morning I went to the abbey. I did mean to go back there; then I suddenly thought I should like to come here instead. I was once one of the assistant clergy at this church."

"I know," said Gwynneth. She would not deny it. That was why she had so often thought of coming to All Souls'—only to resist the temptation time and time again. Why, to-day of all days, had she been unable to resist? Why had she thought of him this morning, and why had the thought been so strong? These were questions for a lifetime's consideration. Now she was walking at his side.

"It was strange to go back there after so many years," pursued Carlton, with the fine unguarded candour which he had brought back with him into the world; "that service, in particular, was very strange to me. I did not care for it at first. It seemed so artificial after our simple service in the country. Then I looked at the faces of the men near me, and I saw how narrow one can get. It was not artificial to them; it was only beautiful; and there lies the root of the whole matter. Simple services for simple folk—that is my watchword now—but beauty, brightness, elaboration by all means for those who need it and can appreciate it. It is the right thing for these rich congregations of hard-worked professional men and busy society women; the trappings of their religious life must not compare meanly with those of their daily lives; let us order God's house as we would our own. But the opposite is the case—though the principle is the same—with a primitive country parish like ours at Long Stow . . . And yet I had not the wit to see that when I went there first."

He was musing aloud as men seldom do unless very sure of their audience. How came he to be so sure of Gwynneth? They had seen nothing of each other; this was the first time they had been alone together long enough to exchange ideas; yet in a moment he was revealing his as few men do to more than one woman in the world. And the one woman's heart was singing at his side.

She was with him; that was enough. Already it was the sweetest hour of all her life; for the thought of him had haunted her for months, and was full of pain; but in his presence all pain passed away. That was so wonderful to Gwynneth! So wonderful was it that she herself was aware of it at the time; it was her one great discovery and surprise. To be with him was to forget all that he had ever done, all that she had never before forgotten—the good with the evil. It was to sweep aside the earthly and the palpable, to feel the divine domination of spirit over spirit, and the peace which comes with even the secret surrender of soul to soul. Hers was a conscious surrender, and Gwynneth made it without shame. Since it was her secret, why should she be ashamed? She was exalted, exultant, and yet serene. She might carry her secret to the grave; her life would be the richer for it, for these few minutes, for every word he spoke. So she caught each one as it fell, and laid the treasure in her heart, even while she listened for the next.

But in a minute they were come as far as he intended to escort her; there were the palings and the stark trees close upon them in the fog; and an omnibus passing, huge as a house. Gwynneth had been treading thin air; now she was back in the sticky streets, inhaling the raw mist, to exhale it in clouds under a microscopic magenta sun. They had stopped at the corner; he was hesitating: her breath disappeared.

"I have to get over to that side sooner or later," he said. "I may just as well walk across with you, if you don't mind."

"I shall be delighted," said Gwynneth, frankly, brightly; but her breath came like a puff of smoke, and she felt her colour come with it as they crossed the road.

"I want to tell you about the church," he said, as they entered upon the broad walk. "This is the first Sunday that I haven't taken service there since the beginning of August."

"The first!" exclaimed Gwynneth. "Have you actually gone on up to now without a roof?"

Carlton turned in his stride.

"But we have a roof, Miss Gleed!"

"You have one?"

"It has been on some weeks."

Gwynneth was standing quite still. "Do you mean to say that the church is finished?" she cried, incredulous.

"Yes," said Carlton; "thank God, I can say that at last."

"But it seems such a short time! I don't understand. It seemed impossible to me—by yourself?"

"Oh, but I have not been by myself. I have had help."

"At last!"

"I wonder you have not heard. Everybody has helped me—everybody!"

"Do you mean—my people—among others?"

And Gwynneth preferred walking on to facing him here.

"Is it possible you haven't heard?" exclaimed Carlton, incredulous in turn.

"Not a word," replied Gwynneth, bitterly. "They never write."

But her bitterness was new-born of her indignation, not that they never wrote, but that they had not written to tell her this. He told her himself with much feeling and more embarrassment.

"Why, Miss Gleed, I owe everything to Sir Wilton! It is the last thing I ever—I can hardly realise it yet—or trust myself to speak of it to you. My heart is so full! But it is Sir Wilton who has finished the church; he came to me, and he took it over. He called for tenders; he poured in workmen; the place has been like a hive. So the roof was on in a month; and we never missed a Sunday, we had one service all the time; but now we have three and four—thanks entirely to Sir Wilton Gleed!"

He paused. But Gwynneth had nothing to say, and his embarrassment increased. It was so hard to speak of Sir Wilton's magnanimity without alluding to his previous attitude, and thus indirectly to its notorious cause; and Carlton could not see that his companion was entirely taken up with his news, could not realise the surprise it was to her, or apprehend for a moment what impression it had made. He might, however, have had some inkling of her view from the manner in which Gwynneth eventually said that she was glad to hear her uncle had done something.

"Something?" echoed Carlton. "He has done everything, and it is like his generosity that you should hear it first from me!"

Gwynneth shook her head unseen, though now he was looking at her, his eyebrows raised; but she seemed intent upon picking her steps through the thin mud of the broad walk.

"And what that is like," continued Carlton, "from my point of view, you will see when I tell you why I am in town to-day. It is the first Sunday I have missed; but Mr. Preston of Linkworth and other friends are kindly dividing my duty between them. Sir Wilton has arranged that, by the way. He telegraphed yesterday to save me the journey; for I was going down for the day, and returning to-morrow. Yet I came up last Monday, and am still hard at work—buying for the new church."

Gwynneth asked what it was that he had to buy; but her tone was so mechanical that Robert Carlton did not at once reply. He was beginning to feel strangely disappointed, to wish that he had gone his own gait to Charing Cross, or at least held his peace about the church. But there was one point upon which he felt constrained to convince his companion before they parted; he might do more than justice to an absent man; but she should not do less. And the spire of St. Mary Abbot's was already dimly discernible through the yellow haze.

"There is nothing we have not to buy, for the interior," he said at length. "The lectern is the one exception, and I have had it straightened and lacquered into a new thing. Sir Wilton wanted me to keep it as it was; but that would never have done. However, he would have an inscription to the effect that it is the same lectern which was in the fire, which is quite a sufficient advertisement of the fact. I was in favour of restoring the communion plate also, but Sir Wilton insisted on presenting us with a new set, which I have been choosing among other things this week. The other things are too numerous to mention—carpets, curtains, collecting-boxes, alms-bags, a Litany desk, and the hundred and one things you take for granted as part of the church itself. But each has to be chosen and bought, and I only wish that I had had your help. I have found the best things most difficult to choose—the plate and a very handsome cross and candlesticks of polished brass—all of which are my choice, but Sir Wilton's gift. So is the organ which is being built for us. Can you wonder, then, that his generosity has moved me more than I can possibly tell you?"

"Indeed, no!" cried Gwynneth, in her own kind voice; but her honour was all for the man who claimed it for another; and, until she opened them now, her lips had been pursed in mute rebellion. She could fancy so much that the true generosity would never even see! Gwynneth had not that sort herself; she did not profess to have it. On the other hand, she was anxious to be fair, even in her own mind; so she asked a question or two concerning the hired and skilled labour which had been thrown into the scale with such effect; and, after all, it appeared that Sir Wilton Gleed had not paid for this.

"But he wanted to," said Carlton, quickly. "It was not his fault that I would not hear of his doing so; it was my obstinacy, because I had set my heart on rebuilding the church myself, in one sense or the other."

"Yet you said he took it over from you!"

"So he did, Miss Gleed. He lent me his influence and support; that was much more to me than the money, which I had and didn't want. Besides, he is a business man, which I am not, and he did take the whole business off my hands. That is what I meant."

Gwynneth wondered whether it was what the countryside understood; but said no more about the matter. She had other things to think of during their last moments together; for she had stopped at the corner near the palace; nor did she mean to let him accompany her any further. She was still so decided and serene. She was still exalted and strengthened out of all self-knowledge in the quiet presence of the man she loved, and must love for ever, even though her love were to remain her heart's prisoner for this life. This life was not all.

So it was that she could look her last upon him, perhaps for ever, with her own face transfigured and beautified by a joy not of earth alone: so it was that she could speak to him, and hear him speak, without a tremor to the end.

His church was to be consecrated that day week—Advent Sunday. The bishop was coming to perform the ceremony; his voice softened as he spoke of the bishop, who was to be his own guest at the rectory. His face shone as he added that. It was going to be a very simple ceremony. And here something set him twisting at one of his gloves; then suddenly he looked Gwynneth in the eyes.

"You don't happen to be coming down, Miss Gleed?"

"I don't think it very likely."

"It—it wouldn't of course be worth your while—"

"It would! It would! It would be more than worth it; but, to be quite frank, I don't know that I shall ever come down again, Mr. Carlton."

Was he sorry? He did not even show surprise; and not a word more: for he had heard stray words in Long Stow concerning Gwynneth's departure and its reason as alleged. "I should have liked you to see the church," was all he said.

"And do you know," rejoined Gwynneth, speaking out her mind at last, "that I am in no great hurry to see it? I know it is foolish of me—for no one man could have finished such a work—no other man living would have got as far as you did without a soul to help you! Yet somehow I don't so much want to see the church that they came in and finished; it would spoil the picture that I can see so plainly now, and always shall—of the stones you cut and the walls you built with your own two hands—and every other hand against you!"

She was holding out her own. Carlton looked from it to her face, a strange surprise in his eyes. He had wriggled out of one of his gloves, and was twisting it round the iron paling at the corner where they stood.

"May I come no further?" he said.

"No, I could not think of taking you another yard out of your way. And it is really not so very many yards from where we stand!"

Gwynneth smiled brightly; but her voice was the very firm one of this half-hour of her existence. And ever afterwards she was to marvel why neither smile nor words were an effort to her at the time: so his presence supported her to the end, when the clasp of that indomitable hand, now bare, and horny even through her glove, left Gwynneth outwardly unmoved. She returned his pressure with honest warmth; her smile was kind and bright; then the cold mist fell between them in a widening yellow gulf, with a diminishing patter of firm footsteps, that Carlton could hear when the nurse's streamers had quite disappeared in the fog.

And he stood where he was to hear the last of her; and still he stood, wishing he had disregarded tact, and persisted in his escort, whether it embarrassed her or not, if only to find out where her hospital was. He felt inclined to call before leaving town; already there was something that he wished he had said; he kept saying it to himself as he wandered back through dark gardens and a desert park.

"So you prefer to think of it before the roof was on, as I managed to make it by myself! You are the first to say that or to feel it—except me! And I have put the feeling down; thank God, I have got it under; yet it is a help to know that one other felt the same. Perhaps it was a human feeling; but in me at least it was unworthy. God help me! But in you it is sweet, and to me very wonderful . . . that you should understand and sympathise . . . a young girl like you!"

This whole fatality left the man sadly unsettled; tired and yet restless in body and soul; humbly thankful for a woman's sympathy after so long, and so much, yet the prey of a new depression. A woman's sympathy! Or was it only a woman's pity? No, she understood; but it mattered little to Robert Carlton; there could be no second woman in his life. That he had always felt; but he was not sure that he had ever before defined the feeling. It was a part of his eternal punishment; but he was quite sure that he had not previously regarded it in that light.

A coxcomb Carlton had never been; he had no suspicion of the kind of impression he had made upon Gwynneth; his sole concern was the impression which she had made on him. Like the rest of the world, she was flying to extremes; only in her case, if she especially magnified the good, it was because she was still ignorant of the original evil. It could be nothing else; but his feeling about himself was more complex. He alone knew how much or how little of the highest and the best in him had redeemed that passion born of passion which had blighted his life. It was of further significance that for years Carlton had not looked upon his life as blighted. The blight fell upon the shining vision of the woman he could have loved. And all had been so sudden that the man was dazed.

He could not eat, though he was hungry; nor rest, though tired to the bone. He would go out again. It was good to be out, even in a London fog, which was nothing to the fogs he remembered, for there was no question of groping one's way; one could see it for fifty yards, often for more. But now there was not even a small magenta sun; it was the middle of the brief December afternoon when Robert Carlton left his hotel; and near its close before he found himself in Kensington Gardens once more. He hardly knew what brought him there. It was partly, but not altogether, a sentimental impulse. Carlton had also some idea of finding the hospital if he could, some hope of seeing Gwynneth again, if only to assure himself that his imaginings of the last few hours had made her other than what she was. And then he could rectify those omissions of the morning; but neither was this all; a strong inexplicable attraction drew him straight to the spot where he had stood so long after Gwynneth was gone.

And Gwynneth herself was standing there again!

He was almost upon her before he saw her in the dusk, then those long lawn streamers leapt like lightning to his eyes; and now he was creeping backwards across the path. But she had not heard him, or she did not heed: her back was turned, and bent, for she was leaning over the iron paling which he had grasped before. And she shook with tears.

Carlton was shaking, too; passion had taken him by the shoulders, and was shaking the strength out of his heart. Horror had driven him back, passion was spurring him on again. If she loved him—if she loved him—then the hand of God was in all this.

He was back upon the spot where recognition had come. Oh, yes, it was she! She had given a little cry; she was stooping lower over the paling; her voice was unmistakable. Then she rose, half turning, and he saw her profile plain. She was raising something to her eyes; in another moment it was at her lips, and she was kissing it, and sobbing over it, whatever it might be.

Carlton thought he knew what it was, and conceived a new horror of himself in his involuntary capacity of spy. Yet instinctively he was feeling in both overcoat pockets at once; in one there was a single glove; in the other nothing at all. Cold with shame, but shivering with excitement, the man stood torn between the newborn desire of his eyes, and the fixed resolve of his soul. But he could not tear himself from the spot—nor was it any longer necessary. Gwynneth was gone herself; gone without seeing him; out of sight this time in an instant. And Robert Carlton, white, trembling, but himself—the man with a will at least—was listening a second time to the failing music of her feet, his own planted firmly on the walk.

CHAPTER XXXI

ADVENT EVE

The bishop arrived on the Saturday afternoon. He was still the same little old man, with the side-whiskers and the long mouth, the queer voice and the ungainly limp; and Robert Carlton found him neither more nor less cordial than at their last dread interview; but he asked to see the church before it was too dark.

All was in readiness at last. But the cocoanut matting in the aisle and transepts, and the maroon axminster in the chancel, had only been laid that day. As yet there was no stained glass, and only the east window and the west were mullioned as of old; but through the latter a wintry sun poured thick red beams, already too much aslant to touch the floor, but just falling upon the altar with its glimmering candlesticks, its rich green cover, its violet frontal, all three gifts from the hall. The bishop heard this without remark, his mouth a mere seam. But he approved of the rows of rush-seated chairs in place of pews, and he admired the simple pulpit of pitch pine. There was a pleasant smell of pitch pine in the church. All the woodwork was of this wood, including the ceiling and all panelling; and the pores of the fragrant timber were not stopped up with varnish. The new red hassocks looked very bright under each chair, and the new black prayer-books shone like polished jet on the book-rests behind them. In the south transept, a space was boarded off for the new organ; and here chaos had still a corner to itself; nor was either the lighting or the heating apparatus quite complete. Oil-stoves were already burning, however, at various points, and their odour compared unfavourably with that of the pitch pine.

"I do not want you to catch cold to-morrow," said Carlton, as he locked the door behind them when they left.

"Tut!" said the bishop, "I am not such an old man that you need coddle me."

Nor did he look a day older for all these years, as they went out together into the raw red sunset. But Robert Carlton seemed almost to have caught him up: he had come back from London so haggard and hollow-eyed.

They talked very little until the evening. Carlton had servants now, that very widow who had been the first to desert him being head and chief once more; and she signalised the occasion by serving one of the soundest meals of her career. But it was in the long low study, now a study pure and simple, and an infinitely tidier one than aforetime, that the bishop smoked his after-dinner pipe like any deacon, while Carlton also tasted his first tobacco for five years and a half. And still they were strangely silent, until the occurrence of an incident, little in itself, but great with suggestion.

There was a tiny patter on the worn carpet, and all at once the bishop beheld a big brown mouse seated upright within a few inches of his companion's boot. The bishop exclaimed, and the mouse fled with a scuttle and a squeak.

"I tamed him," Carlton explained with a slight access of colour. "The house is overrun with them, but this fellow lets none of the others in here."

The bishop was slow to follow up his exclamation. He certainly was a man of fewer words than formerly.

"You ought not to have made yourself such an anchorite," he said at last. "You might have smoked your pipe—you say that's your first—and written to me sooner!"

So that still rankled. Carlton was not altogether surprised.

"My lord," said he, "how could I? You had advised me to live anywhere else, and yet here I was!"

"The circumstances justified you, Mr. Carlton. I could not foresee such circumstances, I assure you. I heard of them, however, at the time."

Carlton had never written till the five years were nearly up, when it became a necessary preliminary to the resumption of those offices from which he had been debarred; but, when he did write, he had done so to such effect that certain other preliminaries had been foregone.

"Though you did not write," continued the bishop, "Sir Wilton Gleed did. We had some correspondence about you, and we disagreed; that is one reason why I declined his invitation and accepted yours. I would not mention it, only you are now such excellent friends. And I understand that he himself makes no secret of his former attitude towards you."

"On the contrary, he has expressed the most generous regret for the line he took."

"He may well regret it," said the bishop.

But Carlton had accepted his old enemy's aid, and would not hear ill of him, whatever he might think. "It was natural enough," he murmured.

"What! To prevent you from making the one reparation in your power? To have you boycotted right and left? To trump up a criminal charge? To force you, a clergyman, to remain in your own parish, labouring like a convict by the year together? To trample the cloth underfoot in the eyes of all the world?"

"Oh," groaned Carlton, "it was I who did that! I alone am to blame for that—I alone!"

He leant his elbows on the chimney-piece, his face in his hands; for stand he must if he was only to hear harsh words—that night of all nights! Carlton was unprepared for such severity at this stage; and infinitely hurt; for at his worst, when he deserved no sympathy at all, the bishop had shown much more. But behind his back the blazing eyes were quenched, and the long mouth relaxed.

"No, no," a softer voice said; "you have done just the opposite—just the opposite. You have been hard enough upon yourself; but the world was harder on you—once."

There was kindness in the rasping voice, but no enthusiasm. None other had made so little of the mere physical feat of this man; and to him the tone was unmistakable.

"I know what you mean," said Carlton, turning round, his own eye alight. "You think the world is going to the other extreme!"

"It generally does," replied the bishop. "I do not mean to be unkind."

"You are not, my lord—unless you think I haven't seen this for myself!"

The bishop nodded gravely to himself.

"You would see the danger. I am sure of that. You must want to hear the last of what you have done; superhuman and heroic in itself—I am the first to admit it—it is nevertheless the last chapter of a book which you must want to close once and for all. The last chapter recalls the first. Close the book; put it behind you; start afresh."

Robert Carlton stood looking down with a curious smile upon his haggard face.

"That is exactly what I am going to do," said he.

"But the parish must do the same; they must help you. Let them also think no more of the past, either remote or immediate."

"They must think of what they will," rejoined Carlton, queerly. "They cannot help me much longer, nor I them. I am resigning the living, my lord."

"Resigning it?" cried the bishop.

"I intend to do so to-morrow night. It always has been my intention. But you are the first whom I have told."

"I'm glad to hear that!" the bishop exclaimed, as he scrambled to his feet another being. "You have taken my breath away! My dear fellow, let me dissuade you from any such course."

Carlton shook his head.

"My work here is done."

"It is just beginning!"

"No, it is done. I have given my parishioners the church I owed them, since they lost their last church through me. I set them once an example for which I shall pray to be forgiven till my life's end; but now, please God, I have at least shown them that because a man falls it need not be utterly and for ever. He can rise; or, at any rate, he can try. God knows I have tried; and they know it; and it may help them in their own day of bitter trouble. But it was you, my lord, who first helped me, by bidding me never despair. I have tried to teach your lesson; that is all."

"But you have not finished," the bishop urged, gently. "Go on teaching it—go on."

"No. It is no sudden thought. I undertook in the beginning, when Sir Wilton Gleed wanted to turn me out forcibly, to go of my own accord when I had built the church. He may forget it, but I do not."

"Then I devoutly hope he will not accept your resignation!"

"He must. I have made my arrangements. There is need of clergy in the far corners of our empire, greater need than here. There was an Australian at the hotel I have been staying at in London, and he has shown me my field. I am going out to offer my services to the Bishop of Riverina, and I am relying upon a word from you for their acceptance. I hope to sail at the beginning of next month; my passage is already taken."

"I suppose you took it when you were in town?" the bishop grumbled. Carlton coloured in an instant.

"I did—but I had long been thinking of it," he said, hastily. "Oh, my lord, in my place you would do the same! How could I continue here to be smiled on by these poor people? It was easier when they looked the other way, when I lived in this room alone, doing everything for myself, and not a soul came near me. How can I settle down again to a prosperous life—here of all places—with my child in the parish, and his poor mother . . . That is what they all forget in the generous warmth of their reaction; but the more they forget, the more keenly I remember. Ah! do you think I ever have forgotten—for an hour—for a moment—since I left off working with my hands?"

One of these was stretched in the direction of the churchyard; and the bishop read its touching testimony for the first time.

"There," whispered Carlton, in strange excitement, "there lies one . . . whose ruin and whose death are at my door. I don't forget—I never have forgotten. I have paid, and I will pay till the end. And there shall be no other woman . . ."

His tongue failed him; his face was grief-stricken; the whole man was changed. So then the human being, his bishop, knew that there was another woman in his heart already; recalled the most terrible part of this man's confession to him, years before; and presently plucked him by the sleeve. And the voice that Robert Carlton heard, as he leaned once more with his elbow on the chimney-piece, and his face between his hands, was the voice of their last interview, at the bishop's palace, in the blank forenoon of a wet summer's day.

"Forgive me," it said, "for I also have misjudged you in my turn. But now I see—but now I see, and am ashamed . . . Your life has been hard, my brother, but it has been brave! You have been through the depths, but you have also touched the heights, and I think that God must be very near you to-night. I see now that you are right to go; you are both nobler and wiser than I thought; may happiness, and peace, and love itself go with you first or last. Let us kneel together before I leave you, and humbly pray that it may still be so!"

When the bishop retired, Robert Carlton returned to his study, and prayed by himself until a knock at the outer door brought him to his feet, much startled; for it was eleven at night.

He was still more startled when he reached the door, for there stood a soldier straight and tall, sunburnt and jaunty; a medal with clasps and the Egyptian star upon his scarlet breast; a smile behind the trim moustache; right hand at the salute. It was only after a prolonged stare that Carlton recognised the smart young man.

"George Mellis?" he cried. "Come in—come in!"

"That's me, sir," said George, entering like a machine. "But—can it be you, Mr. Carlton?"

And his smile vanished as the lamplight fell upon the grey hairs and the deep furrows which made the clergyman look nearly twice his years.

"Yes, George. I have aged a little. But so have you."

"Oh, I'm all right," said the young soldier with his fine eyes on the other's face; "but I want to kill somebody, that's all!"

"I should have thought you'd done enough of that at the wars," rejoined Carlton, smiling. "Come, George, it's you I want to hear about. Of course I have heard of you. So you enlisted in the Grenadiers, and you got straight to Tel-el-Kebir; and that's the clasp, and not the only one! And now you're a colour-sergeant, and certain of your stripes, they tell me; you're a great hero in the village, George; and yet I have heard them complain that you never even came back to show yourself after the war."

"I haven't come back to show myself now, Mr. Carlton."

And the young fellow looked rather grim above his brass and scarlet.

"I didn't mean to hurt your feelings."

"Nor have you, sir. But can't you guess why I've come back for the first time to-night?"

Carlton considered, and suddenly his hollow eyes lit up; but those of the grenadier had lighted first.

"Was it—was it really to—to be here to-morrow, George?"

"That was it, sir—and nothing else! I'd heard how you were building it up with your own—"

"Never mind that, George."

"I heard it from Tom Ivey, who found me out in barracks not long since, and gave me all the Long Stow news. That's how I came to hear of the consecration to-morrow. He said he was coming down for it, and I said I would too if I could get leave; and I did; and we've come down together to-night."

Neither of them had dreamt of intruding at that hour; but Mellis had seen the old light in the old window, and felt he must just come up to shake hands. Yes, he would come in gladly after church to-morrow. No, he had seen no one else to speak to as yet, except Mrs. Musk; and the grenadier stood confused.

"Where did you see her?"

"Driving away from the Flint House."

"That old woman at this time of night?"

"Musk is bad, and she was going for the doctor herself. I offered to go instead, but she had the girl with her, and there was no stopping them."

"Bad!" echoed Carlton. "He has been bad for weeks; he may be dying—and all alone!" He dashed from the room, but was back next moment in his wideawake. "I must go to him, George! He will hate it, but I must go. Open the door, and I'll put out the light; if he's dying I shall stay."

It was a clear keen night with a worn moon curling in the west; and the hard road rang like a drum as red-coat and black ran elbow to elbow down the village, jerking a word here and there as they went.

"Been bad long, sir?"

"Sciatica for years; only just taken to his bed."

"Sciatica shouldn't kill."

"This must be something else. The man is old—and the one enemy I have left!"

They ran on. Before the Flint House came first its meadow and then its garden wall, with the gate left open, and a rude drive twisting through trees to the side of the house. "This way," said Carlton; and in half a minute they were at the side door. This also had been left open. Carlton lowered his voice, his hand upon the latch.

"You wait here, like a good fellow. If he will not let me say one word—if he orders me out—then you must come up instead. If he is so ill that his wife goes herself at midnight for the doctor, then he is too ill to be left with no one in the house but a child of five!"

Carlton's concern was not a little for the child. Suppose he had awakened to call and call in vain—perhaps to run for succour to a corpse! The thought made Carlton shudder as he found his way through passages with which he had been permitted to become familiar after Georgie's accident. At the head of the stairs there was Georgie's room; the father had to pass it; and could not, without peeping in.

For this door was ajar, and a night-light burning on the chest of drawers. Georgie was breathing gently in his cot. Carlton approached on tip-toe, and stood gazing downward with clasped hands. Boisterous and robust upon his feet, the boy looked still a baby in his sleep; his face was so round and innocent; his hands seemed such toys; and the light hair, too seldom cut, was lightest at the roots, and still curly at the ends, as it lay upon the pillow where his last movement had tossed it. It was a sweet face, even with the great eyes closed; the eyelashes looked so much longer and darker against the pure skin; they were many shades darker than the hair; and the eyebrows were assuming a very delicate definition of their own. The mouth was beautiful. That brown little hand was perfectly shaped. Carlton bent over, and kissed the warm smooth cheek with infinite tenderness; then went upon his knees, and prayed over the child, and for him, and for his future, out of the fulness of a brimming heart. He forgot that Musk's death would make a difference to the child and to himself; for the moment he forgot that Musk was in any danger of dying, and that this was his house. He and his child were alone together once more, it might be for the last time, one never knew.

"God keep you, my own poor boy, and lead you not into temptation, but deliver you from evil, for ever and ever, Amen."

He stooped once more over the cot, pushed the long hair back, running his fingers through it gently, and kissed the pure forehead again and again. And it seemed to Robert Carlton—but the night-light was very dim—that at the last his son had smiled upon him in his sleep.

CHAPTER XXXII

THE SECOND TIME

In Musk's room there was more light. It lay under the closed door like a yellow rod. Carlton knocked gently. There was no answer. He knocked louder. Not a sound from within. Then the chill fell on him, and he entered ready for any discovery but the one he was to make.

Neither the quick nor the dead lay within.

A fire was burning as well as the lamp; the very bed looked warm, but was not; the sick man must have left it some minutes at least.

The lame man, the man who could not walk, had left his bed if not the house! Carlton caught up the lamp to go in search. And even on the landing a voice came hailing him from the region below.

"Mr. Carlton! Mr. Carlton! Quick, sir, quick!"

George Mellis was still at the side door, and in the lamplight the other could not see an inch beyond.

"Have you found him, George? He's not in bed!"

"Who—Musk? No, sir, no!"

"Then what have you seen?"

The grenadier had a wet skin, a quivering lip, a starting eye.

"Oh, I can't tell you, sir! I may be wrong. God grant it! But give me the lamp, and go outside and look for yourself!"

In sheer perplexity Carlton complied; and for an instant imagined some outrageous freak of nature; for the trees of the Flint House drive, black as night a few minutes before, now stood etched against the reddest dawn that he had ever seen—at midnight in December! Then a flame shot upwards, and another, and another; and Mellis was left standing, lamp in hand, a brilliant patch of light and colour, yet less brilliant every instant in the face of that unearthly glare in the east. Swift feet were pattering down the drive; and had such a start, before the soldier found his senses, that it was only in the churchyard he caught them up.

Long Stow church was on fire for the second time, and burning faster than it had burnt between five and six years before. The crackle of the pitch pine was loud as musketry already. The roof was already burning; its destruction had been the climax of the former fire.

Robert Carlton stood with folded arms heaving on his chest. The bishop was there already, in his overcoat and rug, with the whiter and the sterner face. The servants had called him: they also were there, in pitiful case, but no more had arrived as yet.

"It is no use their coming. The roof's on fire in three or four different places. He has done his work better this time; more oil for him, with those stoves!"

The voice was Carlton's, because his lips moved, and those of the bishop were compressed out of sight. Otherwise Mellis, for one, would never have recognised so sad a discord of heartbreak and devil-may-care.

"Some things might be saved," said the bishop.

"They might and shall! George, run to my study for the key; it's on a nail beside the fireplace. And to think I locked up myself lest something might happen at the last!" cried Carlton, with a single note of high hollow laughter, as the soldier vanished. "But I never thought of you! No, you have cheated me very cleverly this time. You almost deserve your triumph—over me!"

"Do you mean to say you know who has done it?" cried the bishop.

"Yes—the man who did it before."

"But was that ever known?"

"No; but I knew. I found his hat in the church."

"And you never told?"

"Nor shall I now. But I do wonder where he got in! And he was well enough to climb a ladder—my dying man!"

Carlton said no more; he was sorry he had said so much. Yet this time it was sure to come out. There was the empty bed. Mellis would speak of it, though he had not seen it with his own eyes. Was the malingerer back in it already? What hellish artifice! And the house emptied for the nonce! The man's own wife would never have suspected him.

Carlton was quite calm. There was nothing to be done. The roof was flaring at either end and in the middle. Only a fire-engine could have put it out, and there was still none nearer than Lakenhall. The mind will often puzzle over an immaterial question in the face of facts too terrible to be realised at once: the known is blinding, but the unknown is the dark, and it is a relief to grope there even for that which is useless when discovered. So Robert Carlton was still wondering how the incendiary had got in, and out, and exactly what he had done inside, when Mellis came running with the key. In a few moments they were in the church.

Nothing could have been less like the corresponding impression of the former fire. Then the pews had been discovered burning; but now rush-seated chairs and pitch pine stalls stood equally intact; and a first glance did not reveal the source of the dull red light which filled the church. On the other hand, a badly-broken window in the north transept satisfied Carlton's curiosity on the immaterial point; and supplied another, pregnant with irony; for it was the window whose arch he had been building when Georgie first swam into his ken.

But now Mellis was looking straight above him, and calling to Mr. Carlton to do the same. In three places the ceiling was on fire, and burning planks beginning to drop; in another a spreading patch of brown burnt through even as they watched. Almost simultaneously came a shriek from the women and a roar from the men now gathering outside; it was Tom Ivey who came rushing in.

"There's some one overhead! He's smashing the skylight over the north transept! That's the man that done it—that's the man that done it—fairly caught!"

The saddler came on Tom's heels.

"Gord love us all, that's Jasper Musk!"

Carlton darted into the south transept without waste of words, and in an instant had disappeared in the part that was boarded off until the new organ should be established in its place there; meanwhile the very ceiling had not been carried to the end of the transept, and a ladder led to the natural loft that it formed. Up this ladder the incendiary must have climbed, and up this ladder the rector was running when Mellis and Ivey, with the rest at their heels, reached its foot.

"Come down, sir, come down, for God's sake!"

"I am not coming down alone."

"Then I'll fetch you," roared Ivey; "you are not going to risk your life for him!"

But the red-coat was first upon the ladder, and in a few seconds both young men were in the triangular tunnel between the ceiling and the roof; a space so confined that under the apex alone was it possible to walk upright; and that only for the few feet dividing them from the nearest flames.

"Look out!" cried Tom Ivey from the top rung. "It wasn't made for a floor; get on your hands and knees, and the weight won't be all in one place." So they crept into the centre of the cross; and there they knelt upright to see over a fringe of fire that burnt their eyelids bare as they gazed.

Roof and ceiling of chancel and of nave, both were in roaring flames to right and to left of them; through the flaming barrier in their faces, and the hole already burnt, they could see the pulpit and the chairs in the north transept thirty feet below; and across the gulf, Jasper Musk and Robert Carlton face to face. Carlton had made the leap; they could not; already the flames were driving them back and back.

In the steady roar and crackle they could hear no words. Musk was crouching under a skylight all too narrow for his gigantic shoulders, a tell-tale oil-tin overturned at his feet. His face was livid, but fearless, and his light eyes gleamed with hate. Carlton's back was turned to the watchers, and for a second motionless; then he looked round, saw them through smoke and flame, and clapped a hand to his mouth.

"Down, both of you," he shouted, "and round with the ladder to the outside here, and one of you fetch up an axe. The skylight's too small—we must make it bigger!"

Musk's lips moved, and his eyes flashed their own fire; the others could almost see the words.

"Well?" said Mellis.

"Come on; it's our only chance."

In an instant they were down the ladder, and had it horizontal in a minute. Then Ivey began to fume.

"It'll take some time getting through the porch!"

"Shove it through the broken window."

"Good man! Stand by, out there, to haul out this ladder!"

The red-coat ran round, his medal twinkling in the glare, while Ivey rushed for the axe.

"Up with her, comrades! That's it—altogether—now!"

The ladder was up outside. Ivey, axe in hand, had leapt upon the fourth rung at a bound, and was taking the rest two at a time. Below it was light as day; the naked trees stood brown and brittle in the glare; the upturned faces white as the curled moon. A whiter face peered through the skylight.

"Look alive with that axe, Tom; he can't breathe, and he's being roasted!"

"He deserve ut! Do you come through first, sir. There's room for you as 'tis. He can bide his turn."

The white face flushed indignant dominion.

"Unless you obey me, you are my murderer too!"

A stifled curse came from under the tiles.

"There, then! Would you save him after that? Leave him the axe and through you come, you that can, or else I'll pull you through!"

And his great arm thickened as he thrust it out, and grabbed at the straight white collar, before relinquishing the axe from his other hand; but at that moment there was a crackling groan, and a sudden unbearable weight on Ivey's hand and arm, as the frail inner roof gave way; then a blinding flame in his face, a crash below, and a cry of anguish from a hundred hearts rent as one.

The axe tumbled as Tom Ivey flung both arms round the ladder, and so descended like a drunken man, a crumpled collar still warm and tight between the clenched fingers of his right hand.

CHAPTER XXXIII

SANCTUARY

Long Stow church rose salient from its knoll at the eastern extremity of the village, still in its wintry network of a million twigs. It was not the ruin it had been before; but the new roof had vanished; and the chancel was in the condition to which the first fire had reduced the whole edifice. The other walls still stand as their builder built them, and as they stood on that December day when he was laid to rest in their shadow. The grave is in the angle of the north transept and the nave, not a dozen paces from the site of the shed. The stone was not up when Gwynneth visited it, but the grave was as easily identified as it is to-day. It lay beneath a cairn of dead flowers, picked out with many fresh ones. The cards still fluttered upon some of the wreaths, and Gwynneth could not help seeing the surprising names upon some; but the humble little home-made offerings, the bunches of snow-drops and the early crocuses, touched her more. Yet she showed no feeling as she stood and gazed. She had brought no flowers herself. There was no pretence of mourning in her dress. She shed no tears.

From his own observatory the saddler had seen who was in the covered fly, when Gwynneth got out. He was at his usual work upon the latest newspaper, and he took it up again for a minute. But Gwynneth was more than a minute, and more than five; the saddler lost patience, and wandered across the road.

"Where did you bring that young lady from? Lakenhall?"

"Yes."

"And are you going to take her back again?"

"Yes, in time for the 5.40 train; and she only got down by the 2.10."

Gwynneth, who had not stirred a feature or a limb, started indignantly at the sound of a profaning step; but had forgiven Fuller before he reached her hand with his own outstretched. There had seemed so much that she might never know, could never ask; it would not be necessary with the saddler.

"Why, Miss Gwynneth, is that you?" he cried, when he had crushed her hand; and his eyes widened with concern.

"Am I so much changed?" asked Gwynneth, smiling gallantly.

"Changed! Gord love yer, miss, you're the shadder of what you was."

"There is plenty of substance still, Mr. Fuller."

"And where's your colour, miss?"

"In London, I suppose."

"That's it," cried Fuller; "that London! I wouldn't live there, not if you paid me: nasty, beastly, smoky, overcrowded sink of iniquity and disease! If I was the Government I'd pull that down and build it up again on twice the space. That isn't good manners to run down the place where you live, miss, I know; but I never could abide that London, and now I shall hate it more than ever."

"But I thought you were never there, Mr. Fuller?"

"And never mean to be, miss, and never mean to be! I've too much sense. Look at me: sixty-eight I am, and a bit over, and not an ache or a pain from top to toe. That's because I live in the pure air and know what I eat; now in London, if you'll excuse my saying so, you never do. Where should I be if I'd been swallerun London fogs and adulterated milk and butter all my life? In my grave these thirty years! Do you take the advice of a man of my experience, miss: shake the soot of London off your feet, and come you back to good living and good air, and you won't know yourself in a week."

Gwynneth let the saddler run on; a more sensitive man would have seen that she was not hearkening to a word. Her eyes were very hard and bright; they rested once more upon the faded flowers and the fluttering cards.

"So this is Mr. Carlton's grave!"

The belated words told nothing at all. Fuller removed his cap.

"Yes, miss, there lie the biggest and the bravest heart that ever beat in this here parish or anywhere near it. And I have a right to say so. Many has come back to him this last twelvemonth or so. But I was the first."

"Were you at the fire, Mr. Fuller?"

"Was I at the fire! Why, it was me that saw that first, Miss Gwynneth. Young George Mellis, with his red-coat and his bamboo cane, he would have it that it was him; but there are some folks that fare to be first in everything, and General George'll be getting too big for his uniform if he don't take care. You see, I hadn't closed an eye when I saw the first flicker on the ceiling; but an old man like me have to get on some clothes before he can run outside in the depths o' winter. Meanwhile, Master George, who haven't been near his old friend all these years, he can come down fast enough when the reverend's got the ball at his feet again; and there were the two of them at the Flint House, inquiring after Jasper Musk, said to be at death's door at the very moment he was setting fire to the church."

"Fiend!"

"You may well say that, miss, for it was the second time he'd done it; and the reverend had known, all these years, and that must've been Jasper's hat he flung into the first fire when Tom Ivey come, puttun two an' two together. What make that worse, it seem old Jasper used to say he hoped to live to see the new church consecrated; and some say he'd smile as he said it; but now we know what he meant. And he used to limp up and down his room, for practice, when even the doctor thought he couldn't set foot to the ground; for the servant girl heard him at it. Yes, Miss Gwynneth, he was deep and strong and cruel, like the sea, was Jasper; that's what the bishop said himself, for I heard him; but I will say this for him, he asked no more quarter than he gave. Tom Ivey heard his last words through the skylight, and they aren't fit for a young lady like you to hear, but they were a man's words whatever else they were. The worst is that the dear old reverend could've squeezed through himself if only he'd have let Jasper slip; but that he wouldn't; so they both went through with the ceiling and were killed."

"For his enemy!" whispered Gwynneth, an unearthly radiance in her poor hard eyes.

"Yes, for the man that burnt the church down twice, and deserved to burn himself; that was the worst of it."

The listener's lips were consistently compressed, but at this they parted again.

"Oh, no, it was the best. It was the best. A great death, a glorious death!" And the pale thin face was white-hot with a pride which consumed all else.

"The bishop said his life was greater still. You should ha' heard his sermon, out here, at the open grave, when it was all over. There never was such a funeral in the countryside before, and there never will be another like it. The place was packed. I stood where you are standing now, miss. I was one o' the bearers; and Ivey, Mellis, and Jones the schoolmaster, they were the other three. Then you should have seen the clergy; there was a rare procession of the clergy from all round; the Reverend Scrope from Burton Mills, the Reverend Preston from Linkworth, and Canon Wilders, and a lot more. But the bishop was in all his toggery, and I never see a man look so fine; he's little and he's lame, but the face he preached with, across this here open grave, you'd have said that belonged to some old giant. And what a sermon! That didn't make us cry; that dried our tears, an' made us want to build churches and be killed ourselves. You might guess the text: 'Greater love hath no man than this, that a man lay down his life for his friend.' I kept waitun for him to point out that Musk was not the reverend's friend, but his worst enemy; but he never did. I would have done; otherwise, he said just what I would like to have said myself, let alone the one thing that took the whole lot of us by surprise. And I tell you, Miss Gwynneth, the place was right black with people; not only in the churchyard, but across the fence in the medder as well; there was hardly a blade o' grass to be seen."

"What was the surprise, Mr. Fuller?"

"He'd made up his mind to resign the living! He had told his lordship. He meant to resign next night—I can't for the life of me think why!"

But Gwynneth could; and, with the second sight begotten of her love, read the dead man even in his grave, divining immediately some of the very reasons which he had given to the bishop in his last hours. She was never to divine them all.

Meanwhile the saddler, having imparted a satisfactory amount of information, was beginning to look for some return in kind, and supposed Miss Gwynneth would be going to the hall. No, they were all from home; indeed, Gwynneth had waited for that. Yet she made her answer with a candid look, the prelude to a gratuitous admission.

"I am going on to the Flint House," said she.

"Well, there!" cried Fuller, "if I hadn't forgot to tell you where Musk lie! He don't lie here, miss; he left it that he would go to Lakenhall cemetery, in onconsecrated ground, some say. And Mrs. Musk—you won't have heard it—but she's fair lost her know, poor thing!"

"Yes, I had heard. Poor thing, indeed! Yet in her case it seems almost merciful. But I am not going to see Mrs. Musk."

"Then haven't you heard about little Georgie? That's a grand thing, that! There's a lady in London (that's the only part I don't like), some young widder with none of her own, that's going to adopt him instead."

"I know that, too," said Gwynneth, flushing slightly as she smiled. "The lady is a friend of mine; she heard of Georgie through me. We were in a hospital together, but now we have taken a flat—for I am going to live with her too. And it is for Georgie I am come to-day."

Her companion had served her purpose; but would not go; and a hint might betray that which had obviously never entered the saddler's head. So Gwynneth looked her last upon her own heart's grave with the same pale face and the same unbending carriage; but the bright eyes were softer now, though radiant still with a heavenly pride. So his ashes exalted her as his living presence; so his undying soul still strengthened hers.

It was a pale February day, the grass very green, a subtle gloss of life upon the bough; but it was man's handiwork that appealed to Gwynneth; and all at once an astounding fact forced itself upon her vision and understanding. The church was almost exactly as she had seen it last. The east end was the worst; the roof was not begun. It was just as it had been six months before; and only the work of the hireling had perished after all; that of the self-taught mason, the pariah, the penitent, still endured as an oblation and a sacrifice for his sins, and as a monument to the man for all time. Gwynneth could have gone down on her knees in thanksgiving for this miracle; as it was she saw his resting-place but dimly for the last time. At that moment the starling which had entertained him in life began a gossip in the elderbush at his head; a jealous sparrow poured abuse from every tree; and so she left him, at rest where he never rested, on the field where that rest had been won.

A married Musk with many children, one of the sons who had quarrelled with their father, had already established himself and family in the Flint House. He had thankfully accepted Gwynneth's proposal, made, however, in Nurse Ella's name; and Georgie was ready when Gwynneth called for the second time on her way back from the church. He was also in tremendous spirits, leaping upon his lady like a wild beast, and, later, roaring his farewells through the fly-window, as they drove away towards a watery sunset, Gwynneth sitting far back on the deeper seat She let him shout till he was tired; by that time she was mistress of herself once more, and the dusk was such as to destroy all present evidence of another character. So at last she could take him on her knee.

"And are you glad to come away with Gwynneth, darling?"

"I should think I are; jolly glad; but I thought there was anunner lady too?"

"We shall find her where we are going. Do you know where we are going, Georgie?"

"Course I do. We're goin' to London to see the Queen. I wish we would soon be there!"

"So we shall, Georgie."

"In a minute?"

"No, not in a minute; we have to go in the train first. Have you ever seen a real train, Georgie?"

"No, never. I know I haven't," Georgie averred. "You are kind to take me in one! I do love you, I say!"

"Do you, darling?"

"Yes, really. I love you bestest in the world. I know I do!"

They were entering Lakenhall, and it was quite dark in the fly; but now Georgie knew that Gwynneth was crying, for she was kissing him at the same time, and as he never had been kissed before.

"And you always will, Georgie—you always will?"

"Course I will," said Georgie, gaily.

"And go to school when Gwynneth sends you, and turn into a great strong man, and be good to poor Gwynneth then?"

"Gooder'n all the world," said Georgie.

E. W. Hornung – A Short Biography

Ernest William Hornung was born on 7th June 1866 at Cleveland Villas, Marton, Middlesbrough. He was the third son, and youngest of eight children, to John Peter Hornung and his wife Harriet née Armstrong.

By the age of 13 Hornung had joined St Ninian's Preparatory School in Moffat, Dumfriesshire before enrolling at the exclusive Uppingham School, in Rutland, in 1880.

Hornung suffered from a general state of bad health, including asthma and poor eyesight but managed to be well-liked at school and to develop a life-long passion of cricket. He loved to play despite the obvious fact that his talents were rather limited.

At 17 his health worsened, and he left Uppingham to travel to Australia, where a sunnier climate was deemed to be better for his various ailments.

Upon arriving he worked as a tutor to the Parsons family in Mossgiel, in New South Wales. As well as teaching he spent time working in remote sheep stations in the outback and began to contribute materials to the weekly magazine; The Bulletin. It was also at this time that he began work on his first novel.

After two years of very valuable life experiences Hornung returned to England in February 1886, a few months before the death of his father, in November, whose deteriorating business interests had become a constant worry.

Hornung found work in London as a journalist and story writer. In 1887 he published his first story under his own name, 'Stroke of Five', which appeared in Belgravia magazine. His work as a journalist coincided with the reign of terror brought about by Jack the Ripper's grisly murders. From this Hornung developed an interest in criminal behaviour.

He had completed the manuscript of the novel he brought back from Australia and, between July and November 1890, the story, 'A Bride from the Bush', was published in five parts in the respected Cornhill Magazine. It was released later that year in book form. This, his first novel, was well received by critics.

Hoping to further his talents in cricket Hornung, in 1891, became a member of two cricket clubs: the Idlers, whose members included Arthur Conan Doyle and Jerome K. Jerome, and the Strand club.

Hornung knew Doyle's sister, Constance ('Connie') from when he had visited Portugal. Connie was described as attractive, "with pre-Raphaelite looks ... the most sought-after of the Doyle daughters".

They were married on 27th September 1893, although Doyle was not at the wedding and relations between the two writers were occasionally difficult. The Hornung's had their only child, a son, Arthur Oscar (but always called just Oscar), in 1895.

In 1894 Doyle and Hornung began work on a play for Henry Irving, on the subject of boxing; Doyle was, at first, eager to begin and paid Hornung a £50 advance but then withdrew before the first act had been completed: the play was never finished.

Like Hornung's first novel, 'Tiny Luttrell' had Australia as a backdrop and the device of an Australian woman in a culturally alien environment. This theme ran through his next four novels: 'The Boss of Taroomba' (1894), 'The Unbidden Guest' (1894), 'Irralie's Bushranger' (1896), in this Hornung introduced the character of Stingaree, an Oxford-educated, Australian gentleman thief. In 'The Rogue's March' (1896) Hornung began to show a growing fascination with the motivation behind criminal behaviour and was sympathetic to the criminal hero as a victim of events. It was different thinking but caused some consternation for others.

In 1898 Hornung's mother died and he dedicated his next book, a series of short stories; Some Persons Unknown, to her memory.

Later that year Hornung and Connie spent six months in Posillipo, Italy. An account of this trip was published in the May 1899 issue of the Cornhill Magazine.

The fictional character Stingaree was re-written to become his most famous creation; A. J. Raffles; the gentleman thief, first used in six short stories published in 1898 in Cassell's Magazine. Modelled on George Cecil Ives, a Cambridge-educated criminologist and talented cricketer who, like Raffles, lived in the Albany, a gentlemen's only residence in Mayfair. The first tale of the series 'In the Chains of Crime' was published in June that year, titled 'The Ides of March'.

Another account adds to the richness by asserting that Raffles and his sidekick, Bunny Manders, were based not only on Doyle's Holmes and Watson but also on his friends Oscar Wilde and his lover, Lord Alfred Douglas. Whatever the exact amalgam the characters were warmly embraced by the reading public who turned it into both a popular and financial success, although some critics echoed Doyle's own fears of the dubious nature of a criminal being used as a hero.

In early 1899, the Hornung's returned to London, and resided in Pitt Street, West Kensington, for the next six years.

After publishing two novels, 'Dead Men Tell No Tales' (1899) and 'Peccavi' (1900), Hornung published a second collection of Raffles stories, 'The Black Mask', in 1901. The critics again complained about the criminal aspect. The public who bought them had no such qualms.

In 1903 Hornung collaborated with Eugène Presbrey to write a four-act play, 'Raffles, The Amateur Cracksman', which was based on two previously published short stories, 'Gentlemen and Players' and 'The Return Match'. The play was first performed at the Princess Theatre, New York, on 27th October 1903 and ran for 168 performances.

In 1905, after publishing four other books in the interim, Hornung brought back the character Stingaree. Later that year, in response to public demand he published a third collection of Raffles stories in 'A Thief in the Night', in which Manders relates some of the earlier adventures he had had with Raffles.

In 1909 the final Raffles story was published, the full-length novel 'Mr. Justice Raffles'. It was poorly received. The Observer reviewer asking if "Hornung is perhaps a little tired of Raffles".

It seems not. That same year he partnered with Charles Sansom for the play 'A Visit From Raffles', which was performed in November that year at the Brixton Empress Theatre, London.

Hornung turned away from Raffles thereafter, and in February 1911 published 'The Camera Fiend', a thriller whose narrator is an asthmatic cricket enthusiast and his attempts to photograph the soul as it leaves the body. This was followed by 'Fathers of Men' (1912) and 'The Thousandth Woman' (1913) before 'Witching Hill' (1913), a collection of eight short stories in which he introduced the characters Uvo Delavoye and the narrator Gillon. In 1914 his fictional works ceased with 'The Crime Doctor'.

His son, Oscar, left Eton College in 1914, and was due to proceed to King's College, Cambridge later that year. However, the terrors of WWI were about to unleash themselves all over Europe. Oscar volunteered, and was commissioned into the Essex Regiment. He was killed, aged a mere 20, at the Second Battle of Ypres on 6th July 1915.

Although heartbroken Hornung edited and issued privately a collection of Oscar's letters home under the title 'Trusty and Well Beloved', in 1916.

Around this time Hornung himself joined an anti-aircraft unit. He also joined the YMCA and did volunteer work in England for soldiers on leave. In March 1917 he visited France, writing a poem about his experience afterwards—something he had been doing more frequently since Oscar's death—and a collection of his war poetry, 'Ballad of Ensign Joy', was published later that year.

In July 1917 Hornung's poem, 'Wooden Crosses', was published in The Times, and in September, 'Bond and Free' appeared. A few months later he was accepted as a volunteer in a YMCA canteen and library just a few miles behind the Front Line.

Hornung was concerned about support for pacifism among troops and wrote to Connie about it. She spoke to Doyle and, rather than discussing it with Hornung, he informed the military authorities. Hornung was naturally angered by Doyle's action and relations between the two men were further strained as a result. He continued to work at the library until a German offensive overran the British positions and he was forced to retreat, firstly to Amiens and then, in April, back to England. He stayed in England until November 1918, when he again took up his YMCA duties, establishing a rest hut and library in Cologne.

In 1919 Hornung's account of his time spent in France, 'Notes of a Camp-Follower on the Western Front', was published. Doyle later wrote of the book that "there are parts of it which are brilliant in their vivid portrayal". That year Hornung also published his third and final volume of poetry, 'The Young Guard'.

Hornung finished his YMCA work and returned to England in early 1919. He worked on a new novel but was hampered by poor health. But Connie's was of greater concern. In February 1921 they took a holiday in the south of France to recuperate. Whilst travelling there on the train Hornung fell ill with a chill that progressed to influenza and finally pneumonia.

Ernest William Hornung died on 22nd March 1921, aged 54.

He was buried in Saint-Jean-de-Luz, in the south of France, in a grave adjacent to that of George Gissing.

E. W. Hornung — A Concise Bibliography

Periodicals
Stroke of Five (1887, Belgravia)
Spoilt Negative (1887, Belgravia)
Nettleship's Score (January 1890, Cornhill Magazine)
A Bride From the Bush (5 Parts. July-Nov, Cornhill Magazine, 1890)
Thunderbolt's Mate (4 Parts. March 1892, Chambers's Journal)
Kenyon's Innings (April 1892, Longman's Magazine)

The Burrawurra Brand (November 1893, The Idler)
The Unbidden Guest (6 Parts. May-Oct 1894, Longman's Magazine)
The Governess at Greenbush (4 parts. February 1895, Chambers's Journal)
After the Fact (3 Parts. January 1896, Chambers's Journal)
The Ides of March (June 1898, Cassell's Magazine)
A Villa in a Vineyard (May 1899, Cornhill Magazine)
No Sinicure: More Adventures of the Amateur Cracksman (January 1901, Scribner's Magazine)
A Jubilee Present: More Adventures of the Amateur Cracksman (February 1901, Scribner's Magazine)
The Fate of Faustina: More Adventures of the Amateur Cracksman (March 1901, Scribner's Magazine)
The Last Laugh: More Adventures of the Amateur Cracksman (April 1901, Scribner's Magazine)
To Catch a Thief: More Adventures of the Amateur Cracksman (May 1901, Scribner's Magazine)
An Old Flame: More Adventures of the Amateur Cracksman (June 1901, Scribner's Magazine)
The Wrong House: More Adventures of the Amateur Cracksman (Sept 1901, Scribner's Magazine)
Chrystal's Century (June 1903, Atlantic Monthly)
Charles Reade (June 1921, London Mercury)

Novels and Short Story Collection
A Bride from the Bush (1890) Novel
Under Two Skies (1892) Short story collection
Tiny Luttrell (1893) Novel; two volumes
The Boss of Taroomba (1894) Novel
The Unbidden Guest (1894) Novel
Irralie's Bushranger (1896) Novel
The Rogue's March: A Romance (1896) Novel
My Lord Duke (1897) Novel
Some Persons Unknown (1898) Short story collection
Young Blood (1898) Novel
The Amateur Cracksman (1899) Short story collection
Dead Men Tell No Tales (1899) Novel
The Belle of Toorak (1900) Novel; published in the US as The Shadow of a Man
Peccavi (1900) Novel
The Black Mask (1901) Short story collection; republished as Raffles: Further Adventures of the Amateur Cracksman
At Large (1902) Novel
The Shadow of the Rope (1902) Novel
Denis Dent: A Novel (1903) Novel
No Hero (1903) Novel
Stingaree (1905) Novel
A Thief in the Night (1905) Short story collection; republished as A Thief in the Night: Further Adventures of A. J. Raffles, Cricketer and Cracksman
Raffles: The Amateur Cracksman (1906) Short story collection; stories taken from The Amateur Cracksman and The Black Mask
Mr. Justice Raffles (1909) Novel
The Camera Fiend (1911) Novel
Fathers of Men (1912) Novel
The Thousandth Woman (1913) Novel
Witching Hill (1913) Short story collection

The Crime Doctor (1914) Short story collection
Old Offenders and a Few Old Scores (Published posthumously) Short story collection

Plays
Raffles, The Amateur Cracksman (27th October 1903) By Hornung and Eugéne Presbrey; first performed at the Princess Theatre, New York
Stingaree, the Bushranger (1st February 1908) First performed at the Queen's Theatre, London
A Visit From Raffles (1st November 1909) By Hornung and Charles Sansom; first performed at the Brixton Empress Theatre, London

Non-Fiction
'Trusty and Well Beloved', The Little Record of Arthur Oscar Hornung (1915) Privately published
Notes of a Camp-Follower on the Western Front (1919)

Poetry
Ballad of Ensign Joy (1917)
Wooden Cross (1918)
The Young Guard (1919)